1787

# 1787
*A Novel*

SEAN MICHAEL BAILEY

**FIVE STAR**
*A part of Gale, Cengage Learning*



GALE
CENGAGE Learning™

Detroit • New York • San Francisco • New Haven, Conn • Waterville, Maine • London

Set in 11 pt. Plantin
Printed on permanent paper.

**LIBRARY OF CONGRESS CATALOGING-IN-PUBLICATION DATA**

Bailey, Sean Michael.
1787 : a novel / Sean Michael Bailey. — 1st ed.
p. cm.
ISBN-13: 978-1-59414-636-7 (alk. paper)
ISBN-10: 1-59414-636-5 (alk. paper)
1. Airlines—Fiction. I. Title.
PS3602.A5533A615 2008
813′.6—dc22 2007041919

First Edition. First Printing: April 2008.

Published in 2008 in conjunction with Tekno Books and Ed Gorman.



Printed in the United States of America
1 2 3 4 5 6 7 12 11 10 09 08

This book is dedicated to the late Professor Emeritus James B. Crowley of Yale University: a scholar, gentleman, patriot, longtime consultant to the Central Intelligence Agency, and the warmest Cold Warrior I have ever known.

# PROLOGUE

Artie cursed under his breath, shaking his head in disgust inside the cramped quarters of the airplane lavatory. His broad shoulders hunched forward, he looked down at the commode with the round stainless steel bottom that he had failed to fill with liquid. It's my own fucking fault, Artie thought. The urologist had told him to lay off the spicy food, not to mention chocolate and caffeine. The night before, Artie had loaded up on spicy Hunan hot shredded beef in Chinatown and washed it down with cold beer, chocolate ice cream and a gallon of tea. For months, he had been eating all the stuff that irritated his chronic prostate condition, making his urination frequent and unsatisfying. It was tough to stop eating hot Mexican food when he flew to Mexico from New York and back several times a week. The caffeine and chile peppers were reliably homing in on the stupid little gland, swelling it and creating the feeling of always having to go to the bathroom, but being unable to achieve blessed emptiness. I'm too young for this shit, Artie thought, as he adjusted his concealed gun rig under the jacket that held his SIG 228 nine-millimeter pistol and two other ammo clips. I'd kill for a good piss, he thought, with a smirk. He gave up and pressed the little FLUSH lever in the bulkhead in front of the tiny steel sink. Blue liquid whooshed loudly around the bowl and was sucked out the bottom of the head, as the round bottom cracked open, the negative air pressure pulling at the atmosphere in the flying water closet, tugging at Artie

Flagler's eardrums. He zipped up and turned to the shiny toy sink, catching his reflection in the small mirror. I don't look very healthy, Artie thought, regarding his face. It was probably the rancid light from the cheesy fluorescent bulb, activated by sliding the inside door bolt to OCCUPIED, Artie told himself. He had been feeling tired recently. That probably meant he would again need antibiotics to kill what was obviously an inflamed prostate. It also meant giving up anything that had any flavor, any kick. That sucked. On ice. Artie snugged his blue and gold rep tie in the mirror, straightened his gold-buttoned blazer. It was another day at the office for Artie. He had been a FAM, a federal air marshal, for five years. Looking again at his clothing, his black crew cut, Artie chuckled. Time to blend in. It was absurd for him to be dressed like this but his superiors insisted. Any asshole could see that Artie and his partner Ed were cops because they dressed like cops. The jackets, the ties, the regulation haircuts were worn, so that, in case of action, the passengers would believe they were marshals—not hijackers—and any FAM who looked otherwise was in big trouble. After they had been hired in the crazy days after 9-11, Artie and Ed had tried to grow their hair longer and dress casual—like undercovers should. A cop who was made by the bad guys was a dead cop. For months, they and the other marshals had rebelled against the official memos, hiding from the bosses, communicating with the office only through phone calls and their personal digital assistants. Artie had gone for that blue jeans, blue collar, tattooed look. Ed had grown his hair and beard and taken to wearing a Harley-Davidson leather jacket. They took down exactly one nasty drunk and one mental case, who had to be cuffed and sedated because she had freaked out. Their undercover getups worked great until the big boss in Washington took some congressman aboard the same regularly scheduled Anytime Air flight from New York's Kennedy Airport to Mexico that Artie and Ed were now on, Flight 1787. On that flight, Ed and Artie's PDAs buzzed with a priority message that they were to identify themselves to the gentleman in a particular seat on the plane. When they saw who it was, they knew they were fucked. It was the boss—the head of the service, known as the CFAM—who went bananas because the congressman did not quite grasp the concept of going undercover. He was shocked to see grungy marshals who looked like a construction worker and a Nazi biker. Apparently every adult male in the U.S. government had grown up watching dumb movies about Wyatt Earp and expected all federal marshals to be dressed to the nines. Since that day, it had been Macy's Men's Shop and a Marine Corps haircut—or else. Artie had also been officially reprimanded for going to the bathroom too many times during the flight—a security risk, according to the Potty Patrol, because it put him out of touch with Ed.

"Fuck it," Ed told Artie later. "The war's over. We kicked their ass in Afghanistan and the ones we didn't send to Paradise crawled off to we-don't-know-where-istan. It's over. We haven't been attacked here since September 11th and that means one thing—they can't. The action now is in Iraq and other places. Planes are the last place they will go now because we hardened up the target. If they come, they'll come after a softer one—a nuke plant, chemical plant, shopping mall, the Super Bowl, a Tupperware party, whatever. We're lawn jockeys with guns. Enjoy the ride, partner."

Artie knew Ed might be right, but they still had to do The Job, even if the suits made it tough. Artie sometimes wondered about Ed. He didn't seem to care as much anymore, like it was just a job to him. It made Artie nervous. If you started to think like that, where would it lead? If it was just a job, then you might act like any other asshole on any shit job. In the rush to protect the unfriendly skies after the 9-11 hijackings, the government had not been too picky about hiring, failing to make background checks. Some real clowns and oddballs had gotten through. Quietly, the bosses were trying to weed out the unqualified. Artie thought he knew Ed, but there was always that doubt because they had never seen any real action. If Ed thought it was just a job, not The Job, could he be trusted? If things got hot and hairy at thirty-seven-thousand feet, you needed a partner you could depend on.

Someone rattled the folding door of the bathroom, trying to open it. He heard voices outside.

"Just a second," Artie said, using his I'm-just-another-friendly-guy-on-vacation voice to the impatient jerk, who obviously could not read the OCCUPIED sign on the outside of the door. Probably another business traveler with a fucked-up prostate, like me, Artie chuckled at the thought. He quickly removed his gold wedding band and placed it to the side of the small stainless steel sink. He squirted soap onto his large hands, hit the little lever for a dose of water and rinsed. He reached down for paper towels from the dispenser in the front of the sink and dried off. He put the damp towels into the slot not yet jammed open by the dozens of passengers who would follow him into the first-class lavatory, and slipped his ring back on. As he slid open the door, he looked down to make sure his jacket was closed over his piece.

Something hard bumped him in the forehead and he stopped in the doorway.

"Sorry. I . . ." Artie looked up, into the black hole of a black pistol inches from his nose. Artie recognized the bright red tritium sight. It was Ed's piece, his SIG, an exact duplicate of his own weapon, which was still tucked under his right arm. There was only one other gun on the plane.

"Ed! No, don't . . ."

Artie began to reach for his gun. He was fast but, as his hand grasped the grip of the SIG, he felt and saw the exploding gas of the first shot, more than heard it, although it was quite loud. The CQTF bullet, a Close Quarter Totally Fragmenting 91 grain projectile, struck Artie on the bridge of his nose. The specialized, rounded blue slug instantly passed through his skin, nose cartilage and through his sinus area. It flattened against the front of the marshal's skull before his eyes could blink. Liberated, the load of a dozen round, number-six birdshot pellets inside the special bullet sped through Artie's brain like lead bees at 2,100 feet per second.

Artie didn't hear the second shot.

# 1.

Ruby led the way, as usual, scampering ahead of her parents down the airport skyway ramp toward the front port-side entry of the Boeing 767. As she ran, red lights blinked on and off on her pink sneakers.

"I'm sorry," her dad, Jim Donovan, apologized to a very pregnant woman and her husband just ahead of them.

"That's okay," the woman said.

"She's excited," said an elderly woman with cotton-candy hair behind them, who was wearing a white "ATLANTIC CITY" sun visor on top of the pink confection. "Is this her first time?"

"No," Jim replied, "but she was too young to remember, so, I guess it is. She's thrilled."

"I wish I was," Emily Marco confided. "Flying scares me, always has. How about you?"

Jim smiled politely, anxious to end the conversation, to pretend the woman hadn't hit a bull's-eye.

"No, but I haven't flown in a while," Jim said, hurrying to catch up to his rambunctious daughter, who had disappeared around the corner. Jim did not say his fear of flying dated from September 11, 2001. From their Brooklyn apartment porch, he and his wife, Anna, had watched the Towers fall, rocked by fear and anger and helplessness. As Jim caught up to Ruby at the entrance to the aircraft, he remembered the sharp smell of the pillars of smoke from the fires that seemed like they would never stop, the smell of death and defeat in his lungs.

Ruby was standing at the open cabin door, checking out the three crew members inside the cockpit, readying for takeoff.

"Good morning," one of the tanned, white-shirted men said to Ruby. "Welcome aboard Flight 1787, young lady. What's your name?"

"Ruby. I'm not a young lady, I'm a girl."

"Of course you are."

"Are you the captain?"

"Yes, I'm Captain Cornell, and we'll be taking you to sunny Meh-hee-ko this morning," he grinned. "How old are you, Ruby?"

"Eight-and-a-half."

"Well, you're a big girl. You look older."

"I don't want to be older."

"Really? Why?"

"Too much homework," Ruby said, dead serious.

The captain chuckled and Ruby's dad also smiled. But Jim was smiling at the new fortified steel cabin door that made it impossible for hijackers to get into the cockpit once it was closed. He had read about them but it was the first one he had seen. He drew a deep breath for the first time that morning.

"Ruby, I told you not to run off," said Anna, coming up behind Jim. She knew her daughter did not hear her because she had disobeyed and failed to wear her hearing aids again.

"Hi, I'm Liz. Boarding passes, please," said Elizabeth Atocha, a strikingly pretty flight attendant, with soft onyx eyes that spoke of her Mexican ancestry. Liz beamed at the Donovans.

"Thank you. First class, row C, seats three, four and five. Welcome, Ruby, you and your folks will be flying with me. We're going to have fun. Your seats are down the far aisle, last row, on your left and the middle seat," Liz said, pointing with a long-nailed finger. The first-class cabin was small, containing just fifteen seats in three rows of five. Each side of the plane had three pairs of seats along the windows. In the middle of the double aisles were three single seats.

They stowed their schlep bags in the overhead compartments and took their nice, wide seats in the last row on the far side of the aircraft. Ruby, of course, insisted on the right-side window seat. Her mother sat next to her on the aisle and Jim sat across one of the two aisles in that row's lone, center seat.

Jim's full salt-and-pepper hair was brushed back and curled over his collar like a man who did not have a 9-to-5 job, which he did not. He pulled the large plastic emergency card from the slot in front of him. He confirmed that the equipment on the flight was a 767-400 aircraft. He scanned the color cartoons which showed the emergency exits and information about floating seat cushions, life vests and oxygen masks that dropped from the ceiling. He silently noted how far away the emergency exits were, which one they would go to. He was always trying to anticipate dangers, hoping they might somehow avoid them. Jim glanced at his watch. It was 8:11 a.m.

Next to him, his wife, Anna Horowitz, with her long, curly auburn hair and peasant blouse and antique silver earrings, looked like a jewelry designer from Woodstock, which she was not. Anna was preoccupied with a military problem, which she had been attacking for the past five years. In her mind, as she fastened her seatbelt, she ran and reran all the possible scenarios, logistics and possibilities that had to lead to the same inevitable outcome. Theory was easy. Reality was more difficult, less predictable. She would get only one shot at it when the time came.

For the first time, the Donovans were flying first class, courtesy of a ticket upgrade purchased by points scored by years of extensive use of an Anytime Airways credit card, which racked up miles as they spent dollars. They were also getting three free days of car rental in Cabo San Lucas to drive up the Baja to a little town called Todos Santos to visit the new home of their best friends, a pair of expatriate New Yorkers. It was the special event that got Jim on a plane and out of the country for the first time in years.

Jim's seat felt like a wide, comfortable leather recliner, not a cramped airline seat. There would be no banging elbows on the narrow armrests with anybody, especially strangers, no climbing over anyone, no one climbing over him. Jim preferred aisle seats and he now had an aisle on either side, down which the unfortunates with seats in coach were now passing, sneaking envious looks at Jim's first-class throne, assuming he was some rich guy. King for a day. He loved it.

"Would you like a pillow or blanket?" Liz asked Jim and Anna.

"Maybe later," Anna replied.

"Can I get you a drink? Would you like to see the wine list?"

"I want a Shirley Temple, with cherries," Ruby chirped.

"It's a little early for wine," Anna said. "Maybe with lunch. I'll take an orange juice, please."

"Sure, we have fresh-squeezed. And you, sir?"

"Do you have Pellegrino?" Jim asked.

"Yes sir, with lime?"

"Great."

"I like this," Anna said, as Liz left to get the beverages, dodging her blonde colleague, Jane, the other first-class flight attendant.

"This is obviously the only way to fly," Jim agreed.

As he settled into his seat. Jim's tension began to lift and he wondered why he had avoided air travel all this time. This was great. All it took was money. If you had to spend five or six hours on a plane, this was the way to do it.

Jim smiled as the little old lady with the cane he had spoken to in the skyway passed in the aisle, along with a bunch of other little old ladies, all wearing sneakers. She smiled back and Jim felt a tiny twinge of guilt that this handicapped senior was shuffling toward the uncomfortable cheap seats. It quickly passed.

As she limped through the port aisle of the first-class cabin on her aluminum cane, Emily noticed the young family who had passed her, sitting in the last row, to her left, a nice middle-aged couple with a beautiful little Chinese girl, obviously adopted. On the right, in the last row, two men were already seated, which was curious. Where did they come from? In the aisle seat was a husky man of about forty with straw-colored hair pointed in a wedge down his forehead. Behind him was the bulkhead wall between first class and coach. Next to him was another husky man with a big forehead, thick black hair and dark, shifty eyes. The sandy fellow smiled at her as she passed. His smile had mischief in it and reminded her a little of the brittle black-and-white photographs of her dad in uniform from the war. But this man looks a bit like a devil with blond hair, Emily thought. She wondered how the sandy-haired Satan had gotten there before her. She was certain she had been one of the first onboard, along with the family and a pregnant woman.

Jim saw Emily looking at the men and wondered the same thing. Jim solved mysteries for a living. Where had the two bruisers come from? One was wearing a navy blazer with gold buttons and the other was wearing an olive-colored linen sport coat. They were the most dressed-up men on the plane and they were the only two people in first class from whom Liz the flight attendant had not yet taken a drink order. A light bulb went off in Jim's head. They must be sky marshals, or whatever they were called now. Of course. Maybe. Jim wanted to ask but did not think he should.

"Hi, howya doin'?" the blondish guy in the seat across the aisle said to Jim.

Jim realized he had been staring at him. "Uh, hi. Great. Vacation. You, too, I guess?" Jim asked, lamely.

"No. Business, but we'll be sneaking in some golf and some fishing, if we can, right, Artie?"

"What? Oh, yeah, definitely," Artie recovered, his eyes flicking from passenger to passenger. "Always."

Jim smiled. He didn't believe a word of it. They even sounded like cops. Not only do we have an impregnable cockpit, but we have a personal armed escort. Things have really changed for the better. Jim turned away as Liz arrived with the drinks—in real crystal glasses, not plastic cups. Jim put down his tray table and Liz set down his icy water, a real napkin and a little porcelain dish of honey-roasted cashews—not peanuts, like in coach. Jim took a handful of nuts, a sip of liquid and settled into his soft seat. As he exhaled, all the remaining fear and tension drained from his body. He turned to Anna and Ruby, who were also sipping their drinks. Ruby's had a red umbrella in it. She was using the parasol toothpick to spear cherries.

"The vacation has officially begun," Jim announced, smiling.

Federal Air Marshal Ed Boetsch turned to his partner Artie Flagler. "The guy across from me just made us," Ed said under his breath.

"Definitely," Artie agreed.

It was not the first time they had been noticed. Just another day at the office. So much for blending in. Ed turned back to the aisle and eyeballed everyone, smiling at each passenger who passed, starting with the nice old lady with the cane and pink hair. You could tell a lot from a smile. Or even a nonreaction to someone else's smile. Any good cop could. When full, the plane held more than 200 passengers, everyone with their own lives and secret thoughts. Too bad I can't read minds, Ed thought.

Law enforcement would be so much easier if I just knew what was in their heads. Many of those lugging stuff toward their seats ignored Ed and did not smile back but that was fine. Indifference was okay. Fear of the weird smiling guy or embarrassment was cool. A watcher noticing a watcher was not okay. That's what Ed was looking for. There were a lot of little old ladies, some kind of tour, a lot of families with kids, the plane not quite half full. It was off-season for Mexico. In first class, it was the usual assortment of the privileged: a Chinese or Korean executive type, some white guy with big shades and polo shirt, who looked like a movie producer. A very pretty, very pregnant woman with long black hair and a squirrelly-looking husband in Gucci. An older married couple wearing enough gold to be charged for extra baggage weight, and a crunchy granola couple with a cute Chinese kid. There was also a huge black guy, and a shorter white guy, and a hipster with long hair at a computer. Everybody seemed to be carrying those bottles of personal spring water these days. Why was everybody so thirsty all the time? Ed didn't remember people being that thirsty when he was a kid. Why were they now? Water and other liquids were available almost everywhere. Why did they need it in the car, on the street, all the time? Maybe they didn't trust the tap water. Ed had one alert on today's flight, the ranch run, a flagged passenger in seat 18A, the girl. There she was. He recognized her from her mug shot as she walked through first class toward coach. Brown hair, twisted into pigtails, farmer-Bob coveralls. Pretty, except for the stupid eyebrow ring and the six stud earrings in her ears. Her last bust had been for smashing windows during a political protest in Seattle or some shit. Speaking of busts, nice rack, he thought. She did not smile back at Ed, she glared, her eyes challenging. Did she think he was hitting on her or was it something else? Ed chuckled. He just realized. Her name. Antoinette D'Anza. Toni D'Anza, like the guy, the actor.

What a hoot. If I said "Hi, Toni," she'd freak, Ed thought, smiling all the more.

Antoinette stared right back at the guy in first class who was leering at her, staring at her breasts under her stone-washed safari shirt. Pig. First class was for swine. She detested flying. It required submitting to the fascist machine, the humiliating searches, the probing, the questions. The illegitimate, unelected right-wing regime of America needed the myth of foreign terror to support their power, their lies. It was all fake. The war was over in Afghanistan, or it would have been over, if they had had the guts to trap or kill the Taliban and Al Qaeda, to face the fighters directly, like men. But no, that would have made it impossible for them to invade Iraq—if the war was over already or if they had captured Osama bin Laden. None of this was about Islam, or so-called terrorism, it was about the corporate coup d'état of America, about making the world safe for the Halliburton Corporation, about making America safe for Republican campaign contributors, the polluters, the pigs in first class.

She should be the worst I ever have to deal with, a big-mouth activist, a kid, Ed thought as Antoinette passed. A spoiled rich bitch on the way to visit her rich parents. So far, it was all boring, thank God. This was his last ranch run before his own vacation, two weeks in Vermont—fishing and camping and no airplanes. He and Sharon needed some time alone. Ed shifted his weight in the seat off his pistol in the hidden holster in the small of his back, under his shirt and looked at the middle-aged rich couple up front, typical first-class passengers. Loaded. The wife was a nice sight, pretty and with a body that probably had a whole Olympics of exercise in it. The marshal admired her hair, which had obviously not come out of a bottle. It looked like a frozen blonde hurricane stuck on a long, tanned neck. Ed did not even try to read her mind.

The blonde woman, Danielle, was thinking about shoes and sex. She was angry because she definitely did not have enough shoes with her. She never did. She would have to supplement but she hated depending on fate, on the unlikely possibility that the small resort shops would have what she needed. And all the colors of her shoes and clothing would look different in the tropical light, she knew they would. She could never get it right, never get it perfect. She would have to design her own shoes. It was the only way. She would start in the morning. If there was time. Danielle tugged at her neck and removed a hunt-print Hermès silk scarf. She patted her reddish-gold hair, which was done up in a perfect swirl. Danielle folded her scarf into her burgundy leather Coach bag on her lap and ordered an apple martini with Ketel One vodka. She wondered if the resort still had that masseur, the one who came to your villa? What was his name, Enrique? The one with the amazing hands.

Next to her sat her husband, C. Gordon Pope, who never used his first name. Charles was his father's name, not his. He didn't want it. He was stuck with the initial C but everyone called him Gordon. Of course, he was the spitting image of his dead dad, black hair gone gray, the round face, puffy jowls, cold blue eyes. He sounded like his father, moved like him and was just as unfaithful to his wife as Charles was to Gordon's mother. But Gordon was not thinking about any of that. As usual, as he arranged himself in his first-class seat, Gordon was thinking about chemicals and interstate transportation. And politics, of course. And money, always money.

Ed looked again at the pregnant woman up front on the other

side. Please, God, do not let her give birth on the flight. Somewhere in the underbelly of the jet, a steel door slammed, vibrating the cabin.

Instinctively, one of Maria's finely manicured hands reached to caress her swollen belly under her white, Ralph Lauren silk top. She gently stroked the warm skin and said a prayer. With each tiny stroke, she prayed, consciously pushing away her fears about the future. Her husband, Joey, smiled kindly at her and took her hand. Slowly, she responded. Her lips, as red and wide as Julia Roberts's, parted and exposed perfect teeth that gleamed brightly, like virgin ivory.

Bob Ipswitch, a man of average height and looks, slid into the next-to-last row in first class, right in front of Ed, who smiled at him. Bob's frosted brown hair and mustache were trimmed neatly, giving him the look of a professional, such as a government official or an engineer, and he was both. Bob took the window seat because he knew Lester needed the aisle seat. Both were in their forties but Lester was a head taller than Bob, with twice the muscle mass, a large powerful black man with a shaved, glistening head. Bob and Lester both feigned indifference to each other, a long-practiced habit in public. Soon it would all be over, the lies. This flight was the beginning of the end of the lies. Everything would change. Everyone would know. Bob smiled, blushing like a bride, giddy at the thought.

Lester noticed and returned the secret smile.

Matt was working on his laptop, multitasking as usual, under his personal screen name GHOSTBOOTS, in touch via instant messaging with two assistants at his company, Van Hellsing Security Associates, in Manhattan, and two of his operatives, one in Seattle and the other in Boston. They were discussing a threat made to a new client in California. Several other of Matt's security team were on-site in Hollywood, working with the customer. They were discussing a sensitive Phase Three attack, using multi-encryption software to keep their plans for illegal behavior private. He bailed out of the IM session and into his official e-mail moniker, VANHELLSING1, in order to reassure the corporate CEO under blackmail threat that everything was being done to guard against the menace. Matt explained that they were in Phase One, in which defensive measures were being readied against the threatened attack, while the threat was being traced back to its hidden source. It was important, at this stage, as the countdown proceeded, to determine, if possible, whether the danger was a random external assault by a professional, an inside job, or if a competitor had hired a professional to cripple or kill. Phase Two was fighting off any assault and alerting authorities about the attacker, hoping for an arrest. There was a Phase Three but Matt would only discuss that in person with the client. He would never commit it to paper or, worse, to a computer. Phase One and Phase Two had made his company very successful. Phase Three, the stake-through-the-heart phase, had made him a millionaire before he was thirty-five. Matt was sitting in the single seat just in front of Jim. The younger man held a first-class ticket but he had purchased it for almost the price of a coach seat on the web, by pretending to be a travel agent. Matt loved music and he looked like a geek disguised as a rock star. Just thirty-six, he wore faded blue jeans, brown leather Top-Siders without socks and a faded short-sleeved T-shirt with a picture of a meditating Buddha on the front that featured the words "Inquire Within." Over the T-shirt, he wore a black leather vest, unbuttoned. Encircling his left bicep was a barbed, interlocking black Polynesian tattoo. Finished with business for the moment, he adjusted his John Lennon shades that emerged from his long black hair and logged off his laptop and closed it.

"Here's your Diet Pepsi, sir," Liz said, handing over the can and an iced crystal glass.

"Thanks. What did you say your name was?"

"Liz, Mr. Newton."

"Please call me Matt. May I say that you are the most beautiful woman I have seen in a long time?"

Liz smiled. "Yes, you may say it, Mr. Newton. Thank you."

"And what about me?" Matt asked, pouting.

"Okay," Liz said, with a grin. "You are also the most beautiful women I have seen in a long time."

They both laughed.

"Okay, I deserved that but it's the simple truth. I'm sorry if my social retardation has offended you or your husband, or your boyfriend," said Matt.

"No you haven't offended any of us."

"Good, thanks for the liquid."

"You're very welcome," Liz said.

Matt was sure her eyes were saying just that.

"So, what are you working on?" Liz asked politely, nodding at his laptop.

"Bots and Zombies and their evil masters who send their herds out across the world to destroy."

"No, seriously."

"Seriously," Matt said, smiling back. "The shadow world that most people do not know exists, even though most of them are pawns or victims. International blackmail and terrorism."

"You're in the FBI?"

"No," said Matt. "But I have had extensive dealings with them. Enough, in fact, to last me a lifetime."

"Oh. Okay, enjoy," said Liz, walking away with a friendly smile, wondering if she should point him out to the marshals.

★ ★ ★ ★ ★

She digs me, Matt thought. As he watched Liz walk away, Matt fondled a small platinum rectangle hanging from a platinum chain around his neck. It was a sophisticated storage device he had designed, which contained several virulent viruses. The federal TSA employee at the security gate at the airport had noticed the shiny pendant but thought it was some kind of charm, "a cute little toy harmonica," she called it.

The security officer never asked Matt to play a tune.

# 2.

Paul pulled his U.S. Marine Corps Zippo lighter out of his uniform pocket with his right hand and flicked the stainless top open with a pleasing ring. He flicked the flint wheel with his thumb but got only a spark and that dry, sharp smell of metal against flint—no flame. He thumbed the wheel several more times without fire.

"Sarge, give me a break," moaned Officer Cindy Bernstein from behind the wheel, as she pulled away from the two-story white blockhouse of Building 61, Port Authority Police Headquarters at Kennedy Airport in Queens. "If you're going to smoke one of those turds, at least open the window," Cindy said, waving her left hand in front of her face, her diamond wedding ring flashing. She glanced over at Paul's beer belly, which covered his seat belt. Gross.

"Turds?" Paul asked indignantly, rummaging in the glove compartment of their marked RMP. "This fine see-gar costs all of a dollar."

"It's disgusting and against departmental regulations," said Cindy, a nonsmoker, although she was only half-serious.

"I thought you were a vegetarian? Or is it vee-gan? This is a vegetable. I have more, if you'd like a nosh," Paul offered, waving the fat Primo like a pickle.

"No thanks."

Paul located the yellow can of lighter fluid in the glove box and squirted a few drops onto the wick, closed the bottom of his lighter and replaced the can of fluid in the glove box.

"I thought cigar smokers only used matches to preserve the flavor of the tobacco?" she asked.

"You have obviously mistaken me for a rich cigar twit," Paul replied. "I started smoking these babies in the bush, in 'Nam. It was like a steam room there. Matches didn't work."

"That stuff is a fire hazard. Why don't you use a disposable butane lighter instead of that stone-age torch?"

PAPD Sergeant Paul Ambrosino fired up his stogie and flipped his lighter shut. He puffed blue smoke out the open window and looked back at the younger officer as if she were insane.

"Because of the smell. Haven't you been listening? Butane tastes like sucking a gas pipe. Ruins the smoke. Lighter fluid smells like. . . . like . . . Victory," grinned Paul, a movie fan, as he savored the smoke.

Cindy rolled her eyes. She noticed again that Paul ran his hand over his shiny bald spot whenever he thought he had been funny. She wanted to tell him that the hair wasn't there anymore but she never did. Cindy turned into a security gate. She waved to the guard and then accelerated across the tarmac, toward the Anytime Airline terminal.

"Unit 1632 to Central, 10-85 on the tarmac at Anytime, bay 18, 'kay?" a voice said over the car's radio.

"Yeah, 1632, got it, three no-shows. We're enroute to bay 16," Paul replied, keying the radio mike. "Continue supervising baggage removal."

"They're done already, Sarge. They're just buttoning up and preparing for departure."

Booked passengers not showing up for flights was not very unusual. As a security precaution, however, the plane had to be held and the baggage checked—to make sure no one had put a suitcase containing a bomb on a plane they were not on.

"No, Sarge, 16 and 14, we got two no-shows, three each on two different flights."

"You're on 16, 1632?"

"Affirmative. 1809 is at bay 14. I can see him from here."

"Okay, I'll be there in five," Paul told the officer.

When Paul and Cindy arrived, Unit 1632, Officer Gina Torres, waved and walked over to their car.

"The baggage handlers already double-checked the compartments in both planes," said Torres. "No big deal, the gates say none of the six people on either flight checked in or checked any bags. Total no-shows."

"Good. I'll go say hi," said Paul.

He stowed his cigar inside a shiny metal tube, screwed the cap on and left it on the dashboard. He got out and strode over to the companionway 16 door, opened it with a swipe of his security card pass and mounted the stairs of the skyway and walked up to the gate. There were two pretty women in blue and white uniforms behind the Anytime Airways Gate 16 counter, one with a blonde pageboy haircut and the other with a chestnut ponytail. The blonde, who had one of those beauty marks near the corner of her mouth, like that model Cindy Crawford, was on the phone. She was very pretty but didn't look like Cindy Crawford, who had brown hair. Her partner with the ponytail looked more like her. Actually, Paul thought, neither one looked like that model but Anytime had the prettiest agents and stewardesses. Paul felt older than his fifty-five years. His daughter was in high school, almost as old as these young career women. It bothered him that they were so young and so busy, with little experience or time to spot problems. He asked the girl with the ponytail for a printout of the names of the no-shows on the flight to Washington, strictly routine. He glanced at the computer printout when she handed it over the white countertop. They were code M for males and all three had Arab-sounding names.

"Were there any holds or alerts on these guys?" Paul asked, now a lot more interested. "Were they on either of the CAPPS lists?" he asked, referring to the Transportation Security Administration's Computer Assisted Passenger Prescreening System.

"No and no," the clerk replied. "None of them were on either the 'No-Fly' or the 'Selectee' TSA lists. So, if they had shown up, they would be onboard by now. But they're not." She yawned. The same scene had been enacted dozens of times before, without incident. People missed a connecting flight, or they overbooked to get standby seats. It could have been for many reasons. The CAPPS lists were the bottom line in airline security. The two big watch lists, with several hundred thousand names in the databases, had been compiled and updated from the FBI's data on terrorist names. The no-fly list was just that. A person who was identified as being on that list could not get on an airplane. Anyone who appeared on the Selectee List could fly—after they received an extra level of fine-tooth-comb security.

"Okay, thanks," said Paul, thanking the ticket agent with the ponytail.

He walked down to Gate 14 and went through the same thing with another ticket agent. The printout there showed three different names for a flight to Boston. They were also all Middle Eastern male names. What are the odds, Paul wondered? Was it coincidence that so many guys with Islamic names failed to show up for two flights on the same airline, almost at the same time on the same day? Probably. If they had shown up and gotten on the planes, Paul would have never heard about it. They would be gone.

Paul checked with the TSA supervisor by radio, who told him there was nothing unusual at the security checkpoints. The

Homeland Security guy had rechecked all of the names through the computer and they were all clean. Case closed. Paul radioed his captain and told him what he had learned.

"Good. All wrapped up?"

Paul did not answer at first.

"All wrapped up, Paul?"

The captain had heard this silence before. Paul's two brothers, a firefighter and an NYPD lieutenant, had both gone down in the Towers. The captain had seen Paul make vows to two different closed caskets that it would never happen again, that his brothers' fatherless kids would be safe. The captain waited.

"I just want to ask around a bit more, just to be certain, Cap."

The captain sighed.

"Somebody may be doing a dry run on us, Cap. What are the odds? One of these days . . ."

"Okay, Paul. I already put these names through channels. When you're done, there's a CAPPS no-fly hold at Delta Gate 11 but it looks like it's unfounded."

"Who's the hold?"

"Some seven-year-old boy from Staten Island has the same name as a forty-six-year-old Belgian Islamist and TSA and Homeland Security don't want to let him board."

The captain could hear Paul laughing over the radio. About once a day at the airport, someone who had a name similar to one on the 257,000-name terror watch list had to be checked out, no matter how silly it was. But Paul knew the bastards, the terrorists, would try again—because they already had. Paul had knowledge of several plots that had been foiled that the public did not know about, like that poisoned baby formula thing in Queens and Brooklyn. Paul radioed Cindy down in the car and ordered her to call all the airline security chiefs on her cell phone, to see if anything out of the ordinary had happened

# 3.

Emily hated flying more than diabetes, more than her sluggish left leg, even more than the cane she needed to drag the hateful sausage forward. For weeks she had dreaded the flight, the bus ride from New Jersey to New York's Kennedy Airport, ruining the anticipation of a tropical vacation with her women's club. If Lou were still alive he would have distracted her, teased her out of it. He would not have let her use his death as an excuse. Emily often turned to speak to Lou or ask him a question. Two years ago, right after his massive stroke, Emily would often call out to him in the house, "Lou! Where did you put the . . ." and stop and sob. Now, she only turned to look for him and, when she remembered he wasn't there, she still felt only a slight flutter of pain, where she once had felt a stab. Then she would just know what Lou's answer was. It wasn't like a ghost or anything. At the funeral, the priest had said that everyone who loved Lou had part of him in their hearts. Emily thought it was a bland cliché but she came to realize it was true. Part of Lou had stayed here with her. She smiled to herself and spoke silently once more to her dead husband. The only problem, Lou, is that you took your part of me with you.

Emily's fellow coach section passengers were stowing their bags in the overhead storage compartments, and clicking their seatbelts. A nice, tall young boy with freckles in a bright red "U.S.A." T-shirt helped Emily put her bag away. Someone was discussing today's newspaper story about the next presidential election, how the Democrats would use the upcoming senate hearing and the possible corruption charges against the vice president. Politics did not interest Emily. Everyone seemed so calm, Emily thought, as her friends from the club chatted and gossiped about one of the ladies who didn't come on the trip. They all think hurtling through the air inside a metal tube at more than four hundred miles an hour is normal, routine. Look at all these lovely children, Emily thought. Nothing bad could happen with all these lovely kids here, could it? It's just not possible. God would not allow it. Across the aisle, a handsome young uniformed soldier stowed his bag above her head and said hello to Emily. He was army, not navy, like her dad. Her heart beat faster. She took a deep breath and closed her eyes, like she had learned in her Yoga for Seniors class. Was it the uniform? No, it was the plane, the old fear. Again she saw the same imagined scene in her mind's eye: the silver bullet plane on the beautiful sunny day, the red flames exploding with a sound louder than the ears could hear, the religious suicide, the murder. It was so long ago, that bright day, but it never went away. She opened her eyes and began chatting with her friends, refusing to give in to the pulsing fear in her chest.

Specialist fourth class Angel Cruces was on leave from the army but it wasn't the same thing as a vacation. He was heading home to Mexico, to visit his family. It was great to be heading home to the same family, the same town, the same jokes, even the same arguments. His dad would never understand why he fought for America and wanted to be an American. He could hear his father's repeated question: "What kind of man lays his life on the line for people who don't think he's good enough to be a citizen?" But there would be his mother, hugging him and crying, cooking. He could almost smell the burnt pinon tree heat of the desert, the tang of the salt air on the tongue, the mouthwatering burn of the chiles verdes.

Emmett Hazlett, Jr. also scanned the boarding passengers filing onto the plane in the coach seats. Some were laughing; one family was squabbling. None of them was thinking of God, Emmett thought. Except him. They were sinners, so many of them nonbelievers, the enemies of God, seekers after smooth things. All seemed unaware that He could take them at any moment—especially in the air, in the heavens, so close. Were they ready? Emmett thought not. He was. Ready to vanish in an instant, ready to be gathered unto Paradise, all in a rapture. Emmett took the Good Book out of his bag before he stowed it, intending to read The Revelation of John again. Emmett looked at a young couple across the aisle. They were seriously making out, hot and heavy, not an easy task while wearing seatbelts. They couldn't keep their hands off each other and didn't care who saw them, almost fornicating in their seats. "Disgusting," Emmett whispered in his wife's direction.

Emmett's wife, Valerie, glanced at her husband as she reached for the in-flight magazine. She saw that familiar hateful look on his face and she knew what he was thinking, angry that his thoughts played openly across his face like a screen. She sighed. Could the other passengers see his thoughts? Would they guess? It was obvious from the wedding rings, the new haircuts, new clothes, that the beautiful young couple entwined in each other's arms he was glaring at were honeymooners. A long time ago, Emmett did not think such behavior was disgusting or sinful, Valerie thought. Soon, it wouldn't matter. This flight is taking us to heaven or to hell, she knew. She ignored her husband and began flipping through the photos of luxury gifts on the shiny magazine pages.

Emmett averted his eyes to his open Bible, still convinced he was the only one onboard thinking about God.

He was wrong.

The plane jolted slightly, as the tractor connected to the front landing gear and overcame the inertia of the red, white and blue aircraft's 74,000 kilograms in preparation for takeoff. Large TV screens descended in the front of each passenger section, flickering. A videotape played, showing the usual safety lecture about fastening seatbelts, emergency exits, flotation devices, and oxygen masks. Only a few passengers watched. They were issued earphones for the built-in television screens in the seat backs. The kids quickly tuned to the Disney Channel, Cartoon Network, movie channels, or logged onto an interactive video game that everyone on board could play, their own internet. Adults surfed a range of television channels, networks and cable stations like the History Channel, news stations like CNN and Fox and even a navigation channel showing their route, direction, outside temperature and altitude and a map showing a little stationary plane, covering most of Long Island, just east of Manhattan. There were no built-in cell phones, the ones with a credit card slot. Passengers had to use their own, which they were told to turn off, along with all other electronic devices and get ready for takeoff. In first class, Matt Newton shut off his powerful wireless laptop and stowed it in its case under his seat. Only Ruby and several other kids farther back were fascinated by the taxi along the concrete runway but most of the adults watched the takeoff. A few, like Jim and Emily, gripped their armrests with white knuckles.

The 767 banked to the southwest as they steadily climbed to a cruising altitude of thirty-seven-thousand feet, Captain Cornell announced in a deep, calming sonorous voice. Once they had leveled off, a few passengers got up to use the bathrooms, including Marie, waddling behind her swollen belly. Artie watched her, as her husband assisted the pregnant woman through the folding door of one of the two first-class lavatories.

From his seat next to Artie, Ed Boetsch also noticed the expectant mom. It made Ed nostalgic, thinking of when Amy was pregnant with the boys, back when things were simple and open, before having drinks turned into drinking and screwing around. Ed's sponsor at AA said he had to tell Amy everything. Only one problem, Ed thought. If I do, she'll leave and take the kids, sure as shit. The boys will never look at me the same again. It made no sense to destroy something in order to save it, he was sure. He had already done most of the heavy lifting. He had left NYPD after fifteen years in, quit the drinking and other stuff. He made a new start with this sky marshal job, even though it was nothing but one boring flight after another. There has to be a way around the bullshit. Criminals get a second chance but cops and husbands don't. I want a do-over, Ed thought, with a bitter smirk. Life should come with a fucking reset button.

# 4.

Kevin faintly heard the phone ringing across the lawn, inside the red-shingled house in Centerport, Long Island, above the hissing of a sprinkler. He turned back to the game on the portable color TV on the umbrella table next to his chaise lounge by the pool. Kevin was still damp from doing his fifty laps, glowing from the exercise in the summer heat, a rare moment for him. He was sipping an iced tea from a hard plastic glass dripping with condensation, the tart smell of the lemon wedge in his nose. On a small, portable color TV on the table, the Mets were at bat at Shea Stadium in Queens. For Kevin Toomey, who always worked six or seven days a week, it was a rare Saturday off, a day many big bosses at NYPD and other police departments routinely took off. At work, Kevin was known as the NYPD Deputy Commissioner for Counterterrorism. Kevin watched, as the batter stepped up to the plate for the second time. It was the player's first time back in the starting lineup in the month since he had been injured. The first time, he had belted one into the right field stands for a homer. It wasn't looking good for the Astros. The pitcher wound up and fired one down toward the plate. The batter went down, the horse hide bouncing off his batting helmet. The game stopped as people rushed to the fallen player. A replay showed a slow-motion white ball ricocheting off his helmet and him staggering away like a wounded soldier.

"Son of a bitch!" Kevin said to the set.

was the only one onboard thinking about God.

He was wrong.

The plane jolted slightly, as the tractor connected to the front landing gear and overcame the inertia of the red, white and blue aircraft's 74,000 kilograms in preparation for takeoff. Large TV screens descended in the front of each passenger section, flickering. A videotape played, showing the usual safety lecture about fastening seatbelts, emergency exits, flotation devices, and oxygen masks. Only a few passengers watched. They were issued earphones for the built-in television screens in the seat backs. The kids quickly tuned to the Disney Channel, Cartoon Network, movie channels, or logged onto an interactive video game that everyone on board could play, their own internet. Adults surfed a range of television channels, networks and cable stations like the History Channel, news stations like CNN and Fox and even a navigation channel showing their route, direction, outside temperature and altitude and a map showing a little stationary plane, covering most of Long Island, just east of Manhattan. There were no built-in cell phones, the ones with a credit card slot. Passengers had to use their own, which they were told to turn off, along with all other electronic devices and get ready for takeoff. In first class, Matt Newton shut off his powerful wireless laptop and stowed it in its case under his seat. Only Ruby and several other kids farther back were fascinated by the taxi along the concrete runway but most of the adults watched the takeoff. A few, like Jim and Emily, gripped their armrests with white knuckles.

The 767 banked to the southwest as they steadily climbed to a cruising altitude of thirty-seven-thousand feet, Captain Cornell announced in a deep, calming sonorous voice. Once they had leveled off, a few passengers got up to use the bathrooms, including Marie, waddling behind her swollen belly. Artie mouthwatering burn of the chiles verdes.

Emmett Hazlett, Jr. also scanned the boarding passengers filing onto the plane in the coach seats. Some were laughing; one family was squabbling. None of them was thinking of God, Emmett thought. Except him. They were sinners, so many of them nonbelievers, the enemies of God, seekers after smooth things. All seemed unaware that He could take them at any moment—especially in the air, in the heavens, so close. Were they ready? Emmett thought not. He was. Ready to vanish in an instant, ready to be gathered unto Paradise, all in a rapture. Emmett took the Good Book out of his bag before he stowed it, intending to read The Revelation of John again. Emmett looked at a young couple across the aisle. They were seriously making out, hot and heavy, not an easy task while wearing seatbelts. They couldn't keep their hands off each other and didn't care who saw them, almost fornicating in their seats. "Disgusting," Emmett whispered in his wife's direction.

Emmett's wife, Valerie, glanced at her husband as she reached for the in-flight magazine. She saw that familiar hateful look on his face and she knew what he was thinking, angry that his thoughts played openly across his face like a screen. She sighed. Could the other passengers see his thoughts? Would they guess? It was obvious from the wedding rings, the new haircuts, new clothes, that the beautiful young couple entwined in each other's arms he was glaring at were honeymooners. A long time ago, Emmett did not think such behavior was disgusting or sinful, Valerie thought. Soon, it wouldn't matter. This flight is taking us to heaven or to hell, she knew. She ignored her husband and began flipping through the photos of luxury gifts on the shiny magazine pages.

Emmett averted his eyes to his open Bible, still convinced he election, how the Democrats would use the upcoming senate hearing and the possible corruption charges against the vice president. Politics did not interest Emily. Everyone seemed so calm, Emily thought, as her friends from the club chatted and gossiped about one of the ladies who didn't come on the trip. They all think hurtling through the air inside a metal tube at more than four hundred miles an hour is normal, routine. Look at all these lovely children, Emily thought. Nothing bad could happen with all these lovely kids here, could it? It's just not possible. God would not allow it. Across the aisle, a handsome young uniformed soldier stowed his bag above her head and said hello to Emily. He was army, not navy, like her dad. Her heart beat faster. She took a deep breath and closed her eyes, like she had learned in her Yoga for Seniors class. Was it the uniform? No, it was the plane, the old fear. Again she saw the same imagined scene in her mind's eye: the silver bullet plane on the beautiful sunny day, the red flames exploding with a sound louder than the ears could hear, the religious suicide, the murder. It was so long ago, that bright day, but it never went away. She opened her eyes and began chatting with her friends, refusing to give in to the pulsing fear in her chest.

Specialist fourth class Angel Cruces was on leave from the army but it wasn't the same thing as a vacation. He was heading home to Mexico, to visit his family. It was great to be heading home to the same family, the same town, the same jokes, even the same arguments. His dad would never understand why he fought for America and wanted to be an American. He could hear his father's repeated question: "What kind of man lays his life on the line for people who don't think he's good enough to be a citizen?" But there would be his mother, hugging him and crying, cooking. He could almost smell the burnt pinon tree heat of the desert, the tang of the salt air on the tongue, the

# 3.

Emily hated flying more than diabetes, more than her sluggish left leg, even more than the cane she needed to drag the hateful sausage forward. For weeks she had dreaded the flight, the bus ride from New Jersey to New York's Kennedy Airport, ruining the anticipation of a tropical vacation with her women's club. If Lou were still alive he would have distracted her, teased her out of it. He would not have let her use his death as an excuse. Emily often turned to speak to Lou or ask him a question. Two years ago, right after his massive stroke, Emily would often call out to him in the house, "Lou! Where did you put the . . ." and stop and sob. Now, she only turned to look for him and, when she remembered he wasn't there, she still felt only a slight flutter of pain, where she once had felt a stab. Then she would just know what Lou's answer was. It wasn't like a ghost or anything. At the funeral, the priest had said that everyone who loved Lou had part of him in their hearts. Emily thought it was a bland cliché but she came to realize it was true. Part of Lou had stayed here with her. She smiled to herself and spoke silently once more to her dead husband. The only problem, Lou, is that you took your part of me with you.

Emily's fellow coach section passengers were stowing their bags in the overhead storage compartments, and clicking their seatbelts. A nice, tall young boy with freckles in a bright red "U.S.A." T-shirt helped Emily put her bag away. Someone was discussing today's newspaper story about the next presidential anywhere in the airport, without waiting for the usual delay in reporting. Paul used his personal cell phone to call the desk officers at the local precincts around the airports but it was just the usual daily mayhem. Nothing suspicious. Paul called the Queens FBI office and left a message for the agent in charge, who had been taking longer and longer to return his frequent calls. Cindy called back to tell him that none of the other airlines reported anything unusual this morning, except for someone vomiting in a restroom.

"Wait, did you say all the other airlines? Did you call the guy for Anytime Airways?"

"No," said Cindy. "I thought you already spoke to those people."

"No, I didn't. Just the ticket agents. Never mind, I'll do it by land line from the gate up here," Paul said.

But when he walked back, the blonde and brunette at Gate 16 were gone, off to other assignments. Paul walked to the next gate, Gate 18, where he saw a lone female agent under a sign that said "Flight 1787 CABO SAN LUCAS nonstop."

Paul identified himself and asked to use the phone to talk to the airline's security chief. The young woman punched in four numbers and handed Paul the phone. The head of security was not in today but his deputy said it was dull as dishwater, nothing unusual at all, except for the no-shows Paul already knew about.

"It's as dead as Kelsey's nuts," he said.

Paul thanked him and hung up. On September 11th, Paul had been off-duty but he knew that if he had been working, he would have had no clue about the terror plot. He raced into work and, later, to Ground Zero, in Manhattan, to hunt for the bodies of his brothers. Paul also knew he would never be the same kind of cop again—waiting for something to happen. He felt everyone on the job had to question everything, every day, and hunt for that out-of-place event or person or detail. Any loose thread had to be tugged on right away, in case it wasn't loose, wasn't random. In case it was attached to something.

Paul thought for a moment. He reopened his cell phone and dialed his sister's house on Long Island.

"Wait, he's back in the game. He's taking his base."

"Good for him. Look, Kevin, this may be important."

"Paul, don't tell me you're not coming to the party. Dina will be very upset. She's already pissed I'm watching the game."

"Kevin, I'm sorry to call on your day off. I'll be there. I just had to let you know about something happening here. Just in case."

"Okay, Paul, no problem."

Kevin listened as Paul quickly detailed the events of the morning. It was not the first time Paul had used the back door to advise Kevin of doings at the airport, outside of channels. It was impossible to dismiss Paul's worries as mere paranoia because Paul had pulled that poisoned baby formula tip out of some guy caught coming in with hashish from Istanbul and it turned out to be true. Paul always jumped to the worst conclusion, which is why Kevin sometimes did not feed his paranoia. He had never told Paul about the intelligence reports that said Osama bin Laden used to be, and still was, the best agent the Saudi Secret Service ever had. Paul related the morning's incident, explained that he had run the names through the computer and they were not on any watch list. He also listed the checks he had made, all negative. He had done everything required and more. Kevin waited and did not reply, the silence building on the phone.

"I have a feeling about this one, Kevin."

Shit, Kevin thought, don't say that. He knew that Paul was such a good cop, he could sometimes seem psychic. He made more felony collars than anyone in his department as an officer—because he could spot who was holding a weapon or dope from thirty paces away.

"You also had a funny feeling about that guy with the shoes and the belt," Paul pointed out. "Just because he was a Moslem. You have to be careful about profiling lawsuits, Paul. I mean,

His younger blonde wife, Dina, in a turquoise bikini appeared over Kevin, holding the portable phone, and saying his name loudly.

"Sorry, what? Did you see that?"

"No. It's Paul for you."

Dina's eyebrows went up as she handed over the phone and walked away. Kevin winced. Dina had told him she was happy that Paul was spending the day home. It was her birthday and her party was set for that night. Now Paul was calling. For him. That could mean only one thing. Kevin sighed and put the phone to his ear.

"Hello? Paul? You watching the game?"

He knew Paul was not watching the game.

"No, I'm still at work. Listen, I think you need . . ."

Kevin explained how the Astros pitcher had beaned the player on his second time at bat. "Looks like his comeback might be over. I think he's out of the game," Kevin said.

"What did he do first time at bat?" Paul asked his brother-in-law.

"Homer. Right field."

"They beaned him on purpose, before he could do it again. Did the coach talk to the pitcher before the pitch?" Paul asked.

"I think so, but you don't know if . . ."

"They beaned him to knock him out of the game or make him gun shy. He's too good. It's the smart move," Paul said.

"How can you . . ."

"Kevin, are you suggesting that a guy who gets paid millions of dollars a year to place a ball accurately in space missed by that much? By accident?"

"The pitcher's arm may have just given out. It happens all the time," said Kevin.

"Bullshit," Paul replied. "Listen, Kevin, we have a situation that . . ."

just because his belt was black and his dress shoes were brown, I mean . . ."

"Okay, I was wrong. Once," Paul laughed. "He wasn't a terrorist—he was only a currency smuggler. He was still a bad guy. We locked him up. No lawsuit."

"That's because you are a lucky guy. Okay, Paul, let's hear it before the next inning."

"This is, like, the third time this has happened—once at Newark and once at MacArthur in Islip," Paul reminded Kevin. Paul had jumped on the Newark thing, even though he wasn't assigned there. Paul only knew about the Islip thing because a guy in his volunteer fire department in Center Moriches was a cop there and mentioned it. He certainly didn't get it from the feds. Kevin and Paul both considered feds lawyers with guns, politicians. In each case, several people who had made reservations failed to show up and did not, in fact, exist. They all had Arab names.

"Somebody is probing us, I'm sure of it," Paul said.

Kevin's stomach churned. This was his daylight nightmare—Islamist terrorists slipping in and attacking without tripping any alarms. Their jobs had a built-in failure. They had to foil every plot before it happened, every time—and they had. So far. But the bad guys only had to succeed once. After the London Underground attacks, the terrorists might think they were overdue for a success here. It was only a matter of time.

"Or, maybe it's a fourteen-year-old boy on a computer, like that one in Connecticut, making fake reservations and pretending to be Al Qaeda in Darien," countered Kevin.

This time, Paul waited in silence.

"Okay," Kevin relented. "I'll have the D.O. call you. Thanks. See you later," Kevin said, hanging up the phone, setting it down on the table next to his glass. He looked back at the screen. The Astros were at bat. The runner had not scored.

"Goddamnit," Kevin said out loud, dialing.

# 5.

Ed noticed the tanned guy with the shades get up from his seat and walk forward. The passenger looked at the OCCUPIED sign over the lavatory door handle and waited his turn. He probably had never been on a 767 before. Ed felt like telling him there was another head around the corner but, of course, he did not. Liz and Jane, the other attendant, were already taking lunch orders and refilling beverages, wine glasses. Not surprisingly, the pregnant girl was in the bathroom for some time. Again, Ed said a little prayer that she was just taking care of business and not going into labor. He was relieved when she emerged more than five minutes later, looking fine. After she left, the guy with sunglasses went in. By then, the Asian executive guy had arrived and gotten on the unnecessary line. Then someone else went into the other lavatory. The Korean or Chinese guy went in next and stayed even longer than the pregnant girl. Ed lost interest. He did not notice that the executive and the guy in sunglasses both took their carry-on bags and plastic water bottles with them into the bathroom but came out without them. Ed got up and pretended to stretch his legs, taking a look back at the coach passengers as he did so. Nothing weird.

"I gotta hit the can," Artie alerted Ed, emerging from his seat.

Ed sat back down in his aisle seat, his back to the bulkhead, and fastened his seatbelt, as procedure dictated when his partner was out of pocket. Artie entered the bathroom and closed the folding lavatory door. The little "OCCUPIED" sign flipped on.

Matt had finished his drink and was back on his wireless laptop, using the tray table as a desk. He noticed the Korean guy across the aisle had also opened his laptop computer and was working. Matt glanced around, from habit, to make sure no one could see his screen. He logged onto his executive chat room for a secret, encrypted cyber-chat with his staff.

**Matt:** What's up with the attack?

**Tyrell:** I'm ready to fuck this hack. Ivan is going down.

**Matt:** How?

**Tyrell:** Virus cocktail first, Shanghai Lil, to stop him in his tracks and disconnect him from his zombies. This dude has, like, a zombie zoo of 16,000 machines attacking the sites and servers.

**Fiona:** Then, second, a 300% power spike, courtesy of the local Vilnius Power Cooperative, to toast his hardware to a rich golden brown.

**Melanie:** Then a visit from the friendly local militia, who have been informed by a good citizen that our friend has been delinquent in his bribes and is heavily into kiddie porn and heroin and has lots of American dollars to confiscate.

**Matt:** Is he? Does he?

**Melanie:** Silly boy. This is just to make him play somewhere else. He's just a hack for the mob over there, a drone.

**Matt:** I want them, the bosses.

**Jerry:** No way. Matt, that is, like, totally impossible. You do not want to meet these guys up close and personal. They don't just kill servers.

**Melanie:** A third-country sting is the only way but these slugs do not leave home.

**Matt:** We'll talk about it later. Nice work. Call me when the smoke clears. Also, Tyrell, round up his zombies while he's down and put them in a corral. We'll use them to stampede over him if he pops back up.

**Tyrell:** You got it.

**Matt:** Do it, guys. Pretend I'm on vacation until you have a body count.

Matt took great pains to avoid contact with the dark side of his business: the Russian Mafia, Singapore Tongs, Japanese Yakuza, Nigerian officials, Costa Rican gangsters and the rest of the United Nations of extortionists that provided him with a great living. And business was good. He was about to check his e-mails when his laptop screen flashed. He was blown offline and a red rectangular error box popped up. "CONNECTION LOST." Matt rebooted but got "UNABLE TO FIND HOST" and "DIALING . . ." with a little spinning satellite phone symbol, but no connection. That had never happened before. His laptop was way beyond state-of-the-art. It was edge. The wireless equipment was a satellite phone, not a cell. He had used it on most continents: while boating on the Amazon River, hiking in the Three Gorges in China and in a cave on Kodiak Island off the coast of Alaska. It worked everywhere. Matt tried again and ran a diagnostic program. Everything was supposedly working fine. But it wasn't. In a heuristics subroutine in the communication machine language, he found an odd error message:

"ELIMINATE EW INTERFERENCE OF D MASER TRANSCEIVER DEVICE(S)!"

He clicked the "OK" box but the same message kept popping up. "What the hell does that mean?" Matt said under his breath.

He thought he had seen every computer error message known to man.

"That's a new one."

# 6.

Kevin touched the speed dial function on his cell phone and waited for the duty officer at the Executive Command Center at One Police Plaza, NYPD headquarters in Lower Manhattan, to answer the hotline. The large room contained banks of phones manned by detectives, a huge conference table covered with angled phone sets. On the wall above one end of the rectangular table was a giant flat screen TV, which showed four video scenes of key locations around the city and kept changing every few seconds: the entrance of the Midtown Tunnel entrance in Queens, inside Grand Central Terminal, outside Penn Station, atop the Empire State Building. Above that screen was a wider black rectangle displaying local times in Los Angeles, New York, London, Paris, Tel Aviv, Baghdad, and Kabul in regular and military time. Elsewhere, other banks of screens silently played cable news channels from around the world, Fox, CNN, Al Jazeera, and BBC. The readout on Lieutenant Kathy Small's phone console told her the DCCT was calling the secure line from his cell phone, making it unnecessary for Kevin to identify himself. She glanced at the personnel status board on the wall and noted that the DC for Counterterrorism was logged at his home on Long Island for the day and evening.

"Yes sir?" Smalls asked, picking up the line.

"PAPD at JFK needs a priority fast-track check on six subjects," Kevin ordered, as if the request had come through channels—not from his brother-in-law.

"Yes sir."

Kevin gave her Paul's cell number and directed the lieutenant to feed the names of the no-shows through the computer. The check would quickly turn up any arrests by NYPD. An NCIC check would pull any wants or warrants from around the country. A comparison of the names to NYPD's own master terror watch lists would reveal whether they shared a name with a known bad guy—an unlikely event because they had already been cleared by CAPPS. Smalls would also make ID checks, for license, car registration, addresses, properties owned, businesses owned, neighbors, relatives, and whether they had boats or pilot's licenses, among many other data. A web check would also pull up any websites or NEXUS press clippings containing those names.

"Do you have any other priority jobs working now?" Kevin asked her.

"No sir, just some background checks, a few calls, nothing hot," she replied.

"Put your first team on it right now. When you have a first-read, call me on this number with the results as soon as you can."

"Yes sir," the duty officer said.

Kevin was about to hang up but hesitated. "Where are the Hercules teams today?" Kevin asked, referring to the three highly trained and highly armed antiterror squads.

The lieutenant sat up in her chair, scanning her log. "Hercules Red is at the Guatemalan Parade in Manhattan. Hercules Blue is at City Hall and Hercules White is on Atlantic Avenue in Brooklyn."

"Those are all precautionary, not specific threat-based assignments, correct?"

"Yes sir."

"Fine. Redirect White to JFK forthwith. Redirect Blue to La-

Guardia. Red remains at the parade but advise them to be ready to move."

"Yes sir," the lieutenant said, wondering what was going on. "Anything else, sir?"

"No, that's all."

Kevin flipped his cell phone shut. His wife, Dina, was standing over him, staring.

"What's going on?" she asked, even though she wasn't supposed to ask.

"Nothing," Kevin replied a bit too casually.

It wasn't the fact that Dina had overheard her husband moving the troops around, that was not very unusual. It was his concerned tone that caught her ear. She just looked at him, one hand on her hip, one corner of her mouth crooked. It was her I-don't-believe-you pose.

"Are you leaving?" she asked, finally.

"No."

"Is Paul coming?"

"As far as I know," Kevin said, hopefully. "He hasn't said anything about being late."

Dina looked across the lawn at the blue pool, diamonds of sunlight dancing on the surface, with the weeping willow behind it. Above the tree, the sharp pastel blue sky was empty. Not a cloud in sight. It was a beautiful, cloudless morning. Like that day. The day Dina lost two of her brothers. So many other families had been destroyed; it seemed like half of the world—during that year after the attacks, an entire year of funerals, tears, bagpipes. The terrorists had even poisoned beautiful days, she thought, because now nothing was impossible—and it could happen on any beautiful day.

"I'm just checking some more stuff for Paul. You know your brother," Kevin told her.

"Yes, I know my brother," she said, with a nod, as she turned back toward the pool.

*And I hope to God he's wrong*, Dina silently prayed, feeling the cool blades of grass between her toes.

# 7.

Ed was not watching anything on his personal video screen, but he noticed that the large TV screen in the middle of the front bulkhead had gone blank. Not blank, really, but white with snow. If the geese couldn't watch the tube, it could get ugly, Ed chuckled. On one flight the previous year, the system broke down and the geese did a lot of squawking. It was important to keep the geese calm.

"Excuse me, is this your briefcase? It was lying in the aisle."

Ed looked up from his seat. A large, smiling blond guy, tanned like a surfer, in a loud shirt and shades, was standing next to him in the aisle, holding a black, hard-case Samsonite attaché case. Where had he come from?

"No, I don't . . ."

The surfer slammed the corner of the case into the bridge of Ed's nose. Ed saw a flash of light, felt a spray of pain. It snapped his head back into the seat.

"Unhhh!"

Ed instinctively blocked with his closest arm, his right—his gun hand, reaching for his seat belt with his left. The case came down hard again, as Ed turned. It glanced off his forearm but clipped him on the right side of his head, knocking him sideways in his seat. Ed realized his mistake and reached for his piece with his left hand. Ed could shoot with either. Kill the motherfucker. His hand met another set of hands behind him. Two other guys had materialized from behind the bulkhead, from coach, and were all over him, on top of him. He couldn't get the SIG free. One guy held Ed's wrists and put his weight on them. The other was on top of Ed, a knee in his side, pushing the air out of his lungs, pinning him, pushing him down in the seat. Ed felt the pistol being pulled out of its rig in the small of his back. One of them had it.

"Artie! Go hot! Artie!" Ed sputtered, spitting blood out of his mouth. "Goddamnit! Halt! I'm a federal air marshal!"

"Yes, we know," one of them replied. "Get his cuffs."

"Motherfuckers! Artie!"

Ed saw the blur of the briefcase swinging toward his head again. He tried to turn but they had him nailed tight, his seat belt still on. Ed heard and felt the back of his head dong like a rusty bell filled with mud. He was spinning but he could still feel the bastards gripping him. They were squatting on him, holding him down, but his head was twirling off by itself. He heard a shot.

"Fuck you!" he snarled, bolting every way he could with all his strength, still trapped.

Ed felt another echoing impact on his skull and heard another shot. The sunlight in the cabin went down like it was on a dimmer and Ed heard running water, coming closer, a comforting sound. Where's the light? Shit. There's supposed to be a light. Ed stopped fighting and fell over the edge of a dark waterfall, dry, black water rolling him around and down.

Jim didn't hear the commotion at first. He had earplugs in and was sipping his drink, watching a cop action movie with a car chase and shooting, when the screen went white, a hiss in his earphones. He was pushing buttons, trying to get the movie back when he felt bumping through the floor. He looked up from the screen and saw a blonde first-class flight attendant, rushing down the left aisle, gaping at something, with a strange look on her pretty face. On the right side, up front, the other beautiful flight attendant, Liz, was standing frozen at the entrance to the galley. She also had a peculiar expression on her face. Jim realized it was fear. He turned away from the empty screen and was startled to see three men nearby, struggling with a man in the seat across the aisle. The sky marshal guy. Jim was stunned and just stared. Were they hitting him? What was going on? The blonde stewardess arrived, right next to Jim, and was saying something. It was loud but Jim couldn't make it out. Realizing he still had the earplugs in, hissing static, Jim pulled them out. Instantly, he heard a rush of voices, the marshal cursing at the men, saying he was a federal air marshal. They were definitely beating him, and the stewardess was yelling at the men. One of them pulled out of the huddle and pointed something at the blonde stewardess. It was a black gun. She put up her hands but the man brushed her aside, like a football block, knocking her down onto a seat, as he rushed forward, waving the pistol. He pointed it at Liz, who now had a phone in her hands. She dropped the phone to the floor and also put up her hands. He's got the marshal's gun. Oh, my God. Jim's legs finally worked and he tried to jump up. He jackknifed painfully, the wind knocked out of him. He went nowhere because he still had his seatbelt fastened. His chest hit his seat tray, which was still down. He unsnapped the damn belt and leaped across the aisle, sending his glass flying. As he did, he heard a loud bang, an explosion followed by involuntary gasps and screams from around the aircraft. Then it was totally silent.

"Ruby! Hide! Get under your seat! Stay there!" Jim hissed, desperately. "You, too, Anna! They're shooting."

"Jim, they're hijackers," Anna said evenly, holding Ruby's hand. "What good will it do to hide?"

"I don't know. I don't know what else to do," Jim told her, his voice choking in his throat.

Ruby scampered under the seat, her legs sticking out. Anna squatted down on the floor by the window. Jim crouched low in front of Anna's seat. He looked back to the left. Only two aisles and his empty seat away, the air marshal he had spoken to maybe half an hour ago, while they were boarding, was either dead or unconscious, his face all bloody. Two large men in polo shirts and jeans were handcuffing his hands behind his back, tying his ankles with something. Did they shoot him? The far window seat was empty. Where was the second marshal? Jim peeked forward over the seat. A blond guy in a Hawaiian shirt, the guy with sunglasses and the gun, was pointing it with both hands into the bathroom on the other side of the plane, advancing into the open door. He was shooting at someone in the lavatory? The other marshal, had he gone to the bathroom? The Hawaiian-shirted guy fired again, the noise earsplitting. Jim yelled, as if he had been shot. Won't the plane explode now, depressurize, the air sucked out and us with it? Jim wasn't the only one yelling. There was a lot of screaming. Dozens of passengers were crying out and shouting, all at once. Jim turned his head and looked back to the main passenger cabin. He could hear every one of their voices, every question, overlapping, cascading out of the frightened mouths down the aisle behind him at the same time:

"What's happening?"

"Oh my God, was that a shot?"

"What was that?"

"What's going on?"

"Was that a gun? Who has a gun?"

"Who's shooting?"

"Are we being hijacked? Are they Arabs?"

"How did they get a gun onboard?"

"Are we going to crash?"

"What's happening?"

"Stop shooting, you want to kill us all?"

"What should we do?"

"What's happening?"

Jim wasn't sure if the few passengers who met his eyes expected him to answer but he didn't reply. Maybe it wouldn't matter. If they couldn't get into the cockpit, maybe it wouldn't matter. Maybe they could still be safe. We have to lay low, Jim thought. He saw the two men in jeans who had attacked the marshal in his seat walking forward down the far aisle, one blue polo shirt, one white. They each had a black object in one hand. They looked like those black hand weights that some joggers use, but these glistened. What were they? They met the blond guy with the Hawaiian shirt, who emerged from the bathroom with a gun in each hand. He handed one of the pistols to the big guy in the white shirt. The gunmen swung the guns around the cabin but there was no one to challenge them. One pointed a handgun at Liz and ordered her to the floor. The short Asian man in the far aisle seat on the left side closed his laptop computer and put it on the seat next to the window, under a seatbelt. He stood up with a black bag and joined the group. Four of them. Two rows ahead, up front, the pregnant woman, Maria, and her husband Joey stood up. No, Jim, thought. Stay down. Jim was about to whisper to them, to warn them, when he saw they had black things in their hands, also. Oh, my God. They're part of it, too. That made six of them. But the cockpit door was bulletproof, Jim had read. They still couldn't get in. Unless they started killing us and got the crew to open the door, Jim thought, the breath catching in his throat. They won't do it.

The short Asian man with the bag walked up to the cockpit door and dropped it on the blue carpet. He leaned over and began pulling out little plastic Evian water bottles, one at a time. Jim noticed that they contained a viscous, white substance, not water. More like tofu. The man lined the six bottles up on the floor in front of the closed armored door to the cockpit. He pulled out a little pump spray can, no bigger than a lipstick, and took off the plastic cap. Jim could not read the label but it looked like one of those mint-flavored breath sprays. The man carefully squirted each Evian water bottle, working quickly. The plastic of the bottle partially melted and flattened on the side he had sprayed. He then produced a BIC Click pen and stuck it through the top of the bottle. He repeated this procedure with five more pens on each of the other five bottles, in a line on the floor. He then removed a pair of scuba diving gloves and put them on. He picked up one of the bottles and pressed it upright onto a spot on the line of the closed cockpit door, where a hinge might be, the pen sticking out of the top.

They're going to blow open the door, Jim realized, his stomach dropping.

The bottle stuck to the vertical surface when the man pulled his gloved hand away. Working calmly, methodically, he placed three bottles along the hinge side of the door, one at the top, one at the bottom and one over the recessed metal door handle. He nodded silently to the others and they moved away from the door. Then he reached up and clicked the top pen. He quickly clicked the others in sequence and then backed away, muttering a phrase over and over.

The five others—the two big men, the Hawaiian shirt guy, and Maria and her husband Joey—took up his cry, repeating it softly, which made it even more terrifying:

"God is great," they chanted. "God is great. God is great . . ."

Behind Jim, in the coach section, some people were standing up in their seats but most were just sitting in place, their eyes wide, frozen with fear. Jim was beyond frozen. He was sick to his stomach with it, shivering with bone marrow fear, like he was naked in the snow.

Jim looked down at his family, huddled into a little ball on the floor of an airplane, up against a curved wall. It was the only thing between them and a sunny, sub-freezing heaven outside. His heart ached with cold, as they waited, helplessly, for whatever was going to happen. Anna, he realized, was hugging Ruby and softly singing in a soothing voice to her daughter. Jim could just barely make out the words:

"We all live in a yellow submarine, a yellow submarine, a yellow submarine . . ."

# 8.

Paul heard his cell phone going off in his jacket pocket, a tinkling electronic version of the Marine Corps Hymn. He flipped open the electronic clamshell and saw his sister's phone number displayed in the little window. Paul took the cigar out of his mouth. It was Kevin calling him back.

"Hey, Kevin," Paul said, putting it to his ear.

"Paul, I have your stuff. It's being sent to your people. They can send it to you on the modat in your car. All six guys are real. They're taxpayers. Two of them own businesses. They have money. And lawyers. One does business with the city. He even got a PBA award last year for donating vests to the department."

"And?"

"And nothing, Paul."

"Are they citizens?"

Kevin hesitated.

"Kevin?"

"No, they're resident aliens but they all have green cards. No hits on any lists, no arrests, nothing. But in the London suicide attacks, most of those guys were British citizens. That didn't prevent them from blowing themselves up on subway cars during rush hour."

"Exactly. Proves my point. What country, Kevin? Where are they from?"

"They're all Saudis."

"Thanks, Kevin," Paul said, sarcastically. "That's all I needed to hear. Our favorite oil allies from across the sea. Friends from the friendly Kingdom."

"Paul, be careful. If you step on too many toes, you might be asked to leave the dance floor. Do what you have to do to investigate this but remember these guys didn't get on the planes. Find out if it was some kind of test of the system. Nothing has happened. No one is in danger."

"The computer says so. Computers have been known to be wrong once in a while. I'm just going to find these guys, make sure they're on the ground, doing God's work," said Paul.

"Are you familiar with the term racial profiling, Paul? I agree you should run this down a bit more but be careful. Don't get your ass in a sling."

"Not unless it's worth it. Are you sending units to their home addresses?"

"On what grounds?" Kevin asked. "We don't have a complainant, or a crime."

"I'm the complainant. We're worried about them. They're missing. They didn't show up for their flights. By the way, they were nonrefundable tickets. Why would they not show up and lose the money?"

"I don't know. They're Saudis, maybe they're rich and it's just chump change to them. Paul, you know we can't go to the next level. We gave all the information to the feds. These guys are now on the screen list—they won't be able to fly in or out of the country until the hold is removed. Just check it out. Your department has jurisdiction over the airports. You can do that."

Paul often complained that the Port Authority Police Department was too small to perform such tasks outside the airport on a regular basis. Only NYPD could do that. They had had the same discussion many times in the past. Kevin knew that Paul's bosses were not eager to pull officers from necessary duty to chase possibilities. That was the job of the FBI and Homeland Security, the CIA.

But NYPD had taken over many such tasks since 9-11 because Kevin was convinced that if the city didn't defend itself, no one else would. Kevin had been battling the dumb juggernaut of the federal government since before September 11th. He was used to malignant secrecy, and multiplying, competing, and overlapping bureaucracy in federal police and intelligence agencies. Instead of making law enforcement information more efficient and getting the CIA and FBI to talk each other, the response to the terror attacks had been to create the largest expansion of the federal government and police groups in history, an explosion of competing, armed kingdoms. The alphabet soup of new agencies spawned confusion, as tens of thousands of new federal cops struggled to learn their new jobs against an enemy most of them could not see or find. The feds now routinely either gave NYPD too much information or none at all. The national government was still in the middle of a gigantic restructuring that started with the creation of the unwieldy bureaucracy of Homeland Security and was thrown into further confusion by the appointment of a federal intelligence tsar. After careful analysis, NYPD concluded that the only useful information about terrorism came from the huge, rapidly expanding U.S. military spy apparatus, which seemed to have taken over the job of the CIA, both foreign and domestic—and the military wouldn't even talk to NYPD. Kevin knew for a fact that the National Security Agency was literally tapping and screening every phone call and cell phone call in the country every day, without warrants. They used ESCHELON XT word and speech recognition computer software—hoping to snare bad guys. The idea was to catch any terrorists dumb enough to use key words, in several languages, about weapons, bombs or other nasty subjects on an unscrambled phone. If history's largest electronic fishing expedition had caught any major threats, Kevin had not heard about it.

"Fuck jurisdiction," Paul said. "We have to do this, Kevin. There's nobody else. You know that. The feds fucked it up the first time and they'll fuck it up this time."

Kevin sighed before responding.

"There is no 'this time,' yet. If your nose is itching, you need to do the job. Get me something, and I'll ring the bell," Kevin told his brother-in-law. "Get me more than a feeling, Paul."

# 9.

Captain Dean Cornell glanced at the new upgraded RNP autopilot for the 767. He had just finished checking the revised jet stream wind data when he smelled the sharp fumes.

"What is that, Ramon? Do you smell that?"

"Yes sir. I do. It smells like ammonia," his copilot replied.

"Going to Oh-two," Dean said, lifting his black full-face oxygen mask with the large, curved clear plastic faceplate and pulling it into place. The copilot did the same, as did the navigator, Selim, in his rear, side-facing position.

"New York Center, this is Anytime 1787, heavy," Dean said, his voice muffled by the mask. "We have a strong smell, possibly ammonia, in the cockpit, crew have . . ."

"Captain," Ramon interrupted. "Look at the door. Can you hear that?"

Dean turned and saw white smoke pouring in all around the cockpit door. He heard a hissing sound, getting louder. It was also getting hot in the cockpit.

"Affirmative. New York Center, this is Anytime 1787, heavy, we have smoke or fumes of some kind pouring into the cockpit. Unknown if it is a fire. Crew on Oh-two. It sounds a bit like a smoke grenade but how . . . Oh, Jesus . . ." Dean said, as he turned to look at the security video screen that showed the passenger cabins. It was chaos. People were standing in the aisles. "Selim, call Liz or Nancy, find out what . . ."

"I tried. No one answers back there."

"New York Center," said Dean into his radio. "We have a situation. We have . . . oh Jesus . . ."

Dean stopped in mid-sentence, looking at the video screen of the outside of the cockpit door. There were objects on the door.

"Christ, they're blowing the door! There are marshals on-board. What the hell is . . . I'm flipping the transponder to distress, Ramon."

"Affirmative, Captain, still negative . . ."

"New York Center, please acknowledge," Dean said, keying the radio again. There was no response. He tried again and again. Nothing. He reset his radio to an emergency frequency but again received no reply.

"I'm sending on the board," Ramon told him, typing into a keyboard that sent typed messages through a back-channel via a microwave transmitter. "I sent it but I'm not getting any confirmation of message sent, or a response."

The hissing noise became a loud whooshing and the three crewmembers could barely see each other.

"I'm trying on the SSB, also negative," said Selim. "I can't hear anything on any channel, sir, just clicking and buzzing on all frequencies. The SAT phone says connection lost."

"Sounds like military jamming, Captain," said Ramon, who had served in the Air Force on an AWACS plane. "But they're not jamming the FCS," he said, referring to the FCS 700A flight control system, the new RNP autopilot, which was engaged.

Dean was silent, while he quickly weighed the situation. Autopilot on, smoke through the door, no communications. Smoke alarms in the cockpit and in first class began sounding. There was no nuclear war, so that was not the reason they couldn't get through to anyone, it was no EMP, electromagnetic pulse. It was impossible but it had to be a hijacking. Dean had an instant of regret that neither he, nor any of his crew, had opted to be trained to carry a gun in the cockpit. They were helpless.

"New York Center, this is Anytime 1787, heavy. I think they're blowing our cockpit door with some kind of pyrotechnic device. Our communications, all channels seem to be jammed except the FCS. If you copy, I'm declaring an emergency, apparent hijacking. There are federal marshals onboard. I can now see at least one armed man in the cabin but I do not, I say again, I do not know if it is a marshal. If you do not acknowledge immediately, I will change course and drop altitude to twenty seven angels to get your attention. Acknowledge. Ramon, I think a course and altitude change is the only way we can call the cops, I'm going to disengage the . . ."

His voice was drowned out by a loud noise behind them. The door snapped down like a drawbridge and hit the deck with a crash, after glancing off the back of Selim's chair. Two large men were right behind the door, filling the smoky air above the crew. One had a gun in his hand.

"Get out of my cockpit!" Dean yelled.

# 10.

Paul walked back to the Anytime Airways counter where he had last spoken to the cute brunette employee with the ponytail, the one who had given him the printout of the names of the Saudi no-shows. The counter was empty, no passengers around. He noticed activity at several other gates further down the concourse and strolled down. Behind the counter at Gate 18, he found the woman with the ponytail, alone and obviously very busy setting up for another departure of a flight. The red sign on the board behind her said it was an Anytime Airjump flight to Albany. Passengers were beginning to trickle in, rolling black bags on wheels and finding seats in rows of attached chairs in the secure area. Every civilian Paul could see had already been screened for weapons through magnetometers and the new Explosives Detection Trace Portal, a device that used puffs of air to sniff for explosives, and also run through the electronic sieve of the security lists. Nothing had happened since 9-11 but Paul didn't feel particularly secure, mostly because nothing had happened in so long. There was always a way around and, looking at the growing crowd milling about and coming and going, something else occurred to him.

"Hi, uh . . . Paulette. Hey, that's my name, too," Paul told her, reading her nametag.

"You're name is Paulette, Sergeant?" Paulette asked, smiling.

"Paul, almost the same. Look, I need your help again."

"I'm sorry, we're shorthanded, Sergeant. Can't it wait until I move this flight?"

"No, sorry, it can't. You were at the other gate, with that other beautiful lady, the blonde, right?"

"Right," she said, her eyes down on the computer screen, as she typed.

"Did you or anybody see anything unusual this morning? Out of the routine?"

"You mean other than the bag checks we talked about?"

"Yes, other than that. You know, like groups of Middle Eastern men?"

Paulette looked up from her screen. He had her attention. She was thinking about it for real.

"No, I don't think so," Paulette replied, keeping her voice low. "The only Arab guys I know about were the ones on that list. But, you know, I don't keep track."

"I know. Did you see anyone matching that vague description getting on any of the flights this morning? You know, those types of names, facial appearance?"

"I don't think so. No, not that I noticed, now that you mention it. Why?"

"Could you just check your other flights and see if any of the names on this list got on any other flight at all today?"

"I already did that before. When I spoke to you earlier," she said, obviously not happy at the request. "They didn't. You have to check with the other airlines, to see if . . ."

"Oh, I didn't realize you had checked. That's great, thanks. That's good. I already checked with the other airlines. I guess you did that on the computer?"

"Of course," she replied.

"Here's the deal. Don't you guys also have a paper trail, you know the boarding pass stubs that go into those machines at the gate, as the passengers board?" Paul asked.

"You know we do," she said. "It's a triple-check. The bar

codes get read by the sensors at the gate, they go in clear plastic bags that we keep, so we know it's the same, that everything reconciles. The computer says those men on the list never checked in, never showed up."

"Right. But could maybe people switch at the gate, after check-in and go on the plane with somebody else's ticket? I mean, this isn't a closed-in area. There are about two dozen gates on this concourse. If that happened and the other people just left, we might end up with what we had this morning—six no-shows with Middle Eastern names. Couldn't that happen?"

"Why would anybody switch tickets? Oh, I get it. I guess it's possible. But so what? Even if everybody switched tickets and got on different flights, what difference does it make? Nobody gets on a plane without passing through security, so no weapons or explosives. Everybody gets checked against the lists, so no bad guys. We don't stamp the bar codes onto people's foreheads. That's not my job," she said, making it clear whose job it was.

"Too bad. About the bar codes, I mean," Paul said with a friendly smile. "You're assuming that nobody was using an assumed name. Could you please just check once more? Just between us? You know, look at the boarding pass stubs, just to make sure. Sometimes computers can do funny things. It's very important. I can't say any more than that," said Paul, who didn't have any more than that but figured if he sounded like he had secret information, it might help.

"I can't. I'm alone here." She waited, obviously hoping Paul would go away. "Besides, the bags with the stubs are back at those gates until later."

"I'd be glad to clear it with your supervisor," Paul said. "I'd owe you a big one—how about lunch?"

"I don't eat here," Paulette said.

Paul knew that her supervisor would slow things down. It could take hours because the airline was very concerned about lawsuits and privacy and liability. They would be very deliberate and slow, while they made him wait. He had been there before. Paul couldn't waste the time. Paulette was his best shot. He said nothing. The young woman stared back at Paul. People began crowding behind him, as if he were at the beginning of the line, as if he was a passenger in a police uniform, with a gun. Paulette glanced at the passengers and impatiently back at Paul, who had nothing left but charm.

"The fact that you don't eat here proves your beauty is equaled by your intelligence," he said, with a smile.

"Look, Sergeant, this is an Airjump flight, with small equipment, a light load. I'm on break after this one. I can do it then—otherwise, you need to go downstairs and talk to my boss, or the security guy, okay?"

"Okay, that'd be fine. I appreciate it. Thanks, Paulette. I'll be back soon."

Paul stepped away from the gate and used his cell phone to call Cindy, who was still sitting in their vehicle on the tarmac, and ordered her to meet him at Gate 18 on the concourse.

"What's up, Sarge?" Cindy asked, arriving a few minutes later.

"I'm waiting to get a passenger check after this flight leaves. Go down to Anytime baggage and the Lost & Found downstairs and see if they have any unclaimed bags, packages, anything—in or out."

Cindy rolled her eyes. He was keeping this off the air, off the radio. They both knew she would find nothing.

"I'll buy you a coffee when you get back," Paul promised.

"You know I don't drink coffee."

"Not even decaf? How about a nice jelly doughnut?" He knew Cindy would rather eat plutonium.

"Sarge, do you know what a Snark hunt is?"

"No, never heard of it," Paul replied, with a grin. "But I'll know it when I catch the motherfucker."

# 11.

Jim watched in horror as white smoke hissed out of the bottles against the outside of the cockpit door. It was happening. The bastards had figured out a way to do it. His mind was racing, his stomach seizing, as he watched them do it, like it was a movie. He heard a woman back somewhere in coach, muttering over and over that it was just a dream, a bad dream. Was she talking to a child, or to herself? Or to all of us? He had to do something, he thought, as he watched the blond guy in the Hawaiian shirt sweep the black gun slowly back and forth over the top of the first seat on the far side of the plane. He held the pistol with both hands, swiveling at the hips, like he was on *Hawaii 5-O.* Jim remembered his cell phone clipped onto his belt. He slowly reached for it but stopped when his wife spoke to him.

"Jim, look," Anna said, peeking above the seat. "She's not pregnant anymore."

She was right. Maria, the hugely pregnant woman was pacing with one of the curved Eskimo blades they were carrying, like shiny black crescent moons in their fists. What did they call those? Maria's big white shirt, worn loose before she went into the bathroom, was now tucked into her pants, a belt cinching the loose material around her slim waist. Her stomach was almost flat. How could that be? Maria seemed to be Hispanic. Her husband Joey looked Italian, maybe. The Hawaiian-shirt guy looked like a WASP surfer. The Asian man was giving orders to the other two big guys. One of the big guys, the one in the blue shirt, was a light-skinned black man and the other one might have been Irish. Six of them. They spoke English to each other. They looked and sounded like Americans. But they couldn't be.

"They're not Middle Eastern," Jim observed.

"That doesn't mean they aren't Moslems," Anna replied.

Jane, the blonde stewardess from business class, was still standing, talking back to the hijackers, to the Asian man. Jim couldn't hear what she was saying over the hissing, which was louder now. Was it a fuse? Was it going to explode? The Asian guy waved the back of his hand in a dismissive gesture and Joey grabbed Jane from behind. She tried to punch him but he spun her around easily and yoked her around the neck with his left arm and dragged her toward the far aisle, her shoes dragging on the carpeting. Joey was very strong. The Hawaiian-shirt guy stepped sideways, pointing his gun toward the ceiling, to let Joey stand at the head of the left aisle, with Jane before him, half a head lower.

"Everybody to da back of da plane!" Joey said, in a Brooklyn accent.

Nobody moved.

"I said, EVERYBODY TO DA BACK OF DA PLANE! NOW!"

Joey took his crooked arm from around Jane's neck and roughly grabbed a handful of her straw-colored hair. His right hand, with one of those shiny black things, darted around her neck from her right and quickly vanished back that way, like a magic trick. Jim didn't understand until he saw a large, red mouth gape open on Jane's pale throat. Jim gasped out loud, an indistinct "Ahhhh," which merged with groans from other passengers, men and women. Red exploded from the wound, some of it hitting a young man with long hair up front, spurting like a garden hose around the cabin. The man bolted out of his seat, strangely carrying a laptop computer, and sprinted back down the aisle. Jane's eyes were impossibly wide, like a tethered horse who hears a rattlesnake. She gurgled for breath, her arms clawing at the obscene wound, bubbling red, frothing, brimming between her helpless fingers. Quarts of it. Joey, cold, held her by the hair and her jacket from the back. He wanted everybody to see. An arc of dark liquid hit Jim's pants. It was hot, steaming, like red coffee, soaking through to his leg. He jumped up.

"Out!" Jim ordered his family, pulling them from their hiding places. "We're going now!"

Anna pulled Ruby out and into the aisle, as Jim kept his body between them and the horror. They ran, not seeing Jane's pretty blue eyes roll up into her head, as her life leaked away, Joey dropping her drained body in the aisle, motionless on the dark blue carpet, wet with her blood. They ran past screaming or frozen passengers all the way to the back of the plane.

"Where do we go now, Momma?" Ruby asked when they got to the open area with the bathrooms and galley.

The young man with the long hair and the computer was there, sitting cross legged on the floor with his laptop opened, busily hitting keys. His clothes were soaked in blood and he was cursing under his breath, apparently because his little computer wasn't doing what he wanted. Was it even turned on? Seeing someone lose it like that made Jim think he had to do something, anything. He opened a lavatory door and ordered Ruby and Anna to go inside and lock the door, for safety.

"There is no safety, Jim," Anna said, refusing to budge, hugging Ruby. "This isn't the *Titanic*. We have to do something now."

"I know, but what?"

"Attack. We all have to attack now. There is no other choice."

"But they have guns and knives. How can we attack them, they . . ."

"Your wife is right," the young man with the computer said from the floor. "Everything is jammed, not that it matters to us," he said, closing his laptop. "I'm Matt. Your wife is right."

A new wave of screams in front of the coach section drew their attention forward, over the rows of blue-and-white cloth seats. In coach, there were many more seats, seven across, with the same two aisles leaving three seats in the middle and two at each window. The Hawaiian-shirt guy with the pistol had appeared in the open space in front of the white screen in the front of the cabin. He was holding two other male flight attendants at gunpoint. Both attendants had their hands in the air and each one had a cell phone in one hand. Maria and Joey and one of the two big hijackers, the brown-skinned man in the blue shirt, all had those strange knives. Joey's shirt and face had been sprayed with the blood of the woman he had killed. The dark blue curtains had been drawn across the aisles up front on both sides, making it impossible to see what was going on in the front of the airplane. The sharp smoke had dissipated but everyone's eyes were still watering from it. Joey went forward and then came back with Liz, pushing her ahead of him. When she tried to join her colleagues, Joey yanked her by the elbow and ordered her to the back of the plane. Her other co-workers started to follow her but the Hawaiian-shirt guy jerked his gun at them, ordering them to move back to where they were. He nodded at the others and Joey and the man in the blue shirt came over and pulled them away, until each was standing in front of an aisle. Joey slapped the cell phones out of their hands.

"Don't look, Ruby," Jim said.

"No cell phone calls!" Joey yelled at other passengers.

Jim pulled his daughter down to the floor with him. Anna followed and they hugged in a ball on the floor. Jim was fighting not to cry. He didn't want Ruby to see he couldn't protect her. Suddenly, a loud voice came from above.

"Ladies and gentlemen, this is your captain speaking. Several people have taken control of this aircraft but please do not panic. Everything is under control. They tell me that we will continue to Mexico, as scheduled, because they want to free their Moslem brothers in a prison there. No one else will be harmed if everyone cooperates and follows instructions. They tell me that once their brothers are released, our plane will be refueled and we will fly you safely to a third country, where you will all be released, unharmed. Thank you. God bless you."

When the announcement stopped, Jim heard Joey shouting again.

"NO CELL PHONES, NOTHING! THIS IS WHAT HAPPENS TO ANYONE WHO USES A CELL PHONE!"

Screaming and crying erupted again. Jim didn't stand up. He knew what Joey and the other man were doing to the flight attendants, who had obviously been caught trying to alert their airline about the hijacking. Jim knew when he looked up and saw Matt's face twist into a grimace and turn away. Jim could actually smell the odor of rusty blood in the air. Then he also heard someone vomiting, a woman sobbing hysterically. Then Joey was yelling again, saying that all cell phones and BlackBerrys had to be handed in. Anyone caught with one would die. Hijackers fanned out, with knives in one hand and plastic bags in the other—collecting all the cell phones. Before the killers arrived at the back of the plane, Matt was back sitting on the floor, his laptop hidden underneath him. Matt handed over a cell phone, as did Jim and Anna, almost everyone. Anyone who didn't surrender a phone was searched. They filled all the bags with phones and went back to the front of the coach cabin. Maria carried the four heavy bags, two at a time, out of sight, through the curtains toward the front of the plane. Again, Jim heard someone yelling and Matt tapped him on the shoulder. Jim stood up. A man in an army uniform was standing in the aisle up front.

"Every adult on this plane has to attack now!" the soldier was shouting, his back bravely to the terrorists. The guy in the loud shirt had the gun pointed at his back.

"Every American, every man!" Angel Cruces yelled at the top of his lungs. "Stop them now, before they kill the pilots! Don't believe a word they say! You know what they're going to do!"

Jim and Matt looked at each other. Jim swallowed a lump in his throat and he and Matt and others started forward toward the soldier, as he spoke. Other men and several women also stood up. Lester Littleton and his partner, Bob Ipswitch, who had come from first class, stood up, as did C. Gordon Pope. Some wives pulled at their husbands' clothing to try to make them sit down, other women stood up beside their men, like Anna. Antoinette D'Anza stood up, all five feet one of her. Emmett Hazlett, Jr., not much taller, stood up. When seventy-six-year-old Emily Marco stood up, even more men took to their feet. Almost half of the passengers tentatively stood, unsure.

"Sit down!" Joey yelled. "Sit down!"

"Help me!" Angel Cruces pleaded, one more time, ignoring Joey, who was closing in.

"Now! Now!" Angel crossed himself, spun and bolted down the aisle. He tackled Joey and they both went down. The guy in the blue shirt, who was twice Angel's size, slashed at Angel's back several times, as the passengers moved slowly forward. He fought like hell but the two men overpowered Angel and stood him up, the back of his tan uniform blotting with blood.

"Hold him still!" said the Hawaiian-shirt guy.

The armed hijacker squatted low on the floor in front of the prisoner and pointed the pistol up at Angel, who was pinioned between Joey and the big guy. The gunshot was incredibly loud.

Half of Angel's head burst like a red balloon onto the ceiling and his deflated body crumpled. One long scream by a hundred people filled the space. Everyone who had been moving forward stopped and staggered instinctively away from the savage firepower. The gunman stood up and pointed the gun down the aisle where Matt and Jim were. Several men in front of them stampeded back onto them and everyone went down. The man in the wild black-and-purple flower shirt advanced toward them down the aisle, pointing the gun down at them, picking a target.

"NO! STOP!"

It was the Asian guy, yelling. He had appeared behind the gunman, walking quickly.

"No! No firing down! Only up! I told you! Only up!"

The gunman raised the muzzle of the weapon and backed off. Jim, Matt and the others scrambled to the back again. The killers had a conference, as some passengers continued to cry and pray. Then the killers ordered all of the passengers to move as far back in the seating as possible, filling up all seats. No one would be allowed to sit up front, only in the back half of the seating area or in the open area near the back bathrooms.

As everyone moved back, the two biggest hijackers dragged one of the sky marshals back down the aisle, his hands tied behind him. His head was bloody, his eyelids were almost closed and he was mumbling like a drunk. The thugs dropped him unceremoniously onto the floor in the back and walked away.

Then they ordered Liz, who had tears streaming down her face, to unlock two of the food and beverage carts from their recessed spots in the galley, one bearing beverages, the other loaded with lunch trays, already heated. She was directed to move the heavy, narrow metal boxes, one after the other, into each aisle, just ahead of where people were now seated—and to lock the wheels. When she did, both aisles were totally blocked with the bulky gray aluminum rectangles.

"No one comes forward of the carts," the Hawaiian guy warned, waving his gun around. "Anyone does, I'll blow your head off."

Jim was ashamed he didn't go to help the soldier sooner. Maybe if he had, it would have been different. He felt like a coward for running away. Again. He saw the same burning self-reproach on many other downcast faces around him. Jim sat down and hugged Anna and Ruby, as he cast his eyes around at their new situation. They were in a dead end. Ahead, beyond the barricaded aisles, over rows of empty seats, were murderers, on guard with guns and knives. At their backs were several doors but they led only to bathrooms or to the open sky.

# 12.

Paul went back to the airline counter after the passengers had boarded. He and the agent, Paulette, walked down to the other gate. She unlocked a vertical white bin behind the counter, took out two clear plastic bags and dropped them on the counter. Then she logged onto the computer set into the counter.

"Can I help you go through these stubs?" Paul asked.

"No, first we check the final boarding list in the machine," Paulette replied. "Then, if we have to, we reconcile with the stubs."

She didn't get it, Paul thought. She was so used to looking at computer screens, they were more real than anything else.

"Uh . . . look, Paulette, the whole point is that . . ."

"That's weird," Paulette said, interrupting him.

"What?"

"Your names. Can I see your sheet?"

"What about the names?" Paul asked, coming around behind the counter and handing her the list.

"Yeah, they're all here. How could that happen?"

"They're all where?" Paul demanded, looking over her shoulder, alarmed. "Did they get on the flights?"

"Yes. No, I mean they got on another flight, an earlier one. All six of them. As standby passengers, but that's impossible," she said, clicking keys. "1787 to Cabo at Gate 18. I was there with Jen before the other flights with the bag checks and I don't remember six Arab standbys. The standbys weren't . . ."

"Hold it," Paul snapped, pulling out his large, black leather notebook and pen, writing.

"You're telling me half a dozen guys with Middle Eastern names had tickets to two different flights today and then suddenly all became standby passengers on an earlier flight to Mexico? One that has already left? Flight 1787 to Cabo from Gate 18? These guys who were going to two different cities suddenly all got a plane to Mexico?"

"Yes. They did. I don't understand it. It's here in the computer. We don't need to check the stubs. Maybe Jen boarded them. If they had Arab names, I don't think they looked like . . . I mean, I don't remember . . . This shouldn't happen . . . It's impossible. The computer said before that they never boarded. How could they . . . unless . . ."

"Sergeant One to Central," Paul said into his radio. "Captain, are you on the air?"

"I'm on my way," the captain said, after he heard about the strange development. Paul next called Cindy, who had found nothing downstairs.

"10-85 me up here forthwith."

"You okay, Sarge?" Cindy asked.

"Yeah, get up here. I think I found your Snark."

Paulette was still confused, typing on the computer and shaking her head.

"Paulette, I need you to call your security guy on your land line right away. Get him down here; my captain is on the way."

She made the call and hung up.

"I don't understand it," she said, still peering, unbelieving, at the screen. "This is impossible, unless . . ."

"Look, Paulette, no system is perfect. Nothing is impossibl and computers are just . . ."

"No, it's not that," she said. "This is impossible unl someone changed it. In the computer."

"Who can do that?" Paul asked. "Only the agents working the gate?"

Paulette did not reply.

"So," Paul said, writing again, "what you're telling me is that computer records of your airline have been altered. Any idea who could have done that or why?"

"No, I mean, I certainly didn't. I'm not accusing anyone, I . . ."

"Neither am I," Paul said. Not yet. "If you didn't do it, who else was with you at the gate? That pretty blonde girl, the one with the beauty mark?"

"I didn't say Jennifer had anything to do with . . ."

"Jennifer what? Spell her last name, please."

"Koslowski, with an i, but she would never . . ."

"Where is Jennifer Koslowski right now?" Paul demanded.

"I don't know, I . . . she . . ."

"Paulette, this could be very important. We don't have time for bullshit."

"She went home sick. She said she was going home. That's why I was alone at the gate when you came back."

"She left right after I came over and got the list from you?"

"Yes."

Paul mouthed the word motherfucker, his top teeth biting his lower lip, but did not say it out loud.

"We need to speak to her right away to straighten this out," Paul told her. "Where does she live?"

"Um . . . here in Queens, Forest Hills, I don't know the address."

"Okay, we'll get that from your boss," said Paul.

He found out Jennifer was twenty-seven years old and had only been working there for about seven months.

"What kind of car does she drive?"

"Why would you need that?" Paulette asked.

"Look, you have been great but you know what might be at stake. We are on the same side, right? What kind of car does she drive?"

Paulette said her friend and co-worker drove a Volkswagen.

"What about the model, the color, anything that would help us to find her quickly?"

"Why not just call her cell phone and ask her where she is?"

"Okay, good idea. Do you have it?"

Paulette took out her phone and hit a speed dial button.

"NO, don't call her!" Paul said. "Hang up!"

She flipped her phone shut and read the number to Paul.

"Thanks. What about the model of her Volkswagen, like the color—anything that would help us to spot her quickly? So we can ask her about the computer glitch?"

"Pink, a hot-pink VW beetle," Paulette said.

"The ones with that little flower pot on the dashboard?" Paul asked.

"Bud vase," Paulette corrected him.

"You are terrific. I don't suppose you also know her license plate number?"

"Actually I do but it's not numbers, it's letters."

"You mean a vanity plate?"

"Yes. JEN JOY."

"What kind of flower is in the bud vase?"

"I don't know," Paulette said.

"Thanks."

And thank you, Jesus, Paul thought. A good witness, and a subject in the wind in a bright pink chick-mobile with a flower and a vanity plate. She might as well be driving a clown car with an ARREST ME flag on it. Please, God, let her be behind the wheel. The vanity plate would give them her home address but Paul already knew she wouldn't be there. As the airline security chief strode quickly toward them, Paul got on his radio to his captain and broadcast a physical description of a female white, 27, five-foot-five, blonde hair, blue eyes, beauty mark on face. He described her vehicle and plate. The security guy asked him what this was all about. Cindy also arrived.

"Sergeant, obviously there's some computer problem. But I know for a fact that Jen could never be involved in . . . in whatever this is."

"And why is that?" Paul asked her.

"Because she's very religious."

Paul wanted to laugh but he just shook his head and spoke to the security man.

"I need you to contact several of your flights in the air, forthwith, to confirm their status. Paulette has the information. Hold on one minute," Paul told him, flipping open his cell. He dialed his sister's number on Long Island again. Kevin answered after the first ring.

"Paul?" he asked, obviously anxious at a call he was hoping not to get.

"Kevin, I've got a situation. Those six Arab guys who never showed up for those flights? They're all together, somehow, on an earlier flight. At least, that's what the computer now says, which is different from what it said before. The airline has no clue. A ticket agent says somebody monkeyed with the computer. Maybe one of their ticket agents—a female who went AWOL after I showed up and started asking questions. Jennifer Koslowski, age 27, possibly a bogus ID. We're putting out her scrip and her vehicle info now. It looks like these guys are onboard Anytime 1787 to Cabo San Lucas, Mexico. I don't know what we got here, but something is definitely going on. We're sending everything out to your department, FAA, everybody. My captain is here."

"Goddamnit!" his brother in law responded. "We need to talk to those three crews and nail this down."

"Yeah, we're on it, buddy. We're going to the tower now, to see the FAA people about that. I gotta go," Paul said. "Kevin, ring the bell. Ring the motherfucking bell."

# 13.

The pilot sat back down in the port cockpit seat and checked the dials on the green, center instrument panel, as he looped his throat mike around his neck. He did not grasp the stick, the brown bull horns in front of him, attached to a rectangular black column that disappeared into the deck between his legs. The FCS, he noticed, was nominal, holding the aircraft on course, altitude and speed. He checked the GPS position reading with the figures on his handheld. When he had confirmed that they agreed exactly, he sat back in the chair. He looked out the side and front windshield. The blue sky ahead was clear. It was a beautiful day, glorious. The pilot smiled.

A short time later, a call came over the radio speaker above his head.

"Anytime 1787 heavy, this is New York Center, over?"

"New York, this is 1787 heavy, go ahead," the pilot replied.

"Anytime 1787 heavy, we have been advised of a security alert situation at your originating, JFK, in regard to several passengers possibly onboard your aircraft. Please say your status immediately, over?"

"Status optimal, New York. What situation are we talking about here?"

"Anytime 1787, I need your personal sign immediately, please. Over?"

"Certainly, New York. This is Captain Dean Cornell. Sign follows: Zebra. Zebra. Zebra. Over."

"Thank you, Anytime 1787 heavy, that is confirmed. Stand by."

The pilot waited for the air traffic controller on the ground in Pennsylvania to get back to him for a minute before he keyed his mike to transmit.

"New York, this is 1787 heavy. What is the problem? Please advise."

"Anytime 1787, your people are sending you data on the board concerning six passengers who may be on your aircraft. We need seat checks immediately and advise you go to lock-down while you do it. Copy?"

"Copy, New York. Talk to me. What the hell is going on?"

"We're not sure yet, 1787. There is confusion about half a dozen men with Middle Eastern names on your flight, over."

"Affirmative, New York. Going to lockdown immediately. Please be advised we have FAMs onboard. Thank God. We will alert them about the lockdown and the seat check."

"Copy, 1787. That's good news. I will also advise the FAMS desk to also contact their marshals."

"Thanks, New York. Please tell me what is going on. Should I declare an emergency?"

The ATC hesitated.

"No, not at this time, 1787. This is an alert. Apparently the Port Authority Police and your airline are concerned that some people may have been playing musical chairs with tickets and could have switched flights."

"You had me going there, for a minute. That's it, New York?"

"Yeah, that it, 1787."

"Are they sure this is not some kind of computer foul-up? You know, we've had those before."

"Unknown, 1787. Talk to your people about that. Please proceed and advise us soonest, copy?"

"Copy, New York. Will do. Out."

# 14.

Paul listened to the ceiling console speaker inside the JFK Tower, as the Air Traffic Controller in Ronkonkoma on Long Island spoke to Flight 1787. The square tower had great views of Jamaica Bay and the Manhattan skyline but Paul's eyes were glued to the black speaker. He was frustrated that all they could do was listen in, while someone two counties away spoke to the airplane. At least they had answered, which Paul was afraid would not happen. Also, they had air marshals on the plane, more good news. The pilot had seemed very nervous and asked if he should declare an emergency, which was good. When the pilot said the word Zebra three times, Paul asked an FAA supervisor what it was all about.

"The pilot gave his correct green PCS, his personal code sign letters," said the FAA man. "Flight crews all have two each—one red, one green."

"So, green means good and red means bad?" Paul asked.

"Right. Green, in this case, zebra, zebra, zebra, is normal. Red is emergency or means the crew member is under duress but can't say so."

"Like when there are hijackers."

"Affirmative. Also, they have not flipped their transponder to hijack mode. He's squawking normal onscreen."

When Paul heard that federal marshals were onboard the plane, he heaved a sigh of relief. That was a stroke of luck. Paul noticed his captain glaring at him, when the pilot asked if he should declare an emergency. Under the cool, even pilot talk, the guy sounded scared. When Paul and his captain and Cindy had arrived, the tower personnel were calm but you could feel the tension in the air. As they listened to the exchange between New York Center and Flight 1787, more and more faces relaxed and reacquired most of their coolness.

The pilot signed off to check on the passengers and tip off the marshals. Now, nobody was looking at Paul. Except his boss.

"Now what?" Paul asked.

"We wait for 1787 to get back to us," the FAA supervisor said. "Fran and Emile here are on with the two other flights now but the pilots already responded with green codes. We can still talk to them directly because they're closer. They took off later. There are no marshals on those other two flights but all seems to be normal. All three cockpits are now in locked-down, secure mode. They will all respond after their seat checks are complete."

They were shooting Paul's alert down, but that was okay. When the 1787 pilot had started to suggest over the radio that it was all a computer fuckup, several air traffic controllers had nodded their heads in agreement. They had been there before, apparently. Maybe that new girl had simply screwed everything up before she went home sick, Paul thought. That was Paul's point—garbage in, garbage out. A computer wasn't reality. More and more people in the tower went back to their business, as if it was all over. Paul didn't care. They could call him Chicken Little from now on, if they wanted to. He wanted to be wrong. But, even if he was wrong, he knew he had done the right thing. He would do it again. Besides, it wasn't over yet. The music had stopped but they still didn't know who was sitting in which seats.

# 15.

The pilot in Flight 1787's cockpit switched on his throat microphone again.

"New York Center, this is Anytime 1787 heavy, over?"

"Go ahead, 1787."

"I'm happy to say we struck out. The marshals were unable to find anyone with those names onboard, although they are still talking to the passengers in the seats you flagged. Our hard copy manifests onboard agree with our head count and ticket stub check. Be advised that half of the folks in those questioned seats are children, so it looks like somebody down there got his wires crossed somewhere, over?"

"Copy, 1787. Thank you."

"If it helps, New York, the marshals haven't found any group of men like you described earlier. One of the marshals told me he will so advise his people. And the airline has informed us that we will be met by security at the gate upon arrival at Cabo, as a precaution."

"Affirmative, 1787. Sorry for all the excitement. We were not the source but we had to relay it."

"Copy, New York, I understand. Better safe than sorry. No problem. The customers were a bit ruffled by the whole thing—the marshals were a bit dramatic—but our people are giving out free margaritas now, so all's well that ends well."

"Yeah, it had our full attention down here, as well. Thanks

for your cooperation, 1787. Have a good flight. New York out."

The pilot switched off his mike again. Hearing footsteps behind him in the cockpit, the Asian pilot turned and smiled at his colleague.

"How did it go?" the guy in the Tom Selleck Hawaiian shirt asked.

"Perfect. No problems. We are right on schedule. Everything okay back there?"

"It's okay now. That soldier had to go."

"Of course," said the pilot. "There was no other way. We knew we had to make examples up front. We're lucky it was only five people. If you have to shoot again, please remember your fields of fire."

"I will. The rest of them are all penned up in the back."

"Good, then everything is just fine," the pilot replied.

"Yeah, everything's good."

The guy in the Hawaiian shirt paused before speaking again.

"I can't wait."

"I know what you mean. I can't either, but it's just a few hours away. We have to be patient and do our jobs," the pilot said. "Come, my brother, look at the sky on this wonderful day. Isn't it beautiful?"

"Yeah," said the gaudily dressed killer, smiling for the first time that day. "It's beautiful."

# 16.

Paul listened as the pilots of the planes winging toward Washington and Boston and Mexico checked in with air traffic controllers by radio and reported they had no such people on board and that all was well. They had all given their secret ID, all-is-well code phrases. The Boston and Washington flights were already in the traffic patterns to land at those airports and would be on the ground soon. The Mexico jet, of course, would not be landing for hours. The airline had not yet found out why the computer now showed the Saudis on board.

Paul stared out the huge windows of the JFK control tower at the Manhattan skyline in the distance, the spike of the Empire State Building rising in Midtown. His eyes drifted left, downtown to the Wall Street area, a silhouette notable for what was no longer there, an absence that always caused a physical pang in Paul's gut. Lower Manhattan looked incomplete without the brother buildings, the Twin Towers. Kids born after the attacks won't know there's a big hole where the biggest buildings used to be, where thousands of lives used to be, he thought.

"Can I talk to these cops onboard, the marshals?" Paul asked, turning back to the FAA bosses. "You know, cop-to-cop, just to make sure everything's okay?"

He ignored his captain's withering glance.

"No, I don't see how," the FAA official replied. "They communicate with their agency using their secure PDA's."

"What is a PDA?" Paul asked.

"You, know, a personal digital assistant? It performs scheduling, e-mail and other tasks?"

"Oh yeah, those little computers with the cute little sticks," Paul said.

"Correct. Except this one has secure communications. They have already e-mailed their desk that everything is secure," the FAA man said.

"You guys ever see that *New Yorker* cartoon, the one where a dog is at a computer," Paul asked, "and he's saying to another dog that 'on the Internet, no one knows I'm a dog'?"

"Paul . . ." his captain began.

"Sorry, Captain. Just a few more quick questions. So I can't speak to one of the marshals. Did any of you speak to either of these marshals? Do you maybe have a cell phone number for these guys I could dial?"

"No, we don't normally speak directly to the marshals. They're not under our jurisdiction."

"Let me get this straight," Paul said. "Nobody here in this room, or anywhere else, has actually spoken to the armed law enforcement officers who are on the Mexico flight? The marshals sent a fucking e-mail to their office. Great. The pilot is just a voice on a radio and we're just going to take his word for it? There's no live video camera from the plane or the cockpit, so nobody has seen these guys, or the pilot, for that matter? Just a voice on the radio and an e-mail? That's it?"

No one answered Paul for a moment. His captain had stopped giving Paul the evil eye and turned toward the feds for their answer.

"No, that's not it," said the head guy. "The pilot reported the correct non-duress code. That is secret. Only that pilot knew that code."

"Really?" Paul asked. "Then how did you guys know it was the right code?"

The FAA guy actually sniggered before answering.

"Well, obviously, Sergeant, we knew the code, as well."

"You knew it by heart?" Paul asked. "Do you know Captain Dean Cornell personally? Does the controller in Ronkonkoma know him? Did you recognize his voice?"

From the look on his face, the FAA guy was apparently trying to decide if Paul was being sarcastic—or was just incredibly stupid.

"No, of course not. There are hundreds of pilots, thousands of them, and dozens of airlines . . ."

"So, in the matter of airline safety, the federal government is willing to take an e-mail at face value and just take the word of an anonymous voice on the air?" Paul asked.

"It's not anonymous. They all have different codes, two each, but we can access that very quickly."

"Access it where?" Paul persisted.

"In our computer."

"Exactly," Paul said, triumphantly. "A computer, a nationwide computer system. And who has access to this computer information? Thousands of people? Anyone in the FAA? The TSA? Homeland Security? FBI? Department of Agriculture? Any teenager with a computer?" Paul said, his voice getting louder. "Sounds real secure. You think that if I were responding to a hostage situation, that I would just make a phone call, instead of going in to see for myself? You think that if some unknown voice told me everything was okay—that I would just go away?"

"That's enough, Paul," the captain said.

"I don't think so, Captain. Think about it. These guys do a great job but they're not cops. That's not what they do. That's what we do and we don't know shit. We don't know who's alive or dead or who is really on that plane or what is going on. Eventually, we'll find out—but what might happen between then and now? We need a pair of eyes up there to see what's going on. If we don't get better proof, it's time to scramble the jets, sir."

"I don't think so, Paul. That's not our decision, anyway."

"The Boston and Washington flights are on the ground," one controller said.

"Captain," Paul pleaded. "We need better information. Now."

"Actually, I agree, Paul. I'm going to work on that here. Respond back to the concourse."

Paul opened his mouth to protest but thought better of it.

"Yessir," Paul said, turning to leave.

Cindy followed Paul out the door.

"Sarge, I'm starting to get scared," Cindy said to Paul as they rode down alone together in the elevator.

"Worried the captain is going to fire me?"

"Hell, no. That would be fine by me. For the first time, I'm worried that, this time, you might be right."

# 17.

Anna, even though she was hugging Ruby on the dark blue carpeting at the back of the plane, had the distinct, terrible and paralyzing sensation of being utterly alone, of hurtling down a narrowing tunnel with everyone else at the darker edges, an unmoving tornado of fear. Anna Horowitz had studied battle most of her life and now she was, suddenly, impossibly, inside one without a moment to think, to evaluate. I can't protect Ruby by holding her, Anna decided. That's not the way. If there is a way, it's beyond yes or no. It's something else. She looked around at those standing above her and down the right aisle toward the front of the cabin. As she did, the dark tunnel moved with her head, like she had blinders on. How odd. It was as if someone had also flipped a switch in Anna's brain and her mind went into high gear, racing. It felt like being high, like that time at a New Year's Eve party in college, when she snorted some cocaine; that rush of energy, time speeding up. Except this time she felt outside herself, above herself, floating. She had read about this state of mind her whole life and now it was her whole life. As she looked around again, Anna noticed her field of vision widening and getting brighter. She took a deep breath. They collected our cell phones so the world would not know—until they do whatever they're going to do, wherever they're going to do it. Anna noticed that many people still in seats were changing channels on their little screens—even though all the channels were blank—looking for news of what had happened to them. One man in an aisle seat stared, unseeing, at his white screen, like a zombie. He looked dead but Anna noted that he was still breathing, his chest slowly pulsing. Shock, Anna decided, her eyes darting around for more information. One person was asking others for a cell phone, despite the fact that they had all been collected. Anna could smell the panic as her eyes jumped from sobbing women, rambling men, people crying and praying out loud. She also smelled excrement and vomit and food and fresh coffee. She saw one man who had an aisle seat next to the beverage cart taking one little bottle of booze after another and pouring them down his gullet. He didn't even look at the labels, vodka, whiskey, gin, bourbon. He passed some to a woman next to him and she did the same. They dropped their empties on the floor. Everybody was still in their own tunnel, Anna knew. But she was coming out of the tunnel. To where? Her blood felt warm, coursing through her body. She knew everything, clearly. She knew she could do anything. Kill anyone.

"Anna?" Jim asked, looking strangely at her face.

She ignored her husband and, instead, listened to the bloody trussed-up marshal behind her on the floor, demanding to be untied. Liz, their flight attendant produced a small jackknife and corkscrew from her apron pocket and cut his bonds. He tried to stand up and fell back down on his butt, obviously dizzy, blood dripping out his nose. Sitting on the floor, Anna watched him reach into an inside front pocket of his jacket and remove a small, black, flat notebook. He flipped it open along the long edge. It was one of those personal digital assistants. He punched the little buttons, waited, and did it again.

"Shit!" Ed hissed, still trying to do something with the little computer. "C'mon, c'mon."

Some looked toward Ed with obvious hope on their faces, still waiting for someone else to rescue them. Obviously the marshal could not even stand up, probably because of a concussion. He was also trying to get someone else to help them. There was no one else, she knew. There was only one way. Ruby was trying to tell her something about the captain, about his voice, but Anna was too busy thinking to listen. Anna looked down the aisle again and around at the others, about a hundred people in the seats or standing or sitting in the rear of the plane. No one was doing anything. Jim was sitting and talking to the guy with the laptop computer, talking about how they had to do something.

"Well at least they can't get to us here," said one young man on the edge of the crowd in a white T-shirt with "USA" on it in big red letters. His right forearm was covered with a dirty arm cast, which was signed and decorated in different color markers. He was one of many people talking in the rear area at once.

"This isn't a fort, it's a prison," snarled Matt.

"No, it's not a prison, either," said Anna, correcting Matt loudly and evenly, in her professional voice of authority.

She stood up and squared her shoulders. "Our situation is the prison. This," she said, gesturing to the carts in the aisles, "is an incredible gift from our enemies. From the gods. This is a plan. This is our plan."

Jim looked at the carts. His face opened in understanding and he looked back at Anna, nodding his head.

"Yes," Jim said, also standing up.

No one else said a word for several seconds—even to ridicule her. Then the kid in the USA T-shirt and arm cast spoke up.

"A plan for what?" he asked her.

"For taking back this aircraft, for killing them. A counterattack. As soon as possible. It's that, or die. All of us. We have no choice. Our enemies have not only given us the plan, they have positioned our equipment for us."

"Equipment? What the hell are you talking about?" asked the

kid in the USA shirt. "They have guns and knives. What can we do?"

"Nothing or everything," Anna said, evenly. "Nothing gets us dead. Everything may get us out of this prison."

"She's right," said Matt, standing next to Anna and Jim. "Like on 9-11, those people on the plane in Pennsylvania. They fought back. We have to do something right now, before it's too late."

"That plane crashed," the guy in the T-shirt reminded Matt.

"Yeah, but they made it all the way to the cockpit. The bad guys crashed the plane because the passengers had won," Jim said.

When someone else began to quibble, Jim exploded.

"NO!" Jim roared. "NO! NO! NO! This cannot happen again! I will not let this happen! No! I won't let them kill my family! No! No! NO! Do you want them to kill your kids?"

Matt joined in, also saying the word no, over and over. Other men and women also said it out loud. They looked at each other and said it louder, in unison, stomping their feet and vibrating the floor. Others joined in the chant and no longer felt alone.

"NO! NO! NO!"

"QUIET!" the guy in the Hawaiian shirt yelled, waving his gun at them.

They stopped yelling and crouched down, drawing into a huge football huddle.

A Latin phrase from Virgil's *Aeneid* popped into Anna's head. She translated it out loud to no one in particular.

"The one salvation of the vanquished is to abandon all hope of salvation," said Anna. "It means we are now the moral and spiritual equals of the terrorists."

"It means we're all dead," someone snapped.

"Exactly," said Anna. "The dead are free of fear."

"She's right," said Lester, ignoring the other comment. "We have nothing to lose. Fuck fear! Fuck the bastards! We are as dangerous as they are and there are more of us. It doesn't matter how they got onboard or why or who they are—the only thing now is how to stop them—fast."

"We're going to listen to a woman?" someone shouted.

"Anna is an expert on military tactics and strategy," Jim shouted back. "She teaches at the Pentagon and even the CIA. Listen to her."

"She's right. It's the only way," said Ed. "I am a federal air marshal and I'm telling you that we have to fight. It doesn't matter whose idea it is. It's my idea, too. We have to act now, before it's too late. I haven't been able to reach my desk. We have nothing to lose and very little time. She's right."

"Yeah but they have . . ."

"Shut the fuck up!" Ed ordered from the floor. "What plan?" he asked, turning back to Anna.

"The carts become our battering rams," she explained calmly. "We unlock them and run them down the aisles into them and then kill them. All of us at once, a frontal assault," Anna explained. "It would be better for us if we could have fog or a smokescreen but this is the ground we have been presented. We improvise whatever weapons and shields we can now and attack as soon as possible. Two groups of at least six each behind the carts to attack the enemies here, two more of the same behind them to rush forward down each aisle and retake the cockpit and rescue the pilots. Four groups total. Two dozen in the main assault, followed immediately by, well, everyone else. No reserves. All or nothing the first time. Wait, no. We go down the left flank first, with two groups. If all of the enemy goes left to engage us, the other two groups rush down the right, using the cart as a shield, and run forward to the cockpit. That's better. The priority is speed, to overwhelm them with our numbers, no matter what happens, and recapture the guns, use them against the enemy and take back the cockpit. No matter what happens. To anybody."

"Yes," Ed said. "That's smart. I agree. Those carts are very heavy."

"I was a captain in the reserves," Gordon said. "Your plan is that we just keep rushing them until they run out of bullets? You're talking about twenty or thirty of us dead?" Gordon asked.

"Whatever it takes. You're dead already," Anna told him. "We all are. This is the only way to live. Some of us will die. I will go in front of you, if you like. We also have to make weapons and armor ourselves as best we can. But nothing that takes longer than ten minutes. Or if they change course. We can't let them do what they want. If you have a better plan, we're all listening."

Gordon said nothing. The many conversations had stopped and everyone was gathering around, straining to listen, as Anna explained her plan again.

"Will they shoot at us?" Gordon asked. "I thought we all get sucked out if a bullet hits the plane?"

"They'll shoot," said Ed. "They already have. They obviously know how to do it the right way, to minimize the risk of depressurization. They also know we marshals have special ammunition, to minimize that risk. Stay very low, so they have to shoot downwards or straight back. Maybe they'll flinch or hesitate. Use some trays or anything hard as a shield, to break up the rounds. You'll have a better chance that way."

Everyone began throwing ideas around, going through their bags, searching the cabin for weapons, ideas. Jim pulled a life vest from under a seat, put it on and inflated it by pulling the cord, just like they did in the preflight safety demonstrations.

"What's that for?" Matt asked.

"I thought it might protect me from the knives a little, around the neck and chest," Jim explained.

"Not a bad idea," said Matt, pulling out more vests. He put one on and handed another to Anna. Others did the same.

"Anyone got cigarettes and matches?" Jim asked.

"I do," said Gordon, pulling out a hard pack and matches.

Jim quickly emptied the pack on the floor, dumping ten cigarettes on the carpet. He pulled the aluminum foil pack lining out, crushed the smokes in one hand and wrapped the crushed tobacco and paper inside the foil, making a tube. Then Jim pulled all but two of the paper matches out by the stems and placed them in the top of the foil tube, with a few red match heads sticking out. He stuck the shiny tube back in the box, crushing it to hold the tube snug, like he had done as a prank in grammar school, and held on to the match pack, with its two remaining matches.

"Okay. One smoke bomb. Anna, we have some fog. Anyone else have cigarettes?"

Reluctantly, Gordon's wife, Danielle, turned over her pack and matches and Jim made a second one.

"Can you use this?" Emily asked, handing her aluminum cane to Lester.

"Yes, thanks," said Lester, pulling off the black rubber tip and exposing the metal tube. He handed it to a man standing next to him.

One high school student produced several shiny CDs and snapped them in half, suggesting they might make good knives.

"No," Ed told the teen. "Don't waste time. Get their knife."

Liz suggested hot coffee from the galley as something to throw.

"Your pitchers are a bad delivery system," said Anna. "They're made not to spill. If we put them in water bottles, we could squirt it in their faces and scald them. Who's got bottles?"

Liz got busy with that when a woman crawled over with two

hard plastic baby bottles.

"We really need our own pepper spray, something to blind them," Jim lamented. "They got knives onboard—anybody happen to have any Mace with them?"

"How about these?" Emily asked, pulling a small can of Right Guard spray deodorant and another, smaller tube of Breath Fresh mint breath spray.

"Actually, that is great," Jim said, taking them. "Chemicals and alcohol—that's got to burn the eyes, thanks."

Jim wrapped someone's jacket around his left arm, to protect it from the black blades. Several people were taking Ed's advice and were shoving layers of plastic meal trays down their shirts.

"It's not a bulletproof vest, but it may help," Ed said from the floor. "It would be better to hold them out in front, the farther away, the better, so the shot has a chance to spread out. Remember, stay low, below the gun at all times."

Anna was giving out assignments, separating the volunteers into four teams of the youngest and strongest and the immediate reserve. Once in four groups, she told them who was to go for the weapon, who had the legs, the head.

"Go for the guns first, then the knives. You two punch him, poke his eyes, choke him. Anything. You two go for the woman's knife hand," she ordered. "Everyone—pin them, get the weapons and use them immediately against them until they are dead. All of them."

Groups three and four were given the task of going to the cockpit, to stop them from crashing the plane, to free the pilots. They passed the word quietly to the moms—all kids under the seats. Anna and Jim hugged Ruby and each other one last time.

"Jim, go down this aisle, the right aisle in the second wave," said Anna. "Stay behind the cart and then on the right side of it, if you can. Keep it between you and the guns. Get up front as fast as you can."

Emmett stepped forward and began a prayer, beseeching his maker for victory against evil. Many people bowed their heads.

"Dear God, guide us in our hour of need, oh Lord, have mercy on us . . ."

"God is what got us into this shit," Matt muttered to Jim.

Ruby, who had been hovering outside the circle, had listened to her mom and dad and then gone to the galley by herself. She found the plastic bag she was looking for and a plastic cup. She sat on the floor and got busy like everybody else, like she saw in a cartoon.

"Daddy, I made some pepper spray like you wanted," Ruby proudly announced when she was done, holding up a translucent cup half filled with brown powder and handing it to her dad.

Jim saw the pile of dozens of ripped tiny white paper packets of ground pepper on the floor that Ruby had emptied into the cup. "No, honey, when I said we needed pepper spray, I meant the kind . . . wait, you know, this is great, sweetheart! We'll throw it in their eyes! Thanks."

He hugged Ruby, kissed her and told her he loved her. As Jim crouched forward behind the cart, he realized both hands were full, with the cup of pepper and the small aerosol breath spray. He asked the man behind him if he had a free hand.

"Yes. I'll take the spray, okay?" he smiled at Jim. "I'm Matt."

"Right. I'm Jim," he said, as they shook hands.

"Unlock the wheels and light the smoke," Anna said, ordering the front teams to crawl up behind the two carts.

Everyone was looking at her.

"We have to do what they did to us," Anna told them. "Attack them, take their weapons and use them against them. But we have to kill them all. All of them. All of them. Ready?"

# 18.

Paul's cell rang as he and Cindy were getting out of the JFK tower elevator. He flipped it open when he saw his sister's home number displayed.

"Kevin, you would not believe how fucking stupid these . . ."

"Paul," Kevin interrupted. "Listen up. I've got something for you. Just got it."

"What?"

"The wife for your number-four guy—she walked into the one-twelve this morning and reported her husband, Ali Akbar Whalid, missing."

"This morning?"

"Actually she called the precinct yesterday, because he didn't come home Friday night but a desk officer told her to wait twenty-four hours to file a missing persons report."

"Goddamnit!" Paul said. "I'm going to the precinct."

"No, Paul, don't bother, my guy there said she's clueless. She claims she never heard of the other guys on your list. Her husband was last seen going to their mosque on Woodhaven Boulevard, to pray."

"Shit," Paul said. "Give me the address."

Paul jotted the address in his notebook and told Kevin he was going there.

"I've got a Hercules team on the way, crime scene, you name it," Kevin told him. "Oh, your girl, the Anytime employee? She's not home, place is empty, we're talking to the neighbors and the landlord. Her car's on the air, top of the hot sheet. Nothing yet."

"The feds are calling it off because they spoke to somebody on the plane but it's bullshit," Paul said. "They don't know what's going on aboard that plane, the Cabo flight. So, you rang the bell, yes?"

"Yeah but here's the thing," Kevin said.

"What thing?" Paul asked, hearing Kevin's cell phones ringing in the background, along with his sister's voice and other men.

"The feds are also going on alert," said Kevin. "They were calling us while I was calling them—but not about these guys, about another set of males out of state, from Georgia. We have nothing on their guys, they're clean. We had to tell them about your stuff. Get this—they're bumping up the alert status two rungs but they won't tell us why and they're not going public. Never happened before and they're telling us shit. They're going red, Paul. They're buttoning up. I've got to go into town, my people are here. Do what you can. I don't know what else to tell you because I don't have anything else yet. Good luck, Paul. And thanks."

He hung up.

"Cindy, we're going to this mosque on Woodhaven," Paul said, after telling her what Kevin had told him. "Lights and sirens."

"Okay, boss," she said, taking the piece of paper.

Paul broke into a run, his equipment jangling, Cindy dashing behind him. They both raced for the exit. Cindy was surprised that her older, heavier boss beat her to the skyway door. In the car, Paul pulled out his cigar tube, extracted his old cigar and lit it with his Marine Corps lighter. Cindy said nothing. She would have been hard to hear over the siren noise.

"Sarge, what are we going to find out there that NYPD

can't?" Cindy asked.

"I have no idea."

"Okay. What the hell is going on?"

"I have no idea but, if somebody doesn't figure it out soon, we are totally fucked. Maybe we're fucked even if we do figure it out."

After she straightened out the vehicle and floored it, Cindy pulled out her cell phone with one hand.

"I know we're not supposed to, Sarge, but if we're fucked, I'm going to call my husband. He's in Manhattan today. I've got to warn him."

Paul looked at her.

"I won't tell anybody, Cindy, I've got a family, too, but what are you going to tell him?"

"I have no idea," she said, putting the phone away.

"Exactly," said Paul.

# 19.

Matt and Jim crouched tight together behind the dull aluminum food cart in the right side, starboard aisle, Jim on the left, Matt on the right, waiting. In his left hand, Jim held the plastic cup of pepper Ruby had given him. His hands were wet with cold sweat. Matt had the little can of Right Guard deodorant from the old woman with the pink hair.

"Stay low. Wait until I tell you to go," Anna whispered to them again. "The left goes first to engage them. Then you go as fast as you can all the way up to the front. Stay behind the cart for cover. Don't stop for anything. Others will be behind you. Don't look back. Don't stop."

Matt and Jim looked into each other's eyes and nodded at each other. Anna and Jim hugged and kissed again and told each other they loved each other. Then Anna crawled to the rear and directed four others right behind Jim and Matt, two teenaged boys and two older men. They all had seat cushions held in their left hands, as shields from the black blades. Jim realized they didn't know each other's names. He and Matt and the others introduced themselves and they all shook hands. Jim didn't hear any of the names but he heard and felt his heart beating against the orange life vest, drumming it up and down.

"Let's do this," said Matt.

"Yeah," said everyone else, together. "Let's do this."

Jim heard his wife's voice at the other side of the rear area, on the left, giving more low key orders to the other groups. She was directing the first group behind the beverage cart in the left, port aisle to go first, the second group behind them. Lester and Bob were pushing the cart, seat cushions on their outside arms. Bob clutched Emily's steel cane. Behind them were Gordon, Toni, Emmett and seven others. On the right, Matt and Jim and the four others were the third group, with a fourth group waiting behind them. Anna was telling the fourth group to rush down the right aisle behind Jim and Matt's group and attack the hijackers from the left.

"Wait, I need six more," Anna said to more volunteers. "I need one more group to go up the right into business class and hang a left through the seats. You'll be hidden by the barrier and you'll go from the right aisle to the left aisle, double back, and come up behind them, as fast as you can. This is crucial. That way, we will hit them from the front, their left flank and then their rear. Okay?"

Jim heard the marshal agreeing, and telling people to stay low, move fast and not to get trapped in the aisles. There were more orders, and then Anna said to light the cigarette packs and throw them. Jim lit his match and torched the crumpled pack. It hissed and he chucked it over the cart, as far as he could, into the open aisle in front. Someone on the other side did the same thing. They waited. Jim closed his eyes and tried to catch a breath.

"All kids flat on the floor," Anna said in a stage whisper.

Nothing happened. He and Matt looked at each other. Then Jim smelled burning sulphur, paper and tobacco. White smoke drifted up over the far seats but it was thin and not hiding anything. Jim's smoke bomb had apparently gone out.

"Never mind, never mind," Anna was saying. "GO, ONE! GO NOW!"

Four hijackers, who had seen the smoke bomb, were yelling threats on the left side of the open area. Joey, Maria, and the two big guys, including the one with a gun, were taking menacing steps toward the left aisle when the passengers launched their counterattack.

"GO! GO! GO!" the men yelled, giving Jim a chill, as he peeked above the seat tops. Jim's feet felt the heavy cart rumbling forward, too slow, shouting, screaming, crying.

"Faster! Faster!" Anna yelled. "Second group GO! Behind them!"

Was that us? Jim wondered. No, I think we're three. The nose of the plane dipped slightly down and the cart on the other side jerked forward, as Lester and Bob grunted and pushed it even faster.

"NO! Shoot up! Not down!!" Joey yelled to the big guy with the gun.

The gun went off twice, as the terrorist fired into the cart, apparently trying to hit Lester and Bob crouched behind it, but the cart kept going. Men and some women staggered and ran down the aisle toward the terrorists, who stood their ground. The cart shot out of the aisle and rammed right into the two big guys. The one with the gun stumbled back and fired into the ceiling as he went down. The shooting stopped for a moment but the yelling was loud, as a dozen passengers flooded into the open area, hands, arms, cushions flying. Over and over, Jim heard screams and moans as the smoke suddenly got thicker in the cabin and so did the noise, the screaming, the crying, the rumbling . . .

"Jim, GO! GO!" Anna yelled behind him. "GO!"

Jim and Matt pushed the cart forward, gaining momentum as they leaned into it, faster and faster. In seconds, they were out of the aisle and pushing the cart across open carpet toward the next opening. The men behind them crowded around and helped them push the cart faster. Anna was shouting orders to other groups as they left her behind in the haze, thicker now.

Jim heard more bangs, snapping noises over his head, screams. Jim and Matt reached the entrance of the next aisle and kept pushing the cart into the narrow space, forward through business class, their legs straining. And then they were there, passing the seats where they had been sitting in first class, breaking into the open again near the lavatory and forward galley. They had made it. Jim turned to look over his shoulder but the four other men were gone, nowhere to be seen. He and Matt were alone. They stopped the cart in the open area, near the front bulkhead, beneath the white screen, almost to the far left aisle. Other men were moving behind them, through the seats in business class toward the other side, including two young teenagers. They were sneaking up behind the hijackers, Jim guessed. The guns started firing again in the rear and then stopped. Jim heard men chanting.

"NO! . . . NO! . . . NO! . . ."

"Let's go!" said Matt, jerking his thumb toward the cockpit.

"Get back!" the Asian hijacker ordered them, appearing from around the right lavatory, his knife raised in his right hand.

Jim and Matt instinctively recoiled. Matt hit the bulkhead wall and Jim backed into the cart. They were trapped between the wall, the cart and the man with the knife. Jim looked at the crumpled translucent plastic cup in his hand and pulled the mouth open with his fingers.

"We're not trapped, Matt," he said out loud, remembering his partner's name.

Jim threw the cup of pepper into the shorter man's face, like a dry, brown drink.

The hijacker quickly lashed out, hitting Jim's arm and his life vest. His eyes closed, and he put one hand to his blinking, burning eyes, swinging the blade wildly.

Matt fired his deodorant spray and also got the little man

right in the eyes and mouth and nose, the chemical foaming on his skin.

The hijacker, spitting, flailed in Matt's direction but missed. He screamed and dropped the knife, grabbing his eyes with both hands.

Jim leaned down and grabbed the weapon. It was black as obsidian but man-made, like a pair of brass knuckles with a blade in place of the knuckles. Jim hefted it, and looked at Matt. Matt nodded and Jim swung it in his fist, back and forth. The terrorist, who was rubbing both eyes, grabbed his throat, and fell over backwards. He lay on the floor, near the right aisle, blind and bleeding, choking, like they had done to that poor blonde stewardess on the other side, when it all began. How long ago was that?

"Let's go, Jim," said Matt again.

Before he could move, Jim caught a blur of black flowers coming around the forward corner of the left aisle, behind the cart, behind Matt. He saw a black object in front of the black Hawaiian shirt and ducked, as the gun went off like a bomb. Jim and Matt crouched back behind their cart but it was the wrong reflex. A second bullet exploded through the cart and sprayed them with red. They each jerked away from the explosion, flat on their backs. The cart was no protection.

The guy in the Hawaiian shirt moved to the left of the cart, and spotted his prone pal on the floor. He saw what they had done to his partner and his face bloomed into fury. His lips curling away from his teeth, like a dog, he stepped around the cart for a better shot at them, bringing the weapon to bear on Jim. Jim should have scrambled up, attacked or turned to run but he just lay there, frozen by the face that would kill him. Matt futilely threw his little deodorant can at the gunman. It missed and sailed out of sight.

The gunman, still moving to his right at the head of the left aisle, aimed directly at Jim's face.

Jim's hands went up, defensively up—as if they could stop bullets.

The gunman jerked sharply to his left, back the way he came. His body flew sideways and the gun went up and to his right. He fired as he fell hard onto the floor, with a grunt, and disappeared just behind the cart.

"Quick!" Matt yelled to Jim.

Matt had scrambled up and was pushing at the side of the cart.

"Push it over!" he yelled.

Jim rolled up and hit the cart with his shoulder and they both shoved as hard as they could. It went over on its side, heavy as a tree. The whole plane shook from the impact. They both jumped back but the guy in the Hawaiian shirt was gone. One of his legs, with a Top-Sider on it, was sticking out from under the left end of the cart. Jim stepped back further and saw another leg, without a shoe, protruding from the right end, covered in thick, brown fluid. It didn't seem possible.

"Look!" Matt said, walking around the right side.

Only part of the Hawaiian shirt was visible, along with the gunman's head. His shades were gone. The handsome man stared at the ceiling without blinking, a peaceful look on his face. Blood had sprayed out of his nostrils. For some reason, he had done a split on the floor, like a gymnast, allowing them to topple the cart, which had crushed his torso impossibly thin. He did not move or breathe. He was broken. Matt looked back at the Asian guy, who was also motionless on the carpet.

"I don't see the gun," Matt said.

"How did he fall?" Jim asked.

"Here it is!" Matt said, holding the pistol in his hand.

Jim looked again at the foot covered in brown stuff. Then he looked at the big dark spot on the carpet. The flight attendant's pool of blood. That's what made him go down.

"Matt! Blood!" Jim said, pointing at Matt's left side. There was red everywhere. Matt ran his hands over his body and neck, smearing the red. He tasted it.

"Bloody Mary mix," he decided.

Jim and Matt were alone with the two bodies. Shrieking and groaning and cursing and wailing and crying continued to come from the smoky rear of the plane. They could not see what was happening behind the blue curtains, only a hazy, writhing mangle around the edges and dark shapes below. Had the others won or were they all being slaughtered? Matt put his hand on Jim's shoulder.

"We have to go, man," Matt said again.

Jim turned away and they both went forward, Matt in the lead, pointing the gun. No one else was up front. The cockpit door was lying on the floor at the left, near the entrance to the plane. Holes had been melted in it. On top of the door, at the end of a smear of dark blood, was the body of the blonde flight attendant, whose slippery blood had just saved them. The hijackers had hung a curtain over the cockpit. Neither Jim nor Matt were sure how many hijackers there were or where they were. Matt stood at the curtain, aiming the gun at the dark blue material. Jim, to the left, grasped the cloth.

"I don't think you should shoot, unless you . . ."

"I know," said Matt. "Do it."

Jim snatched the curtain away. It came off in his hand. Matt stood there, the pistol pointed into the cockpit. He took a step forward, into the doorway, swinging the gun. He seemed confused, his eyes darting all over. Jim stepped behind him to look.

The cockpit was completely empty. The yokes of the twin controls moved slightly, silently, as the FCS autopilot made minute corrections for wind currents and drift. Outside, on the other side of the windshield, it was also peaceful and devoid of life. A bright white carpet of clouds stretched ahead, to meet a sharp ceiling of blue. The sun, above and behind them, cast a soft shadow of the plane onto the pure, snowy landscape below.

# 20.

Alice sat in her usual leather seat at a corner of a very long conference table, dropping her files on the glassy mahogany surface. She tugged her U.S. Army captain's uniform tunic straight with both hands and pulled a long thin gooseneck microphone toward her, until the golf-ball sized black end of the mike pointed at her mouth. Captain Alice St. Thomas scanned the opposite wall. An image of herself, clearly showing her smooth ebony skin, long eyelashes, and small gold studs, double bars, like the bars on her uniform, sparkling in her ear-lobes, appeared in high definition inside a tiny inset video box on a wall-sized 40-foot-wide video screen. She gave the date, time and location. The large center screen was a live video of an oval conference table with a presidential seal on a white wall behind the table. The chair at the head of the table was empty but several people were taking seats around the table. Eight smaller screens, two on either side, also showed similar tables with different seals on the wall, and people taking seats. Signs under each video screen identified the locations, as PENTAGON, WHITE HOUSE, STATE DEPT., HOMELAND SEC., FBI, CIA, FAA, and TSA. Alice pressed a button on the built-in console and began speaking. A preset video camera was recording her voice and image in three different media as she ran through her usual spiel, although one item was obviously non-routine.

"The following is an unscheduled, triple delta clearance briefing and meeting of the National Security Council at the DC BLUEGRASS site," she said, looking directly into the camera, as if she were reading the morning news. "There are three items on the agenda. This site is currently under full security alert, with nothing to report. Video telelinks are established to the TX HAYLOFT site and eight secondary sites, as seen onscreen. NOFORN and NOCON distribution is authorized at this time. The following meeting may contain Secret Compartmentalized Intelligence, SIGINT recordings and/or transcripts, NSA CRYPTO data and phased array NRO imagery, as well as sensitive and secret U.S government policy deliberations. Review by persons not authorized to receive such information is unlawful. Disclosure of any or all of the above is a federal crime punishable by ten years in a federal prison and a fine of $10,000 for each violation. Thank you. Zero nine thirteen, local. Please stand by."

As Alice began to list the participants arriving in the secure room, the vice president of the United States, George Franklin Yarwood, dropped his considerable weight into the captain's chair at the head of the table, where the president would sit if he were in attendance. Yarwood's puffy, round face was more florid than usual. The red bloom extended above his forehead, cresting onto his shiny bald dome. The only things not pink on the vice president's visage were his silver mustache and his bright cornflower blue eyes. Before Yarwood on the table was a white NSC briefing portfolio with a bright diagonal red stripe and a large red triangle. Inside the pyramid was an NSC seal over a "DELTA3" logo.

Already seated next to Yarwood, intently reading from the portfolio, was National Security Advisor Sheila Preston, who bore a remarkable resemblance to Paula Abdul. As Preston read, she had the habit of fiddling with her black Montblanc pen, dangling it between her fingers.

"Admiral, what the fuck is going on?" Yarwood demanded with his customary shyness, flipping open his portfolio. "This had better not be a COG drill, I think I've been through enough of those. I feel like this place is my second home. Turner tells me you wouldn't tell him shit on the phone on the way here. I warn you that you took me away from a lovely breakfast, so I'm a bit cranky. In fact, Alice, get some food in here, please. The chef knows what I like."

Rear Admiral Roger Sherman waited until he was sure the VP had finished speaking. Sherman's predecessor had interrupted him once. Sherman also glanced at the VP's chief of staff, Turner Black, but he did not speak. Technically, since the president had not yet come online and his chair on the V-Tel screen was still empty, they should wait, but, obviously, today was going to be different from other days.

"As you will see from your folder, Mr. Vice President, we have issued a NUWARN directive, specifically, a QUIVERWARN alert to all branches of the military, after several pieces of information came to us this morning. This meeting is to discuss my recommendation that we upgrade the QUIVERWARN to an MTQUIVER as soon as possible, sir."

Turner Black, who always wore a black Italian suit, leaned toward his boss and whispered in the VP's ear.

"I know what a Nuclear Warning alert is," Yarwood snapped at his subordinate. "But, Admiral, what the Christ is a QUIVERWARN?"

"As explained in the executive summary, sir, that is a warning that strategic or tactical nuclear weapons could be compromised or even stolen. The alert, which I have already issued, triggered increased security and . . ."

"Hold it—you issued this already? Are you kidding me? Do you know what the media will do with this?"

The admiral was used to the VP insisting on verbal briefings first.

"Uhh . . . well, sir, as you can see, I urgently recommend that we elevate that warning to the MTQUIVER status because it looks like we have an unprecedented situation on our hands. Of course, the alert is top secret, so the media should not . . ."

"Well thanks for checking with the executive branch before you went forward with this, Admiral," Yarwood, said, his voice dripping with sarcasm. "What does this mean, exactly?"

"Sir, I am sorry to report that, at this early stage of an investigation by the National Command Authority, we have high confidence and multiple credible sources that report that two tactical nuclear weapons from the U.S. arsenal are missing, specifically, two M-27 dial-a-yield devices."

"Fuck!" said Yarwood. "Fuck!" he said again, louder, pounding the table with his clenched fist.

"Oh, my God," said a man in a gray suit on the TV screen labeled CIA.

"Hey, Woody, whose ass you kicking now?" a smiling President Stanton Westport III chuckled from the video screen, as he sat and joined the video conference from his Texas ranch. "What's goin' on, fellas?"

Unlike most previous occasions, no one laughed at the president's joke. He was wearing blue jeans and a polo shirt with the presidential logo over the left breast. The leader of the free world dropped a white cowboy hat on the table in front of him and rubbed his nose vigorously, a nervous gesture of his. In the underground bunker room with the vice president, Sheila Preston was the first to respond.

"Mr. President, we have a very serious situation that needs immediate attention," Preston said from her chair inside the Maryland mountain, looking directly at the screen. She stated the problem simply and starkly, as the president listened.

"Well, how sure are we about this?" the president asked.

Yarwood and Preston turned to the admiral, who spoke to the screen.

"Mr. President, the secretary of defense is on the way, he asked me to tell you he was reading-in and would be along shortly, so I will brief you, sir. The deputy commander of the eighty-third infantry task force at Fort Benning in Georgia pulled the hard-wired fiber optic alarm inside the weapons storage area at 8:27 this morning. The MPs are still gathering information but they found the bodies of two marine lance corporals inside the storage area guard room about a half hour after they failed to report a tour change at oh-eight-hundred."

"Somebody broke in and killed two marines and took nukes?" the president asked, standing up in his chair. "Who?"

"We're not sure, Mr. President. There was drug paraphernalia and hypodermic needles and evidence of, well, a party, sir. It's possible they overdosed but the fact that two devices are unaccounted for makes that conclusion suspect. Also there are several other personnel who work in the storage facility, or act as Marine guards, who are, as yet, unaccounted for."

"Who?" the president asked.

"Two other Marines working the prior shift, sir, among others."

"Who are they?" the vice president demanded.

The admiral glanced at his papers. He read off two names, Tariq Aziz Taylor and Muhammad Ali Jones, their ranks, serial numbers and detailed their ages and home towns, how many kids they had. Yarwood cut him off.

"Admiral, you're reading the file backwards. What's their pedigree? What's recorded against them? My sheet says they are both Moslems—is that true? You had two Moslems guarding a nuclear arsenal?"

"They do list their religion as Islam. Yes sir, they are apparently Moslem, but they have exemplary records and they would not be there unless an exhaustive security process determined that they were . . ."

"Where are they?" the president asked. "How much head start do they have?" he asked.

"That's some of what we don't know, sir," the admiral answered. "They have been unable to reach the commander, who is on leave, as well as several previous security shifts at the facility—to nail that down."

"Who is the commander?" the president asked.

"General Andre LeBoef, sir," the admiral replied. "He's on vacation. Camping somewhere in Yellowstone Park, I believe."

"I know Andy Beefcake. He's a good man. I'll have my people get a hold of him," the president declared.

"What, exactly do we know and what, exactly do we not know, Admiral?" Preston pressed.

"Ma'am, as you see in the briefing, we cannot yet confirm the last moment when the devices were electronically secured by a security team. The status panel at the facility shows such confirmations were apparently not recorded for about . . . seventy-two hours—although that could be an error. We've had problems like that before. We won't know for sure until we audit the system and track down all the security teams who are on leave, or whatever, and pin it, sir. I have dispatched NEST and they are enroute, Ma'am."

Preston shook her head and threw her Montblanc onto the table.

"Admiral Sherman," the vice president said loudly. "I'm glad you put the Nuclear Emergency Search Team on this but are you telling us that you have more missing soldiers and that the bombs could be missing as long as three days?"

"I'm not sure yet if the personnel are missing or simply unavailable, sir. Yes, it is, at this moment, still possible that the devices have been gone that long, although I doubt that very much. And actually, they're not bomb ordnance, sir."

"I'm confused," said the president. "I though you said they were nuclear bombs?"

"Yes, but not for air drop, Mr. President. They are special-use transportable devices."

"You mean they're backpack nukes?" Preston asked.

"Yes, Ma'am, if you want to call them that."

"In other words, they are small, suitcase bombs. With a yield of what?"

"Each has a variable yield, adjustable from 18 to 36 kilotons, Ma'am, as noted in Appendix A."

"If I may, Mr. President. I have virtually our entire local field office heading to the base," said FBI director Dick Bassett, a husky black man with a square jaw and salt-and-pepper hair. "A planeload with a special team will lift off from Dulles within the hour. We are researching the backgrounds of those involved and I hope to have an interim status report for you by midday."

"Thanks, Mr. Director, I appreciate that."

"Mr. President, I think we all hope these weapons have not been stolen but I believe we have to act as if they have been," said Preston. "I suggest we immediately order wartime levels of security and an inventory of all nonconventional military weapons."

"Ma'am, that would require an elevation to DEFCON 4, in order to get it done soonest."

"Whatever it takes to secure these weapons, Admiral," Preston said. "Mr. President, I recommend you order the increased security and the elevation of our defensive posture."

"What do you think, Woody?"

"I agree, Mr. President, but I'm concerned about the press getting hold of this, which is much more likely if we panic and notify every soldier, sailor and Marine to report back to their units immediately. This has to be done discreetly, without causing public alarm. But I think we have no choice but to immediately initiate the Continuity of Government plan—certainly until we know what we're dealing with. I also think you need to increase security around yourself, sir. Did you hear me, John?" the vice president asked John Langdon, the head of the president's Secret Service detail.

"Loud and clear, sir," the Secret Service agent responded.

"Okay, Woody, Sheila, let's go with it but let's keep it low key, 'til we're sure we're not goin' off half-cocked," said the president. "Woody, I think you like being underground so much, you must be part gopher," the president chuckled. "Let me know as soon as we have anything further. Thanks, folks."

Alice motioned to the admiral, who spoke up.

"Mr. President, we also have two other lesser items that have come up that were not in your daily briefing. The second item is an AIRWARN bulletin that NYPD has expressed concerns about some men with Arab-sounding surnames that may or may not be on a jetliner out of JFK Airport in New York."

"Oh yeah?"

"Mr. President, it's John Blair from the FAA."

"Hey, 'Air Blair,' howya doin'?" the president said.

"Fine, sir, thank you. Hope you're enjoying your vacation. There seems to be some confusion about a manifest on an Anytime Airlines flight but my people tell me the pilot has reported that there are no problems onboard. In fact, there are two armed federal air marshals on the plane, sir."

"So, what's the problem?" the president asked.

"Uh, Mr. President, it's George Read, from Homeland Security. Actually, NYPD has just told us that they are investigating the possibility that some Saudi nationals might be on that plane. And, uh, John? My folks want to ask your people to please reconfirm the status of the crew. NYPD says one of the men, a Saudi national, has been reported missing. The Federal Air Marshal Service is trying to reach their marshals now but they seem to be having a problem with their communications."

"Mr. President," said Preston, fiddling again with her pen, "I don't think we're ready to recommend anything on this yet, until we get a better reading, sir. The pilots have not signaled a hijacking or anything like that."

"Alrighty, then. We'll talk after lunch, or whenever? But you're not saying these things are related, are you?"

"Mr. President," the vice president interjected. "We don't know yet but it couldn't hurt to put all our air wings on alert, get them in the air—just in case. With live ammo."

"Okay, Woody," said the president, reaching for his hat.

"Mr. President," said Admiral Sherman. "We also have a third item. Our COMPSEC people are reporting multiple foreign cyber attacks on DOD websites and servers. The computer attacks are in depth and are coming from multiple foreign sites, sir. Slowdowns and a few shutdowns but no damage yet."

The president dropped his hat and sank back in his chair.

"Uh, Woody, what's your take on this? Is it serious? Does this computer thing have anything to do with the other two things?"

"There's no reason to think they are related but I don't think we can say. We've had these kinds of random computer hacker offensives before and they have never been related to anything in the real world, isn't that right, Admiral?"

"So far, that's been true, Mr. Vice President."

"Mr. President," said Preston. "Perhaps this is best left tabled until later, when more information becomes available. Obviously the first item is urgent and that is our highest priority."

"Okay, thanks. Let's get right on this. That is very troubling. I want immediate action," the president said, putting on his cowboy hat.

"Yes sir," the admiral said, sitting at attention.

The president ambled out of the video frame. The officials on the smaller screens relaxed. Most stood up and walked away from their tables.

"Mr. Vice President, why wasn't NYPD linked into the conference?" the FBI chief asked.

"Weren't they?" the vice president asked. "I'm not sure. Maybe we can get them onboard for the follow-up, if we need them, Mr. Director."

"Thank you, sir."

The FBI director left his seat, as his screen went to black and the other screens winked off.

"What was that about?" the VP asked his chief of staff, Turner Black.

Black looked around at the screens and reached over and flipped his boss's microphone to OFF.

"Sir, the director has noticed that we have been excluding NYPD from this level of conferencing for some time," said Black. "He thinks they're good. I guess he thought this situation might be an exception."

"Like hell," said the VP. "NYPD is a sieve. They have no need to know. If they were plugged in, this would be on TV before I could take a leak."

"Yes sir," said Black. "By the way, why wasn't the SOD here?"

"Because the secretary of defense is a smart customer, Turner. He wants the admiral to give the boss the bad news. Then he rides in to clean up the mess in his own stable—he hopes. Look, Turner, we have to knock this fucking nuke thing down as quickly as possible, no matter what it takes, before it gets out. Get everyone on this. If it's true, that Moslems have grabbed the weapons, that's bad but at least it gets us off the hook. It would be better if we can come up with an Al Qaeda or terrorist link to these men before we have to go public, if we have to. But keep everything as quiet as a mouse fart for as long as you can. This is one big, smelly shit sundae and I do not want to have to eat it, live, on CNN. Clear?"

# 21.

Matt, the heavy gun at his side, just kept looking around the deserted cockpit but the surreal scene did not change. He was thinking, trying to remember something, but he couldn't. It just kept slipping away in his brain.

"It's on autopilot," Jim said, behind him. "We should call somebody. What do we do?"

"Nothing, for now," Matt answered.

"Yeah, but where's the crew? They didn't get off."

Neither one voiced the obvious, as they left the cockpit. Without a crew it didn't matter who won. Jim looked toward the lavatories, the only possible remaining place they could be imprisoned.

"That one has the marshal in it," Jim reminded him, pointing with a bloody hand still holding the black blade.

"I know," said Matt, moving toward the other, starboard head.

The two-piece accordion door was closed flat but not locked. The little rectangle read "VACANT."

Matt jerked it open. It was vacant. Except for the toilet. He leaned inside. The shiny stainless steel plate on the bottom of the toilet bowl was depressed, revealing the top of a pile of cell phones soaked in blue liquid below.

"What the hell?" he said.

Jim walked back and opened the other bathroom door. He staggered back, a gorge rising in his throat. It looked like a butcher's freezer without hooks. The walls had been squirted with reddish brown squiggles, like dripping Arabic script. Bodies were clumped like wood, three, four, maybe five of them, filling the small space. The floor was a bathtub of dark liquid. Most of the corpses wore uniforms.

"No!" said Jim, banging the wall with his fist.

"I don't suppose you're a pilot?" Matt asked, closing the door on the sight.

"No," said Jim, looking down at the body of the Asian terrorist. "But I'll bet he was."

"Yeah," Matt agreed. "I think you're right."

"Matt, thanks. I'm going back to my family," Jim said.

"Yeah, let's go back to help."

Both men turned toward the terrible noises coming from the rear and walked quickly back the way they had come. Added to the chaotic crying and groans, there were also high pitched whistling noises and more wretched smells.

Who won?

As they approached the curtain, there was another loud shot and they both jumped. Jim could hear Anna and the marshal yelling the word stop, over and over.

It wasn't over.

Matt brought the gun up again, his finger on the trigger, and went through the starboard curtain into the coach section. Jim was right behind him, his left hand on Matt's back, his right brandishing his blade. Matt was aware of piles of bright red clothing all over the floor in the open area in front of the seats, some of it piled quite high on the port side. Bodies. Some of the piles were moving, most were not. It smelled like blood and coffee and a backed-up toilet. Matt swung the pistol around to his right, as he turned the corner of the wall where the big front video screen was mounted. The yelling and crying got louder. He saw Anna and the marshal, Ed, standing near the piles, shouting at someone to the right.

"Anna!" Jim shouted.

Matt saw none of the hijackers. He started to lower the gun. One person sitting on the floor near the biggest pile was wearing a USA T-shirt but the white behind the red letters had blotted bright red. Matt recognized him as one of the young passengers. He was pointing at Matt. No, he was holding something out, blocking his face. Then, oddly, the passenger winked at Matt and kept one eye closed.

Matt was jerked backwards. As he fell, the bulkhead near his head shredded with a loud noise. The floor rushed up and slammed into his back. His head hit Jim, who had yanked his collar and pulled them both down onto the floor, painfully. Fiberglass snow was fluttering down around them and there was more yelling inside.

"He tried to shoot you!" Jim was saying. "That passenger shot at you!"

They both scrambled off the floor and crouched behind seats. Matt swung the pistol wildly to one side and then the other of the bulkhead wall, unsure where to point it. The guy had not been winking at me, Matt thought, he was sighting down the gun.

"Anna! It's us!" Jim yelled. "We got them! They're all dead! Don't shoot!"

They heard the marshal calmly commanding the young passenger to give him the gun, calling him son, saying it was all over. Anna appeared at the curtain. Jim jumped up and hugged her.

"Jim, careful," Anna said. "The knife."

Jim peered curiously at his right hand. He still grasped the savage blade in his blood-wet fist. His hand did not want to let it go. He used his other hand to pry the weapon from his grasp and place it on a seat table tray, smearing it red. His shaking palm bore a rut from clenching the object.

Ruby flew through the curtain and hugged her parents, almost knocking them off their feet. Jim winced. His leg hurt. The marshal, somewhat unsteady on his feet, was behind Anna, leaning against the wall. Ed held an automatic that was a twin of the one in Matt's hand, except the top slide was all the way back, Matt noticed. Out of bullets.

"You men okay?" Ed asked, pulling a clip off his belt and reloading the pistol.

They both said they were.

"You got them all?" Matt asked.

"Yes," said Anna, "but so many people . . ." she began to cry.

"They're all dead," Ed agreed. "Someone got their gun but went down. Then the boy recovered the gun and finished them off. That kid has guts. What about the rest?"

"He almost finished me off," said Matt.

"We got two," Jim said. "They're dead. No more up front. It's . . . over . . ."

"Good job," Ed told them, holding his other hand out for Matt's handgun.

Ed, Matt noticed, was wearing his badge, which hung from his front jacket pocket. Matt turned over the weapon. His hand felt suddenly light, naked. Ed walked back into the coach area and announced the good news. The passengers erupted into cheers and applause from those still in their seats who had witnessed the carnage in coach.

The tall boy in the blood-soaked USA shirt, who looked like a high school kid, appeared. Large, pink ears protruded from his short, black hair, which was wet, tousled. There was something on his baby face, brown and red spots. Matt realized they were freckles and blood spatters.

"I'm really sorry, man," he said to Matt. "I thought you were one of them. Sorry. I was really scared. I'm glad I missed, man.

I'm Teddy."

You didn't miss, asshole, Jim moved my head, Matt thought. But instead, he said, "That's okay, Teddy. I'm glad you missed, too."

Matt reached his hand out to shake but he wanted to punch the jerky kid. He took his hand and turned back to Jim.

"Jim, thanks for pulling me back."

"No problem. I think I twisted my leg."

"Oh, my God, Jim," Anna cried, noticing blood all over Jim's yellow life vest and his clothing. "Both of you are covered in blood."

"I'm okay. It's not my blood but I've got a cramp in my left calf," said Jim, limping a few steps to a seat and sitting on the armrest. "From when we fell. Matt's head hit me."

"I've just got Bloody Mary mix all over me," Matt said, evoking odd looks from the others, including Liz, who had joined them.

Anna had Jim take off his life vest. There was blood underneath, from a wide but shallow gash across his chest that had sliced and deflated half of the vest. His left arm hairs were dripping blood from a lesser cut there, which Jim also had not noticed.

"I think your life vest may have saved your life," Liz said. "That was a good idea."

"Maybe," said Jim, as he reached down to massage his cramping calf. His pants were wet. He looked at his red hand in puzzlement.

Ed returned, one loaded gun in his hand, the other bulging from a holster under his jacket. He crouched down next to Jim and pulled up his trouser leg.

"You caught a pellet, amigo," Ed told Jim. "You get a purple heart. Doesn't look too bad. It's probably in the muscle. Wrap it up and stay off your feet. We'll get you help when we're on the ground."

"You got these two?" Ed said, standing and pointing to the Asian guy and the Hawaiian shirt under the cart up in front of first class. "Great job," Ed said, walking forward. "I've got to get up front, to see how . . ."

"Marshal, wait," said Matt.

"What?" an impatient Ed asked, returning from down the aisle.

The loud cheering was still going on back in coach, prayers and sobs of joy mixed in. Some thanked God, some thanked each other.

"We did it!" someone shouted in triumph.

"God bless America!" someone else shouted back. And then they began to sing.

Matt and Jim looked at the brave, smiling faces around them and then at each other.

"Tell him," Jim said.

"Quick," Ed demanded. "What is it?"

# 22.

Paul and Cindy didn't have to look for street numbers as they sped toward the mosque. They could see the flashing lights of the precinct cars and a street full of emergency vehicles ahead. Two blue-and-white RMP's had blocked off Woodhaven Boulevard and two uniforms were standing on the pavement in front of the cars. One cop had a shotgun, the butt resting on his hip. Cindy rolled around the blocking cars and stopped the car in front of the mosque, just behind an A&E Bomb Squad truck. Two officers were suiting up in heavy green armor as Paul and Cindy got out. A dozen men were spread-eagled on the sidewalk in front of the blue and green dome of the mosque, a large, stone corner building with a big ball atop it. The suspects were guarded by ESU officers with machine guns. The cops were not pointing their weapons safely into the air. They were pointing them at their prone prisoners. The bearded men had different colored robes and little caps. One looked older, with a longer, white beard. Cops in uniform and in plainclothes were sprinting into the building. A huge crowd was gathering behind the perimeter barricades. People were leaning out of apartment house windows for a better view. Fire sirens were approaching.

"Whoa," said Cindy, surveying the scene.

Paul spotted a boss, an NYPD deputy inspector, and walked toward him.

"Inspector, Sergeant Ambrosino, PAPD. Deputy Commissioner Toomey sent me, sir. I called this in from JFK. What have you got?"

The DI would have loved to brush the sergeant off but Paul had invoked the name of a DC, a deputy commissioner.

"We're not secure yet. Some guy locked himself in a bathroom in the basement. I'm just about to evacuate the area until I know what I've got."

"Any weapons, explosives?" Paul asked.

"We don't know. We're doing a preliminary search of the premises while a couple of anticrime guys and an ESU team isolate the guy in the toilet."

Paul asked him if he had the names of the men on the ground and the boss looked at him like he was nuts.

"Names? Not yet, Sergeant. As soon as we have everything secure. Stand by."

The Deputy Inspector spoke into his handheld radio.

"Are you serious? Here? Now?"

A black chopper appeared overhead and descended rapidly. Civilians at the barrier shouted and some ran away. The downwash from the blades increased to hurricane level, whipping up fast food wrappers and gravel from the gutter. The unmarked helicopter stopped forty feet above the sidewalk, just above the level of the dome of the mosque. Black lines spidered out of the craft and six people in all-black riot gear and helmets slid down the lines to the ground.

As he had learned in Vietnam, Paul turned and faced away from the pelting dirt churned up by the blades and held his hat. The wind died and Paul turned around. The chopper was already climbing and banking away over buildings. Five of the Hercules Squad hit the dirt and pointed small black MP4 machine guns at the mosque. One saluted the DI and Paul and asked for a status report. He was wearing a black ski mask. The commando had grenades hanging from hooks on his chest rig but no nametag or insignia of rank. The boss repeated what he had said to Paul, word for word. He added that the bathroom was at the bottom of the stairs, on the right. Then the officer in the ski mask saluted again. He thanked them and announced they would make an entry forthwith, leaving a boss with his mouth open. It was his scene. Before the DI could protest, the man in black gave a hand signal to his men and they vanished into the building. Recovering, the NYPD boss got on his radio and announced the arrival of the Hercules Team to his troops. Not ninety seconds later, Paul heard thumping from inside the building. Shotgun. Slugs. All the cops tensed. They were blowing the hinges on a door. If anything was going to happen, it would be now, Paul thought. Another two bangs, louder. Flash-bang grenades, Paul decided. There was silence for several minutes and then uniformed cops dragged out a skinny, naked, bearded man. Paul heard doors being kicked in by combat boots inside the building, glass smashing. The Hercules Team was clearing the building. Those boys did not waste time. Paul went inside, stepping over scattered shoes and sandals just inside the door. The commandos were flinging open every closet and every drawer, like ninja burglars. They found nothing but boxes of Korans, piles of Saudi newspapers, stacks of videos, toilet paper, boxes of jasmine tea. No arsenal, no bomb factory. Paul went back outside to the men on the ground. He pulled out his list of names and read the first out loud. No response. He read them all loudly, asking each time if that man was present. No one volunteered.

"They worship here," said the older man with the longer beard. "They are good men. Why are you doing this?"

"They all go here? You recognize all of these names?"

"Yes sir, what have they done, please?"

I wish I knew, Paul thought. The guy was scared, not defiant.

"Do you remember when you saw them last?" Paul asked.

"Uh . . . please, sir, I'm not sure. Last night? No, maybe last week? I'm not sure."

"You did not see them last night?"

"Please, I'm not sure; I don't think so, sir."

The old guy thought they were going to shoot him. As they spoke, Paul noticed a group of women at the sidewalk barricade. They were dressed in black, flowing traditional Saudi dress, but without the veils over their faces. One was wearing dark horn-rimmed glasses, which, for some reason, struck Paul as funny. She was fingering a string of dark worry beads, like a fat rosary. All of the women also seemed terrified and worried. Were the men on the ground, under the gun, their husbands? Probably. They were talking and watching Paul and the other cops intently. He called to Cindy to come with him over to the barricade.

"Excuse me," Paul said to the woman in the glasses. "Are those men your husbands?"

First they froze. Then they shot each other glances and then vigorously shook their heads.

"Please don't be scared. Do you speak English?"

They all shook their heads no but Paul didn't buy it. One of the women was talking in a foreign language quickly and insistently. Paul didn't need to speak Arabic to understand the tone. Every cop understood that language. They heard it every day. It was the don't-talk-to-the-cop tone of voice. Paul consulted his list and read the first name out loud to them. One of the women gasped.

Bull's-eye.

Then he read another name. Another woman clapped her hand over her mouth. Paul looked at Cindy and nodded his head back toward the troops. Cindy casually walked away.

"When did you last see your husbands?" Paul asked them.

No answer.

"I know you speak English. I have news about your husbands. They are fine. I just need your cooperation for a few minutes so we can clear up all this confusion, okay?"

He read the fourth name, Ali Akbar Whalid, and said Whalid's wife was already over at the precinct, already helping out. The other women looked at the woman in glasses. Paul smiled but they just stared at him. He noticed that Cindy and a dozen other cops were quietly, slowly surrounding the women behind their backs.

"Look, we need your help, please, so we can reunite you with your husbands over at the precinct, as soon as we can clear up this mistake. We appreciate you help."

"Is my husband okay?" asked the young woman in glasses, breaking the silence.

"Here, ladies, let me move this saw horse for you," Paul said, opening the barricade. "When did you last see him, Ma'am? You are Mrs. Whalid?"

The woman in glasses was stunned he knew her name. The wives now thought Paul was all-knowing and began to talk. But the wives knew less than Paul, which they made clear in British-accented English he thought was better than his. All of their husbands were last seen leaving for the mosque on Friday night. Four of them drove there. They all denied their men were radicals or terrorists and declared that they were hardworking family men. Cindy interrupted to whisper to Paul that NYPD had located cars belonging to some of the husbands parked on the surrounding streets and was taping off a crime scene for each one. Paul excused himself from the wives and called Kevin to update him.

"Kevin, they all went to the same mosque and were last seen last night before or after Friday prayers. They're all Moslems from the same mosque here. I found the wives, they're clueless. They say their husbands would never do anything wrong but it's not a coincidence. They must be on those planes. Are they on the ground yet?"

"Uh . . . two are but no, the feds are not moving on that yet. I rang the bell but they did nothing. The third flight is still in the air. This should do it."

"What the fuck are they waiting for? Ground everything, take the system down."

"I told them that, Paul. It hasn't happened yet but I'm going to make it happen, one way or another. Soon."

"Your people have found four of their cars nearby. The bomb squad is checking them out now. Your Rambos found a guy shitting his pants in the bathroom of the mosque. Looks like he thought your army was Immigration, come just for him. If he's a terrorist, we're safe. What are the feds freaking out about?"

"I can't tell you over this line, Paul."

"That doesn't sound good."

"They're looking for people and they're looking for something but they don't want to tell us what that something is. It's as bad as it gets, I think. That's the only thing that would explain what's going on. They're keeping it a secret, Paul."

"Even from you?"

"Yes."

"Jesus. Kevin, are we talking about something very bright and very, very loud?"

"That's what I'm afraid of, Paul. I gotta go."

"Fuck," said Paul.

"Yeah," said Kevin. "Fuck."

"Where? When?"

"We don't know. Work your case, Paul. Pull out all the stops, buddy. This is the case. This is the one. Be safe."

Kevin hung up, leaving Paul alone in the middle of Woodhaven Boulevard.

Paul realized he had no more leads, no where else to go to.

He had to do something, but what? He looked around at his brother and sister officers doing the job and at the thousands of fat, dumb and happy civilians on the street and in the windows. A short Puerto Rican man with a big silver ice box attached to his three-wheeled bicycle was already working the hot crowd of gawkers, selling little paper cups filled with shaved ice and topped with their choice of brightly colored bottled syrups. One brown-eyed kid in a red shirt was licking his ice and peering over the blue wooden barricade. The boy smiled at Paul. His teeth were blue.

# 23.

Matt took a deep breath and gave Ed the terrible news, as Jim, Anna, Ruby, Liz and Teddy in his bloody T-shirt, listened in the aisle.

"They're all dead up there," Matt said. "We got two bad guys but not before they killed the crew. We won, but it's over . . . unless you can land this plane, Officer? It's on autopilot, apparently, but . . ."

"Motherfucker!" Ed spat, punching seat backs with a fist. "Motherfucker!"

Matt took that as a no. Ed was not a pilot. Liz, the only one who knew the murdered crew, began crying. Anna was silent, hugging Ruby and stroking her hair. She was staring out a window. Jim reached out to Anna and held her hand. Teddy was also silent. Ed bolted up front to see for himself, his pistol ready. Matt and Liz and Teddy followed. Liz screamed when she saw Nancy's body. Matt took the curtain that had been over the cockpit door and placed it over the woman's body. Ed went into the cockpit and started pushing buttons, trying to work the radios. He began cursing again.

"We are still on the same course. I think the radios are working but nothing is going through," Ed explained, shaking his head, confused.

He said his PDA also didn't work. Everything seemed to be sabotaged or jammed and there were no cell phones.

"We're totally fucked," Ed concluded. "Totally fucked."

"Oh man," Teddy said. "So we did all that for nothing?"

"You got it, kid," Ed replied.

"So the plane will keep flying?" Teddy asked.

Ed told Teddy he was right.

Matt had been hoping that, somehow, Ed, the authority figure, would figure it out. Apparently not. It was a problem without a solution. The Kobayshi Maru Scenario episode on *Star Trek,* the always-fatal exercise. And no Captain Kirk in sight to save the ship.

"Maybe there's a passenger who's a pilot?" Jim suggested, approaching with a limp, aided by Emily's cane, which was dented and slightly bent from use as a club.

Ed made a face, as if he should have thought of that or already had. Anna joined them, Ruby peeking around her.

"Maybe, but this is a 767, not a fucking Cessna," Ed said. "Besides, that would mean telling the passengers."

The passengers looked at each other. Matt wondered if Ed's head injury was worse than it seemed. He must have a concussion. And he had both guns.

"Uh, Marshal, we're passengers. Are you seriously suggesting you intend to hide this from everyone else?" Matt asked.

Ed said he didn't want a panic on his hands, especially if there was nothing to be gained. Anna spoke up and pointed out that, if there was nothing to be done, everyone, especially those whose loved ones died, had the right to know the truth. They had earned it and they had the right to prepare themselves, to say goodbye to their families.

"Marshal, you won't know if there is a pilot onboard who can land this plane, unless you ask them," Jim pointed out.

Ed reiterated that he did not want to reveal the fact that no one was flying the plane, that it would cause panic. As he spoke, he still held the gun. Jim suggested that Ed simply not reveal all of the bad news.

"What if you said that the copilot was killed or wounded, and was there anyone with flying experience who could help up front, no big deal?"

Ed liked that idea but nobody else did. Ed rehearsed his speech and then insisted on collecting all the hijacker knives first. He had Teddy collect them and report back. Ed had Teddy chuck all six bloody blades down the toilet that contained the cell phones, so no one could use them. Then he ejected the clip from the pistol in his hand and threw the second gun down into the blue cesspool. Now there was only one weapon on board.

While Ed was busy, Matt wondered why he was bothering. The hijackers were all dead. It didn't matter. Why was he afraid of us? Matt noticed a closed laptop on the seat where the Asian hijacker had been sitting, peeking out from under a glossy *Anytime, Anywhere* magazine. Matt picked it up, sat down and opened the computer on his lap. The screen was gray, in sleep mode. He hit the mouse pad and the screen flashed back on. It was a brand new Toshiba but Matt did not recognize the software banner at the top. "breadcrumbs Ver. 7.77." Fields of colored bar graphs appeared. Most of the charts were unmoving but three were animated, bobbing slightly up and down. Each column was divided vertically, the left on each was labeled REC and the right was labeled TRANS. At the bottom of the columns were numbers and letters like 221.00 MGHZ, 447.05 MGHZ, 57.870 GGHZ and a toggle on/off box. The columns that were moving had been toggled ON. When he hit the Page Down key, more bars appeared, more frequencies. There were screens and screens of them. On the right was a menu of options like. STAT, DISTOR, ECHO, HI, LO, FEED, XGAIN, BLAST, ALL.

"Marshal," Matt asked Ed when he emerged from the lavatory. "Do you know what frequency your personal digital assistant transmits and receives on?"

"What? My PDA? I have no fucking idea. I just know it

doesn't work."

Matt then asked about the frequencies of the radios in the cockpit. Ed did not know that, either. He explained that he had found what he thought was a hijacker computer that was jamming the radios and he was going to shut it down. Ed looked over Matt's shoulder. Matt pulled down a file task bar and clicked on EXIT.

"Hey, Marshal, if he's right, that's cool but what if he's wrong? What if this thing is, like, what's keeping us flying?" Teddy asked.

"You mean it might shut off the autopilot?" Jim asked.

"Hold it," Ed said. "He might be right."

A status box with three options popped up: "Are you sure you want to exit breadcrumbs? Yes. No. Cancel."

Matt did not agree. It made no sense. But then, again, he knew nothing about airplanes, except for a Tiger Squadron computer action game he used to play. Matt tuned out the argument between the others and focused on the problem in front of him. If he listened to the marshal, they might do nothing at all. Like he did with all major decisions in his life, Matt consciously pretended that he was a character in a role-playing video game, something he did extremely well. He imagined he was playing software that placed him on a plane with hijackers and now he had reached a decision tree about the hijackers' jamming computer. Did the jamming come from the laptop itself? Possible but doubtful. May not matter. Would shutting off the jamming crash the plane or free it from the hijackers' control? His gut told him yes, so he clicked the yes box. The program vanished and a desktop appeared. There were several breadcrumbs program logos, with a tiny cartoon of a smiling blond boy and girl on the laptop desktop screen, along with other program logos.

"Shit. Did you hear what I said?" Ed was shaking his

shoulder, the gun in his other large hand. "I told you not to turn it off until I can . . ."

Matt and everyone else literally jumped when all the video screens, big and small, and speakers, suddenly blasted from white, hissing static into living color and sound.

". . . declined to comment on the report in *Tinsel* magazine that she was pregnant with her married co-star's child. His publicist denied the report."

On the large screen, a redheaded TV commentator was beaming into the camera. Red CNN letters floated over her considerable cleavage.

"Goddamnit, I told you not to do that," Ed said, looking around, like he expected the plane to spiral out of control. It didn't. He put his hands over his ears, the gun pointing up, and ordered Liz to shut the noise off. Liz turned away.

"I have a newsbreak," the beautiful woman on the screen said. The word NEWSBREAK appeared across her breasts. "Police in New York have surrounded a mosque in Queens and are searching the building. Shots have been heard and we have a crew on the way to that scene. A law enforcement source has told CNN that authorities are investigating the possibility that several people who attend that mosque were aboard a passenger jet that took off from New York this morning. Officials have lost contact with that aircraft, however no hijacking has been reported yet. We will have more information on this breaking story in a few minutes. Now this."

She was replaced by a commercial about a female cop who had to urinate all the time. Ed told Liz not to turn off the TV news, after all, just turn down the volume. A surprised Ed grabbed his waist, reached inside his jacket and pulled out his PDA, which was beeping. He put his gun back in its hidden holster and held the PDA with both hands, peering at the screen.

"Eighteen urgent messages. Yes! It's working."

He began pushing buttons on the device, mouthing the words as he typed with his stubby fingers.

"Plane taken over by six hijackers, partner KIA, plane retaken by myself and passengers. Crew is dead."

"Wait," said Matt. "I don't know if you should send that message."

Ed ignored Matt.

"Marshal, don't tell them there was a hijacking yet."

"You don't want me to lie to the geese but you want me to lie to my superiors?" Ed asked sarcastically, still typing on the tiny keys.

"The geese?" Matt asked, again wondering about Ed's mental status.

"The passengers."

"Oh. Yes, that's exactly right. Don't tell your office. Just wait a minute. You may think it's the right thing to do, Marshal, but it is definitely the wrong game move."

Ed pressed a button that caused a tinkling, ascending song. Matt knew that sound. He had sent the message.

"Wrong game move? What the hell are you talking about?" Ed demanded.

"You sent it?"

"You bet your ass I did," Ed said. "I'm in charge here, pal. Not you. In an emergency, I have to . . ."

"Oh, my God," said Jim, getting it.

"Yeah," said Matt. "If they hear we've been hijacked . . ."

"They'll shoot us down," Jim completed his sentence.

"Right," Matt agreed. "Any message is better than that one. Can you UNSEND on that PDA?"

"I told them we had taken the plane back," Ed protested. "It's clear we now have control."

"But we don't have control," Anna interjected. "A machine is flying the plane."

"If I didn't send that message, they might shoot us down. Now they won't," Ed declared, touching his clotted head wound.

"I guess we're going to find out," Matt said.

"Maybe now would be a good time to see if there's another pilot onboard?" Jim suggested, after an uncomfortable silence, except for the TV sound, which Liz had lowered.

Ed agreed and strode a bit unsteadily toward the coach section. Matt whispered to Jim as he passed, quoting an old Who song:

"Meet the new boss. Same as the old boss."

"That's not true," Jim replied.

"Maybe not, but I don't like bosses," said Matt. "A boss who makes bad decisions is almost as bad as the bad guys. Either way, we end up dead."

"Nothing has changed. We're still dead," Anna corrected him, with a sigh. "It's up to us to find our own path back to the land of the living."

Matt looked at Anna and wondered if she always talked like that.

"Are we dead, Momma?" Ruby asked.

"No, sweetheart, that's just a way of speaking. But our adventure is not over. We have some more big problems to solve before we can go home. Maybe you can help us?"

The group moved back into coach, back into the fetid stench of battle and death. Matt looked down at the two boys and two men who had been behind him and Jim, the rest of their attack group. The two older men were on their right sides, with their legs folded under them, dead, blood staining their left sides. One of the teenagers was face-down, dead, but Matt could not see a wound or blood. The other teen was on his back, pale-faced, holding his bleeding elbow, which was shattered. A woman was wrapping a tan shirt around the wound.

"The guys behind us were shot," Jim, with tears in his eyes, said to Matt.

Jim was crying because he was happy Ruby and Anna were alive. "That's what that buzzing and snapping was."

Matt didn't remember any buzzing or snapping. Liz had produced several first-aid kits and people were bandaging bleeding passengers. Others were dragging dead, soaked bodies around under Emily's direction.

"No, he's one of them," Emily said to two teenagers who were lifting Joey's body. "Don't put that evil man next to our heroes. Put him over there with the rest of them."

Emily had the remains of the hijackers dragged over to the port side door and dumped into a tangle, where their stained bodies lay entwined in orgiastic slumber. Matt saw Maria's long hair over her pretty face.

"Wait," said Emily limping over to Maria's body.

Emily reached down and roughly pulled up Maria's blood-soaked blouse. The skin on her abdomen was wrinkled and loose but not swollen, as it had been when she came aboard.

"What the hell?" Danielle said. "Where's the baby?"

"What baby?" asked another woman.

"This one was pregnant when she got on," Emily explained.

Emily unzipped Maria's black pants and tugged them open to her crotch.

"Look at that," said Emily. "What is that?"

She exposed a small blue plastic plug protruding from the pale skin just above a shaved crotch. The small tube was in the middle of a horizontal red line, an incision that had been surgically stitched.

"It looks like a hospital thing, you know, like an IV plug . . ." said Danielle. "There was no baby. She's not pregnant."

"So what was in her belly?" Emily asked.

"The explosive, probably," Jim suggested, peering over the shoulders of the women. "The stuff they used to melt the door."

"You mean she smuggled it inside her . . . her . . . womb?" asked Gordon. "Incredible."

"I don't know," said Liz. "The stuff in the bottles they used was mushy, almost liquid. But she and the men in First all used the same bathroom just before it started."

Bob kneeled and touched Maria's cold belly with his right hand.

"I can feel something," Bob Ipswitch, the engineer, said. "You're right, Jim. I think she had the stuff concealed inside some kind of bladder under the skin," said Bob. "That's why her skin is all wrinkled—because it was stretched and became loose after the liquid was drained. This is brilliant. They must have done this a few days ago to get around the explosives detector at the gate. Maybe the explosive was a binary, the kind where there are two stable elements that become explosive when combined."

"Brilliant?" Emily asked. "It's sick. Cover her up."

The passengers who had died in the assault were lined up in a place of honor against the wall beneath the video screen in the open area. Their bodies and faces had been respectfully covered with blue curtains and jackets. The mound of heroes was twice the size of the group of hijackers, and growing. Someone had placed a single white rose on the bier. Emmett had created a large cross atop the dead, using rolled-up lap blankets. He was leading a few folks in prayer, while glaring at Lester, the large black guy, who was hugging his friend Bob. Both men had been slashed on their arms and legs and their clothes were stained with their own blood. Bob's left hand was bandaged. They kissed on the lips several times, causing Emmett to stare at them each time, his expression turning most unprayerful when he did. Obviously the men were a gay couple. Matt noticed that even Emmett had been cut in the battle, on his arm and shoulder.

"Dear Lord, we thank you for delivering us from our enemies

in the Valley of the Shadow of Death," Emmett intoned.

Most people stopped and bowed their heads, including Jim and Anna and Tim and Ed. Matt did the same, out of respect. "Please welcome these brave souls into your everlasting heavenly peace, that they may sit by your side forever and ever in Glory, Amen."

Gordon came over to shake everyone's hand. He welcomed the marshal and praised Anna for her successful battle plan and Jim for his jury-rigged ideas. He actually called for a cheer and people cheered Anna. The marshal did not seem pleased at being left out.

"Where were you an officer, Anna?" Gordon asked. "Marines? West Point?"

"Oh, I was never in the service," Anna told him, with a smile.

She explained that she was a full, tenured professor of ancient history at Hunter College in Manhattan. Her specialty was paleomachism, the study of ancient wars.

Gordon reacted like he had been slapped.

"But your husband said you lectured at the Pentagon and the CIA."

"True. I was just down at the Pentagon last month, speaking to some officers about the Battle of Leuctra in 371 B.C."

Stunned, Gordon turned to Jim, asking about his work, hoping for someone who outranked him.

"Actually, I was a conscientious objector during the Vietnam War, until I won the draft lottery with a really high number. It's the only lotto I ever won," Jim smiled.

He explained he was the author of a somewhat popular children's problem-solving book series. Gordon's pain was palpable. He, a former artillery captain in the reserves, had followed the orders of a woman college professor and an author of kiddie books.

"Maybe you've heard of my books?" Jim asked. "I write the

'What If . . .' series. My best seller was *What If . . . There Was a Hippo in the House?*"

Gordon said no, he did not know the books.

"My dad's only slightly famous," Ruby explained to Gordon.

"I'm glad we didn't know that before," said Gordon, laughing, and shaking Jim and Anna's hands again.

"Gordon, ideas do not have genitals, they only have merit or they do not," Anna said, as if to a slow student.

They all laughed until Ed asked for everyone's attention. Liz was standing at his side. Ed announced all the hijackers were dead, something that everyone already knew. He told everyone who he was, which they also knew, although most did not know his name until he said it. He said he was in contact with the U.S. Federal Air Marshal Service on the ground and they were just fine now. He said that the copilot had been wounded and anyone with flying experience, especially any pilots, would be of service to the crew. No one came forward. Ed scanned the cabin.

"My husband is a pilot," said a red-eyed woman in her forties sitting in the front row of seats, one away from the window on the left side.

Ed walked over to her. She had bloodstains on her dress and was holding the hand of a chubby bald man sitting in the window seat next to her. His seatbelt was fastened. His eyes were open and he was looking toward the video screen in the seat back in front of him but he wasn't watching it. He was dead.

"Just leave her," Emily said quietly. "Monica wants to be with her husband."

"Is there anyone else?" Ed asked, looking around again.

There wasn't.

Ed turned and walked stiffly toward the front, holding his head again. He swayed, steadied himself on Teddy, and kept walking, as people began asking him questions.

"The pilot's okay, isn't he?"

"What's going on?"

"When are we going to land?"

No one was answering the questions. Ed stumbled and fell, falling to his knees. Teddy helped him sit up, his back against the bulkhead. He said he was okay, just dizzy. There were tears in his eyes.

"Oh, my God," Danielle wailed. "Who's driving the plane?"

She was standing in the aisle leaning forward and she could see all the way up front. "Why don't I see anyone up there?"

"What the hell's going on?" Gordon demanded.

Lester and Bob and Emmett and Toni and others crowded around, demanding to know. Ed said nothing but he pulled his pistol out.

"Nobody goes up front," he ordered.

"They killed the crew," Matt said. "The plane is on autopilot. We're the *Flying Dutchman.* We can't land."

Danielle screamed very loudly. Her husband Gordon stood over Ed, peppering him with questions. He wanted answers. Slowly, casually, Ed pivoted his pistol until it was pointing at the large man above him.

"Don't you train for this kind of thing?" Gordon demanded.

"Keep your voice down," Ed said, finally. "Yes we do and we are exploring our options now. We'll get back to you shortly. Please stay calm."

Gordon looked to the others. Matt was shaking his head. Jim shrugged.

"Well, Marshal, what do you do when this happens? What do we do?"

Ed said nothing.

"I don't think he knows," Matt said. "Also, he obviously has a concussion. I don't suppose there's a doctor on board, either?"

No one was a doctor.

Ed was saying something and shaking his head. He laughed bitterly and then spat out some red saliva.

"What did you say, Marshal?" Gordon asked. "Care to share the joke?"

"You want honesty? You got it. I said, in all of our drills, the cockpit crew and the pilots were still alive. None of the training scenarios envisioned the possibility of them getting through the cockpit door. That's what's so funny. We're off the playbook, here, sports fans."

No one laughed. Emmett began praying out loud again, something about divine punishment for wickedness and perversion. Ed swiveled the gun in his direction.

"Praying might actually be a good idea," Ed said, closing his eyes.

"I'd rather think," Matt said. "I'll pray after I'm dead."

"The fighting is over," Anna said in a calm tone. "We need to think and to communicate. Especially with someone who has answers, if there are any. We have to work together. Together, we can do the impossible, as we just did. That's the only way we're ever going to come back from the dead."

Everyone nodded their heads but no one could think of anything to say yet. Emmett continued to pray, joined by others. Matt looked at the poor woman holding her dead husband's hand and talking to him tenderly. In front of her, a man was staring blankly at the little TV in front of him. He had his headphones on and was ignoring everything going on around him, preferring the reality of the tube. In the back, the honeymoon couple stepped into a bathroom together. The pretty blonde bride had already removed her blouse and bra, which she held in one hand. They closed the door. Matt saw an older couple seated together, slugging back tiny bottles of booze and tossing the empties. They were babbling in slurred English to each other, arguing and giggling, drunk as skunks.

Maybe Ed was right about the panic thing. But Anna was definitely right, Matt decided. People were opting out to their personal oblivions. They were all dead. And it seemed to be contagious.

# 24.

George Franklin Yarwood listened to newly arrived Secretary of Defense Gerhardt Veissbrott brief the president and the rest of the NSC teleconference on the latest news from Georgia. Two little girls heard a cell phone ringing in a culvert under a roadway. They saw a foot protruding from the gulley and told a passing local cop. Two bodies in "chocolate chip" fatigues were found in the culvert, apparently the two missing Moslem soldiers. The FBI and base MPs were there. The vice president marveled at Veissbrott's luck. He had avoided delivering the initial horrible news to the boss and here he was now, by a stroke of good fortune, pulling his fat from the fire.

"So, Pappy, what you're saying is that the two missing soldiers were also killed by somebody else?" the president asked Veissbrott. "They didn't steal the bombs? It was terrorists?"

"Well, Mr. President, we don't yet know for sure but it certainly looks that way right at this moment in time," Veissbrott responded, addressing the bunker screen image of the boss. "The likelihood that it was terrorists is much stronger, rather than our troops gone bad, that is."

"Maybe someone wanted it to look like it was our troops, Mr. President," the vice president volunteered. "Or maybe they were recruited by Al Qaeda and then eliminated once they handed over the weapons. Apparently someone calling repeatedly on a cell phone on one of the bodies led to the corpses being discovered sooner, rather than later. This is a break, sir."

"Where the weapons are is more important at this moment in time than who is to blame," National Security Advisor Preston said.

"Yes," Veissbrott agreed. "But, Sheila, the 'who' will lead us to the 'where,' or rather, it should lead the FBI to where. Hopefully, soon."

The vice president smirked. Veissbrott had passed his hot potato to the FBI.

"Yes, Mr. Director." The president asked the FBI chief, "Where are you with this? Where are the weapons?"

The director took a deep breath. Maybe rushing his local agents there hadn't been such a good idea after all. He was being asked what he had done with Veissbrott's nukes.

"I don't know where they are yet, sir. The Naval Investigative Service has told my agents that the two dead Marines found on the base had some problems. One has a very bad gambling problem, the other has used heroin before, although we don't know if either problem has anything to do with what happened. Unfortunately, my agents do not have radiation detectors at the local level, as you know. We have to wait for the Department of Defense to get their Nuclear Emergency Search Team up and running there."

Veissbrott launched into another defensive volley but he was interrupted by Preston.

"Excuse me, Mr. President," Preston interjected. "Immigration and Customs Enforcement has just sent a priority teletype message. It's on your screen. One of the marshals onboard, uh . . . Flight 1787 from JFK in New York has just reported that there was, in fact, a hijacking."

"So we do have a hijacking, also?" the president asked. "Oh, boy."

"Yes sir," the vice president responded. "I suggested earlier we alert all our air wings. I recommend we now intercept this flight as soon as possible and do whatever we have to do."

Veissbrott fumed at the vice president but recovered quickly.

"I'm doing that right now, Mr. President," Veissbrott said. "I'll have a report for you soon."

"Since the media has already gotten wind of this, I also suggest we ground all flights around the country as a precaution," the vice president added, further angering Veissbrott, who was on the phone. "I understand New York City is closing down all bridges and tunnels and the subway system, even though we have not recommended they do so. Turner tells me the cyber attacks on government computers have tripled in the last hour or so and they are serious. I have a note here . . . air bases, Pentagon computers, uh, Secret Service, FBI, a lot more. Mr. President, until we get information otherwise, I think we have to consider all of this, the stolen weapons, the hijacking, the computer assaults, as all part of a coordinated attack on this country. I think we are at war."

"Shit," said the president. "I thought we already were at war? Okay, unless anyone disagrees, I guess that's probably true. We have to assume that, right?"

No one disagreed.

"Okay," the president said. "I have to give the order to shoot down the jet, right?"

"That is correct, Mr. President," the vice president told him.

"Excuse me, Mr. President," Preston interrupted. "My understanding, according to my screen, is that the Air Force's 102nd Fighter Wing at Otis Air Force Base in Massachusetts is already in the air and is being ordered to perform an escort only. If you look at the message from the marshals, sir, you'll note that the marshal aboard the hijacked airliner has also communicated that he and the passengers have already taken back the aircraft. His name is Edward Boetsch and he reports that all of the hijackers are now dead."

"Really?" the president asked. "That's great!"

"Bullshit," the vice president snapped. "Don't believe it, Mr. President. How do we know it's true? How do we know that marshal is even still alive?"

"I thought he was talking to us on the radio?" the president asked.

"Actually, he used his personal digital assistant, as he is supposed to," Preston said. "I believe they are directing him to the cockpit radio for further proofs. He said that multiple shots were fired during the takeover and the fight to regain control. Quite a few people are dead. Interestingly, he said the hijackers jammed all communications. But now it may have stopped. We need to confirm this, of course. The fighters can take a look and . . ."

"Bullshit," the vice president repeated. "The fighters can't board that aircraft. We can't take anything from this point on at face value. Nothing, sir. Sheila, tell ICE to message their marshal and order him to tell the crew to land that plane at the nearest airport. Any action short of that is just talk, sir."

"I agree, Mr. President," Veissbrott said.

"Makes sense to me," the president said.

"Mr. President," Preston countered, "the message from the marshal also claims that the crew, unfortunately, was killed, as it says on your screens. If hijackers are still in control of that aircraft, why would they tell us that? Wouldn't that be an invitation to treat them as a danger and shoot them down? Why would they say the crew was dead and they could not land? Wouldn't they tell us, instead, that there was no hijacking at all? Or that the crew was fine? Doesn't that make more sense, sir?"

Preston spoke to her assistant, who dialed a phone. The vice president gave her a cool look but said nothing.

"I don't know, Sheila. Maybe they are lying," the president said. "How can they go shooting guns off inside a jet, without blowing a hole in the fuselage?"

"I'll get you an answer on that, Mr. President," Preston said, nodding to her assistant.

"Wait," the president said, "if the crew was killed by the terrorists, how can they land the plane?"

"That will be a problem," Veissbrott said. "As tragic as it is, Mr. President, we may have to take it down, if the aircraft becomes a danger to any populated area."

"Yeah, sure, we would have to do that, if we have to, sure."

Veissbrott informed the president that he had a Special Forces officer by the name of Lieutenant Colonel Gunning Bedford, Jr. on the speaker phone from the Pentagon, to answer his question about firing guns on a pressurized aircraft. He informed Bedford that he was talking to the president and the NSC.

"Mr. President, the FAMs, the marshals on those planes, use special ammunition in their pistols, like little shotgun shells with buckshot inside," said Bedford. "The slugs would free the grape shot when they hit any hard surface or the human body—to scatter and make much smaller holes—to guard against a serious fuselage breech. That way, there is less chance of ripping the skin of the airplane or severing nonredundant hydraulic fluid lines or electrical relays. If you travel in a balloon, Mr. President, it's always a bad idea to play with pins, sir," said Bedford.

"Yes it is, Colonel, thank you," the president chuckled. "Have you been briefed on what this marshal claims has happened, the hijacking and this claim of taking it back?"

"Yes, Mr. President, I have."

When he said nothing else, the president asked Bedford for his assessment.

"Well, Mr. President, if it is true that they retook the aircraft, and there were casualties, then American heroes have been made today, sir. I salute them. But if the crew is dead, then so is everyone else aboard. We have the unpleasant duty of deciding where and when, sir. Unfortunately, they are now a bomb looking for a target. But now, instead of the target being chosen by the hijackers, it will be chosen by the guy who decided how much jet fuel to put in the tanks. Also, sir, how do we know this is not a cover plan, disinformation designed to get us to hesitate, to stop you, Mr. President, from doing exactly what you need to do—take it down? I don't think we know who we're talking to. We don't know who is or was a terrorist or what they really intend to do. One turd in the punchbowl is enough for me, sir. Also, Mr. President, if I had planned this mission, and by that I mean the hijacking, I would plant a sleeper agent among the passengers to guard against just such a possibility of successful counterattack. If the passengers overwhelmed the terrorists and they thought they were secure, a sleeper could emerge at the right time and complete their mission, whatever it might be. Ideally, the identity of the sleeper or sleepers would not be known to the first wave of overt hijackers—just as the drivers of the primary and secondary bomb vehicles in some terrorist land attacks do not know each other. In other words, even if these poor people truly believe they have taken out the terrorists, they may still be under hostile control. I feel honor-bound to note for the record that what they did was a very courageous act. But, all things being equal, sir, I think we have an unpleasant task to perform very soon, which may prevent a much more unpleasant event, Mr. President."

"Damn," the president replied.

"Yes sir," Bedford agreed.

An admiral hissed into Veissbrott's ear and pointed at the huge plasma situation screen of the United States. There was a tiny red plane over Tennessee, with a black line leading back to JFK on Long Island.

"Excuse me, Mr. President," said Veissbrott. "I'm looking at the big board, here. Has anyone other than myself noticed that the hijacked aircraft is on a direct path, heading, as far as I can tell, directly at you, sir?"

The president's head swiveled to and from the screen in his remote situation room in the Summer White House.

"Are you talking to me, Pappy?"

"Yes, Mr. President," Veissbrott continued, "the damn thing is heading right toward you!"

The president stood up, and looked around the room.

"The plane? It's heading here? Shit!"

"Good heavens," said Preston, looking at the red jet pointed toward the little presidential seal in the middle of Texas. "It does seem to be headed in that direction."

"Mr. President, get the hell out of there," said the vice president loudly. "Don't wait for the jets to shoot it down. John Langdon, are you there?"

"Yes, I am, sir," said Langdon, head of the White House Secret Service detail, stepping into the picture.

Langdon yanked the president's elbow. Another agent grabbed the other arm and they turkey-trotted the president away, vanishing from the big video screen, although Langdon could still be heard yelling into his radio, as they ran:

"SKYDIVE! Repeat, all units, SKYDIVE! SKYDIVE! This is not a drill! Longhorn to the ranch LZ now. Longhorn to the ranch LZ now! SKYDIVE!"

# 25.

Ruby was grossed out by all the blood and she was scared. It wasn't like in movies or cartoons. She never threw up from a movie. It was worse than her nightmares because she was already awake. She felt cold and shivery. While her mom and dad were arguing with the other people, Ruby ran back to her old seat in first class and sat looking out the window, hugging herself. Her mom had told her there were no cloudy days up here, because they were above the clouds. Down below, the cloud floor looked close, like she could jump out the window and float down to it, roll around. Would it feel like Marshmallow Fluff? Her dad told her it was way below zero, like the North Pole out there, even though it was so sunny. She found a square of raspberry Dubble Bubble gum in her pocketbook, opened it and popped it into her mouth. As she chewed, she calmed down and imagined living in a space station with other kids. Her eyelids were heavy. Lights flashed on the Fluff, two of them. Flying fish? Two shiny, sleepy silver sharks jumped out of the foamy cloud sea but didn't fall back into the white waves. The sparkle sharks rose steadily up toward Ruby, one right behind the tip of the plane's wing and another one further out. They were smaller airplanes with pointy noses and big bubbles on top. A spaceman was inside the bubble, looking at Ruby. He waved a gloved hand at her. She waved back and smiled.

In the open area in front of the coach section, the adults were still arguing and talking. Lester and his friend Bob said they saw a movie where the government had a secret stealth plane that they used to sneak onto a plane in flight to surprise hijackers. Jim said it did not exist but he wished it did.

"But, wait, I read something awhile ago that these big jets all fly by wire, that they are all programmed with automatic pilots," Jim said. "I think the article said that the computers could take off and fly and land, everything. We need to talk to somebody who knows."

Gordon said that if it was a computerized system, then somebody had to program it, plug in coordinates, things like that—who would do that?

"I have no idea," Jim said. "If *Popular Science* mentioned that, I forgot it."

"The space shuttle works like that," Matt said. "Something like that. They could even upload data back and forth, so no one had to let their fingers do the walking. But I don't think planes like this work like that."

"We need to find out right away," Jim said.

"Momma, come look—baby planes! They look like sharks," Ruby told Anna.

"What?" Anna asked. "Where?"

"Fighters!" Teddy yelled from the starboard side, where he was looking out a window. "Two of them!"

People began to cheer and applaud, as they rushed to the right side of the aircraft and peered out the windows. The cavalry had arrived.

"Thank God!" one elderly woman said, obviously under the impression it was a rescue mission. "What are those spiky things under the wings?"

*"Oy veys meir!"* her husband said. "They're missiles."

Ed did not get up. He was pecking into his PDA with one finger, the gun resting in his lap.

Jim, Anna, Matt, and the others stood looking at each other.

"Marshal, what is going on?" Gordon asked. "What is happening?" he asked again, when Ed did not look up from his machine.

"I think they're here to shoot us down," Matt announced. "We have to do something now or we are all dead."

"Why would they do that?" someone shouted. "The hijackers are dead."

"I told them that," Ed protested, waving his PDA. "I said I was going to try the radio again but they said no. Now, they're not answering me. Wait . . . here . . . my desk is . . . asking for my mother's maiden name? What the hell?"

"They don't believe you're you," Matt told Ed. "I warned you."

Matt ran back to the rear of the plane and found his laptop where he had left it. He sat in a vacant seat and logged on. His machine had a cellular phone with a speakerphone module and a separate webcam built in, among other things. He banged out a short e-mail and didn't bother to correct the mistakes:

> Call news media and fedral government, air force, immedtely. This is not a joke. I am on an 830 anytime flight from jfk to cabo. hijakers took the plane over, we foght back, all of us, we killed them, its all over. Bastards killed the crew, Fighters are here now I think they are here to shoot us down bcause they think its not over. Call everybody or you may never see me again. Cell phone gone we'll run an IM chat on laptop, HURRY
>
> matt

Matt sent it to every employee, customer, supplier and personal friend he had, everyone in all of his computer phone books, which meant that his plumber, his old girlfriends and his parents in San Diego would also get it. They'd freak. He began typing a second e-mail to his staff only.

Everyone drop everything. Get on this, I need everything on this plane it's a

Matt looked around. He rummaged through a seat pocket in front of him and found someone's boarding pass and a large, colored card with cartoons of the airplane, a 767-400. He went back to his typing.

It's a 767-400 find out if the autopilot can land the plane by itself. if so upload all files, Fiona, find me a pilot who knows how to fly it, anything, there's got to be a flight simulator game for this plane. Buy it online now, download and then load in to the site, so I can upload . . . Get jerry to dive into that now, he should cram changing course and landing. If no pilot jerry can walk me through it. its Flight 1787 don't forget media calls, A-S-A-P, also set up virgin website for this and send me a link to e-mail from the site, matt1787.com, something like that so I can download pix, webcam, audio for media. Also, Tyrell you set up a public website, like saveflight1787.com and link it to news organizations, link to search engines, Melanie you weed through that and put anything major on my site. thanx GO!

Matt

Matt broadcast the e-mail and looked up when he heard Teddy shouting. He was calling for paper and pens, markers, lipsticks, anything that would write. Teddy said if we can't talk to the fighter jets we could make signs. Good idea. Maybe the kid wasn't so dumb after all, Matt thought. Adults and kids began making signs on white paper placemats that Teddy found on a cart.

"No, much bigger!" Teddy directed. "They'll never read that. Like this."

Teddy used one of Danielle's dark red lipsticks to block out one word on each placemat and had kids hold one in each window on the side with the warplanes. That's smart, Matt thought, using kids. Teddy ran down the line making sure they formed a single message if the windows were read from back to front, left to right for the pilot just off the starboard wing.

HIJACKERS DEAD MANY WOUNDED HELP US

Teddy was listening to me, thought Matt. He didn't mention the dead crew. Good boy. We can go into that after we call off the dogs. Ruby made one of her own signs with lettering and a rainbow and went up front to her seat. She held it up to the window for the man in the plane to see:

Please Don't Kill Us

Love, Ruby

"We're on CNN!" Toni, the young woman in pigtails and overalls shouted. Matt looked up at the big screen on the front wall. A different gorgeous woman announcer said that at least one plane out of New York, possibly headed to Chicago, had been hijacked. The news anchor said all air traffic was being grounded around the country. They switched to a male reporter standing in front of Police Headquarters in Lower Manhattan, who said that fighter jets were racing toward the hijacked jet and had already been given clearance to shoot it down, if given the order.

"Oh, my God," said Emily in disbelief. "They would actually do that?"

The anchor threw it over to their White House correspondent, a stunning young blonde in a safari shirt, who was with the president, on vacation at his Texas ranch. The reporter, standing in front of a dry, flat treeless landscape, said the president was meeting with several close aides and had not yet made any statement. Her delivery was calm, her face animated, selling the story. A presidential staffer said that communication had been lost with a jet but that it might be simply a malfunctioning radio. They would release further information when it was available. Meanwhile, the president was set to go kayaking after lunch.

"That's not true," Emily said, indignantly, her fists on her hips. "I mean, not the kayaking thing."

Back in New York, the CNN anchor said that New York City Police had reported that no weapons or explosives had been found in a search of the mosque. One arrest was made and their investigation was continuing. They switched to another live shot in front of the mosque.

"Suzanne, I'm in front of the Al Saud mosque in Queens, the scene of a huge police siege this morning. Police descended on this working-class neighborhood, creating a scene that . . ."

His microphone shut off but he kept talking. He zoomed into the background, as the anchor came back on camera.

"I'm sorry, Frasier, please stand by, we are going back to the president's ranch, where we apparently have some kind of breaking development."

The flat Texas scene popped back on-screen. The reporter was waving the hand that did not have a microphone in it. Dust was swirling around her, blowing her long, straw-colored hair into her face. She shouted to be heard over the noise of loud helicopters. She was anything but calm.

"Suzanne? Can you hear me? We have had a development here. I'm unable to confirm this but it appears the president and his family and closest aides have . . . uh . . . yes, just departed the ranch. Several large green Marine choppers arrived a few minutes ago and are now leaving. I've actually never seen this happen before, Suzanne, I think we, Sonny, did you get the shot? Okay, we can feed you this piece of tape showing the president leaving rather suddenly. No one has given us any explanation yet, and, is it running?"

A shaky video of a crowd of people running away from the camera to a fat green helicopter appeared on the screen. You couldn't see their faces but a man in blue jeans and a white cowboy hat was being turkey trotted to the chopper, his feet pumping but not touching the ground. His white Stetson blew off and sailed out of sight. Men pointing Uzis appeared and put their hands over the lens and the tape stopped. The screen went blank for a moment and then the blonde in Texas appeared again. She was facing away from the camera and coughing dust.

"What do you mean they left without us, too? All of them? That's impossible," the blonde was saying to someone off camera. The helicopter noise was gone but large black SUVs with black windows could be seen speeding across a road in the background, ripping up a plume of yellow dust.

"Where are they going?" the reporter demanded. "What the hell is going on?"

"I don't know," a male voice said off camera. "They didn't tell any of us, they just took off. Something weird is going on. Uh . . . we're live."

Clearly, the reporter was rattled because of the confusion but there was something more in her pretty eyes. She was scared. The screen again went black and then returned to New York, where the anchor, Suzanne something-or-other, was looking at the wrong camera and holding her ear plug.

"No, I . . . we're back. Our apologies, we are having some technical difficulties. Uh, obviously our reporter can't hear us, so we'll get back to her as soon as we can. Meanwhile, in New York, outside the mosque, where . . . What? I'm sorry, apparently we will not be going back to our Queens live shot, either. As you saw in that bit of, uh, live television, the president seems to have made an unscheduled departure from his ranch. And, uh, as soon as we have further details we will get them to you. Yes. Right after these words."

She smiled and held the smile but not quite long enough. In the two seconds before they went to commercial, the smile fell away, replaced by an angry snarl and a snapped order that was cut off, probably just in time:

"Somebody better tell me what the . . ."

Then that same commercial about the fat female cop who had to urinate all the time came on. The officer with the bad bladder even had her own cute little theme song. Ed was also looking at the screen but he wasn't smiling at the song or the cute little dance the cop did because she had to pee.

"Oh shit," Ed moaned.

"Oh shit, what?" Matt asked.

"It doesn't matter anymore," Ed said.

"What doesn't matter anymore?" Jim demanded.

"Weren't you watching?" Ed asked. "They just cleared the ranch. The president's ranch. They think we're trying to kill the president. It's over."

"We're not trying to kill the president," Emily said.

"They think the hijackers were trying to kill him. We call this the ranch flight because it passes almost over the president's ranch. That's why my partner and I were onboard . . . to make sure something like this never happened."

"And you did a swell job," Gordon said.

"Fuck you," Ed replied.

"They think we're trying to assassinate him?" Jim asked. "But the terrorists are dead."

"Yeah, we know that," Ed said, "but maybe they don't believe that. Or maybe they do but they're going to drop us anyway, so we don't crash into a city and kill other people. What difference does it make? The fighters are not here to protect us—they're here to protect everyone else from us. We're the bad guys, even if we're the good guys."

"Of course the right-wingers are going to kill us," Toni said. "That's all they know how to do. Anything to cover up their incompetence."

"How is this the government's fault?" Emmett asked her. "You hate cops and soldiers but now you want them to come save you? Are you one of those disloyal nuts who say conservatives cause terrorism?"

"Of course they cause it or they make it up to get reelected. Terrorists are your best friends."

"What? How dare you, you, you . . ."

"What can we do?" Lester asked Ed, loudly, the big man stepping in between Toni and Emmett, cutting off the fight.

"Yes," said Gordon. "What can we do?"

"Pray, if you pray," said Ed. "It'll be over soon."

"Bullshit," Matt said to Ed. "Get off your ass and talk to your people. You have to. This is your job. Are you just going to give up and sit here and cry about it? I know you're hurt, but these kids are doing more with crayons to save our lives than you are. I thought you were a cop?"

"Matt," said Jim. "Anna is right. We are all in this together. No one else is going to save us. We're all going to save each other. There must be a way."

Ed was looking at Matt like he wanted to kill him. Matt didn't care. Ed looked down at his badge on his chest. He took a deep breath and looked up at Teddy.

"Help me up."

Teddy pulled Ed to his feet and the marshal walked stiffly to the starboard side. He sat hard in the empty front row seat and peered outside. The jet was an F-15, fully armed. It had moved forward and was even with the cockpit of the 767. It stayed there for several minutes, floating, and then drifted back towards

Ed, although it felt, strangely, like they were slowly passing the smaller plane. Ed saw the pilot had his left hand up to his open visor and something glinted in his hand. A video camera. The guy was filming and flying with one hand. Ed snatched his badge off his jacket pocket and slammed it against the Plexiglas, under his injured face. The pilot did not notice. He was filming Ruby and her sign. She was waving again. Ed pulled his piece and clapped it flat on the window above his head.

"C'mon, goddamnit," Ed growled. "Over here! I'm a U.S. marshal!"

"He can't hear you," Danielle pointed out, unnecessarily. Someone yelled from the other side that there was another fighter on the other side, too.

Ed ordered those at the windows near him to wave. That caught the pilot's eye. He turned his head and lazily floated back until he was directly opposite Ed.

"Yes! That's right. I'm a U.S. marshal," Ed said loudly and distinctly.

Danielle rolled her eyes but said nothing. Jim was at another window, watching. The pilot stopped filming and put the video camera down. He gave a thumbs up sign and slipped away slowly from them. He waggled his wings like a see-saw and then the big plane seemed to leave him behind.

"Yes!" Ed said, pumping his fist. "He got it! The wing thing meant he got it. It's okay now."

"Hallelujah!" Emmett shouted, falling to his knees and intoning another prayer.

Several other people cheered again but it was much shorter and weaker than the last time. The honeymoon couple was still in the bathroom together. The TV man was still glued to his little screen and the drunken couple were celebrating and singing in sloppy voices. Jim went over to Matt, who was furiously typing on his laptop. Matt had ignored the whole scene with the fighter and Ed. He seemed to be in his own little world.

"Maybe he's just dropping back to shoot?" Jim asked Matt, afraid he was losing him.

"What?" Matt asked vaguely, not looking up from the screen.

Matt hadn't heard a word. Jim started to ask him the question again but Matt interrupted him, without taking his eyes from his task.

"I don't know, maybe. Jim, my man, do you have a digital camera and USB cable?"

"Uh . . . yeah, in my bag up front. The jets are gone. You want to take pictures?"

"You bet. Go get it. Take a lot of pictures. Fast."

"Why? Of what?"

Matt looked up, confused.

"Of what? Of the hijackers, of the bodies, of the marshal, and don't forget to take one of your daughter and her sign. What's her name?"

"Ruby. Why . . . Oh, I get it. You've got a wireless laptop. You're going to send our pictures out. I thought you were . . . to who?"

"The media. All of them, post them on the Web, soon as I can. Don't forget the old people like the lady with the cane. Very important. And our wounded people, our heroes. That's the scenario. We need to get this out as soon as we can," Matt said, looking back to his computer. "They need to know that it's over. We need help to get this plane down and we need to stop them from blowing us up. We are all about to become famous. Let's hope it's not for just fifteen minutes."

"Great. Good idea, Matt. That's just what we need to . . ."

"You still here?" Matt asked, with a grin. "Focus, buddy, focus."

Jim turned and ran forward to get his camera.

# 26.

Captain Charles Cotesworth Pinckney tugged the yoke toward his gut. The F-15 Strike Eagle nosed into the cloud cover above and was enveloped in gray, causing the wing tips to vanish in the soup. His nose radar painted the belly aspect of the heavy target to his left up ahead, and displayed it in the green heads-up display on his windshield. The flare from his double afterburners lit up the surrounding cloud, giving it a pink glow as he climbed, vectoring toward the target.

"Werewolf Two, this is Werewolf One. Bank right. We'll come up on the fatty's starboard," Captain C.C. Pinckney said into his intercom radio to his wingman.

"Roger, C.C., banking right."

"Copy, Werewolf Two," C.C. Pinckney replied. "Stand by. Eyeball first, acknowledge?"

"Copy, Werewolf One. Safety's engaged."

"Roger. Afterburners off, Billy."

"Copy. Burners off, boss."

The interceptors had been scrambled from the 336th Tactical Fighter Squadron, the "Rocketeers," of the 4th Fighter Wing stationed at Seymour-Johnson Air Force Base in North Carolina. Their unit motto was "Fourth but First" and that's what they were doing—beating another unit to the target. Under the scoop belly of each fighter were two four-finned AIM 7M/P Sparrow III air-to-air missiles. C.C.'s radar sweep told him the other fighters were not even on his screen yet. They were first.

Brilliant sunlight exploded into the cockpit, as C.C. popped out of the cloud layer. The fatty, the 767, was 500 feet above, and to the left, the Anytime Airways logo clearly visible on the big tail.

"Werewolf One to Rocket Base. Intercept confirmed. Heavy target undamaged, flying straight and level, course 225 magnetic. Moving in for a closer look, over?"

"Rocket Base to Werewolf One, roger. Proceed."

The gunmetal war birds slowed and closed the distance. C.C. edged closer and sidled up toward the wing tip. There was no sign of a problem, no one at the windows. C.C. nudged forward along the fuselage and saw something at a porthole up front. It was a little face. He leaned it over closer. It was a pretty little Asian girl, staring at him wide-eyed. He instinctively waved and then felt odd, considering his mission. She smiled and waved back. C.C. proceeded up alongside toward the cockpit, setting the dial on a transceiver for the commercial emergency radio frequency.

"Anytime 1787, heavy, come in, please."

There was no answer. C.C. repeated the hail twice but there was no answer.

"Anytime 1787, heavy, this is Captain Pinckney of the 336th Tactical Fighter Squadron, United States Air Force. Acknowledge immediately. I am armed and have been duly informed that you are under hostile control. Acknowledge immediately or we will be forced to engage and destroy you. This is not a drill. Over?"

C.C. was not surprised there was no reply. He was peering down into the cockpit. It was empty. He clicked on the plane-to-plane intercom.

"Billy, there's nobody home," C.C. told his wingman, Lieutenant William Blount. "The cockpit is empty, they're on the robot."

"Shit, C.C., that means . . ."

"Yeah, maybe," C.C. replied, reaching for his digital videocam and flipping up his visor. "Billy, check the port side."

"Oh, man. Roger," said Billy, the father of two young girls, as he tipped over the jetliner and dipped onto the other side of the wide wing.

The captain filmed the nose of the plane and zoomed in on the empty cockpit. It was spooky. He zoomed back out. Sliding back down the fuselage, C.C. paused to film the little girl, who was now holding up something. He zoomed in on her.

"Damn," he said as he read the girl's words.

Please don't kill us. Love, Ruby. Her name was Ruby. C.C., the father of a boy in high school, swallowed a lump in his throat. Then he noticed words had appeared in other windows, US in one and HELP in another. Another, larger message. He moved away to read it, still filming.

HIJACKERS DEAD MANY WOUNDED HELP US

Some movement to his left caught his eye. He drifted further back, still filming. A man with wild eyes and a wound over one eye was holding a badge up to the window. He produced a pistol and also held that up. C.C. wobbled a bit, unsure what was happening. He steadied the stick, as he realized the guy was mouthing words. What the hell? He stopped the video, tipped right and waggled his wings to acknowledge the messages.

"Billy, they've got messages in the windows. They say the hijackers are dead, many wounded help us. They're kids."

"Yeah, C.C., same on this side."

"Billy, I've also got a guy with a gun and a badge. He could be an air marshal or a bad guy. I don't know but I videoed it."

"Roger. C.C., what's going on?"

"I don't know, Billy. Doesn't look good."

C.C. switched back from VOX intercom to radio.

"Werewolf One to Rocket Base, over?"

"Rocket Base, go."

"This is Werewolf One, we have an empty cockpit, I say again, an empty cockpit, the aircraft is obviously on autopilot. No uniformed crew members in sight. There are children, say again, children at the windows with written messages. One message reads 'hijackers dead, many wounded. Help us.' Message ends. One adult male was visible. He was injured and displayed a black semiautomatic pistol and some kind of badge. Are there air marshals on the flight, Rocket Base, over?"

"Unknown, Werewolf One. Uh . . . Please be advised all of your transmissions are being relayed in real-time direct up through the National Command Authority, copy? Stand by."

C.C. grimaced. Their intercom chatter was also going live up the chain of command to the top, to the Pentagon, all the way up the food chain to POTUS, the guy in the windbreaker, the President of the United States. But it wasn't stage fright that was puckering C.C.'s seat.

"Werewolf One, this is Rocket Base."

"Go ahead, Base."

"Your orders are to drop back into attack position. Arm your weapons, paint the target and hold. I say again weapons hot. Hold until further orders. This is a live fire exercise. This is not a drill. Acknowledge?"

"Copy, Base. Dropping back, going weapons hot. Holding until further. This is not a drill. Awaiting further authorized instructions, Base. Werewolf Two, acknowledge."

"Copy, Base," Billy replied, in an unsteady voice, after a few seconds delay. "Acknowledging authorized orders. Not a drill."

Both fighters fell back on flanking positions well behind and to the right of the jetliner, about a mile. The jet receded up front, a tiny winged object, no bigger than a bird, with no human faces visible. Both pilots reengaged their targeting radar and flipped red cowling covers up off the pickle hot switch.

They toggled their Sparrow Missiles on. Why call it a sparrow, C.C. wondered? Why name a state-of-the-art supersonic tube of flaming death after a cute little brown bird? Whose frigging joke was that?

"C.C., are you sure we . . ."

"Werewolf Two, are you in attack posture?"

"Affirmative, C.C. Are we really going to . . . I mean, do I . . ."

"Werewolf Two, be advised again our mission traffic is being relayed beyond the group, copy?"

"Yeah. Yes sir, copy, Werewolf One. But, C.C., you saw those . . ."

"Werewolf Two, knock it off."

"Yes sir, sorry, Werewolf One," said Billy.

Lieutenant William Blount was looking at a photo of his girls in the swimming pool, which was taped to his front instrument panel.

Captain Charles Cotesworth Pinckney, U.S. Air Force, hard-ass Eagle jockey, the great-great-great-grandson of slaves, checked his heads-up display, his grip tightening on the controls. All systems were nominal. He checked fuel poundage but the face of that little girl, Ruby, and her message with the rainbow kept flashing into his vision, like it was on his heads-up display. He had to do his duty. But there had to be some way, he thought. Some way.

Some way he would not have to send a sparrow to Ruby.

# 27.

Matt was in an encrypted instant message chat room with all of his people, getting feedback, as they set up the website and online blog and posted the 800 number and broadcast it in e-mails to a media list and a government list. They were all supreme cyber warriors who made hackers look like sausage thumbs on a kluge but he had to stop them from wasting time with personal messages. Fiona, always emotional, had called him on the voice link, with the webcam. She was crying onto her keyboard. He told her to get off the video link because he needed to work multiple screens and might need the secondary webcam phone channel for other things.

**Matt:** Stop it. I get it that you all like me and want me to live. I love you too. We can do all this later. Hopefully. Now what have you got?

**Fiona:** Sorry. You site is now up. It's matts1787.com. I'm sending you the admin code and web host IP numbers in a separate email. We used one of our peapod sites. I'm sending you an email with the link now. Log on and set up your password asap. We're already getting calls to the 800 line and emails to the public site, also a peapod. Tyrell's on the public site and blog. He's keeping a running log and news links, government links. I called a dozen pilots and also the Airline Pilot's Association but nothing back yet. Still working on it.

**Jerry:** I downloaded the 767 flight simulator program and put it on the site. The thing flying your plane is called the FCS-700A Autopilot Flight Director System. It looks like it can be fully programmed from takeoff to landing but it's complicated. From an initial scan it looks like the plane, if it's been programmed with all the coordinates and GPS data, will just keep flying to its original destination and land. All by itself. Totally cool.

**Matt:** Jerry, I love you. You just saved our ass.

**Jerry:** Remember this is just my first look. I have to get into the nitty-gritty of the simulation, but it does say that yes, I think. It's not as if I'm a pilot or anything. Also, there's stuff about wind and barometric altimeter settings and crap that I just have no idea yet. And there's a note about a new Required Navigation performance add-on that is an improvement that keeps you in an 1800 foot wide path.

**Matt:** Okay, get into it and highlight everything I need to do but only the bottom line, no frills. I'll probably need a screen showing the FCS thing and what the buttons are.

**Jerry:** Already in the pipe, boss, there is a main screen showing the whole instrument panel and sub pages for all the individual system instrumentality. It's already labeled. I think I can highlight that stuff too, if I need to. No problemo. I'll set it up real-time for one user—you—so you can do any moves you have to do on the simulator first and then on the real deal. If you have to. But maybe you don't have to do squat. Maybe you can just coast down to Cabo, dude. Margaritaville.

**Matt:** That would be nice. Who's next?

**Tyrell:** Public site is running, called saveflight1787.com. I threw on a 767 plane photo but I left a page open for your pictures, called faces of Flight 1787. You have to also type in the captions. Log onto the admin link and download your stuff. It will appear as soon as you click the add option, within three seconds, that is, give or take. I'm loading media videos now. Almost done. End.

**Melanie:** Matt, I sent an URGENT email link to news outlets from the public site, using a PR associations national media list. Waiting for response.

**Matt:** Don't wait too long. Melanie, send me an address book of media outlets, so I can broadcast instant press releases.

**Melanie:** Already done, Tyrell put it on your admin page. He loaded his lists already. We'll start a new list of direct lines of anyone who responds, in bold type, ok?

**Matt:** YOU GUYS ARE THE BEST. Hold on a sec . . . something's on CNN now. Let's use them as the prime target, right? Government dickheads all watch it. Stand by . . . go back to work, leave the IM room open. Later . . .

Matt heard people talking and pointing up at the big TV screen in the front of the coach cabin. He looked up. The CNN anchor was back on the screen and a flashing RED ALERT box was blinking on the bottom of the screen. On the top was a bigger blue CNN EXCLUSIVE banner. She was saying that, according to a CNN Washington correspondent, a high government source said that Homeland Security might soon issue a red alert for the first time. They went to correspondent Jake Broom, who was standing in front of the White House. He was wearing a green polo shirt and white shorts. They zoomed in closer and Broom, obviously called in on his day off, said he had learned exclusively that the alert was related to the plane hijacking, separate ongoing computer assaults against U.S. Government websites and a third even more serious threat. Drawn by the sound, passengers began to crowd around Matt to watch the video.

"When pressed what the third more serious threat was, my source declined to answer," said Broom. "When asked what form the most serious threat took, the source said no credible threat had yet been made by any group or individual. But the threat, he said, was believed credible, based on circumstances and apparent capability of an as-yet unidentified group."

"What does that mean, Jake?" the anchor asked.

"Frankly, I don't know yet," Broom replied. "But that kind of language is often the way the military and intelligence agencies refer to a group's ability to carry out an attack, their capability. It may mean they have the means and equipment to carry out a specific attack."

"I understand you have some unusual news about the vice president, as well, Jake?"

Jake looked uncomfortable, as if he did not expect the question, but recovered quickly.

"Uh . . . yes, I do. The vice president was also whisked away from a breakfast meeting at an exclusive Georgetown hotel to an undisclosed location this morning. Secret Service agents hurried him into a large armored SUV and he has not been seen publicly since. A source close to the vice president said the move was purely precautionary during the current alert. The source close to the vice president . . ."

His cell phone went off, playing "Hail to the Chief" in a tinkly tone, throwing Broom off stride for a second. He ignored the ring.

The anchor interrupted Broom, telling him he could answer his phone because they were coming back to the studio for further developments. She said CNN had also exclusively received an e-mail photo and message claiming to be a group of Islamist terrorists who had taken Flight 1787 from New York. A photo of five dark-bearded men brandishing weapons appeared over her shoulder. They had white headbands with black Arabic script on them. Behind them was a wide black banner with white Arabic script. The anchor announced that they were withholding the names of the men, who lived in New York. The e-mail had originated in Bahrain. A government source had told CNN that the five men in the photo were all believed to be men who attended the same mosque in Queens, which was currently the target of a massive police and FBI raid.

"Kirsten?" Broom could be heard over an open mike from his remote stand-up location.

"Yes, what is it Jake?" she asked, as they reverted back to a shot of Broom at the White House.

Broom was tucking his cell phone back in his shorts pocket.

"Kirsten, I can now also confirm that the men in that photo are believed to be the hijackers aboard that flight from Kennedy Airport in New York to Mexico. A source close to . . . that is, a source has just told CNN that those men are believed to be the ones who took over the aircraft. I am told that armed jets are intercepting the aircraft as we speak and are awaiting a possible order to shoot it down, in order to prevent the plane from being used as a weapon. Specifically, that aircraft, CNN has just learned, was apparently headed directly toward the presidential ranch in Texas, which has just been evacuated, I understand?"

"Incredible," the anchor responded, as she came back on camera. "Yes, Jake, the president has been evacuated from his ranch, also, I guess, to an undisclosed location. Um, stand by, please. We are just getting in that the Federal Aviation Administration is ordering the grounding of all aircraft over the continental U.S. for the first time since the 9-11 attacks in 2001. Obviously we are in another crisis and local stations please note we are suspending all commercial breaks. Again, to recap the incredible events . . ."

The anchor recapitulated the new information, as the box with the bearded men appeared again. The passengers were standing around, gaping at the screen.

"Those aren't the guys we killed," Matt said. "That's not them."

"That's not they," Emily, a former schoolteacher, corrected. "I agree."

"Maybe they shaved their beards so they could get through security?" Gordon ventured.

"No," Anna said. "Those are different people. Look at their faces. Besides, none of the men in that picture is Asian and not one is a woman."

Everyone's eyes glanced toward the body pile, with Maria on top.

"We should cover them," Lester said, still looking at the clotted corpses.

"Yes," his friend Bob echoed.

"No," Matt protested. "Jim, get close-ups of their faces. All of them. Clean the blood off. We have to send their pictures down to the FBI and the media. Something stinks. They're showing a picture of five Arab guys with guns but that's not who took over this plane. Americans took over this plane. Even the Asian guy had an American accent. Somebody is playing a major game and they're way ahead of us. We have to get into the game. Jim?"

"Yeah," he said. "Lester, Bob, could you help me move this guy so I can shoot his face?"

"Ewww," Bob said. "Alright, but . . ."

"Hurry, Jim. Close and clear. All of them. Somebody is setting us up."

Matt clicked on the CONTACT box on the CNN site. He typed the landline number into his e-mail address book and clicked onto the e-mail contact. When the e-mail box popped up, Matt typed URGENT EXCLUSIVE FROM FLIGHT 1787 into the subject box. Then he filled in the numbers for his laptop phone, his webcam address and the web address of the new public website set up by his staff. Above all that he hit the caps lock button and began typing in the message area:

> TO CNN: MY NAME IS MATT NEWTON, LOOK UP MY CYBER SECURITY FIRM IN MANHATTAN, VAN HELLSING ASSOCIATES. I AM A PASSENGER ON FLIGHT 1787 AND I AM OFFERING YOU WORLD EXCLUSIVE INTERVIEWS, PICTURES AND LIVE VIDEO FROM THIS AIRCRAFT IF YOU RESPOND AND AIR WHAT I TELL YOU WITHIN 15 MINUTES. AFTER THAT, I GIVE IT TO EVERYBODY ELSE. CLOCK STARTS NOW. FIVE MEN AND ONE WOMAN—ALL AMERICAN, NOT ARAB, TOOK OVER THE AIRCRAFT. THEY TOOK THE MARSHALS' GUNS. WE ATTACKED THEM AND KILLED THEM ALL. MANY OF US DIED AND WERE WOUNDED. HIJACKERS KILLED THE CREW. THE PLANE IS ON AUTOPILOT, NO ONE TO FLY IT. WE ARE GOING TO TRY TO DO IT OURSELVES, WITH HELP FROM THE GROUND. JETS HAVE BEEN HERE. WE ARE AFRAID THEY WILL SHOOT US DOWN SOON. THE PHOTO YOU RAN IS NOT OF ANYONE ON THIS PLANE. DIFFERENT GUYS. SOMEONE IS PULLING YOUR CHAIN. CHECK IT OUT. I WILL SEND JPG PHOTOS TO SAME EMAIL TO PROVE ALL OF THE ABOVE. CALL ME AT NUMBER BELOW OR, BETTER, SET UP WEBCAM, AND I WILL SHOW YOU LIVE. YOU HAVE LESS THAN 15 MINUTES.—MATT NEWTON

Jim arrived with new photos and Matt downloaded them all using the USB cable. There were pictures of Ruby, holding her sign and many others, bandaged, smiling, crying. There were shots of the bodies and then the close-ups of the hijackers. Matt sent those first. Then the passengers, a shot of the empty cockpit, the marshal. Matt sent them off and then dialed the CNN news desk number in Manhattan on his laptop. When the webcam was not engaged, it worked like a simple speakerphone. The line rang about ten times before someone picked it up.

"CNN," a desk assistant said, picking up the line.

"Hi, this is Matt Newton."

# 28.

Paul, standing in front of the Queens mosque with Cindy, heard the Marine Corps Hymn and opened his cell phone. "Private number" appeared on his phone screen. It was Kevin calling from Police Headquarters.

"Kevin?"

"Paul, I had to call and tell you. You did it. You were right. We have a photo e-mail from the bad guys, with guns and a statement. The usual crap. It's your guys. They give their names, all of them. It's on the tube now, the bastards sent it everywhere. It looks like they were trying for the president at his ranch, to crash the plane, but the passengers may have taken the plane back. The hijackers failed, thank God. The passengers are claiming they killed the hijackers but the FBI says the feds don't trust it. They're probably taking them down right now. Not my call, thank Christ. My cyber people working on the computer attacks tell me one of the passengers has actually set up his own website and an 800 number to tell the world not to shoot them down."

"You've got to be kidding me."

"Do you believe it? The FBI thinks it's real but everybody else in Washington thinks it's all part of the plot. I mean, how could they do all that so fast?"

"Right. So, why does the FBI think it's kosher?"

"No idea. No time now. We are hitting every watch-list location we have. That's one hundred and fifty-six addresses, including six other mosques. The airports, subways, trains, bridges, tunnels, are all closed. Don't waste time trying to leave Queens."

"I figured, Kevin."

"Look, Paul, buddy, thanks for everything. What you did was . . . you got us off our asses early, before anyone else. You did the job, man. Let's hope it makes a difference."

"No problem. Kiss me later. What's up with the main show? The loud thing? What can I do?"

"Nothing, Paul. I'm afraid nothing can be done. It's already been done. If it's here, it's here already. We're just waiting for a break. Or . . ."

"Tell me."

Paul could hear Kevin thinking about speaking on the tape recorded line.

"Two weapons are missing from an Air Force base down south. Maybe for two or three days, the FBI says. They have no clue where they are. Soldiers are dead. Marines. The feds won't release it. They're still dicking around, hoping to keep it quiet."

"Maybe they should issue ear plugs? Fuck. Two of them? They got two of our bombs?"

"Yeah. Looks like. On the plane, they may have grabbed the marshals and used their guns to hijack it."

"Shit. These people are cute. That's smart."

"What? Hold on . . . Paul, I gotta go. We got shots fired at a mosque in the Bronx, cops down. Keep your head down, buddy."

Paul looked at his phone. "Call ended."

Goddamn. He looked at the kid with the blue ice. His T-shirt was now stained with the blue stuff but on the red shirt it looked like blood.

Paul strode over to the Mobile Command Post van. Inside, the NYPD boss of the scene was on the phone. Paul could tell from his face that he was getting the same news, the word that this was the big one. His face was pale. The leader of the Hercules Team was looking at a color printout. The fear and rage of his brother officers was palpable in the air, like the time the PAPD suspected that a letter dropped off at their headquarters at JFK had a nerve agent because everyone started itching. It turned out to be itching powder from a magic store but Paul remembered the fast heartbeat, the danger sweat, the fear that anything could happen, the willingness to do anything to prevent it. Some of the guys had drawn their guns, even though there was no one to shoot; like their piece would protect them.

"Is that the picture of the hijackers?" Paul asked the commando.

"Yeah," he replied. "Five of the women ID'd their husbands' faces. Same guys. They say they know nothing. No speak English."

"Yeah, I know. I found them. Five? I thought there were six?" Paul asked, pulling out his printed list. "Can I see that?"

The commando looked at the boss on the phone, who nodded slightly. Paul took the photo, which was actually two pages. On the first, was a picture of five guys with headbands and AKs. Your basic decapitators, terrorists. Why only five? He looked at the second page. It was the message:

> We of the Al Mecca Martyr's Brigade, all sons of Arabia, have taken this major action to strike at the Crusader heart of infidel America, the great Satan. Death to the U.S. and down with their God. Allah be praised.

Short and sweet but vague. Under the brief message were all the names. The spellings were close but slightly different from the ones on Paul's list. Where was the sixth guy? Actually, the one missing was Ali Akbar Whalid, the husband of the woman with the glasses, who had reported him missing. Maybe he took the picture? Or did he get cold feet? No, there were supposed to be six bad guys on the plane. It said "major action." Just one, not several actions. If they had two bombs they wouldn't set them off in the same city, would they, Paul wondered? That would be less bang for the buck. If it were me, I'd nuke Washington and New York. That would really make them dance in Tehran. Paul looked back at the photo, at the terrorists. Why a still photo? Didn't all these fuckheads make videos saying goodbye to mom before they blew up children? There was something odd about their faces. He looked closer. They all looked scared. Also, two of them weren't looking into the camera. One was looking off to the left, another at the ceiling. Scared, not happy.

The commando spoke to the NYPD boss and then left the trailer. Paul followed him. The wives that Paul had found had been herded onto the sidewalk in front of the mosque. The commando ordered the women to strip off their hooded robes, their burkas. They resisted but the ninja commando gestured to several female officers, including Cindy.

"Stay out of it," Paul told Cindy, and she stepped away. "Why are you doing this?" Paul asked the Hercules Team leader.

"For all I know, they're wired with explosives."

The women were stripped of their outer garb by the women officers, while the male commandos held their guns at the ready. One woman, the younger one with the glasses, fought back. The older women cried and prayed in terror. They obviously thought they were going to be raped or killed. One woman was stripped naked in front of the crowd. There was laughter because one of the older, chubby women was wearing lacy, hot-pink underwear. The head commando scolded one officer, telling her he just meant the robes, not everything. The naked woman was allowed to put a slip back on. The others stood or kneeled, trying to hide their nakedness. The one with the glasses, now in just a white sports bra, jogging shorts and sneakers, stood defiantly, as the commandos questioned them. The cops waved the photo and the message at them and they became hysterical. But not the wife in glasses.

"Photo is fake. My husband is not there," Mrs. Whalid protested. "He would never do this. I work with computers, this is garbage, fake. No way, you hear me? Fake."

"Officer, they do not have any weapons or explosives. Let them get dressed, please. Stop this," Paul said.

He looked at Paul and then behind him. The uniformed commander was standing there. He stopped it. The women put their clothing on. Paul walked up to the woman in glasses.

"The government thinks your husband and his friends are going to destroy the city. Why should I believe that he wouldn't do that?"

She glared at Paul and then realized he was the one who spoke up for them. Paul watched her eyes.

"He is good father. His children are here. He loves me. He loves his job. He is good man. And they are not his friends, oh, only one is friend, Monsour. The rest we do not really know. Except from mosque. This is the truth and God knows it."

She believed it. Paul's crap detector did not go off. Damn. But was she right?

"Your husband go on a trip this week? Maybe down south? Any of the others?"

"No. He works, he comes home."

She asked the other women in Arabic and they shook their heads. None of them had been away this week, she told Paul.

"This is big lie, sir. Believe me. We like it better here than at home. We want to be Americans. He not do this thing."

The commando ordered the women taken away. He told them they were being taken into protective custody. Paul looked around. He noticed the crime scene detectives processing two cars down the block. He and Cindy walked down the street.

The crime scene guys were inside the first car, lifting a blue "QURAN" book with latex-gloved hands and dropping it into a plastic bag. Paul and Cindy walked to the next car, a green Honda, Whalid's vehicle. A crime scene guy was taking pictures of something on the driver's side mirror.

"Hey. Whatcha got?" Paul asked, sidling up to the bright yellow CRIME SCENE DO NOT PASS tape next to the car.

"Blood, probably human," the detective answered. "On the side view and the window."

Blood? If these true believers parked their cars, went to pray for maximum body count and then somehow got to the airport, why blood? Paul was getting an uneasy feeling. Everything had fallen into place. Now the pieces were wiggling.

"Any shell casings, spent rounds?"

"Nah, just blood. Not much, also on the pavement. Not dripping. He fell. Probably nothing fatal, see?"

The investigator pointed to the ground, a blotch of reddish brown. Paul squatted down for a better look. At the correct angle, the splotch glistened slightly. Something else caught the light. Colored dots, very small.

"What's with the small confetti?" Paul asked.

"Where?" the detective asked, taking his eye away from his camera.

"There, all around the blood on the cement," Paul pointed.

The detective crouched next to Paul and looked. He pulled out a black plastic magnifier and leaned over, bringing it into focus. He picked out the dots, amid the old, shiny tiny glass fragments on the dirty roadway.

"Shit. Nice catch, Sarge," he said. "It looks like . . . yeah. Wait a sec . . ."

He went to his open case nearby and returned with several things. First, he used a long tweezer to pick up several of the dots and drop them into a small, clear plastic EVIDENCE bag.

There were hundreds of the tiny colored things. As he did that, Paul noticed there were also some in the shallow blood patch. He didn't know what that meant. The detective examined the dots in the bag with the magnifier.

"Yeah. They are. Damn."

"They are what?" Paul asked.

The detective waved a black wand over the ground. The dots glowed slightly in the shade of the car. Then he passed it over the outside of the door and the window. Paul saw nothing.

"Look at that. A void. Neat. It hasn't rained. Excellent," the detective said, talking to himself.

"What's surprising? What void?" Paul pleaded.

"Sorry, Sarge. Thanks. They used a Taser. The dots are Taser ID dots, little markers that are ejected to let us know that somebody used a Taser gun to stun somebody. You know, when the little darts with wires are fired out and stick into someone and pump current through the muscles, causing instant spasm? They have little letters and numbers on them, microscopic, to pinpoint where the Taser was sold and to who. Tasers all have serial numbers. This guy got zapped outside his car while he was standing, creating a void of the dots, and probably fell and hit his head on the mirror and then hit the deck. The void is the shape of his body. He blocked the spray of dots, so there are none behind where he was standing. There will probably be dozens of them on him, wherever he is. Listen, Sarge, I appreciate this but could I ask you a favor, if you could . . ."

"Sure. You found it, not me. No problem. But are you sure?"

"Oh yeah. No doubt. It's really quite cool. I've seen blood voids on shit cases and I've seen Taser dots before but I've never found a void on a major case before."

And you still haven't, Paul thought.

"So somebody used a stun gun on the driver of this car and then . . ."

"Whoa, Sarge. I have no idea who got zapped. I'll get DNA from the blood. If this guy is in a database, we'll nail it. Otherwise, get me a guy with little colored dots on his clothes and in his hair. Or on his body. Then we'll talk."

"Right. Of course. Go for it, the DNA."

"Will do. Also, we'll call the company and trace the stun gun. So, it's okay if I say I . . ."

"Yeah," Paul repeated. "You found it, pal. Thanks. I think."

Cindy asked Paul what it all meant.

"Not sure. But if the guy who got zapped is the guy who owned the car, Whalid, then someone felt they had to immobilize him with fifty thousand volts. Does that sound like a willing suicidal terrorist to you?"

"No," Cindy answered. "Sounds more like a hostage. I'm confused."

"Tell me about it," Paul said.

"Maybe he chickened out?" Cindy offered.

"Maybe. Or maybe his wife is right. It's all a big lie. She said he was not in the hijacker picture. Maybe they had to get rid of him, a weak link. Shit. Guessing does not count."

Paul called Kevin with the news but he had to wait. When Kevin came on, Paul told him about what the wife had said, the oddness of the picture, the missing sixth guy.

"Kevin, that same guy's car has blood on it and next to it. We found little dots and the crime scene guy said they are Taser ID dots from a stun gun. Somebody zapped this guy and he hit his head. Why? How come he's not in the class picture? Something smells, Kevin. I know I shouldn't but I believe the wife. I'm beginning to wonder if we're not being jerked around. Bigtime."

"Damn," Kevin said. "The FBI director told me his people just found the same kind of dots on two of the murdered marines, that they were stunned and then killed. This is getting weird. Are you sure about this?"

"Yup. What's the matter, bro? Don't want to give me a medal anymore?"

"I don't know whether to shit, piss or go blind, buddy," Kevin snapped. "I've got to tell the FBI what you found."

"What's with the jet?"

"Either way, they're fucked. God help them."

"That's bad. Nothing new on my missing blonde airline clerk?"

"No, not yet."

Neither man spoke for a long moment.

"So these bastards took a plane but they got killed by the passengers, supposedly," Paul said. "They took two bombs so they can blow up two cities. Which? When? The computer attack stuff is bullshit. Who cares about websites?"

"You're wrong about that, Paul. It's heavy and it's screwing the government up—just when they need to work well."

"I guess I'm not getting this. Did you say that guy on the plane has an 800 number or a cell phone I can call?"

"Yeah. I can have the lieutenant give that to you. Why?" Kevin asked.

"I don't know. I don't know what the fuck I'm looking for and I don't know where to look for it. I feel like I've got a bag over my head. I'm playing blind man's bluff and some fucker is spinning me around. By the time stuff gets to me, it's old. Like those Taser dots. It's time to cut to the chase, Kevin. We need to know where we stand. Faster."

"How will calling this poor guy on the plane help?" Kevin asked. "He could be one of them."

"It probably won't but I can't just stand here and wait for the flash. I can't think of anything else to do."

Paul got the 800 number, hung up and immediately dialed it. A woman operator answered.

"Van Hellsing Security Associates . . . sorry, I mean, Save

Flight 1787 hotline—how may I help you?"

Paul identified himself by name and badge number and said it was a police emergency call and she should put him in touch with the gentleman on the hijacked plane immediately.

"I'm sorry, sir, I can't do that. May I take a number and have him call you back, please?"

"You've got to be kidding me."

"No sir. I don't have any way to connect you directly. He is on a separate line."

Paul gave her his cell number and asked for the name of the man who would be calling back. Again, he said it was an emergency.

"If he returns your call, his name is Matthew Newton, sir."

"What do mean IF he returns my call?"

"Sir, I don't know who you are but I've already taken more than fifty messages. One guy said he was the head of the CIA and then asked what I was wearing. They put this out on the web and there are four of us and the phones won't stop ringing, so . . ."

"I got it. Look, this is life or death. Just tell him that I'm the cop from JFK who rang the bell about these guys on the plane. I'm standing in front of the mosque in Queens. I heard what he is saying about the hijackers and I now agree with him that something is wrong and I have information for him. Just tell him now."

"What mosque?" she asked.

"Never mind. Just tell him, sweetheart. Tell him I'm going to find the CNN camera and wave my cell phone, okay?"

# 29.

Matt cursed at his computer. CNN was stalling. They had all the pictures and his e-mails but they had not yet put them on the air. Some assistant producer, Tiffany somebody-or-other, probably some kid who answered phones, e-mailed back that they were trying to confirm his information. Confirm it? Then she e-mailed back and said their Washington correspondent had a high level source that said what Matt was saying was not true. He pointed out that they had the pictures and that they had five more minutes to put them on the air or he would go to the Fox News Channel, their big competitor. He again gave her his SAT phone number to set up a webcam interview.

Jim stood over Matt but had to say his name several times before Matt looked up from his computer.

"Yeah?" Matt asked.

"You should come up to the cockpit with us," Jim told him. "The marshal is on the radio with someone and it's weird. You should hear this."

Teddy was standing outside the cockpit when Matt, his laptop under his arm, and Jim arrived. Ed was slouched in the copilot's seat. He was talking into a throat mike he was holding in one hand. He was wearing a headset in one ear, so it was only possible to hear his side of the conversation.

"What about the jets? Where are they?" Ed asked.

Teddy whispered to Matt and Jim that Ed was talking to his boss but the boss apparently wasn't answering Ed's questions.

Jim said that it seemed that Ed's superiors didn't believe him, even though he had told them repeatedly that they had taken back the plane and the hijackers were dead.

"The ranch doesn't matter anymore," Ed protested to his boss. "I saw it on CNN. He's not there! You're going to kill us all for a fucking building? What the hell are you talking about? What? Listen, I'm telling you that picture of those Arab guys with beards on CNN? Those are not the guys who did this. The ones who took this jet do not look like Al Qaeda—more like Up with People . . . doesn't matter anyway—they're all fuckin' dead. What? Who? Uh huh . . . yeah . . ." Ed's face suddenly went white. "Oh, now you're sorry? Just following orders, right? They've already given the order, haven't they? Damn right I'm a good man. Oh, you can't say anymore? I'm compromised? Call Barbara? All you've got to tell me is call my wife? With what? You are one sorry fucking excuse for a . . . hello? HELLO?"

Ed threw the headset across the cockpit and cursed for a full thirty seconds before he emerged from the cockpit and saw the gathering crowd who had been listening: Matt, Jim, Teddy, and now Anna and Ruby and several others. He thought it over and then gave up with a sigh.

"It's over. The jets are lining up," he told them.

"Who told you that?" Jim asked.

"They didn't tell me shit. They say they can't give me any information until further notice. I'm compromised and the aircraft is assumed to be under hostile control until proved otherwise. Rules of engagement. From the top. Motherfuckers."

"They told you they're going to shoot us down?" Matt asked.

"Are you deaf? They didn't tell me anything. But it's a good guess. He did say we're being followed by jets from North Carolina right now and that the Texas Air National Guard may be joining the party at some point."

Toni burst into hysterical giggling outside the cockpit. Everyone turned to look at her in silence.

"Sorry," she chortled. "That's really funny. Sorry," she said, trailing off.

"If they were going to do it, why haven't they done it already?" Gordon asked.

"I don't know. Maybe we're over a city that they don't want to drop a jet on. Maybe they're waiting for a nice open stretch of land where we won't hurt anybody."

"Marshal, tell them that the plane is on autopilot and we can just land at Cabo as planned," Matt said.

Ed asked what the hell he was talking about and Matt explained what he had been doing. Ed admitted that, technically, that was possible.

"But in the real world, it's suicide. It's never been done. The pilots always tweak it and update it and watch it. It's never been done."

"Then why have the system in the first place?" Matt countered. "Because human pilots make mistakes and computers do not." He explained about the flight simulator software. "It can be done and we're going to do it."

Matt trusted computers and Ed did not. They would never agree but all of their lives depended on Matt being right.

"You're not a pilot and you think you're going to land a 767 using a friggin' video game?" Ed scoffed. "You're nuts."

Matt explained it was not a game. It was the same program used to train the pilots who flew the plane. Ed shook his head slowly and explained it was impossible. Pilots always shut off the autopilot to land the plane.

"No, they don't turn it off," Matt said. "They have to reengage and choose the autoland function below one thousand feet. Apparently they do it all the time. No one has ever done it completely hands free without a pilot because that is a risk no one would ever take—unless your lives depended on taking just that risk."

Now everyone was looking at Matt.

"Who's going to do that? You?" Ed asked, with a smirk.

"Yeah," said Matt. "You got a better idea?"

"You touch anything in this cockpit and I'll shoot you," Ed warned. "If we've only got a few minutes left, I'm going to . . ."

"Marshal, there's been enough shooting," Emily said, wagging a finger at him.

"Can you really do that?" Anna asked Matt.

Matt told them about the simulator program, and how he and his staff could try moves on that before he did them on the real thing, how he had his entire company working on the problem. Ed asked what company and Matt explained about computer security and attacking and defending in cyberspace. Ed said the government should be the ones guiding us through this, not computer programmers.

"Well, you work for them," Jim said. "Maybe you can convince them."

"I don't need them but it would be nice," said Matt. "If we can trust them. I don't think we can. The point is we don't need to touch anything now. The point is, Marshal, you should stop threatening me and get back on that radio and tell them to leave us alone and just let us land."

"Let's vote on it," Lester said.

"Yeah," said Bob. "Let's vote."

Everyone else chimed in for a vote. It was obvious everyone except Ed was for it.

"This is not a democracy," Ed snapped.

The marshal glared at Matt for several seconds before biting his lower lip and returning to the cockpit. He began radioing the plan to his people on the ground. He got someone to admit they were listening but they did not respond to Matt's plan. Ed just kept talking. He switched channels at one point and broadcast the same message over the International Distress frequency before returning to the original channel.

Matt noticed that Teddy had the Asian hijacker's closed laptop in his hands. Teddy asked if he could help, maybe using that machine. Matt sat down and opened the hijacker's computer. It was still on but no programs were running. There were several breadcrumbs programs and an America Online logo on the desktop. He asked Teddy if he had an e-mail account.

"Yeah, on AOL."

Matt double-clicked on AOL. It connected, so obviously the hijacker also had a satellite phone system integrated into his laptop, just like his own. He passed the computer to Teddy.

"Okay, Teddy. E-mail anybody you can think of, FBI, cops, your family, the White House, whatever. But just stay on AOL and do not open any other programs, okay—that's very important. Also, don't turn off the computer. You can close it but don't shut it off, just in case there's some kind of security trap. Don't let anybody else play with it, even if they want to send e-mails—you keep an eye on them. You understand?"

"I got it. AOL only, no other programs, don't shut it off, right?"

"Right. Good. Get the word out."

"Matt, can you land the plane so we don't crash?" Ruby asked Matt, who looked down into her dark eyes.

"Well, I'm hoping the computer will do it for me."

"A computer game will get us back on the ground?" Ruby asked.

"I hope so," Matt smiled.

"Can I help, too? I'm really good at Zoombini and Clue Finders."

"Sure," said Matt.

# 30.

Turner Black slipped a note to the vice president telling him that his contact at CNN was calling again. Black had already denied that the hijackers were dead but now the cable news channel had some kind of photos, supposedly from the plane itself.

Black, speaking quietly into his phone, arranged with reporter Jake Broom for the pictures to be forwarded from CNN to him in the bunker command center. Black then called them up on his video screen and gasped.

While the FBI director was telling the NSC group the odd fact that the same kind of stun gun was used on the dead Marines and possibly one of the hijackers in Queens, Black swiveled his screen and interrupted his boss, pointing to the slide show of grisly images of bloody corpses inside an airplane. Faces of men and a woman obviously dead, one of them missing part of his face, flashed in sequence, a slide show.

"You should see this, sir," Black told the vice president.

"Jesus. What the hell is that?" his boss asked.

Black explained that CNN had sent it for confirmation, saying it came from a passenger on the plane. He said the CNN reporter had relayed the information that the passenger was claiming that the hijackers were all dead, but they were not the same men in the photo that CNN was already running, that came with the claim of responsibility.

National Security Advisor Sheila Preston appeared behind

them and asked what they were looking at.

Black said nothing.

"They're just unconfirmed images from the press," the vice president said, dismissively. "Internet crap."

"Excuse me," Preston said, leaning between the two men and punching a console button. The images instantly appeared on a large screen on a side wall. She asked Black to narrate for the group.

The vice president nodded curtly and Black pulled a microphone towards himself. He explained that they were raw images from a television source, supposedly coming from the hijacked plane—but totally unconfirmed.

"Is this stuff genuine?" the president asked from the big screen.

He was sitting in a large airline seat at a conference table, aboard Air Force One.

"I have no idea," said the vice president, "but if they are genuine, it proves only that there has been a hijacking."

A shot of the empty cockpit flashed on the screen. The vice president said that proved the crew was dead and no one—unless some of the hijackers were still alive—could safely land the plane. Besides, he said, there was no way to tell if the photographs were fake or not.

"What if this is an elaborate deception plan designed in advance to accomplish exactly what is going on now? We are hesitating and not acting," the vice president said, his voice getting louder.

From his intonation of the word "hesitating," it was clear that hesitation was a foolish and unmanly thing to do and his inflection of the word "acting" made it clear that was the morally correct choice.

"This new information about the same type of weapon used on the Marines and at the New York mosque also proves that this is all related, a large conspiracy," the vice president declared.

"Well, what do you think we should do?" the president asked the vice president.

"Unfortunately, we have no choice, Mr. President. We have to interdict them before that plane can be used as a weapon. They tried to get you and they failed. Even if they do not attack you, who knows where they might try next? We can't blink, here, let's take it out of the equation and concentrate on the main problem."

The photo of Ruby, holding her sign, flashed on the screen.

"Okay, Woody, I guess you're right, we should . . . oh, shit, will you look at that?"

Preston spoke up to disagree. She said if the pictures were genuine they showed the terrorists were dead and there was a U.S. marshal in charge. They needed to know from the FAA how long the jet could fly with its load of fuel. Contact must be established with the aircraft first. Black whispered in his boss's ear and the vice president announced that, according to the FAA, someone claiming to be the pilot had earlier spoken to air traffic controllers on the ground and lied to them, saying there was no trouble onboard.

"That proves my point," the vice president bellowed, slamming the table with his fist. "They are spoofing us and we cannot fall for it!"

His face grew more and more pink.

"Mr. President," Preston pleaded, "please give us time to confirm this information and give you a better read on the situation and a range of options. Fighters are tailing the plane now. If it does anything threatening or changes course or altitude, they can bring the unarmed jet down in about a minute or two. Bringing down a large jetliner into a populated area might kill more people than . . ."

The vice president broke in to tell the president that his life was probably in danger and the plane might likely follow him and try to crash into Air Force One. Preston pointed out that the hijacked airliner was still heading southwest, while Air Force One was heading north.

"We're wasting time, sir. We have to take this piece off the board now. It's tragic but I don't want to become president today because we didn't do our duty, Mr. President."

"Okay, Woody. This is a damn shame, but you're probably right. Yes, I give that order. Damn. What's next?"

# 31.

Matt glared at his laptop screen, waiting for CNN to air it all. Nothing happened. They kept showing that picture of the terrorists who were not on the plane. He had a brief weird thought. What if I'm already dead? Maybe this is a dream that I'll have until the blood sugar in my brain is used up? He shook it off and looked at his watch. Emily was playing with the kids in the back of the plane, like a little day care center. When the honeymoon couple made too much noise in one of the bathrooms, Emily banged on the door to quiet them down. The drunken couple were also still at it, arguing about who was going to spend their money and live in their house when they were dead. The TV guy was still glued to his tube, his earbuds plugged in, looking at his little TV screen. It's amazing how quickly you can get used to anything, Matt thought.

"Fuck it!" Matt said, his fingers flying over the keys of his laptop.

He e-mailed his employees to send his message and the photos to Fox TV, radio stations—to every news outlet they could think of. He warned his crew what he was about to attempt and to get ready. One of the 800 operators jumped in with an instant message she said was urgent but Matt blew her off. He told her to post it to him in an e-mail. Then he took the 100 Gigabyte USB flash drive from the platinum chain around his neck and plugged it into the front port on his laptop. He accessed two different hacking programs and three nasty little modular computer virus agents, including Trojan Whorz. He easily found the right DSL lines for CNN from an indexed web surfer database and went in through the front door. It took one of his cryptanalysis programs only a few seconds to blow through their password security and for the hijacker viruses to do their work, as fast as blasting alien faces off in a game. A quick pull-down of a HELP menu told him what he needed to do. These people really need my help, Matt chuckled. This is too easy. He downloaded his message and the photos and linked his video line into something called ONAIR READY1 directory. He didn't care if they traced his number. Let them. Let them call the FBI. The virus units, especially Trojan Whorz, would keep them busy long enough for him to run barefoot through their underwear. He hit execute. He directed his message to LIVE CRAWL "A" directory and plugged his webcam line audio and video into LIVE AIR PRIORITY. He got an error message until he realized that he only had to pick MONO or STEREO for audio. Totally unchallenged. The old hacker high lifted him, like a caffeine buzz from a gallon of Starbucks java. After years of fighting the bad guys, it was a kick to go outlaw. Nothing to lose. He clicked default mode MONO and he was ready to rock. He set it in motion and watched the little hourglass figure dance for a few seconds, as the link bounced up and down off the satellites and finally rammed it up a modem at the CNN studio in New York. Matt got a simple "OK" message box and he clicked it gone. He looked up at the large screen but there was a delay as everything bounced back up the line. As he watched the CNN live box on his laptop, it all went black for a full three seconds and then came back on. First the red crawl with a CNN bug, on the bottom of the screen appeared, white letters moving from right to left:

"FIVE MEN AND ONE WOMAN—ALL AMERI-

CAN, NOT ARABS, TOOK OVER THE AIRCRAFT. THEY TOOK THE MARSHALS' GUNS. WE ATTACKED THEM AND KILLED THEM ALL. MANY OF US DIED AND WERE WOUNDED. HIJACKERS KILLED THE CREW, THE PLANE IS . . ."

Matt's message crawled steadily across the screen and he thought he might have to redo that for this format. If there was time. The main screen divided into two equal squares. On one side, the slide show of the dead hijackers and the passengers and empty cockpit began showing, one after the other. No captions. He forgot that. Damn. The other side looked blank, until Matt realized his webcam was pointed at his arm. He adjusted it until his face appeared on half of the TV. I look like crap, he almost said out loud.

Showtime.

"Uh . . . Hi. My name is Matt Newton. We are aboard Flight 1787. As you can see from the pictures on your screen, the hijackers who took over the plane are dead. They are not Arabs. They looked and sounded American. The photo that CNN ran earlier is bullsh . . . uh, it's not accurate. None of those people are on this airplane. We don't know who they are. I may not have a lot of time here, so, hold on. I want to show you some things."

Matt cringed at his ineloquence but it didn't matter.

"What are you doing, Matt?" Jim asked.

"I'm live on CNN," Matt said.

Passengers began noticing the Matt show in front of them. Some laughed and pointed at the laptop screen, which showed the live broadcast, the photos and the CNN logo and the news crawl that Matt had programmed.

"How did he do that?" Danielle asked.

"Damned if I know," her husband, Gordon, replied.

Matt stood up and panned the webcam around, showing the

cabin. He walked over to the corpses of the hijackers, narrating as he went, talking loudly, so the little mike in the front of the laptop would pick it up. He hoped he could be heard. Matt then showed some of the living passengers, who were gathering around. One waved and smiled. People looked at themselves on the little screen.

"This is Jim . . . I'm sorry, Jim I don't know your last name? Jim and I got two of them. Jim was wounded."

"Donovan. Jim Donovan. Matt, you are incredible. Anyone listening out there should call the government and tell them not to shoot us down. The hijackers are dead. The crew is dead but Matt thinks the autopilot can land the plane safely. We need help, please. Now."

Matt kneeled down in front of Ruby and aimed the camera at her.

"Ruby, do you have a message for the President of the United States?" Matt asked.

"Yes. Please don't kill us," Ruby said. "The bad guys are dead. Please help us. My mom and dad didn't vote for you but please help us anyway, okay?"

Toni could be heard laughing again, somewhere in the crowd.

"What the hell is this?" Ed demanded, pushing through.

"This is Marshal Ed . . . I'm sorry, Marshal, I don't know your last name, either." Matt pointed the laptop camera and the live CNN screen at Ed, who did a double-take at his image.

"Federal Air Marshal Ed Boetsch. Is this going out everywhere?"

"Yes it is," Matt assured him. "On CNN. For now. Go for it, Marshal. Just look at the laptop."

"Oh. Uh, believe me, the terrorists are dead," Ed said. "We would not lie. Americans died to take back this plane. Matt here has a good idea about using the autopilot and we need help. I'm asking my superiors in Washington to listen and to . . ."

The big screen went black where Ed's face had been.

"What happened?" Ed asked Matt. "Are we still on?"

A few seconds later, the slide show also vanished, leaving only the crawl with Matt's message.

"No. They crashed it," Matt said shaking his head. "Very crude, but effective. They can't get rid of the crawl, yet, though."

After another thirty seconds, the crawl also went black and then a blue screen with the CNN logo and a message "Technical Difficulties. Please Stand By."

Matt severed the connection. And cleared his screen. Ed asked him how he did it.

"I hacked in," Matt smiled. "I thought we'd have more time. They're better than I thought. They yanked the lines and crashed the whole system. Ouch."

"Computer hacking is a federal felony," Ed told him.

"No shit. You going to bust me?" Matt asked.

"No," Ed said, grabbing Matt in a bear hug and, embarrassed, quickly letting him go. "I may kiss you, you crazy bastard."

"I'll kiss him," said Liz, who planted one softly on Matt's lips, throwing her arms around his neck.

Then Liz did it again and Matt blushed, remembering how much good girls liked bad boys. The others applauded and patted him on the back. Matt was floating from the hacker rush, the applause and the kiss.

"That was good," Ed decided. "You got our message out. To the whole world. I thought you were a total asshole but maybe you are crazy enough to land this thing."

"Let's hope so," said Matt, smiling at Liz.

# 32.

C.C. Pinckney was expecting the order but it churned his stomach when he heard it repeated twice in his ear, as per weapons release protocols.

"Roger, Rocket Base, this is Werewolf One. Engage and destroy target. Acknowledged."

C.C. looked at the target a mile ahead and to the left, like a small white seagull with blue and red markings gliding alone in the sun. He heard Billy curse into his radio.

"Werewolf Two, this is Werewolf One. I will engage. Hang back, copy?"

"Okay C.C. . . . Yes sir," Billy responded, glad for the reprieve.

"Werewolf One, this is Rocket Base. Negative. Your orders from the National Command Authority are for both platforms to engage target with two Sparrow Threes each. Say again, each aircraft will target and fire double Sparrows at your primary target. This is an authorized and valid order. Acknowledge immediately."

Jesus, C.C. thought. Someone at the top is calling the shots. One tube will swim up an engine exhaust, and detonate inside the turbofan. Once the engine goes, that wing tank will detonate before those folks can finish a short prayer. They'll all be dead or unconscious in seconds, as the aircraft explodes, breaks and burns in the thin air. Why do they want four missiles? Somebody up there wants these folks very dead. In pieces, nothing left. What aren't they telling me?

"Werewolf One, acknowledged, Rocket Base. Two weapons each onto target."

"C.C. . . ." Billy began.

"Stand by, Werewolf Two," said C.C., cutting his wingman off. "Werewolf One to Rocket Base. Sounds like overkill. Be advised this is a two-engine aircraft. Any more than two missiles simultaneously may result in fratricide or a runaway at this range. Also, please note that target is above a heavily populated area. Recommend delay to prevent almost certain collateral damage on the ground. Also, I have a question, Base, are we in a state of war at this time? Are there terrorists still alive onboard the target? Please advise soonest, over?"

At first there was no reply, just dead air. They couldn't believe what they just heard, probably.

"Rocket Base to Werewolf One. Stand by. Group is consulting with command."

"Werewolf Two, this is Werewolf One. Stand by."

"Standing by, Boss."

C.C. was working on the problem. Why was he trying to avoid following direct orders in a time of war with the entire military command structure looking over his shoulder? Of course he didn't want to kill unarmed civilians—especially Americans. It didn't feel right, he realized. It didn't pass the nose test. Something stank, but what? Why the rush, why the overkill? A sunny afternoon in Afghanistan was always in the back of C.C.'s mind. He had been ordered to drop a pod of cluster munitions on a confirmed Taliban concentration just west of Mazar al Sharif. It did the job well, with enough hot, flying flechettes left over to shred a van of kids that drove into that street after the weapon was released. It wasn't his fault but he was responsible. He saw the pictures on NBC. C.C. knew about collateral damage. The cluster device, like a Sparrow missile, was not a smart weapon and could not be recalled.

"Werewolf One? This is Rocket Base. We have relayed your, uh, concerns up the ladder. There is a . . . uh, vigorous discussion in progress, stand by for your reconfirmed orders, Werewolf Pack."

Discussion? That was a euphemism for an argument. Between Group and the Pentagon? At least the Group was with me. Maybe. I'm in the shit, now, C.C. knew.

"Werewolf One, this is Rocket Base. Execute your original orders at this time. You are to . . . uh . . . stand by, Werewolf. Check that. Check that. Those orders have been countermanded at this time. Uh . . . stand by. There is a . . . Disregard, Werewolf. Stand by. Do not engage until further. Acknowledge?"

C.C. confirmed that they would do nothing. He let out a breath.

"C.C., what the hell's goin' on?" Billy asked.

"Werewolf Two, stay off the air unless and until I hail you. That is an order."

"What? Okay, Captain. Yes sir."

If I'm going to Leavenworth, no sense in taking Billy with me, he vowed.

"Werewolf One. This is Rocket Base. You are to engage and destroy your target as ordered, immediately. Acknowledge this valid wartime order immediately."

So much for discussion. It was a different voice.

"Werewolf One to Rocket Base. I acknowledge a valid, direct order to engage and destroy target. Proceeding with mission, over?"

"Copy, Werewolf One. Via con Dios, amigo."

"Stand by, Rocket Base. This is Werewolf One. I have bingo fuel. I say again I have bingo fuel alert. Unable to engage, over?"

C.C. was now in free fall. He had just pulled the ripcord on his career. He heard Billy key his mike but he spoke over him before his wingman could point out that they each still had enough gas to get the job done and they had not heard Sadie, the electronic voice, say "bingo fuel," which meant that they had reached half-tank, which meant there was just enough Aviation #1 to get them back home.

"Werewolf One to Werewolf Two, are you also bingo fuel?"

"Uh . . . yeah . . . I think so, Werewolf One. I must have missed it."

"Roger. Base, this is Werewolf One. We are both bingo fuel, unable to complete. Please advise ASAP?"

"Um . . . Werewolf Flight, our computations have you not at bingo."

"Base, be advised afterburners were engaged on first leg and we had a bitch of a headwind, over?"

Everyone knew there was no way to call C.C. a liar and prove it. The pilots could burn off more on the burners on the way back if they had to. This is the way, C.C. figured. No Sparrow for Ruby. At least, not from me.

"Werewolf One, this is Rocket Base. We confirm you bingo. Stand by for direct encrypted transmission from NCA on this frequency, copy?"

Shit, C.C. mouthed the word silently. Here it comes.

"This is the vice president of the United States, George Franklin Yarwood. Can you hear me, Captain?"

"Affirmative, Mr. Vice President, I copy you five-by-five, sir." C.C. threw in the radio discipline term because he knew the hawkish VP was a draft dodger.

"I am ordering you to shoot down that aircraft now. I don't care if you don't make it back to your base—do you understand? National security is at stake. You are to destroy the jet and then find somewhere to land. If you can't, then you eject and hit the silk. Is that clear?"

"Yes sir, absolutely clear. Destroy the target despite low fuel. Roger, sir. May I ask why we are receiving this valid order from you, sir, and not the president?"

C.C. clearly heard a sputtering noise at the other end of the line.

"Air Force One is having communications problems at the moment, not that that's any of your business. In answer to your other question—yes, we are at war. Are you going to obey orders or do we have to shoot you down, too?"

"I will obey any valid order, sir. I apologize for any delay but I was compelled to relay battlefield information to my command. I was always trained that the ultimate smart weapon was a United States Air Force pilot, sir."

"Goddamnit, Captain, stop gabbing," the vice president shouted. "You are not in charge, I am. You are a just a gun. Clear your weapons or I'll have you in front of a fucking firing squad by sundown."

"Uh . . . Werewolf Two to Werewolf One. I have two hard, climbing echoes, eighty nautical, bearing two-seven-zero, C.C. No transponders. They're air breathers on a direct intercept course. Sixteens, boss. They're Falcons—banging hard, burners on. Company's comin'."

"What the hell is he talking about?" the vice president asked, unaware that two F-16s were converging on the Werewolves.

Voices explaining the situation to the vice president could be heard on the radio. It was over, C.C. knew. Why go to Leavenworth over possibly bad orders if some other assholes were lining up to execute them? Why, indeed?

"This is Werewolf One, copy, Werewolf Two. Get them on the air and warn them to break off—they are in our line of fire. Werewolf One to NCA, Mr. Vice President, we are preparing to fire on the target, as ordered, as soon as we get the friendlies out of the way. Was there anything else, sir?"

"Go fuck yourself."

So much for radio discipline.

"I believe I have already complied with that order, sir," C.C. replied.

The captain heard Billy warning the two other fighters, who would have to pull up and break away in a tight, high-G maneuver to avoid being targeted in the coming shitstorm. The Falcons acknowledged the warning and broke off, one zipping above and one below the 767, flashing in front of the big jet faster than speeding bullets.

"Billy, sorry. Werewolf One to Werewolf Two. On me, Billy, stay on my right. Slip in behind. I'll take the port slipstream, you look for the starboard ripple, right? Safeties off. By the numbers, we'll fire up the contrail, okay?"

"Yeah, copy, C.C. Both rails at once?"

"No, Billy. Too risky. Confirm an impact and then release your number two. Can't miss, copy?"

"Affirmative, C.C. I guess they think the terrorists are still, you know. Listen, are you . . ."

"Forget it, Werewolf Two. Shoot straight. Make it quick. Let me know when you have tone."

The two fighters, now with a clear field, tipped left. They lined up behind the 767, which was leaving two parallel tubes of hot gases that quickly froze into ice, making twin white contrails. The fighters bumped over the potholes in the sky created by the turbulent exhaust and ice crystals. As soon as they lit the weapons, they would snake up the icy river in the cold stratosphere at Mach 5, seeking the heat of the engines. They would wriggle right up the pipes of the fat, dumb and happy target. It would be as easy as shooting a puppy. In the back.

A high-pitched piercing tone sounded from the control panel. The tone indicator confirmed lock on target. The missiles had an electronic path to the 767. A kill solution.

"I have tone," Billy said, his voice choking.

"Roger, Billy, I have tone. Wait one."

Still, C.C. hesitated. He had tried his best but here he was, after all, sending a Sparrow to Ruby.

# 33.

Matt sat back down in a cramped front-row coach seat, fastened his seatbelt and flipped his laptop back open. As soon as Emmett had offered up a new prayer of thanksgiving for Matt's hacking into CNN, Matt knew it was time to get back to work. Liz sat down next to him.

"Hi," she smiled.

"Hi."

Because of the narrow seat, her warm, soft arm was resting on his. Coach is better than I remember it, Matt thought, as the pretty flight attendant watched him work. Oh, man.

"You are going to be a challenge, Liz," Matt told her.

"What do you mean?" she asked.

"I can concentrate in the middle of almost any distraction."

"Oh. I'm a distraction?"

"Sort of."

Liz smiled. It was a nice smile.

"Okay, Matt," she said. "Hungry?"

He realized he was starving, ravenous, and she went off to get some food. Matt looked at his watch. Was it possible for so much to happen in one day and it was only lunchtime? He went back to his computer, to check in with his crew. He felt a gentle poke on the back of his elbow from a gnarly hand in between the seats. The TV guy with the headset behind him was trying to get his attention. He was gaunt, bags under his eyes, a burning cigarette in one hand, utterly calm, moving like a tree sloth.

He was pointing like a ghoul at the big screen. Matt turned and saw that CNN was back on the air. The reporter at the Queens mosque was talking to some cop who was holding up a cell phone. Matt couldn't hear what they were saying because so many people were talking and ignoring the screen. Emmett and Toni were arguing about politics again. He couldn't hear. Ruby appeared at his elbow. She was eating a large chocolate chip cookie, her lips smeared with the chocolate.

"The policeman on TV wants to talk to you," Ruby told him, like she said it every day.

"I'm sorry? What are you talking about? Can you hear that?"

"Yeah, but not too good. I don't have my hearing aids in right now. I read lips. Isn't your last name Newton, like Fig Newton? Look, he's saying it again."

Matt looked at the image while Ruby's little voice spoke the words of the big, bald cop, as his mouth moved on TV:

"Um . . . to call me on this cell phone as soon as possible. That's Matthew Newton on Flight 1787. Matthew Newton, the man who has the website and 800 phone number please call me, Sergeant Ambro-something-o. We need to figure out . . ." Ruby hesitated. "The other man is saying something, wait . . . I can't see his lips."

Matt snatched up a pair of headphones on the seat next to him and put it to one ear. He heard the reporter asking the cop for the phone number but the cop wouldn't give it out. He said he had already given it to the operator at the 800 number. It was only for Matthew Newton. It was urgent. Damn. Contact.

"So you can confirm that Matthew Newton, the man who claims to be a passenger, is actually aboard the hijacked jet? The photos he sent us are real?" the CNN reporter asked.

"The ones you just showed me in the truck? Obviously. Anybody can see that. That's why I'm talking to you, Drew."

"Thank you, Ruby," Matt said.

"You're welcome."

Matt turned to the calm TV guy behind him and thanked him, also. The man slowly nodded. His eyes were glassy. The guy was ripped. Matt had to know.

"Excuse me, what are you on, man?"

His face was impassive, as the question worked on him. The beginnings of a slow motion smile started on his face and he vaguely pointed to his bulging shirt pocket. Matt reached over the seat and pulled a pill bottle out. Dilaudid. An Elvis favorite. He put the pill bottle back where he found it.

"Cancer?" Matt asked him.

The man did that half smile again before it fell away. Matt thanked him again. Poor bastard. The guy was probably dying and now he was overmedicating himself or committing suicide. Matt didn't have time to find out which. Too bad he didn't bring enough for everybody. Matt went right to his message board, looking for the cop's phone number. Sergeant Ambro-something . . .

"Whoa! Look at that!" Teddy yelled from up front on the left.

"Did you see that?" someone else on the right yelled. "What were those things?"

A double rushing noise that quickly built to a screeching roar poured into the jet from above and below. It shook everything, rattling the whole plane with two almost simultaneous booms. People began screaming, just as the jet tipped to the right and lurched violently upwards, sending things sliding, stuff falling out of the overhead compartments. Both engines suddenly whined and raced. Then, the screaming increased, as the left wing dropped fast and the plane see-sawed the other way and dove down, sending two dozen people who had been standing or walking sprawling into each other and onto the deck. One of the food carts flew into the left coach emergency door with a loud bang.

Emmett, sitting on the floor, his arms raised to heaven, was shrieking words that might have made up a prayer but they were in no order and made no sense.

"Jesus Deliverance God Savior Blessing Sin Evil Everlasting Hellfire Harlot Mary Kingdom Joseph Mercy Bounty Wisdom Heaven Hallowed Grace!"

A female voice was saying the word "no" over and over again and a man was repeating "this is it, this is it. They shot us down."

Matt closed his laptop. He saw Anna and Ruby on the floor. Anna was holding her child and singing something. His seatbelt tugged hard at his lap. He could not reach them. He wanted to thank Anna again.

"Goddamnit," Matt said to himself. "Not enough time."

He looked around for Liz but couldn't see her. Out the left windows he saw no flames. The plane righted itself and teeter-tottered back and forth. Always a little bit less each time, Matt noticed. He looked out the other side. Also no flames. If they shot us down, we'd be in a ball of fire and ice, falling like Icarus, Matt thought. There was no fire. The see-saw slowed and then stopped. Nothing happened. The autopilot had done its job well. The screaming stopped but there was crying, still, especially several kids who were hysterical.

"Thank God!" Emmett said, in tears.

"Maybe they missed?" Danielle asked, hopefully.

"Those guys never miss, especially a target like us," said Ed. "Those weren't missiles. We'd all be dead."

"They were jets," Teddy said, arriving with a fresh cut on his forehead. "Two of them. That was just turbulence . . . I think. A sonic boom that hit us and the engines."

"They're just fucking with us," Ed offered.

"Why?" Matt asked. "Why would they do that?"

# 34.

Captain C.C. Pinckney watched the other two fighters pull twisting acrobatic hairpin turns on the radar screen to get aft of Billy and him and avoid their weapons, even though Billy told them they would wait until they were clear. They turned to their left when they should have turned to their right. They had shut off their afterburners but were still supersonic when they rocketed under and over the big jet, far too close. You couldn't see it but C.C. knew those boys had piled up a bow wave of lazy air that couldn't get out of their way, invisible breakers that could swamp small boats and cripple big ones. If this was a peacetime exercise, those two Falcon jockeys would get their tail feathers kicked. That was the problem with war and destruction, C.C. mused, it led to carelessness.

"Oh, man," Billy said.

"Boneheads," C.C. said into his mike. "Billy, stand by for wake impact and possible engine restart."

"Roger, boss."

"Uh, sorry about that, Werewolf One," one of the Falcon pilots said, sounding distinctly un-sorry.

If the overpressure wave slammed into the jet's engines close enough, they could throw turbofan blades and destroy the engine or stall them out. It might save C.C. and Billy a job. The airwave broke on the chubby first and she began to rock and roll. The huge aircraft acted as if it had been punched with a right uppercut. Like a cruise ship surfing a tsunami, the 767 crested and rolled and tipped ponderously. C.C. lost his tone. The shimmying had thrown off the targeting computer.

"Werewolf One to Rocket Base. We have lost tone due to target aspect change. Will reacquire. Stand by, over?"

"Werewolf One, this is Rocket Base. The target is now under positive control, over?"

"Werewolf One to Base. Negative, Base. The falcons gave them a bit of a breeze. Wait one."

"An auto can't take that, can it C.C.?"

"I don't think so, Billy. Once it exceeds the angles, it will go. We'll know in a second. Here it comes."

The shock wave hit the Werewolves less violently but it felt like driving over potholes at sixty miles an hour, with a strong wind from the driver's side added in. C.C gave the Eagle a little more gas and ruddered the bird to the left to compensate. After it passed, the fatty was still bouncing and yawing but not as much. Slowly, it calmed down.

"I'm good, C.C. You okay?"

"Copy, Werewolf Two. Both engines green. Target settling down, flying straight and level, and resuming original course of two-seven-zero magnetic. That is one amazing piece of machinery. Shame to waste it. Let's get back above the contrails, Billy."

"Roger, C.C.," Billy responded, trying to sound as frosty as his boss.

As the two jets resumed their positions just above the white contrails, C.C.'s targeting computer reacquired the jetliner and announced it with a loud beep.

"Werewolf One to Werewolf Two. I have tone and a valid command. Safeties off, this is not a drill."

"Copy, Werewolf One, I have tone. Ready to . . . hold it. What the hell is that? No way. Hey, C.C., you won't believe this but I'm getting a NURAD alarm, that high pitched bleeper. I never got one of those before, have you?"

C.C. realized he was also hearing a high pitched intermittent beep that he had only heard in drills. He could barely hear it over his target tone. NURAD. A nose-mounted scintillation counter that detected ionizing radiation in the air, in order to warn pilots of fallout.

"Yeah, Billy, I'm getting it, too. No, I forgot it was there."

"Do we shoot, boss?"

"No, stand by. Werewolf One to Rocket Base. We have NURAD cockpit alarms sounding. I say again NURAD cockpit alarms. We are downstream of the heavy target, ready to fire. Please advise."

"Rocket Base to Werewolf One. Hold. Okay. We uh . . . okay, please reset your NURAD units, I'm told that a good goose . . . I mean an overpressure wave can cause those doohickeys to put out a false positive, over?"

"Live and learn, Rocket Base. Will comply. Stand by. You copy, Billy?"

"Roger, boss."

C.C. leaned down to the left to find the almost forgotten little rectangle on the bottom of his panel with the little radiation symbol, a red dot, surrounded by three triangular pie slices. There was no on or off switch, just three little lights colored blue, orange and red, three little buttons and a tiny screen. A little blue diode was flashing. He pressed the RESET button and the bleating noise stopped. The blue light went out. The screen said RESET. After ten seconds, the screen said RESTART. The bleating immediately started again and the blue light on the left began winking again. The little screen now said GAMMA LOW.

"Werewolf One to Werewolf Two. I have reset my NURAD unit. It tripped again. I say again my NURAD tripped again."

"Same here, C.C. I got a blue light, and a 'gamma low' reading. What does that mean, boss?"

"Fucked if I know, Billy. Either the hard-on from those knuckleheads fried the exterior sensors or something hot is onboard that fatty up there."

"Like what?"

"Rocket Base, this is Werewolf One. We both have reset and the NURADs tripped again, copy? Readout is gamma low. Is there something about the cargo onboard the target heavy aircraft that you would like to share with us, over?"

"C.C., I have no . . . Rocket Base to Werewolf One. I have no such information. Damn. Please stand by while we check it out."

"C.C., I'm getting . . . I mean, I'm just reminding you about my bingo fuel, okay?"

The captain could hear the "bingo fuel" audio prompt gently sounding with the ding, behind Billy's voice. He got the message. Now Billy really was at the halfway mark. C.C.'s bingo also went off and he reset it. Half tanks and no gas station in sight.

"Copy, Billy, I won't forget. I have an idea about that for later, maybe. You heard our orders. We stick, buddy. Hang tight. I don't think that this stuff can get to us, but meanwhile, let's move above it about five hundred feet, okay?"

"Yessir."

Both jets slowly rose out of the backwash of the big jet. The air was calmer out of the turbulence. C.C.'s NURAD alarm stopped beeping. He looked at it again. No lights. The screen simply read ON.

"C.C., my radiation alarm . . ."

"Just went off? Mine, too, Werewolf Two. I think they're working fine, Billy."

"That means there's something on that plane?"

"Yeah, Two, and I don't think it's a cancer patient fresh from radiation treatment."

"Rocket Base, this is Werewolf One. We climbed out of the heavy target aircraft's slipstream and our NURADs have stopped sounding, copy?"

"Copy, Werewolf One."

"Stay here, Billy."

C.C. nosed quickly back down into the wake of the big jet. His NURAD went off immediately, the blue light blinking. Hot damn. He climbed back up next to Billy and it stopped again.

"Rocket Base, this is Werewolf One. I just dropped back in and there is something hot in their trail. The NURAD sounds while I'm in their smoke and stops when I leave. It only goes off when it gets a sniff, over?"

"Got it, Werewolf One. Thanks. Sorry, but hold on. This is above my pay grade, copy?"

"A little information for the working men would be nice," C.C. replied. "Can we talk about the 'N' word now?"

"What? Oh, the other N-word. Points for that one, Werewolf One, that's funny. When I have it, you'll have it, Captain. Stand by. By the way, the Falcons have taken up a position behind you, three nautical."

"Roger, thank you, sir," C.C. said, checking his scope to confirm the other jets were in their six.

"They're behind us?" Billy asked.

"Yup."

C.C. began thinking again. The new arrivals, the Falcon pukes who slammed them, had taken up a firing position behind them, a definite violation of fighter jock etiquette. The vice president was not kidding. Maybe that shock wave was a warning. If they did not drop the heavy when ordered, the Falcons would send some tubes up their ass and then do the big jet. Also, why hadn't the vice president cut in and put his two cents in on this NURAD deal? If I were him, I'd think it was that cheeky traitor Werewolf dude—stalling again by faking a radiation alarm. Why wasn't he doing that? What did Mr. Vice President know that the Werewolves didn't? It was taking them a long time to get back to them and C.C. heard no voices discussing the situation. It wasn't as if the information that something radioactive was aboard a hijacked commercial airliner was boring. How come no chatter? Some Islamist swine got a dirty bomb on a jet? Ho hum. At least they didn't have any nail clippers. But guessing did not count. One thing was certain—it seemed like nobody was in a hurry to discuss the N-word: nuke. It was turning out to be a bad day at the office.

# 35.

Matt quickly found Sergeant Paul Ambrosino's cell phone number on his new personal website bulletin board. He dialed the 917 number on the laptop and looked up at CNN on the big video screen, picking up an airline headset and putting a bud to one ear. Matt heard the reporter still trying to get information out of the sergeant and then he heard music, Marine Corps music. The sergeant looked at the phone in his hand and flipped it open.

"Hello?"

Matt heard the same voice in both ears but the CNN sound was slightly delayed. Matt dropped the ear bud.

"Sergeant Ambrosino, this is Matt Newton. I'm watching you on CNN. It's really good to finally speak to someone down there who can help us."

"Matt? Excellent. Call me Paul. Hold on a sec." Paul told the reporter to excuse him for a minute and walked quickly off-screen. The TV guy protested and tried to follow but a woman cop stepped in the way and blocked him. She smiled. The reporter had to either knock her over or interview her. He began asking her questions that Matt could not hear.

"Matt?" Paul asked.

"Yes."

"Okay. I figured you could tell me what happened up there and I could tell you what's been happening on the ground and maybe we can help each other?"

“I don’t suppose you’re a pilot?”

“No,” said Paul, “but maybe I can hook that up.”

“That might help. Okay. Start at the beginning?”

“Yeah, go ahead,” Paul said.

Matt walked through the events of the morning. As he spoke, the words had a palpable unreality as he described the pregnant woman, Marie, and her husband Joey, the Asian guy, the guy in the Hawaiian shirt, how Marie suddenly wasn’t pregnant anymore, the water bottles and blowing off the door.

“So you think this broad was carrying something inside her that was explosive?” Paul asked, wondering if, despite his precautions, this was a crank call, after all.

“We think so but it didn’t really explode. It was slower, like some fireworks. It made noise but not a bang. There was some smoke and a lot of heat. I have no clue what it was. Are you on the bomb squad?”

“No, sorry. Go ahead.”

Matt described the killings, the half-moon blades, how they attacked one marshal, took his gun and used it against the second marshal in the bathroom. He talked about the pools of blood that slipped up the Hawaiian guy and the slaughtered crew bodies piled in the same bathroom and corrected himself, because that came later.

“Christ,” said Paul out loud, thinking, this is too weird not to be true.

Matt detailed the murders of the flight attendant and the soldier and others and then described how Anna rallied the men and they used the carts and deodorant and pepper and how they killed the Asian and Hawaiian guys and the others, all the bodies, the shooting, the terror, finding the cockpit empty. He threw in the booms and the wild ride and the jets. He told Paul his plan to let the autopilot do the work but Paul said nothing.

"You work at the airport, right? What do you think?"

"Well, I've heard that they use them every flight but no autopilot has ever landed a big jet without human hands, as far as I know."

"So I hear. The marshal said that, too. Well, we're going to try. What else are we going to do?"

"Yeah. You got a point."

Paul relayed his story, the switched names and flights, the missing ticket agent and the siege at the mosque. He quickly got to the point where they found the confetti and the blood near the car of one of the Saudi guys that meant someone used a stun gun on him.

"The wives here don't think the Saudi guys have anything to do with this. That's possible but I can't prove it. The pictures you sent CNN are obviously different guys."

"I'm telling you they're all Americans, not Saudis," Matt said. "So you think one of the Saudi guys got zapped because he got cold feet? So where are the other Saudis? What are they doing?"

"I don't know, Matt. Maybe nothing. Maybe something. Maybe they're dead."

"So you guys don't know who's doing this or why, either?"

"We're sure that the guys you killed were bad guys. We don't know who they were yet. Was there any ID on the bodies?"

"Uh . . . we didn't think of that. We didn't look. They're . . ."

"Get on it right away and get back to me, okay? That's basic."

"Right, of course. So you don't know who and you don't know what?"

"Unfortunately we know what, we just don't know who or where."

"You know what?"

"Yeah. The Marines who were killed at the Air Force base also had that stun gun confetti on their bodies. So we know there's a connection between Queens and Georgia and the . . ." Paul stopped in midsentence.

"Paul, you're breaking up. There's a connection between Queens and what?"

Paul hesitated. It was supposed to be a secret but maybe it shouldn't be a secret.

"Matt? Hell, you have a right to know. Two nukes were stolen from an air base. The government is keeping it secret. Soldiers were killed. Somebody's got them somewhere—we don't know where."

There was dead air between them so long Paul spoke up.

"Hello? Matt?"

"Yeah. I'm here. So the Saudis have two atomic bombs? In New York?"

"Yes, no or maybe. Somebody has them. We have no clue, Matt. That's why I'm talking to you, pal. Did these people say anything?"

"Some God stuff. They could have been Islamists but they sure as hell didn't look like it. Could the bombs be on this plane?"

"That is a possibility, I guess, although I don't see how the hell they could have gotten one onboard. Yeah, maybe they intended to nuke the president. Why not?"

"In which case it would still be here, right? Are there radiation detectors at the airport?"

"We have them but domestic baggage is not routinely screened for radiation. Let's put it this way. If they wanted to get one onboard, they might have done it. Look at what they did. They couldn't get guns onboard but they got knives and got the marshals' guns. They're smart. Anything is possible. Is the marshal there?"

"He's up in the cockpit. On the radio, I think. I'll tell him everything you told me. Shall I have him call you?"

"Please. Don't forget to look for ID or something on the bodies or in their seats or bags, okay? I wish you could print them. Get back to me as soon as you can, Matt."

"Okay, Sarge. Paul. Can you stop them from shooting us down?"

"Not directly but I'm close to someone at the top of NYPD. I'm calling him next. That should help," Paul said, hoping he wasn't lying.

There was another awkward silence. Neither one seemed to have done much to help the other but at least they were talking. Matt had found someone who believed him. He disconnected the call and glanced at the big screen. CNN had moved back to the studio. Matt brooded on the bombs. If they had figured a way to get them onboard, they would have figured out a way to set them off. Unless someone on the ground would do that. Either way, it didn't matter. The hijackers were dead and couldn't set anything off. If someone on the ground was in charge, they couldn't do anything. The fighter planes were more of an immediate risk and Matt had to task his people to get through to the Air Force and the Pentagon and the White House. He sent them an instant message.

"Was that the policeman?" Ruby asked Matt.

"Yes, thanks, Ruby," Matt said, still trying to process what he had just heard and wondering if he should share the paralyzing news with the others. "It's pretty cool you can read lips. Can you see what your mother is saying to your dad over there?"

Ruby turned to look at her parents in front row seats and stared at them.

"No, not really. It's really hard from the side."

Matt looked around and saw Teddy sitting on the far left side of the cabin, his back against the bulkhead near the emergency exit. He was on the Asian hijacker's laptop and was talking, obviously on the SAT phone, like Matt. He was facing in their direction and his mouth was visible over the top of the laptop.

"What's Teddy saying?" Matt asked Ruby, without pointing at the young man.

Ruby looked at Teddy.

"Okay, that's easy. He's saying . . . 'Yes, every Samaritan. The lord is with us. I do not have the cell phone, every Samaritan.' "

Matt had to smile at the little voice, like a comical movie dub of Teddy's mouth movements.

"What's a Samaritan?" Ruby asked Matt. "Now he's saying . . . 'Yes, my life was spared for a larger purpose. Yes sir, in God's time, not man's. We are trying to stop the fighters. Of course. Yes I will. Not yet. Yes, that would do it, every . . ."

"Okay, Ruby. That's really cool. What do they think of that at your school?"

"My teacher once was talking about how the principal was a pain in the ass but now she puts her hand over her mouth."

"So would I. Thanks, Ruby. You are a big help."

Matt closed his laptop, undid his seat belt and walked over to Teddy and sat down next to him. If there was more turbulence, he didn't want to be knocked down. Teddy seemed embarrassed.

"Hey, Teddy. How's it going? Who are you talking to?"

"Uh . . . my minister," the big guy said sheepishly.

"Really?" Matt asked, trying not to sound like he was surprised because he had not taken Teddy for a religious person at all.

"Is this the Matt I've been hearing about?" a deep, sonorous voice with a distinct southern twang said from Teddy's laptop speakerphone.

"Yes, Reverend, it is. He's the one we were talking about."

"Matt, this is Reverend Samaritan. I'm Teddy's spiritual advisor. We were just praying. Would you care to join us in a prayer for your deliverance from evil?"

"Uh . . . no, thank you, Reverend, uh . . ."

"Samaritan. The Right Reverend Aaron Samaritan."

"Right. Sorry, I didn't know you were praying. I'm sorry to interrupt. I was just coming over to ask Teddy to do something," Matt said, trying to be polite and not betray his feelings that people who talked like that were, basically, nuts.

"Well you go right ahead, Matt. God bless you. The Lord has chosen you as an instrument of his divine will. Your life and Teddy's have been spared as part of His eternal plan. You must realize that, for some reason we may not fathom, you have been chosen to ride in the army of God against the forces of evil. And we will be victorious. Are you sure you won't pray with us, Matt?"

"No, Reverend, I'm not much good at that. I'm kind of one of those 'the Lord helps those who help themselves' kind of guys. I just have an unpleasant task for Teddy. I was just speaking to a New York City Port Authority sergeant and he wants us to search the hijacker bodies for any identification. He agrees with us that the people on this plane are not the ones in that picture on CNN."

"Really? Render unto Caesar," said the minister's voice. "Teddy, this is exactly what we were talking about. Your path is lit by His wisdom. Help your shipmates and fulfill His will."

"I will . . . Reverend, thank you. God bless you. See you soon."

Teddy closed the laptop and stood up, as did Matt.

"If you can't do this with your arm cast, I could get someone else . . ."

"No, it's not a problem," Teddy insisted, swinging his right arm, the forearm covered with the signed half-cast, to demonstrate he had use of it.

Teddy, who had been sitting only a few yards from the corpses of the hijackers, began going through their pockets and rolling the bloody dead weight to search for ID. Matt walked forward to the cockpit and found Ed back on the radio. Matt heard a beeping and an electronic voice. "Tur-bu-lence. Dis-en-gage A-L-S now."

"That damn thing goes off every few minutes," Ed said, looking up at Matt. "After our roller coaster ride, it went off continuously for ten fucking minutes."

Matt filled Ed in on his conversation with Paul but left out the nuclear weapons part for the moment. Matt wanted to wait until he spoke to the others before telling Ed, if he didn't already know. He read off Paul's phone number to Ed but he didn't even pretend to write it down or memorize it.

"I can't speak to him. Out of channels," Ed said, dismissively.

"Who are you talking to now?" Matt asked.

"My wife."

"Oh, sorry. When I have hard stuff on the autopilot, I'll be back."

"Yeah, okay," Ed said.

Matt walked back to his seat in coach. He noticed on his right, Teddy still searching the bodies. He saw him put something in his jeans pocket and then continue his search. Matt sat down and flipped his laptop open on his lap. Teddy came over. There was blood on his hands again.

"Nothing," Teddy informed Matt. "No ID on any of them. No wallets or anything."

"What was that thing you put in your pocket?"

"What? Oh, that. I forgot about that. It's not ID—one of them had a cell phone but it doesn't work. I tried it."

"Can I see it?"

"Sure," Teddy said, digging it out of his jeans pocket and handing the bloody cell over. "It's got blood on it. Want me to show you?"

"Sure."

Teddy turned it on and held it up for Matt to see. The screen went on and showed five bars for the battery and five towers for the signal. The words Verizon ENTER PASSWORD flashed on the screen.

"Yeah. There are six lines under the message. That means, maybe nine hundred thousand possibilities. You're right. The cops won't get anything from that for a while. Try display number. Lower right."

Teddy hit the button but the ENTER PASSWORD message just kept flashing.

"I'll play with it, if you want?" Teddy asked.

"Sure, thanks, Teddy. See if you can find their carry-on bags. Okay?"

"You got it, Matt," Teddy said, slipping the cell back into his pocket and walking forward.

Matt went back online to check in on the progress of the autopilot plan and the media and government blitz.

Matt: I'm back. Hold on a sec. I just remembered I've got to call Sergeant Paul back. Hold on. . . . Fiona, in the meantime, google somebody called reverend aaron samaritan for me and dump into the site, okay. Back in five . . .

Matt hit redial on Paul's number. He told him about the missing ID and the locked Verizon cell phone.

"Damn," said Paul. "Keep trying. Look for their bags. Look, I told NYPD what you told me and they also agree. They are on with the feds now, trying to get them to hold off. I also spoke to my captain at JFK. Turns out there are two baggage security guys at Anytime Airways that are also missing. They're in the wind. Something like thirty-five-thousand people work at the airport. It may be a coincidence or it may mean that's how they got it on your plane—or on two other planes. We're working on it."

"But you don't know?"

"Sorry I have to keep saying that, Matt. I've got a call coming in. I'll call you later, okay?"

"Paul, you ever hear of a Reverend Samaritan? Aaron Samaritan?"

"Who? Nope. Why?"

"No reason. It just sounded familiar to me."

# 36.

The president was back on the big screen in the bunker, seated at the conference table on Air Force One. On his left was a uniformed Air Force officer, the one with "the football," the case with the missile codes. On the president's right was his political advisor, Ben Andre. The president explained that he had been updated on the latest news. During the communications problem, the president explained, he had spoken to the Federal Air Marshal Service and told them to tell the marshal aboard the airplane that they would not shoot the plane down for now.

"What?" the vice president demanded. "Why the hell did you do that, Mr. President?"

Even the president was taken aback by the rebuke. Only a month earlier, the president had seen an "Impeach the President" T-shirt displayed on a news channel. The words were printed on the front of the shirt, below a picture of the vice president. The president recovered from the vice president's outburst with a tight smile.

"Well, Woody, I saw that little girl on TV and I decided we could wait a few minutes while we got a dry handle on this thing, here. Those pilots will let us know if the plane starts to do anything funny. Now we're plugged back in, we can chew it out, okay?"

"Yes sir, of course. Just in time." The vice president replied.

"Mr. President," said Secretary of Defense Veissbrott in the

bunker. "I can report that we have no other unusual activity in our armed forces around the world. Except for an overdue Jump Jet in Kuwait, all seems to be quiet."

"You mean, except for the two missing nuclear weapons?" Preston asked.

The Pentagon chief ignored the comment.

"Mr. President, the Special Forces officer who spoke to you earlier, Lieutenant Colonel Gunning Bedford, Jr., has choppered over from the Pentagon and can now give you the facts, face-to-face, so to speak."

The secretary knew the president was only a visual and verbal learner.

"Give him the come-to-Jesus sermon, Colonel," the secretary whispered to Bedford, who began speaking to the president's image.

"Hello again, Mr. President," the colonel said.

"Ahh, Colonel. So what should I do?" the president asked.

"Short version? Shoot it down, Mr. President. Now."

"Okay, Colonel. Why?"

"Dallas and Houston, sir. They'll be flying near those cities soon. They could fly low, open a door, drop one package and be over the other city after a short flight, an improvised nuclear bomber. They missed their chance at you, sir, but they could take out both cities, as backup targets. The tacs they stole are the right size to waste midsized downtowns and make them uninhabitable for quite some time. Millions would die, sir. An air burst would knock down the buildings but create less fallout. A ground level burst would still knock the buildings but spare the suburbs. Of course there would be a lot more fallout. Tens of thousands of prompt casualties from the blast and gamma radiation. Deaths would continue for years, from the effects of plutonium, strontium-90 and cesium-70, hundreds of thousands of cancer deaths over the next few years. As far as the real estate, plutonium itself has a half-life of 26,000 years, sir."

"Holy hell. But I thought all of these bombs had a bunch of locks and stuff."

"Yes sir, but I think we have to assume that if these folks took the weapons, they have a plan to defeat the seven trigger safety system. Although, in the case of these backpack gadgets, there are only five. Obviously these people are committed to their cause and willing to die for it. Also, sir, you should know they could climb the aircraft and detonate the devices at maximum altitude to create a considerable EMP that would cause widespread catastrophic economic damage."

"What's an EMP?" the president asked.

"Part of the double-bang of nuclear explosions, Mr. President. An electromagnetic pulse that would propagate at the speed of light and fry every unshielded electronic circuit in the country, sir."

"Like what?"

"Like every car and truck ignition circuit in the nation. Also every computer—including civilian corporations, police, fire and 911 systems. Civilian Air Traffic Control networks, hospitals, prisons. The power grid would crash, causing blackouts. Every home computer, television, electronic device, burglar alarm, garage door opener, phone answering machine—you name it. Chaos. If detonated at the right altitude and the right strength weapon, it would shut America down. Cars would be useless unless pulled by a horse. Computers from Wall Street to Joe Sixpack's desktop would be toast, sculpture. Brick-a-brack. Personally, I'd drop one on Dallas using the timer function and then climb and do an EMP. More bang for the buck."

"Jesus fucking Christ almighty," the president said.

"Yes sir."

"Shouldn't we warn those people in the cities?"

"That's not policy, sir. Studies say more would be killed after a warning because everyone would be outside, exposed, stuck in traffic."

"Oh. So why don't we just let it go? Let the plane land in Mexico with this autopilot thing like they want? You know, if the terrorists really are dead?"

"If is the biggest word in the dictionary, Mr. President. That probably won't work, it's virtually impossible. If the barometric pressure or wind changes even a little, the autopilot might decide to land either too high or too low or in the wrong place. If it thinks it's on the ground but it's still in the air, the equipment will lower the landing gear, shut off the engines at the wrong time. They'll stall and crash. If the machine thinks the runway is lower than it is, the jet will fly into the ground and explode. Even if it works perfectly, who will reverse the engines, slow the plane down before the end of the runway? What about the thousands of innocent people in other planes in the pattern, on the runways and in the terminals? They could crash into them and take them with them—not to mention the fact that most airports are near major cities. If they are not programmed to land, we could just let them fly until they drop into the sea and recover the weapons later. I am obliged to point out, from a contingency standpoint, sir, that such population centers could be their actual target, as I mentioned. Now that we have confirmed that the weapons, or at least one weapon, is probably onboard, it would be nothing short of treason to allow a nuclear device anywhere near an American city, sir. The devices could be rigged to a timer or an altimeter to detonate when the plane gets below a certain altitude. Or there could be a sleeper agent or a capability to detonate from the ground. They could use virtually any electronic device, a cell phone, beeper, computer, or a baby monitor. Actually, our people have a digital watch and an Apple iPod that can do that. Mr. President, without a pilot, their survival odds are 99 per cent against success, even if there are no hostiles left aboard. They are flying in a coffin, sir. We have to say a prayer, do our duty, and treat them as we would any other nuclear missile aimed by an enemy at our heartland, sir. Knock it out of the sky, before detonation. That is the only option. Do it over a sparsely inhabited area if possible, but knock it down."

"Damn. Woody, do you agree with this?"

"Yes I do, sir."

"Well, I guess, we have no . . ."

"Excuse me, Mr. President," said National Security Advisor Sheila Preston. "I also agree—to a point. It seems their original target was you at your ranch. They failed and they now seem to be dead, killed by the passengers. If that is true, there is no one to set off the weapons. We have time to get to the bottom of this."

"Horseshit!" the vice president stormed. "Weren't you listening? The colonel said we have to assume that there is some kind of fail-safe detonation capability of the weapon or weapons. It is also our responsibility to destroy or retrieve those weapons, if possible."

Preston's aide handed her a note and she picked up her phone.

"What if their plan is now to get the bombs out of the country?" the vice president continued. "What if they're waiting for them in Mexico? Anybody want to sit here and wait for the mushroom clouds to sprout over Los Angeles and San Francisco?"

Preston rejoined the conversation to say she had Mexican president Carlos Vincente on the line.

"His aide, General Gonzago, urgently wants to link President Vincente in to our conference with you, Mr. President. He just told me Mexican forces are ready to back up the American Air Force in our unfortunate job with the plane."

"Can't you talk to him, Sheila?"

"Mr. President, this could be good," Ben Andre said. "If you could avoid shooting down a plane with Americans onboard? If somebody else did it?"

"Hmmm. I don't know. Okay, Sheila, let's talk to him."

Sheila nodded to her aide, who clicked on his computer and added the new video box next to the president on the bunker screen.

"Hello, Senor Presidente," the American president said to his Mexican counterpart, who was seated inside a palatial office with lots of gold furnishings. "Thank you for calling to offer your help. Muchas gracias, mi amigo."

"Well, President Westport, I, of course, do offer any help you need but I am calling first for information. I am told that your hijacked airliner is coming for my country, to Cabo San Lucas. Is that so?"

"Well, yes, that was its, uh, destination, yes. But there are problems, as you've heard, I'm sure."

"Yes, President Westport, but I would like to hear what they are from you, my friend."

"Well," the president replied, looking around nervously. "Hijackers took over the plane but the passengers claim they killed them all. We're trying to confirm all that now."

"Yes, President Westport, my military has told me that. I mean the nuclear weapons, sir. Will you shoot this aircraft down before it crosses the border into my country or would you prefer that our pilots do the job for you?"

The president froze with a half smirk on his face. His political advisor's lips were moving. He was furiously whispering something to his boss.

"Well, Senor Presidente, we have not confirmed that yet, I don't think."

"I am sorry for the confusion, President Westport, but my

commanders tell me your jets have determined that no one is flying this aircraft and they have already threatened to shoot this plane down, no?"

"Well yes, that's true but we haven't done that yet. They're holding off for now because, we are working hard to uh, to figure out . . ." he trailed off, with a chuckle.

The Mexican leader waited but the president said nothing more. National Security Advisor Sheila Preston grimaced. She had heard the president's inappropriate nervous laugh before.

"And they tell me your fighter planes have detected radiation coming from the plane that indicates such a bomb is on board, is that correct?"

In the Maryland bunker, the vice president could be heard faintly cursing, furious that the word was out to another government. Official policy was to never confirm whether nuclear weapons were or were not aboard any ship or plane. It was just a matter of time that the press got it all.

"Well, I believe there was some kind of . . . they did have a kind of . . . what-do-you-call-it?" the president said, again trailing off vaguely.

"President Vincente, this is National Security Advisor Sheila Preston. It is true that an alarm was received but the equipment on those fighters cannot identify specific isotope signatures, so we actually have not yet determined if . . ."

"Excuse me, Miss Preston, my people say they have recorded this and it does mean exactly that. Ah, yes . . . also your own pilots threatened them on an International Distress Frequency and someone on the plane also called on that same frequency. Is this false? Are you denying it?

"President Westport, I must say I cannot permit such weapons into my country. Time is short. If you do not want to do this thing, please give me permission and I will order my armed forces to attack the aircraft. They are in the air."

There was an extended silence on Air Force One, as the president conferred with his political aide. In the bunker there were intense side discussions.

"Hello? President Westport? There are formalities to be observed. There is also a technical issue. Because these are nuclear weapons, I must ask for permission to attack your civilian aircraft while it is still in American airspace. Otherwise, I am told the radioactive debris would fall on our side of the Rio Grande. That I cannot allow, you understand. You, sir, would do the same, yes? If it is your wish that we perform this terrible task, please say so. We wouldn't want any of your countrymen to think Mexico was invading Texas again, no?"

# 37.

Ed appeared in front of Matt and, for the first time, he was actually smiling.

"You did it, you fucker!" the marshal grinned.

"What?"

"I just got off with my boss. He said the head of Homeland Security got the word direct from the president. They're going to let us land in Mexico."

"Seriously?"

"Yeah. They're going to help us—as long as we don't change course or altitude. Nothing that would make them think the bad guys are still in charge. We just have to let the autopilot take us in. 'Look, ma, no hands.' Anything else happens, the fighters take us out."

"That's great, Marshal," Matt said, thinking that Sergeant Paul had done his job. "So the Mexicans have no problem with this?"

"Nobody said anything about the Mexicans. I guess so."

"Terrific. I'm just brushing up on this simulator thing now. It looks like I have to reset the Automatic Landing System when we get between one thousand feet and four-hundred-seventy-five feet. If I don't reset it, it shuts off by itself."

"Shit."

"Right. It looks pretty simple. I'm going to be up there soon to find the altimeter and get oriented, okay? Thanks. According to the simulator, we've got more than three hours to Cabo."

"Okay but look, don't touch. I gave them my word we wouldn't touch anything."

"You got it. Not until we have to. We'll do this together. Later. Thanks, Ed."

"No, Matt, thank you. You done good. I'm the one who should be sorry."

Matt realized the big cop was holding out his large hand. He took it. Ed's grip was so strong it hurt. Embarrassed, Ed turned away. On the big TV screen, CNN was now running the video of Matt and Ruby and Ed on the webcam, over and over again, with an EXCLUSIVE banner. They also ran Jim's pictures in a smaller screen. IMAGES ABOARD THE HIJACKED AIRLINER.

"The other networks are all stealing CNN's feed. Everyone is seeing this," Jim told Matt. "The world is watching."

Jim rushed to tell everyone else, as Matt went back to his staff chat room on his laptop screen. Matt was done celebrating until he could kiss the ground, like the Pope. Why was the government suddenly so helpful, he wondered?

**Tyrell:** Matt, I've got some great numbers and mails from hacker sites. Click on the link and then on the number or e-mail itself. Happy calling.

Matt clicked on the link and found Tyrell's list, a compendium of federal government insider phone numbers. He skimmed down the long list, which ended with cell phone numbers of various hot Hollywood starlets. This stuff was too cool to be on any hacker website. Tyrell had this in his back pocket, Matt decided, but would never admit it. The first group was White House landline numbers, cell phones of top personnel and their e-mail addresses. Excellent. Matt highlighted all e-mail addresses and composed a message thanking them for allowing them to land in Mexico, using the Global Landing function of the autopilot. He again stated that all of the hijackers were dead and that several passengers needed medical attention. He asked for help with the landing. Matt broadcast the e-mail and then copied the same message to the press list. Matt activated an audio link to his CD drive and then went back to the list. Might as well go right to the top. He clicked on one of the phone links. His laptop processed the call and he heard the phone ring.

"Yes?" a familiar, impatient deep male voice asked.

"This is Matt Newton, aboard Flight 1787. Vice President Yarwood?"

"Yes. Who is this?"

"This is Matt Newton. I'm calling from Flight 1787."

"Who? What do you want?"

"What do I want? I want to thank you and the president for allowing us to land the plane safely in Mexico, using the autopilot, now that all of the hijackers are dead. On behalf of all the passengers, I wanted to say that we all are . . ."

"How did you get this number?"

"The Internet, Mr. Vice President."

"Don't call me again!"

"But, Mr. Vice President, we're talking about hundreds of lives. There are kids onboard. We have wounded heroes who need medical . . ."

"I don't give a shit!"

The line went dead and Matt's screen said CALL TERMINATED. In one sense, the chat went quite well. So much for the government helping us, he thought. Matt replayed the digital recording to make sure it was all there. Then he broadcast the audio attachment to every e-mail on his media list, as well as to his staff. Matt dialed CNN and drew their attention to the new e-mail. A female voice, Tiffany somebody, said they wanted to set up a live video link with him as soon as possible.

"Tiffany, you play my little chat with the vice president live on the air and I'll do whatever you want. His personal cell phone number is in the e-mail. Give him a jingle. I'll call you as soon as I see it on the air. Bye."

Ed had reappeared but he was no longer smiling.

"Matt, I need you up here now," Ed said.

"Sure, Ed. What's up?"

"Mexicans. On the radio."

He was right. In the cockpit, a voice with a south-of-the-border accent was hailing Flight 1787 in English. Ed picked up the mike and headset.

"This is Flight 1787," Ed said, in an authoritative voice. "This is Federal Air Marshal Edward Boetsch. Who's calling?"

"This is Lieutenant Luis Hernandez of the Air Force of the Republic of Mexico. Are you in charge, sir?"

"Yes, I am, Lieutenant. What can I do for you?"

"Please be advised that you are on a course that will take you into sovereign air space of the Republic of Mexico. I have direct orders to prevent that, sir. Please change course and do not cross the border. We do not want to do anything bad, sir."

"Lieutenant, I have been advised by my government, as high up as the president, that we have been cleared to land in Cabo San Lucas, as scheduled. You are mistaken. Please consult your superiors."

"I have just done that, Marshal. My orders are clear. I will relay your response to my command but I must warn you again not to violate Mexican air space. Please sir, do not mistake me. I do not know what your government told you, I only know what my government tells me. You have my personal regrets, sir, but this is not, like you say, not a drill. Do you understand?"

"Look, asshole, you'd better not try anything cute. Our guys will wipe you out!"

The marshal needed a little work on his interpersonal skills.

Also on his bluffing skills.

"Ed, that is not a good idea," Matt chided. "Can I talk to him?"

Ed handed the radio rig over to Matt.

"Uh, Lieutenant, my name is Matt Newton. Let me understand this, you have orders to shoot us down if we go into Mexico?"

"That is correct, sir."

"But if we change course and stay in the U.S.—you will not attack us?"

"Correct. Yes, those are my orders now, sir."

"Thank you, Lieutenant. I think the marshal will be talking to our government and will get back to you soon. I will take steps to change our course as soon as possible. Please hold off. We will talk to you as soon as possible. Please understand the pilots have been killed."

"Okay. I understand."

Ed pulled his gun again and pointed it at Matt's chest.

"I told you, don't touch anything!"

Matt froze but winked at Ed, who gave him a curious look.

"Please tell your government that we will do what you ask. Do not shoot us down," Matt said.

"I will tell them, sir. Thank you. This is not something I want to do, you understand?"

"Of course not. We agree on that," Matt said.

"Okay, I await your course change, amigo. Over and out."

Matt handed the radio set back to Ed, who looked very unhappy. He lowered the pistol. The radio speaker came to life again.

"Hello, Flight 1787, this is Captain Charles Cotesworth Pinckney of the United States Air Force, hailing you on the IDF frequency. I'm driving one of the F-15s behind you. Did I just hear that right? Did the Mexican Air Force just threaten to shoot you down?"

Matt and Ed looked at each other.

"What's the matter, Captain, afraid he's going to take your job?" Ed snapped back, feisty but, again, confrontational with people who had guns pointed at them.

"What? Hold on a second, 1787. Okay, my wingman tells me two jets have just crossed the International Border and are on an intercept course with us. This just keeps getting weirder and weirder. Fellas, I have no clue what's going on, here. Who's in charge over there?"

"I am," said Ed. "First you guys told us we can land in Cabo, now this."

"Okay, Marshal, is it? Are all the hijackers dead? Any information about the nuclear weapons onboard?"

"What the fuck? Nuclear weapons? I don't know anything about . . . are you nuts?"

"Actually," Matt said, "I have heard something about that. I heard that some are missing from a military base."

Ed glared at Matt.

"From one of our military bases?" C.C. asked, incredulously. "Shit on a stick. Now it makes more sense."

"No it doesn't," Ed moaned.

"We have detected radiation in your wake. That's the only reason we didn't light you up a little while ago. It looks like there's a bomb onboard. For the moment, it saved your butt."

"Jesus Christ, we're fucked," Ed said, collapsing into the copilot's seat.

"Captain? This is Matt Newton. We have to change course or the Mexicans will shoot us down. I have to get off to figure out how to reprogram the autopilot. Any suggestions?"

"I wouldn't know how to start. They have a different system than we do."

"No, I meant, a destination. Where to?"

"You're asking me? I don't know. I guess away from Mexico but not back toward any major targets."

"You mean, like California?"

"Well, there's a lot of open land on the way out there. New Mexico, Arizona, a lot of desert and mountains. You would be less threatening, I guess, but we have another problem."

"Why not one more?" Matt shrugged. "What is it?"

"If you change course, I'll have to tell my superiors. They're probably listening to us right now. I have orders to fire on you if you change your course or altitude. Sorry."

"So if we do nothing, the Mexicans will shoot us down. If we change course you will destroy us. The choice is between a Mexican missile or an American missile?"

"Probably. But I don't think the Mexicans would be in our territory unless somebody up there gave them the word that it was okay. You see what I mean?"

"No," said Ed. "They want the Mexicans to do it because they don't want to do it openly?" he asked.

"Maybe," said C.C. "You said it, not me. We won't know until you make your move."

"Captain, this is Matt. I'm going to try to change our course. Please do not fire on us. The hijackers are really dead. I'd like to play you a chat I just had with the vice president. Maybe it will change your mind."

"The vice president?" C.C. asked. "What a coincidence. Go ahead, I'm all ears."

# 38.

Paul could not wait for everything to grind its way forward. Procedure would take too long. It was time to make some luck. He told the NYPD boss at the mosque scene in Queens what had to be done. When he ignored him, Paul called Kevin, who called the boss directly and handed him his head. Paul instantly got a free hand. He knew the NYPD guy hated letting him in but probably also saw it as insurance. If there was any fuckup, it would be Paul's fault. And the boss now had a favor from Kevin deposited in the favor bank. That was the problem with these guys. Paul considered anyone above the rank of sergeant too political. They couldn't change their ways, even when there was an earthquake.

The first order of business was to interview all the men at the mosque and find out anything they could about the missing men. That was being done but they seemed to be scared and clueless, especially since the department Men in Black had guns to their heads. Paul didn't mind kicking ass but he had been taught to think first and kick the right ass. The missing six never showed up for Friday night prayer service, that much seemed certain. For some reason, Paul thought of one of his cousins, Gina, the doctor. When she was in medical school, she once told him that sometimes when you hear hoofbeats in your stethoscope it's not horses—it's zebras.

The next thing was to get the wives moving back to their homes to get hair and skin samples from their husbands' hairbrushes to match up DNA, especially with the blood next to the car. That would connect another set of dots. Maybe. Paul convinced the younger wife with the glasses to cooperate, that he felt they might be victims. The women were driven to their homes. Paul made sure one female cop went with each. The Saudi wife thanked him for the courtesy and for his earlier kindness. He made reassuring noises to her but Paul's gut told him it would not end well. Either their husbands were secret terrorists or someone wanted the world to think they were. Either way, Paul did not expect to ever see them alive.

Next, the confetti. The blood and the Taser confetti outside one of the cars showed that at least one of the Saudis had resisted someone. Force, in the form of the stun gun was applied. Did he try to back out of the plan and was zapped by his pals? Or were all six Saudis zapped and he was the only one who got injured—because he happened to hit his side mirror during the spasm that put him down? Paul and the NYPD crime scene guy checked out the other two cars belonging to the Saudis. Neither one had the tiny colored confetti dots near the cars. Did that mean that only one guy had second thoughts and had to be dealt with? Why use a stun gun? If the other five outvoted him about attacking the Great Satan, it would have been easy for the group to kick his butt and drag him away. Why get fancy with a stun gun? The only reason Paul could think of was a Taser put a man down fast and quiet, no muss, no fuss. What worried him was that he was getting the feeling that the bad guys didn't care if anybody found that out eventually. They did not fear arrest a few days or weeks in the future, as detectives and the lab slowly put it together. That meant that whatever they were planning to do was going to take place soon, before Sherlock Holmes could figure it out. Suicide bombers do not fear future arrest.

"There's nothing here, Sarge," the CSU guy sighed, obviously disappointed.

"What if they fucked up with the guy next to his car and they learned from their mistake?" Paul asked him.

"You mean they took the other guys well away from their cars?"

"Yeah, maybe. Less blood. No chance the vics could jump back in and get away?"

"Okay, Sarge. Where? The confetti glows under UV light but in this sun, forget it," the detective said, looking up and down the side street around the second car, a nice silver Lexus.

"Look, we know this guy here was going to the mosque, right? He's going to walk that way, toward the front entrance. We only have to cover the possible paths between here and the front door, but more likely on this side street. Fewer witnesses."

"Okay, Sarge, but this happened last night, right? With alternate side of the street parking, all of the fucking cars here now may not have been here then. Or at least not in the same order. Also, it's not metered spaces, so the tiny dots we're looking for on these dirty streets are probably now under some cars—if they exist."

"Right. Now you're with me. Let's get started. If I were going to grab some guys, I'd have a few men and a van double-parked and zap them in the street or, even better, on the sidewalk."

"Yeah, but in between two cars would also be good. Look, Sarge, my UV lamp won't work in strong sunlight. Too much ultraviolet competition."

"Hmmmm. Got an umbrella in your van?"

"Yeah."

"Get it. I'll give you shade—you hunt for confetti, okay?"

"What the hell."

Paul did not feel the least bit silly, squatting in the sunny street while holding a black umbrella open to shade the pavement while the CSU detective slowly, carefully passed his UV wand over the concrete underneath. Cindy also got her regulation raincoat from the RMP and held it like a curtain over the CSU man while he inched along the pavement. It only took them half an hour to find the first spray on the sidewalk enroute to the mosque, near the curb.

"Son of a bitch!" the CSU guy said, shaking his head. "Watch your feet. It starts here and goes back into the gutter."

"How long do you think it will take to trace the numbers on the dots to get purchase information on the Taser gun?" Paul asked.

The CSU guy frowned. "Today is Saturday, so first thing Monday morning. Also, they're on Central Time. So, ten a.m. at the earliest. Uh, usually this takes a week, at least. We have to get a subpoena, fax it to their lawyer and wait for them to fax us the name of the retailer. Then we go there and check their sales records. Well, not me. Whoever is assigned to the case. You know the drill, Sarge."

"Yeah, I do. Thanks. We're fucked. Look, you need to get home numbers and get the Taser people off the golf course and get that information today. At least give it a try. We have to know. Now."

"Okay, Sarge, you got it. Thanks for the help. Sorry."

"What for? You did great, man. And now we know what we didn't know before."

"That someone used a Taser on these guys."

"Yeah, which means they were victims, not perps. Patsies, not terrorists."

"Is that good?"

"No. Not for them or for us. We still don't know what the real deal is."

"At least we know this is a fake deal, right, Sarge?"

"Right. Now all we need is where and when."

"Where and when what?"

"Nothing good."

Paul flipped open his cell phone and handed the umbrella to Cindy.

"Kevin? Paul. I'm still at the mosque. We have a second patch of Taser confetti here. At least two of the Saudis were zapped with stun guns. They were grabbed, Kevin, it was a snatch. This is a scam. That proves that what Matt on the plane is saying is true. The hijackers were Americans, not Arabs. We're trying to trace the Taser but I don't think that on a weekend, we'll . . ."

"Okay, but what does that bring to the picnic?"

"No lead on what or where or who yet," Paul admitted. "What do you hear?"

"I think I got the feds to hold off splashing the hijacked plane but now it looks like the Mexicans are going to do it."

"What the hell are you talking about?"

"Don't ask. Neither one of us has the time, Paul. Hey, I was about to call you. A Highway Two unit stopped a female in a pink Volkswagen near JFK."

"My girl, the ticket agent?"

"Maybe, but this woman is a brunette. Looks like the Highway guy caught her backing up into traffic and noticed her vehicle was on the hot sheet. He's got her on North Conduit, at the North Belt Service Road, near the airport, cuffed in the back. You want to take a ride and see if it's her?"

"Yeah. I think I'm done here. She can give us the shit, Kevin."

"Maybe. You still at the mosque on Woodhaven?"

"Yeah. I'll get there as soon as I can."

"Bullshit," said Kevin. "We don't have time. Go to the LZ at the mosque now and hop a chopper ride."

"No, Kevin, thanks, I can get there quicker with back streets. It's not far. I'm on my way."

Paul hung up and dashed back to Cindy and told her the

news. They both ran around the corner to their car. This time, Cindy tried to beat him but it was a tie.

"I'll drive," Paul ordered, jumping behind the wheel and flipping on the lights and sirens.

"God help us," Cindy said, strapping on her seat belt.

"That would be nice," Paul agreed.

# 39.

Matt played the vice president's recording for C.C. over the cockpit radio.

"I recognize the voice," said C.C. from his cockpit.

Matt explained that he had sent the recording to the news media, starting with CNN. Ed disapproved.

"Are you nuts?" Ed asked. "They've agreed to help us."

"I don't think so, Ed. At least not him."

"He doesn't know who you are. It was an open line."

"Then why didn't he say that? No, we have to go over their heads," said Matt. "I'm typing a message to the media now about the Mexican Air Force. That's a story, right? Mexico threatens to shoot down U.S. jetliner? There we go. It's on the way. Via con Dios."

Other passengers had begun to gather outside the cockpit and wanted to know what was happening. Matt felt guilty for not telling them about the bombs but he was still wrestling with that one.

"Speak of El Diablo, 1787," C.C. cut in. "This is Werewolf . . . uh, call me C.C. Our friends are here. On your left."

Matt looked out the left cockpit window. A pointy brown and green camouflaged jet was gliding close to the leading edge of the left wing of the airliner. In the middle of the body, the jet had an inverted red triangle. Inside the triangle was white, with a small green triangle. Why would a plane need camouflage in the sky, where there were no trees or foliage?

"Flight 1787, this is Lieutenant Hernandez once more. Welcome to Texas. You have not yet changed your course. I have checked with my command and they have repeated my orders, sir. If you have not made a turn by the time you reach San Antonio, I have clearance to fire upon you."

"I'm working on that new course, Lieutenant. Give me some time to figure it out and then enter it into the autopilot. This is my first day on the job, okay?" Matt said.

"Take your time but not for too long, okay?"

Matt was unsure if that was supposed to be a joke. He looked up at Jim in the doorway and told him to run and get a shot of the Mexican jet. Jim took off and Matt went back to his screen and opened his crew chat room.

"Hola, Mexican Air Force. I'm speaking to the F-5E. This is Werewolf One. You don't have my clearance. Is that clear?"

"Please stop painting me with your targeting radar, sir. I am an invited guest. You need to, how you say it, to call your office, amigo?"

"Werewolf?" Matt said out loud, chuckling despite himself.

"I got it," said Jim, holding up his camera.

Matt downloaded the new shots of the Mexican camo jet and sent them on to CNN and everybody else. He went back to his staff chat room, to the people he had fought many cyber battles with.

**Matt:** I'm back.

**Fiona:** Matt, I hit three cherries on that minister. Check it out. Also some guy has an idea about how you can land.

**Matt:** Not now. Later. OK jerry, you're on. We need a new course. Now. Or the Mexican air force will blow us up.

**Jerry:** You serious?

**Matt:** Stop wasting time.

**Jerry:** Ok, is there a line input into this autopilot thing?

**Matt:** Not that I can see no.

**Jerry:** Too bad. You are looking at the GLU-920 MMR Global Landing System, right? You'll have to punch this in by hand. Where do you want to go?

**Matt:** Away from Mexico for now.

**Jerry:** More specific? Phoenix?

**Matt:** No. I don't think anybody will let us land. Just away but not at a major city. we're in a hurry here . . .

**Jerry:** Ok, you are getting lower in Texas, so you have to avoid that piece of Mexico that sticks up, right? And you're going to keep going for awhile until you enter this and execute, so the closest round number that does that is 340.

**Matt:** 340 what?

**Jerry:** 340 degrees. Like on a compass? Haven't you looked at this stuff yet?

**Matt:** I've been busy. I'm calling it up now. I thought you'd be an expert by now.

**Jerry:** Right. Okay, you bet. I'll talk you through this. You have to hit enter and then punch in the course. Except we have to use the DIVERT function, also.

**Matt:** Have you done this on the simulator program first?

**Jerry:** No, not with that number.

**Matt:** Do it now.

**Jerry:** Ok hold on.

As he waited, a pop-up informed Matt that CNN was calling on the webcam line. Someone else was calling on the phone line. More press. Good. Matt was used to pressure and killer deadlines, defending corporations from criminal onslaughts by hackers but this was the most important defense of his life. He dealt with cyber-extortionists every day. Usually, somewhere behind the geeks in the room with the towers and servers and re-mailers, were some real bad guys: Russian Mafia, Singapore Tongs, Japanese Yakuza, but Matt never actually met them. If he was fast and good, he could track back to the hacker who was running the zombie zoo, the legions of personal computers around the world sitting on clueless consumers' desks. Once under the spell of the Zombie Master, the PCs were slaved to attack the same target and jam it with an avalanche of zombie attacks around the clock, until the firm was out of business—or they paid up. When he could, he spiked the hacker's machines with viruses, crashed their re-mailers, and fried their equipment—which often only slowed them down for a few hours or days. Usually, they moved on to targets that did not bite back. On one job in Singapore, Matt couldn't trace the phone down past the local prefix—so he disconnected all 9,999 lines by telling the phone company computer that no one had paid their bills in a year. Then, he had pinned that on the hacker.

**Jerry:** Ok, Matt, are you ready? Click on this link I'm sending you. This is a sim of how to do it. First, the command appears below the image of the autopilot thing with an OK box. The button you need to push will blink each time to prompt you for the real thing, okay? Got it? Ready to run through? Then you rerack the sim and walk through it again, punching the real buttons as the ones on the sim light up, okay?

**Matt:** Yeah, I got it. Okay, let me try this once.

Matt ran through the game simulation on his laptop. The little image of the autopilot read COURSE: 240.120. First, as directed by Jerry's prompts, Matt clicked the ENTER button. Then the proper MODE choice when presented, which was DIVERT. Next came course. He had to punch in 340.000 and then click ENTER. He clicked with his mouse pad on the laptop and then typed in the numbers. ACCEPT? Flashed on the two-dimensional autopilot on his laptop screen. He then clicked ENTER again. The computer game beeped and told him COURSE ACCEPTED. EXECUTE? Matt clicked on the EXECUTE button.

Nothing seemed to happen on his screen. Then he noticed that the image of the compass on the computer was slowly moving. The level flight indicator showed the cyber plane was banking to the right. Then it leveled off. Barely noticeable.

**Matt:** I think I got it. Let's do it. Throw some clouds in the sky in the sim, Jerry, I can't tell when the plane is turning because the sky is blank.

**Jerry:** You got it. Ready?

**Matt:** No, but let's go anyway.

Matt reset the flight game and started walking through it again—first on the laptop and then in the real world. When he hit the real ENTER button, it beeped much louder than in the game.

"What the fuck are you doing?" Ed said, pulling that damn gun again.

"What we have to do. I'm changing course so the Mexicans won't shoot us down."

"Not until I say so. We have to talk to the ground!"

"Ed, if we wait for them, we'll be dead."

"You don't know what you're doing. Our jets will shoot on us."

"Maybe. I just went through this on the computer and it worked just fine. I've got to do this now Ed. You're not going to shoot me are you? You might hurt the plane."

Ed looked at the gun and put it away.

"Be careful. This is not a game."

"That was my plan, Marshal."

Matt then went through the other steps, first on the laptop and then on the real equipment. The only difference was that Matt's cursor was not sweating as it pushed the make-believe buttons. When he got to ENTER, Matt punched the button and got the beep.

COURSE ACCEPTED. EXECUTE DIVERT A?

That was different than on the computer game. Matt dialed Jerry's voice line on his speaker phone because he wanted his hands free.

"Yeah, Matt?"

"Jerry, this is different. It doesn't say just 'execute,' it says 'execute divert A.' Should I hit execute?"

"I think so. Maybe this is a different model than the sim or the real one has upgraded software. Or the other way around."

"Maybe? Jerry, it's different."

"Yeah. Whatever. I'd go with it. Your move, Matt."

"Hold it!" said Ed, raising his hand like a school crossing guard.

"Banzai," Matt said, pressing the square EXECUTE button.

"Goddamn it, I said hold it!"

Like in the game, nothing happened. Then it did. The huge plane tilted to the right.

"It's working," Matt said, his voice rising.

The floor pitched to the right and kept on tilting. Matt could hear passengers screaming back in the cabin. There were two large bangs.

"Go tell them it's okay," Matt yelled to Jim and the others.

"Is it okay?" Jim asked.

They turned to talk to the other passengers but were knocked off their feet and vanished from the doorway. The screaming got louder as the plane tilted at a forty five degree angle, the nose swinging fast to the right.

"Oh shit!" Matt said, holding on to his laptop and the seat.

A few more degrees and he would tumble down onto Ed, who was cursing a blue streak in the other seat. After a long minute, everything dipped back slowly to where it had been and gently leveled off. The compass read 340.000 and the flight globe lines were level again. They continued to fly straight ahead, but on the new course.

"Hey, that wasn't so bad," Matt said.

"Asshole," Ed replied.

"You okay, Matt?" Jerry asked on the phone.

"Yeah, we're great. It worked. Except maybe we can figure a way to do it more gently next time?"

"Okay, I'll check it out. There must be a slower execute function but that might be more complicated, Matt."

"Get on it. The simple version scared the shit out of us. We were standing on one wing there for a minute."

"Oh. Okay, will do. For now, you're good to go. Like, into nowhere—desert and mountains, badlands. Eventually you end up at uh . . . let's see . . . Eureka, California, and then over the Pacific Ocean. Oh, and then Alaska. How's your gas doing?"

Matt read him the fuel poundage gauges and Jerry had Matt plug that into his laptop also.

"According to the total you have more than 4,600 kilometers

left to go but this is different than in a car. You have to figure winds and altitude."

"No, Jerry you have to figure it."

"Right, boss. I'm on it. Tell me again why you want to fly over the Big Nothing?"

"Jerry, they're afraid of us, afraid we are really still hijackers and want to drive this into a skyscraper. It's better for everyone if we stay away from things for a while, considering what they think we have onboard."

"Which is what?"

"A nuke. Or two."

"Shut up!"

"For real, Jerry, but don't put that out to the press. Yet. If everyone panics and loses it, they won't care what happens to us. We'll be a pariah, total poison."

"Dude, you're that now."

"Thanks for the lift, Jerry."

"No problem. I'll call back on the voice line when I've got this all squared away. Bye."

"Matt you scared the hell out of me. Not only me," Ed said.

"Yeah, sorry. I didn't know."

"Thanks, anyway."

"No problem. That was nothing. The hard part will be landing."

"Thanks, Captain bring-down."

"Hello, Flight 1787, this is Lieutenant Hernandez. I have seen your turn away from our airspace. I have been ordered back to my base. Thank you and good luck."

"Thanks," Ed replied. "Captain? Is the F-16 captain on the air?"

"Yes, Marshal, I'm here. Look up."

Ed and Matt looked up and saw two American jets above and to the right.

"The next time you're going to do that, I suggest you let us, or anyone else know in advance. For your own safety. Was that an autopilot turn?"

"Yes it was," said Ed. "Sorry. I didn't do that. Are we good?"

"Yes sir," C.C. replied. "I have orders to stand down. For now, it's over. Just stay on this course until otherwise agreed, okay?"

"Hear that, Matt?"

"I got it. Sorry, new toy."

"Marshal?"

"Yes?"

"We have to split, we're low on gas. Good luck. Fly the friendly skies. Rocket Base, this is Werewolf One. We are breaking off pursuit as ordered and proceeding to alternate field with fuel emergency. Out."

Matt waved at the jets waggling their wings and he went back to his laptop once more. The computer display panel was tracking their fuel and course and speed. The number agreed with the real ones in front of him. He reduced the autopilot program and clicked on Fiona's posting for him.

> Matt, this has got to be the same guy. He was the president's minister. But then the president dumped him. Is he onboard?
>
> Fiona

He clicked on the link and got a screen full of articles about the Right Reverend Aaron Samaritan. One was a Christian magazine article quoting the then-congressman and future president about how Samaritan had saved his soul and turned his life around. That's why the guy's name was familiar, Matt realized. The article mentioned that Samaritan used to drive around Texas in an old van, wearing a black suit and a crown of thorns. Real ones. The reverend told the magazine how the president was troubled by alcohol and drugs and failure and how his soul was thirsting for salvation. Apparently this historic event took place at a Motel 7 in Yoakum, Texas, and led to the meteoric rise of the president to a congressional seat and thence to the highest office in the land. It was all God's will, courtesy of the Right Reverend Samaritan, the minister explained.

Matt found another, later article in *Newsweek,* in which the president claimed he had actually been subsequently resaved by another less controversial minister. The newly elected president seemed eager to distance himself from Samaritan. Why? The crown of thorns thing? There were more articles listed. Samaritan had a TV show, a real money-raiser. He developed tax problems. Aha. There was one describing allegations of sexual impropriety by an underage girl who had also been saved by the guy with the uncomfortable hat. She told a newspaper the minister told her and other devotees at his church that they had to sin—with him—before they could receive heavenly forgiveness. Another story in *Newsweek* featured charges that Samaritan's church was heavily into survivalism and a theory of government called Unitary Executive. It sounded like total Christian militia stuff. No wonder the president had disowned him.

He sent an instant message to Fiona. He wanted her all over the Samaritan stuff and to send him a summary, with links. As he sent the message, he heard that familiar voice, this time coming from one of the big screens. And his own. Matt walked back into first class and saw a still photo of the vice president on the screen. He heard the man who was a heartbeat away from the presidency say "I don't give a shit!" about the hero passengers.

"Jesus," said Jim. "You spoke to him?"

"Well, mostly he spoke to me."

"Potty mouth!" Ruby chided.

Next CNN ran Jim's Mexican fighter jet photos and their EXCLUSIVE story that foreign jets were flying above American soil for the first time in history, apparently ready to shoot down Flight 1787. The White House declined to comment on the bizarre turn of events. The vice president had hung up on their reporter, the anchor said. That was the deal, Matt realized. They ran his stuff and now he had to call CNN and give them the latest—live. It would keep those bastards in the White House honest. Theoretically. On the way back to the coach cabin, Matt ran into Ruby who was dashing about with two other kids.

"Hey, Matt, I slid all the way across the plane and scraped my knee," she said proudly. "Look."

"Sorry, Ruby," he said glancing at her slight wound.

Matt took Ruby aside and asked if she could keep a secret.

"I can't tell you," Ruby replied, with a sly smile.

"Why?" Matt asked.

"Because it's a secret," she giggled.

"Right," Matt smiled. "Exactly. Just between us, Ruby, I have a secret mission and I think you are just the girl for it."

# 40.

The vice president, speaking from inside the Maryland bunker, was again warning the president, aboard Air Force One, that he was still in danger.

"Mr. President, take a look at the Big Board. Was it a coincidence that the jet turned away from Mexico and toward the section of the country where Eagle One went? I don't think so. I think they are still targeting you, hoping to take you out, sir. I recommend that you do not land at the Nevada air base. I think you should stay in the air and change direction, north or northeast and see if the hijacked jet follows."

As he spoke to the Commander-in-Chief's video image on the large video screen, the vice president pointed toward the adjacent wall, where the giant liquid crystal display showed a map of North America. A circular Presidential Seal was inching its way toward Nevada. Lower on the screen, hundreds of miles behind, the position of Flight 1787 was marked by a target with a red center, surrounded by concentric circles of orange and yellow. Small letters in the center read SIM 36.0KT. The translucent bull's eye was a moving, computerized template that replaced earlier generations of plastic templates used by the military to place over maps. It indicated the blast damage zones and denied fallout areas if the nukes presumed to be onboard were detonated. Just behind 1787, two blinking triangles indicated the pair of F-16s from the Texas Air National Guard still tailing the big jet. Two similar flashing dots protectively flanked Air Force One.

"John, are you with me on this?" the vice president asked the screen.

"Yes, Mr. Vice President, I agree," Secret Service Agent John Langdon replied.

He turned to the president, seated next to him. "I think we should try a course change and see what they do. If they turn toward us, we should take them down."

"Okay, Woody, we'll change direction and see what happens. I should get back to Washington, anyway."

"No, Mr. President. For all we know one of those backpack things is being walked up and down near the White House, waiting for you to return. Until we locate and neutralize them both, I don't think you should even fly near a major city."

No one disagreed with the logic. The president slapped the table in front of him.

"Damnit, Woody! Half the time, the damn video stuff doesn't work and I have to use the phone. What the hell am I supposed to do, fly around all week?"

"Sir, I have a feeling that this will be a long day and night. Hopefully by tonight or tomorrow, we'll know where we are."

Everyone knew that the president's airborne command post could be refueled in the air and kept in the air for weeks. But the press was beginning to figure out that the crisis might be bigger than the government was telling them. Already, the more experienced correspondents were using words that communicated that something big was up—bigger than anyone had ever seen, even though they had no details. The huge military alert and base sealings were being reported, along with the security alerts, first in New York and later in other cities. A ranking Democratic congressman, Robert Morris, went on CNN to denounce the scale of the alert as an overreaction and a possible ploy to distract the country from the president's problems and the vice president's developing scandal investigation.

"Bob Morris just tripped over his dick," the vice president chuckled, when he saw the report.

The FAA chief reported to the group that no major airport would permit the hijacked jet to land because they were all under terror alerts, landing airplanes, and feared the jetliner might crash into the downtown areas, intentionally or otherwise. Except Alaska. Fairbanks said they would permit the landing but a major storm system would probably make such a landing—without a pilot—virtually certain to be a crash. The FAA chief suggested they reroute the aircraft there. It was their last chance.

"Have you been listening?" the vice president snapped. "The states and cities don't know about the missing weapons. We cannot permit nuclear devices near an American city—that would be treason! But that's not a bad idea. Why don't we tell the jet to alter course for Fairbanks? That would bring them over California, then out to sea, toward Alaska, right? That gives us some time. Once they're over water, Mr. President, no one on the ground would be affected if we're forced to take them down. We can recover the weapons at our leisure."

"You're saying we should lie to them, Woody, the people on the plane?"

"We have to assume that they are lying to us, Mr. President. You heard the colonel. We cannot take the chance. History would not treat us kindly if we permitted an entire city to be destroyed because we were weak."

"Okay, I guess, you're right. We can do that but we don't have to decide about shooting it down right now, do we?"

"No sir, we have a few hours to make that decision, Mr. President."

"Okay, that's it, I guess. Is there anything else now?"

FBI director Bassett spoke up at the same time as Sheila Preston.

"Yes, Sheila?"

He sighed as the national security advisor, Sheila Preston, updated him on the status of U.S. forces. There were no other missing weapons and the mobilization was proceeding well. Aside from the one overdue jet from Kuwait, there were no problems except the computer attacks. The allies had been notified and the British prime minister wanted to speak to him right away. The president took the call.

While he spoke, the vice president's aide handed him his cell phone. The vice president looked at the number of the vibrating flip phone, which was not recognized by his caller ID.

"Is this that asshole on the plane again?" he asked Turner Black in a low voice.

"No. Different number. I blocked that one. I'm not sure who it is, sir. It might be more press but I don't think so. It's from your state, I thought it might be your daughter?"

"Who the hell is this?" the vice president grumbled into the phone. "Oh, sorry, R.R., my phone didn't recognize your number. I can't talk right now, as you know . . . yes, well, I can't talk about . . . yes, God bless you too, R.R., I appreciate that. No. Well, you are a merciful man, but if that plane is a threat to . . . really? Well, that's comforting that you . . . R.R., I hope you're right. No, I'm afraid I can't do that right now. Yes, of course, I remember our talk. We'll do all we can to save the people on that plane, of course, but . . . I'm sorry one of your people is onboard. I'm afraid we're a bit busy to pray right now, so . . . I beg your pardon? Are you . . . thanks for your thoughts, but, I can't . . . What are you talking about? Absolutely not, I . . . WHAT? Hello? Hello?"

"Who was it?" Black asked his boss.

"Nobody," the vice president said, handing the phone back to

Black, with a shaking hand. "No more outside calls."

The president finished his call and the FBI director, also holding a phone in his hand, immediately spoke up.

"Yes, Mr. Director?" the president asked.

"I have to disagree with several items just discussed, Mr. President. Everything we have so far points to the fact that the passengers did exactly what they said they did and that the federal marshal is back in charge on that plane. Why can't we find a remote area to let the jet land under full security? The National Security Act clearly gives the FBI jurisdiction here. I'm concerned about letting weapons of mass destruction out of the country and out of our control, not to mention losing most of the evidence in my case, Mr. President."

The president sighed. He hated confusion. He looked at the video image of the FBI guy and used his little memory gimmick to remember his name by picturing him with a megaphone and black beret and those puffy riding pants, a movie director—holding a male bassett hound. FBI director Dick Bassett.

"Well, okay, Dick, but Woody and everybody thinks that there might be more bad guys up there. Why take the chance? I don't want more people to die."

"That is possible, Mr. President, but we have to find out who did this—all of them—and stop them. Then prosecute them. That's my job."

"Your suspects are dead, Mr. Director," the vice president quipped. "Get their DNA later."

"I thought you said there were more suspects on the plane, Mr. Vice President? If you're right, and maybe you are, they are the only ones who might be able to tell us who did this and why."

"That's obvious."

"Is it, Mr. Vice President? Why was a photo of five Middle Eastern men, supposedly Saudi nationals from New York, sent out to all news organizations by an anonymous source? The six hijackers, five men and one woman, were not the people in that photograph, which my people tell me was a fake, with a 75 per cent probability."

"I don't know yet," the vice president replied. "My guess is that the claim of responsibility and the picture were meant for whatever they are going to do with the weapons. Maybe the dead hijackers—if they are really dead—are co-conspirators, recruited precisely because they do not look like Arabs."

"Perhaps, sir, but what if domestic terrorists are trying to get us to jump to the usual conclusions?"

"Did you say domestic terrorists?" the president asked.

"Yes, Mr. President. The information I'm getting is that the passengers on Flight 1787 say the hijackers, even the Asian man, all spoke American English."

"So what?" the vice president interjected. "That doesn't mean they aren't Islamist terrorists. Sheila said all the computer attacks are coming from Bahrain and Indonesia—both Islamic countries. You have no proof."

"Well, Mr. Vice President, I could say the same about your position. You have no proof they are," the FBI chief countered. "Computer hackers can make you think they are in any country they want. In fact, we have just come across very disturbing information that may point to a domestic origin."

"What information?" the president demanded.

"How well do you know General LeBoef, Mr. President?"

"I've known Beefcake for years. He's a good man. A hero and a good Christian, no matter what the press says. He's doin' a helluva job."

"Yes sir. My agents have been unable to locate him."

"I thought he was on vacation."

"Yes sir. In Yosemite Park, according to his base. But he has a satellite phone for emergencies like this. He does not answer, according to the secretary of defense. He's not at Yosemite and no one has seen him," the FBI chief continued, reading from his computer screen. "But we just interviewed one witness, who told us he saw two young women drive into the park three days ago. One was at the wheel of a large recreational vehicle belonging to the general, the other driving a rental car. They registered at the park in the general's name and were gone the next morning. The general's empty 2003 Winnebago with Georgia plates is still there, paid up 'til the end of next week."

"What the hell are you suggesting?" the vice president asked indignantly.

"Nothing yet, except the odd fact that the general, and his family, are missing. Perhaps they have been kidnapped. I took the liberty of putting out a nationwide alert for them just now. His radical personal views, the ones that resulted in him being reduced in rank to a one-star a few years ago, are well known at this table, I believe."

"I spoke to him about that, Mr. Director," said the president. "He's a deeply religious man, a born-again Christian and, well, sometimes the spirit just takes him. That was unfortunate, what he said from the pulpit."

"Unfortunate? Yes sir, it is unfortunate when an American general in uniform tells a church full of white people that the United States is, let me get this right," the dark-skinned Director Bassett said, reading from his screen, " 'that the United States was founded by white Protestant men who called upon God to make Americans his new chosen people. America is and will always be ruled by the divine will of our Lord Jesus Christ and white, Christian men.' Yes, Mr. President, that is very unfortunate, sir, which is why he was busted in rank. I consider it very interesting that such a man, with such strong views, is missing at this critical juncture resulting from the unauthorized removal of nuclear weapons in his trust. My lead agent says the case feels like an armored car job. What he means is that most armored car robberies are either violent assaults in a public area or inside jobs. Sometimes both."

"Oh, my God," said Sheila Preston.

"But you said yourself, he might have been kidnapped," the vice president pointed out.

"Yes, until my agents at the base interviewed troops there. They just told my agents that, except for the two murdered Islamic Marines, every missing soldier from that base, up to eighteen at this moment, had participated in the same weekly group activity at the base involving a rather exclusive prayer group of officers and enlisted men. All white, all Christian. Headed by General LeBoef."

"Hell, Mr. Director, I've prayed with them myself, when I visited the base," the president said. "They are all fine, God-fearing men and all patriots."

"Yes, Mr. President, of that I have no doubt. My fear is that he and the others may define patriotism in a different way than you or I." The FBI director looked toward the vice president, who remained uncharacteristically silent.

# 41.

Ruby skipped around the plane, wondering if all plane rides were this scary or weird.

She wouldn't look at the piles of dead people. It creeped her out. She and her friend pigged out on food from the carts. They ate cookies and candy and their moms didn't say anything.

In the coach section, most passengers had helped themselves to food and collapsed, exhausted, in their seats. Half of them were asleep from the adrenaline crash and even Ruby's skipping and singing could not rouse them. The drunken couple was sleeping it off, as was the handsome honeymoon couple. They had emerged from their cramped bridal suite and were sound asleep in their reclined seats, holding hands.

Ruby knew the couple were sexing in there and giggled every time she saw them. She told the story to the other little girl about her age and pointed at the sleeping pair.

"Ewwwww," Ruby's friend mewled, and they giggled until their sides hurt.

Emily asked Ruby how old she was and said she was a grandma and used to teach kids in school before she retired. She said she hated flying, ever since she was a kid, because her dad was a sailor killed by a kamikaze pilot in World War II when she was ten. Emily explained that a kamikaze pilot was a man who crashed his plane into our ships to kill soldiers.

"Like at the World Trade Center?" Ruby asked.

"Yes, something like that," Emily said.

When the old lady said her husband had died of a heart attack almost three years ago, and other stuff, Ruby got bored and skipped away.

Ruby heard Gordon telling someone that he ran a chemical company and had homes in Darien, Connecticut, and Palm Beach, Florida. Boooring. His wife, Danielle, said she was a designer with a degree in art. Ruby asked if they had kids. Danielle said they had two, a boy and girl, who were at home with their English nanny. Ruby told Danielle that her dad was "slightly famous" for writing a series of children's books and her mom was a college professor. Danielle said she knew that already. Ruby didn't think she was very friendly and walked away.

For a while, she watched Emmett's wife yell at him. She said he wasn't interested in saving their marriage.

"Where did all this come from?" she asked him. "Since we're going to die, I'd like to know, Emmett. Cabo was our last chance and we'll never get there. All you do is pray. You want the Rapture? Here it is. Happy? God knows I haven't been getting any rapture from you."

Emmett was about to discuss blasphemy when he saw Ruby standing there, licking a Tootsie Roll Pop, watching them bicker.

"What do you want, little girl?" Emmett asked.

"Nothing. Are you a rabbi?"

"No," said Emmett, sounding quite offended. "Why would you think I'm a rabbi?"

"Because you pray all the time, like your wife says, and you don't have a uniform."

"No," Emmett's wife laughed. "He's a banker. He repossesses homes."

"What does repossess mean?"

"It means when people don't have money, he takes their homes away."

"That's mean," Ruby said, turning away.

Next Ruby talked to the big man Lester and his friend Bob, who were nice.

"Are you a football player?" Ruby asked Lester.

"Not anymore, but I used to do that in college, until my knee came apart," Lester answered. "Now I sell sporting goods. You know, basketballs, baseball bats, things like that."

"Did they fix it? Can I see?"

"Yes, they fixed my knee. Maybe later. I don't think I should take my pants off, do you?"

Ruby giggled. His friend Bob asked her about school and stuff. He said he was an engineer.

"On the subway? Cool. Can I drive the train sometime?"

"No, I don't drive a train, sweetie, but I do work for the city. I use a drawing board. I design and direct repairs of sewers and pipes."

"Booooring," Ruby said, grinning.

"Yes, it is very boring, Ruby," he agreed, with a chuckle.

"Do you and Lester live together?"

"Yes, we do."

"Are you guys gay?"

"Yes, we are," said Bob. "Is that a problem?"

"No, I know lots of gay people. Even some women are gay."

"So I've heard," Bob said, still laughing. "In fact, Lester and I were flying to Cabo to get married."

"No way."

"Yes, way."

"Do you get to wear the wedding dress?"

"Nah, we're not into that," Bob smiled. "We have matching Mexican wedding shirts."

Later, Ruby said hi to Matt, who was always playing computer games and wouldn't let her play. Neither would Teddy.

"Can I play a game now, Matt?"

"Not yet Ruby," said Matt.

"Are you a Democrat, Matt? We're Democrats."

"No, Ruby, I'm an Independent. I never got to vote for Howard Dean."

"Who?"

"Is your little friend over there also a Democrat?"

"No, I asked her. She said she's Italian. Matt, do you play computer games all the time? Are you in college?"

"No, I run a company that protects companies from people who use computers to blackmail them. In college, I studied making movies."

"They turn their mail black?"

"Ruby, what about your secret mission?"

"Oh. Sorry. I forgot. Everybody's nice, except Emmett and Danielle and Teddy," she said.

"What about that other thing?"

"Not yet," she said, running off.

Ed walked from the cockpit into the first-class area. He diverted to the starboard side to avoid the toppled beverage cart and slippery blood in the aisle where the bad guy in the Hawaiian shirt was killed. Someone had thrown newspapers onto the pool of blood and it was now a carpet of red *New York Posts*. Matt was back sitting in his old seat, using his laptop. The marshal told Matt about Alaska and the government's plan to let them keep flying. As Ed explained what he had been told over the radio, Jim and Anna, who were also sitting in their old seats, came over, as did the others.

Incredibly, there was a weak cheer from the small group up front for Ed's news that an airport was willing to let them land and would feed Ed the coordinates by radio. The marshal explained there was a storm up north but it was their best shot.

Matt hated to be the bad guy but he didn't see the government being very helpful. He felt guilty for withholding what he knew but decided he had to tell them, especially since Ed was not mentioning it.

"I don't trust them," Matt said. "Especially that Yarwood, the vice president. That guy is a total dick. My guess is they want us to continue on this course so they can get us out over the ocean. They could shoot us down without hurting anyone on the ground. We're a pariah because of what they think we have onboard."

Ed tried to interrupt but Jim cut the marshal off.

"What are you talking about?" Jim asked. "That stuff about the hijackers still being in charge? We sent them the pictures. What else do they want?"

"No," said Matt, ignoring Ed. "The fact that some nuclear weapons were stolen by terrorists from some military base down south and they think one or both of the bombs might be onboard, that's why."

"Oh, my God," said Anna.

"You have got to be fucking kidding me," Lester said. "The shit never stops."

"No. I don't know that they are onboard—just that they think that. The cop told me the jets detected radiation coming from the plane. Maybe it's all those little holes from the buckshot bullets that we can hear whistling. It almost doesn't matter if it's here or not. The hijackers are dead, so it will just sit there, right? The point is they think it's onboard—that's the problem. I think we're safe as long as we stay away from big cities and presidential ranches."

"So, we're still dead," Anna said. It was not a question.

"Metaphorically speaking, yeah," Matt said. "But I'm feeling pretty good."

Danielle crumpled onto the floor in a faint. Apparently the

prospect of death by A-bomb was more frightening than dying by any of the other ways they were still facing. Gordon and Lester helped her into a seat. Mercifully, Emmett's praying was barely audible. Ruby asked her mom what kind of bomb it was and she told her daughter she would tell her later.

"Where is it?" Bob asked.

"I have no clue," Matt admitted.

Everyone looked at the marshal.

"I only know what Matt heard. My desk refuses even to talk about it, which probably means it's true."

"They could never carry something like that onboard," said Liz. "I don't believe it. The only place it could be would be in the cargo hold and I don't think they could do that, either. Marshal, don't they check all the baggage for explosives and radiation?"

"No."

"Oh."

"All checked domestic bags are screened for explosives, not radiation," Ed explained. "The problem is passenger planes like this also carry commercial cargo and that is almost never checked for either."

"Can't we get into the baggage compartment and turn it off?" Emily asked.

"No. Only from the outside," answered Ed. "For security reasons."

"Liz," said Matt, "it doesn't matter if it's on the plane or not, the . . ."

"It fucking matters, if it's onboard," Ed disagreed. "Besides, anybody here know how to deactivate a nuclear weapon?"

"What I mean is all that matters is what the government believes or tells the people, which, fortunately, so far, isn't very much. They don't want anyone to know they lost them and are playing hide-and-seek with a Hiroshima and a Nagasaki."

"Dear God in Heaven," Emily said.

No one could think of anything to say for a while.

"So, they could give us the wrong numbers for the autopilot and make us land in the sea?" Jim finally asked.

"No, I'll know if they give me bogus numbers," said Matt, explaining the simulator and his staff working on the problems. "But I think if we don't find someplace to land this plane ourselves, we are all going swimming. Maybe it's time to let the press and the world know the really bad news—but that's a good news, bad news deal. We have to decide. Together."

"What do you mean?" Gordon asked.

"Well," Matt said, taking a deep breath. "I want to tell the press because the government is so big on keeping it a secret, for whatever reasons."

"You mean reasons like mass panic, losing all control, jammed communications, jammed roadways and transit systems, rioting, looting, rape, chaos—reasons like that," said the marshal, sarcastically.

"Yeah," said Matt, "like that."

"If we tell the media, the whole country will go nuts," said Teddy. "They'll want the government to shoot us down. If it gets out, we're dead."

"That's what I'm afraid of," admitted Matt.

"I agree," said Ed. "If they announce it, we're done."

Everyone else in the group nodded their heads.

"I don't think we should tell the others," Ed said in a low voice. "We don't need any panic."

"I don't agree," said Matt. "Everybody has a right to know, but I'll wait until I know more."

Everyone else either shrugged or nodded but said nothing, except one.

"I agree with Matt but I don't want to wait," Toni said. "I don't believe you can protect people by lying to them."

"Keep your mouth shut," Ed warned her, a clear threat. "You've made your dissent, now zip it."

"Congratulations," Toni said, sarcastically. "Our little group of thirteen is now withholding vital information and enforcing it with the threat of violence. We're making life and death decisions that affect all of our lives and theirs but only we have all the facts. We are now, officially, a government."

# 42.

Paul raced west under the elevated subway on Jamaica Avenue in Queens, lights and sirens blaring. Probably in Peoria people got out of the way for cops speeding to the scene of a crime, but drivers in New York mostly ignored them. Even if cops and ambulances and fire trucks could get through the traffic, there were always some city drivers who only let the emergency vehicles pass so they could slipstream behind them and beat the traffic. Normally, it pissed Paul off. Today, he had no time for it. Cindy, strapped in tight and holding on to the strap above the door with her right hand, had the mike in her left hand and was broadcasting over the PA system.

"Police emergency, move aside!" Cindy said over and over, her voice louder than a bull horn.

As they neared Lefferts Boulevard, they hit a bottleneck of cars up ahead, blocked by a cab across two lanes, discharging a passenger. Other cars, trying to go around, were head-to-head and honking their horns at each other in the intersection.

"Police emergency! Move aside!" Cindy ordered through the speaker.

The cabbie ignored the cops, as he was counting change for a passenger in the backseat.

Paul pulled his piece, transferred it to his left hand and pointed it out the window, up in the air, pushing off the safety. He glanced upwards, to make sure he was not aiming at the steel El tracks above.

"Not today, asshole," Paul said calmly.

He fired three shots. They sounded like a cannon and made his ears ring. The cabbie floored it up onto the empty sidewalk. The passenger got out and ran. All traffic stopped and they roared through the intersection.

"Thank you for your cooperation," Cindy announced, as they sped away. "Have a nice day."

They zipped around the traffic and sped west to Lefferts and screeched a left, going south. As they approached the intersection with Conduit Boulevard, they saw flashing lights on an NYPD Highway 2 blue-and-white, sitting at the curb near the Belt Parkway—directly behind a pink Volkswagen Beetle. The New York plate on the VW read JEN JOY. The pink chick-mobile. Bingo. Paul pulled up behind the city RMP and got out.

"Hey, Sarge, you got some hook," waved the Highway 2 guy, who was behind the wheel, talking on his radio.

In the seat behind the cop was a young woman in a white tank top with a gold crucifix around her neck and long, shiny black hair.

"Scotty, right?" Paul replied. "Hey, thanks, nice catch."

"That's the VW. The VIN matches, it's seventeen, all around. No wants or warrants for her, either. Is this your girl?" the cop asked, getting out and jerking his thumb toward the backseat.

"I don't know. Get her out."

The cop opened the back door and ordered her out but she said she couldn't because her hands were handcuffed behind her. He helped her out.

"Hello, honey," Paul said.

The girl said nothing.

"I thought we were looking for a blonde?" Cindy asked.

"We are. I'd know that cute little beauty mark anywhere," Paul said, pointing to the black dot on her face.

He reached up and snatched off the wig, freeing the blonde hair underneath.

"Jennifer Koslowski, say hi to officer Cindy Bernstein."

"I have nothing to say. I want a lawyer," Jennifer said.

"Of course you do, Jennifer," Paul said, handing the wig to his partner. "I want world peace. Cindy, put her in our car, please."

Cindy put a second pair of cuffs on Jennifer and then unlocked the Highway 2 cop's set and handed them back to him.

"Thanks. What about the car?" the highway cop asked. "It looks clean."

He and Paul walked over to the VW. Paul pulled a crumpled pair of surgical gloves from his pants pocket and put them on before he opened the door. A live yellow daisy was in the little bud vase on the dashboard. A black pocketbook was on the passenger seat. Paul snagged it and emptied it onto the driver's seat. There was a red wallet with some money and lots of coins. Credit cards, license. The picture window in the wallet had a picture of a guy with black hair and dark, piercing eyes in a white suit. Daddy? Lots of receipts, none for a bomb, and a zippered bag. Paul opened it. Makeup. A checkbook and an address book. Paul slipped them in his pocket. Pencils, pens, tissues, loose change. Sugarless gum. A cell phone. He took that, too. Nothing else. He walked around to the other door and popped the glove compartment. An owner's manual, a box of Kleenex and a small umbrella. He reached under the seats. Nothing.

"Scotty, pop the trunk, willya?"

"Sure."

Paul lifted the trunk and rooted around. A tire, a jack, her uniform, with her picture ID still clipped on. A travel bag. Only clothes and toiletries inside. No nuclear weapons. No terrorist manifesto. Another box of tissues.

"Fuck," Paul said, slamming the pink trunk.

"Yeah, nothing. I was just told to hold her for you and secure the vehicle for prints."

"Got a screwdriver?"

"Yeah, why?"

"Take off the plates before the press gets here and runs it."

"No problem, Sarge. So, you sticking around for Crime Scene and the FBI?"

"What FBI?"

"My sergeant just called me. He says a bunch of feebies are on the way, too."

"Shit. No, we're outta here. Anybody wants to know, we're transporting her to NYPD headquarters or our headquarters at JFK, you can't remember, okay? Thanks."

Paul got back behind the wheel, flipped the lights and sirens on again and pulled away fast. He told Cindy to put gloves on. Cindy opened the glove compartment. Next to Paul's yellow Zippo lighter fluid can was a flat cardboard dispenser box of surgical gloves. She put two on and Paul handed her the cell phone and the address book and check book.

"Check these out. Start with the phone. Look for last numbers dialed and jot them down. Then the address book, then the checkbook."

"Jennifer," Paul said to his prisoner. "We both know that millions of lives are at stake. I'm asking you once to do the right thing. Please tell us what you know. We need your help to stop this thing. For God's sake, help us."

"You don't know what God wants. I want a lawyer. I have the number in my address book."

"Okay. I was scared for a second you might ask me what I was talking about but obviously you know exactly what I'm talking about, don't you, Princess?"

Paul glanced at her in his rearview mirror. She was biting her lip.

"Aren't you afraid to still be in the city—with those nukes about to go off?" Paul tried. "That why you wigged out and were trying to get out of town?"

In his rearview mirror, Paul could see her smirk and look away to hide her expression.

"So they're not going to set one off here. Okay, thanks, Jennifer. That's good news."

"I didn't say anything," Jennifer protested in a panicky voice, confirming Paul's guess.

"Hey, I'm a cop. You say something, you don't say something—I'm gonna get what I want. I can read you like a comic book, sweetheart. You're in my world now and you're not good at this. The only problem, Princess? Today, I don't have time to be polite."

# 43.

Secretary of Defense Gerhardt Veissbrott briefed the president and other government agency heads about the computer assaults on DOD computers and the U.S. jet missing from Kuwait, via V-Tel link, from the underground Maryland bunker. Veissbrott said that the pilot, Marine Lieutenant Oswald Guiteau, had taken off from Kuwait at 3 p.m. local time, 8 a.m. Washington time. His mission was to ferry his replacement AV-9B jet to the USS *Nassau* helicopter landing ship in the Persian Gulf. Shortly after takeoff, the aircraft descended suddenly and vanished from the radar screen over the Gulf. There was no distress call. A later preliminary air search turned up no floating wreckage. A wider search was underway. The pilot was new to the Gulf, having arrived only three weeks earlier in Kuwait.

"I'm sorry, what was that name again?" FBI director Bassett asked.

Veissbrott repeated and spelled the missing pilot's name, as Bassett typed it into his computer at FBI headquarters. The director asked for the service file of the airman. The two men, the black former police commissioner of New York City, and the white shoe law firm lawyer from Wall Street and longtime conservative fixture in several administrations, had been oil and water from their first meeting.

"Why do you want his file?" Veissbrott demanded, bristling at the invasion of his turf.

"Routine, Mr. Secretary. I'm a cop. A dog runs across my path, I want his pedigree. We must move quickly and leave no stone unturned," Bassett smiled.

"A dog? What are you suggesting?" the vice president asked. "That this poor pilot, who is probably at the bottom of the Gulf, is somehow involved with the terrorists?"

"I'm suggesting we find out what is going on, Mr. Vice President. Mr. Secretary, can you please find out everything you can for me about this pilot and the plane?"

"Of course," Veissbrott said graciously, once the FBI director was back in his place. "But I can already tell you the aircraft was unarmed when it left Kuwait. These Jump Jets have a limited range, so I don't think that . . ."

"Jump Jet?" the president cut in. "The vertical take off and landing jets? They are really cool."

"Yes, Mr. President. But they only have a range of . . . uh . . . what is it, Colonel? Yes, one thousand kilometers, which is not quite 700 miles."

"You're sure it was unarmed?" Bassett pressed.

"Quite sure," Veissbrott said.

"Well," said Bassett on the big screen, "just thumb-nailing on a map here, 700 miles could take that jet over Iran's capital of Tehran, into the Caspian Sea, Baghdad and beyond. He could enter Syria, Jordan, Riyadh in Saudi Arabia and all the way west over to the Red Sea."

"Maybe he flew to Bahrain for tea with the king," Veissbrott suggested, sarcastically, with his well-known bemused grin. "Why would he do that?"

"I don't know. Why would one of your generals and his soldiers steal our own nuclear weapons?" Bassett asked, in the same tone.

"How dare you question me?" asked Veissbrott. "Who the hell do you think you are?"

"Nothing like that has been proved," the vice president protested.

"And it never will be if I don't have full cooperation, Mr. President," Bassett said. "Maybe that's the idea."

"Now hold on . . ." the president began.

"It is much more fucking likely that this is an elaborate plot to make a terrorist attack on this country look like something else," the vice president said, loudly interrupting his boss. "To get us to waste time doing exactly what some of us are doing and to discredit us in public."

"Hey, fellas," the president tried again.

"This government will be discredited in public—five seconds after the news of the missing nuclear weapons is made public," Bassett shot back. "Oh, I'm sorry, Mr. President."

"Is that a threat?" Veissbrott asked.

"Hey, fellas!" the president shouted. "Up here, the guy up on the screen. The one in charge. Mind if I say something?"

The bickering stopped abruptly.

"I agree with Woody," the president declared, surprising no one. "Unless we can really prove it, this is probably the Islamists trying to fake us out. They are evil bastards. But we have to let Dick do his job. We have to work together on this. No way our own people would do this. It just makes no sense."

Everyone waited to make sure the president had finished speaking. Satisfied, the secretary and the vice president sat back in their chairs. Magnanimous in victory, Veissbrott directed his aide to get the information for the director. But Bassett was not finished.

"Mr. President, I beg you to look at the facts. Islamist terrorists have no reason to hide. They are proud of their attacks. They take credit for them and then brag about them to the world. Why haven't they done so for the hijacking?"

"Because it may have failed," the vice president answered.

"So you agree now, Mr. Vice President?" Bassett asked.

"It's possible," he admitted. "But it's also possible they are still on the plane and have delayed taking credit—because they know we will blow their ass out of the sky if they do."

"Mr. President," the director continued. "Terrorists have no reason to be shy. They see themselves as soldiers in a holy war against us. The only people who would have to hide are traitors."

"I'd be very careful with that word, if I were you," Veissbrott snapped at the director.

"Are you suggesting that it is treason to investigate the suspicious actions of anyone in uniform?" Bassett asked.

"No," Veisbrott replied. "I'm reminding you that the definition of treason is giving aid and comfort to the enemy. These terrorist bunnies may be delaying taking credit because they fear the retaliation we will surely take on their bases. They need to get their people out of there before we target them. Also, they could be protecting a second wave of attacks, hoping to confuse us until those are carried out—possibly the nuclear attack itself."

"Or," the vice president continued in the same vein, "Maybe they don't intend to use the nuclear weapons but want them to blackmail us. They could do that in public—or they could use a back channel."

"All that might be true," Bassett agreed. "I agree that anything could happen. That is why I need complete and instant cooperation so we can put this together as soon as . . ."

A phone warbled in the director's command center at FBI headquarters. He excused himself to take the call, picking up a red phone handset.

Veissbrott continued updating the NSC on the computer attacks. The military computers were under assault but had been able to deal with the situation, with a few exceptions, so far. The move on civilian computers was more powerful, however.

Utilities and phone companies, cell phone systems and World Wide Web sites were under heavy attack. If it continued, he said, it could affect . . .

"Excuse, me" Bassett said, off the phone. "Mr. Secretary, could you confirm the spelling of your missing pilot's name and give me his date of birth, please?"

Veissbrott consulted with his uniformed aide, who had the flier's file on his screen. He read the name aloud, along with his date of birth.

"He comes from the same base, doesn't he?" Bassett asked.

At first, Veissbrott did not answer. He only stared at his computer screen, as the colonel whispered quickly.

"It would seem so," Veissbrott admitted. "But he left there last month, so he could not possibly be . . ."

"Mr. President," Bassett said, "that missing pilot's name, Guiteau, is also on the prayer meeting list my agents obtained in Georgia. He comes from the base where the bombs were stolen. He is also missing. He is either the unfortunate victim of an accident or a kidnapping or he is an active participant. We must assume from this point on that the latter is true—until we find evidence to the contrary."

"That what is true?" the president asked, apparently confused.

"I think we have to assume this is also enemy action," Bassett said. "And act accordingly, sir."

"What do you mean, enemy action?" the president asked.

"I don't believe in coincidence, Mr. President."

"That plane is unarmed," Veissbrott protested. "It's impossible."

"So you say, Mr. Secretary," Bassett said. "Yesterday, I'm sure you would have said that the theft of nuclear devices from the United States arsenal was also impossible. Mr. President, this is Impossible Day. We must act swiftly if we are to prevent the impossible from becoming fact."

# 44.

Matt searched online for a place to land but had come up empty. Alaska or the sea? He and the others were exhausted. Physically but, more importantly, they were mentally used up. Matt knew when his brain wasn't firing right. That was not good. His mother called and he had to take it. He lied his ass off, telling his mom he was fine and their safe landing was all set, that the TV people were just exaggerating. Why am I trying to make her feel better, he wondered? After he hung up, Matt got back into the private chat room with his staff. He had to work on the problem. As he typed, Liz asked how he was doing.

"Wiped. Is there any coffee or sugar left onboard?"

"Probably. Want some?"

"Yes, bring it all."

"Okay, Matt," she said.

Matt went back to his computer.

**Jerry:** Any luck on a new landing spot?

**Melanie:** Fuck cable, every network anchor wants you live right now. I'm not kidding. The actual guys are on hold right now. Also Hollywood studios and producers.

**Fiona:** Matt, you have GOT to look at this preacher stuff. Is he on the plane?

**Tyrell:** The zombie attack on government websites has widened to public and civilian sectors. It's huge. It's coming from Bahrain and Indo but it's all re-mailed stuff, laundered clean. Could be anybody, the Disney Organization, perhaps.

**Matt:** Everybody stop typing. The problem we have to solve first is where we land this thing.

**Fiona:** You would not believe the stuff on this guy, look at it now.

**Matt:** No. Later. He's not onboard. My brain is fried. One problem at a time. Any ideas into the public website about where to land?

**Melanie:** Yes, many. We're up to 1300 so far, mostly goofy. But one guy suggests the place where they filmed that test pilot movie, the astronauts in the desert? Here it is, The Right Stuff. Guy claims to be a pilot, says you could land at Edwards Air Force Base in California. He said it's totally flat and goes for miles and you would not have to reverse the engines, whatever that means. He said it is in the direction you are heading, more or less, in the high desert, northeast of Los Angeles. He says it is the only forgiving environment you can find.

**Jerry:** That is one great fucking idea, Matt. If you don't have to worry about doing that maneuver or running off the end of a runway, you might actually be able to pull this shit off, man. All you would have to do is plug in the numbers and then reset the unit when you drop below 1000 feet. Set it and forget it. Then shut off the engines once you're on the ground. Just coast to a stop and split.

**Matt:** I like it. If we don't do it, it won't get done. Get me the GPS coordinates and a course to that spot. Hold it, Jerry, I thought you already said I could do this?

**Jerry:** I lied. I've been trying to figure a way around this engine reversal shit but no dice. To do engine reversal, which you would know if you tried it on the simulator, you have to disengage the autopilot and take manual control. No offense, boss, but if you try that, you're dead. I've tried it seven times now and each time I try the reversal, it all turns to shit fast. Kaboom. Maybe you can do better. You always were the primo gamer. Don't try it unless you have to. This pilot's idea is gold, amigo.

**Melanie:** There is also a guy who says he runs the world's largest aerial firefighting 747 supertanker. He says he is ready to lay down firefighting foam on any runway in the West, so you, uh, don't burn up. Sorry.

**Matt:** I like that idea, too. Not burning is good. My guess is that there won't be any firefighting equipment in the middle of the desert. Let's do both. Tell him we're going to this Edwards desert spot. He can meet us there. E-mail his numbers to me.

**Jerry:** If you go to the desert base, they must have emergency equipment.

**Matt:** They might let us burn. It's like a rubber, Jerry.

**Jerry:** Better to have one and not need it instead of the other way around?

**Matt:** Exactly.

Matt, gulping coffee and chomping dark chocolate squares provided by Liz, told Ed and the others about the plan and the reasons for it. He left out the part about Jerry crashing on the computer but included the information about the 747 supertanker that had volunteered to be their flying fire extinguisher. Everyone was cautiously optimistic. The plan passed unanimously. Ed got on the radio and relayed the request to the government. After a few minutes, they called back to say they would get back to them with GPS coordinates and course information, if the landing plan was approved at the top.

"I don't like you," Ed smiled at Matt. "But you are one smart bastard."

"Gee, thanks, Ed. If I'm so smart, what am I doing on this flight?"

It took them more than half an hour, but the government called Ed back to say the plan had been approved. They relayed a long series of numbers for the course. Matt punched them into his laptop, as he read them back over the phone to Jerry on the ground—who also punched them into his machine. After a few more minutes, Jerry spoke up.

"You want the good news or the bad news first?" Jerry asked Matt.

"The good news," Matt replied.

"These are landing coordinates for a desert location in California."

"What's the bad news?"

"I just checked the map. They're not sending you to Edwards Air Force Base."

"Where the hell are they sending us?" Ed demanded.

"Death Valley."

# 45.

Paul braked hard to a stop at the curb in the southbound roadway of Lefferts Boulevard. The lights atop the PAPD car were still flashing but he had turned the siren off.

"Why are you stopping here?" Cindy asked.

Paul ignored her and hit a button on his cell phone. Cindy heard Paul ask his brother-in-law Kevin if he had anything at all.

"Nothing?" Paul asked. "Yeah, I've got her. No, nothing but my guess is it's not her. No. We don't have time. Don't ask. You know what I used to do."

He closed his phone, and slammed the steering wheel with his hand.

"Cindy, I think I should drop you off at headquarters before I transport our pretty prisoner, here."

"Why?"

Paul sighed and shot a glance back to the beautiful blonde ticket agent handcuffed in the backseat.

"Because I have an unpleasant duty to perform and I don't want you there."

"Sarge, what are you talking about?"

"I don't have time for this. You ever see *Godfather II*?" Paul asked.

Cindy admitted she had seen the movie.

"Remember when Michael Corleone asked Tom Hagen, 'I need to know you're going to come along with me in this thing

I have to do'? It was in the boathouse on Lake Tahoe?"

Technically, he and Cindy were not partners. He was her supervisor. Cindy was pissed he was doing this but she did not say it. Then she got it, what he meant. Paul watched her face as she thought about it.

"You mean, like his father did with the band leader?"

"Very good. Yes, Cindy. I'm going to make her an offer she can't refuse. We have no other choice. Hey, Princess," Paul asked his passenger. "Ever see *The Godfather*?"

Cindy suppressed a smile and winked.

"No, Cindy. No winking. This isn't good cop, bad cop. I'm serious."

The smile vanished from her face.

"But that's not like you, Sarge."

"I know, but it doesn't matter what I'm like. I'm here. I'm the guy. Turns out, I'm the perfect guy. This is the job. Actually, I don't have time to drop you off, Cindy. So, either you get out, call in a personal or a meal or you don't get out and we go. I think you should go."

Cindy looked at Paul for a full minute.

"Where are we going?" she said, at last.

"Just over the line into Brooklyn, a nice little spot on the water I know, near where I grew up," said Paul, as he rocketed away from the curb and onto the westbound belt. "I gotta take a leak."

He got off two exits later and sped through side streets back the way they had come. Cindy knew they were somewhere in the Flatlands section of Brooklyn but had no clue where they were going. She didn't ask. Soon, he went south on a dinky, deserted street. They went back under the highway, past rusted abandoned cars and piles of junk. Through a hole in a chain-link fence, they continued down the single lane, past a NO TRESPASSING sign. Marsh reeds rose up eight feet high on either side of the roadway, which was now a smelly, muddy track, without houses or street lights or people. Paul slowed, avoiding the piles of illegally dumped trash, bouncing in huge potholes in the dirt. A jet roared only two hundred feet above their heads, descending for a landing on Runway 13 Left at JFK, just to the east. The car met a solid wall of green reeds, with brown feather-duster tops, which now surrounded them on three sides, and Paul stopped. He shut off the car and turned to his prisoner.

"You didn't answer me, Princess," said Paul, taking something from the glove compartment. "Did you see *The Godfather*? You're a bit young, but it's all over cable."

Jennifer did not answer. She was looking around at the enclosing wall of reeds, her delicate nostrils flaring at the stench of low tide and sewage.

"No? Yes? Well, there's this scene where three people in a car come out to the reeds in Brooklyn. That's where we are now, and one goes to take a leak and the second guy kills the other guy," Paul said, lighting up a cigar.

The prisoner did not speak.

"So the funny part is Clemenza takes his leak and we hear shots. He goes back to the car and tells the hitman, 'Leave the gun, take the cannoli.' Funniest line in the picture. Remember now?"

Paul could see from her wide eyes that she did.

"Always nice to meet a film lover," Paul said, getting out of the car and opening the back door.

"This is where they filmed that scene, Princess," Paul said into the open door. "We're in a little piece of film history. Pretty neat, huh?"

Jennifer said nothing. Cindy said nothing but Paul was scaring her. She had never seen him like this before. She regretted not getting out of the car when he gave her the chance.

"Jennifer, please do not make me do this," Paul said. "Just tell me everything right now, okay? Things will go easy on you and we can stop this and save a lot of lives. I see you're wearing a gold cross. Obviously, you're not a Moslem. Thou shalt not kill, Jennifer. Jesus wants you to confess. It's good for the soul. What would your mother think? Just tell us where the bombs are and who is doing this."

"I want a lawyer. You have no right. You have no right. This is illegal."

Paul just laughed and dragged her roughly out of the car into a standing position in one motion. Startled, Jennifer whimpered.

"You're hurting my arm! I want a lawyer."

"No problem, Princess, they'll get a lawyer to settle your estate. Did you leave a will?"

Paul giggled as he pulled her toward a narrow cut through the reeds, over a smelly mud path, as another jet screamed by above, one of hundreds landing as America cleared the skies again. Jennifer complained that her handcuffs were too tight.

"You are too much, Princess. Get a boo-boo, did you? You know, I have a pretty daughter about your age. Only difference is, she's not crazy scum—like you. You know, you picked the wrong fuckin' guy to get busted by. A lot of my friends and brothers died the last time, because of human shit like you. And my own brothers. Phil had three kids. Dominic had two kids. Here we go."

They stopped at the edge of a small mud creek littered with garbage. Paul uncuffed his prisoner and turned her around. Her back was to the filthy stream. Paul drew his Glock, flicked off the safety. He pointed the muzzle at Jennifer's pretty face. She closed her eyes but her lips were moving. She was praying.

"Jennifer, tell him what he wants to know," Cindy said. "He's crazy."

"Another thing, shitheel," Paul told her. "You scumbags killed two Marines. I was a Marine. In Vietnam. Did you know that?"

Paul stood there, pointing his gun.

"Paul, what are you doing?" Cindy asked, her voice shaky.

"It's hot. People have their windows open. They might hear the shot for miles. We're waiting for a nice loud plane, aren't we, Princess?"

On cue, a high-pitched whine swept over the reeds and quickly built to a wave of sound, high, low and in between, assaulting their eardrums as it rolled over Canarsie toward them.

"No! Wait, Paul. She's saying something!" Cindy yelled over the din.

Paul could not hear Jennifer, so he lowered the gun and walked up to her. She was babbling the same words nonstop, with her eyes shut tight.

"God help me, God help me, God help me."

Paul removed the cigar from his mouth and put his lips next to her ear.

"God help you? Forget about it, Princess. You're in Brooklyn."

# 46.

Sheila Preston explained the new landing plan for Flight 1787 to the extended National Security Council. The marshal on the plane had requested clearance to land at Edwards Air Force Base in California but Secretary Veissbrott had vetoed the idea immediately.

"I will never open one of our bases to nuclear terrorists," Veissbrott declared. "Let them land in Death Valley or the North Pole but they aren't getting anywhere near one of my bases."

His joke quickly turned into Plan B and the hijacked plane was notified. If there were still terrorists aboard and they set off the bombs, it would happen in the middle of nowhere. The fallout was another problem. At least the weapons, if they were aboard, would not leave the country.

FBI director Bassett reported that agents had arrived at the Idaho home of General LeBoef. No one was home and the neighbors had not seen the family for more than a week.

"He's on vacation," the vice president said.

"I don't think so," said Bassett. "You also know the general, don't you, Mr. Vice President?"

"Of course I do. So does the president and the entire government."

"No, I understand you are social friends, as well, and attend the same church?"

"Well, we used to, yes. I haven't spoken to him in months.

What of it?" the vice president challenged, his face burning pink again.

"My agents from the local field office also stopped by your church but your . . . minister . . . is also away on vacation. Along with his entire flock, it seems."

"It's July, Dick. Aren't you going to Maine yourself in a few weeks?"

"Yes, Mr. Vice President, I was planning on that. It turns out we also have quite a file on this particular man of God. My agents, with probable cause—fearing more possible kidnappings—entered the church buildings, the school and residences. They're all gone. Everything, including the computers. We're talking more than a hundred people. There seems to be a remote video surveillance system in place, the kind you can access from anywhere in the world. Unfortunately, they may already know we are there. In several offices, we found shredded computer discs and a huge amount of shredded and burned documents. Any idea why your church is shredding . . ."

"Former church. No, I have no idea."

"Me neither, so, I Googled the preacher and found several interesting things. First of all, the missing General LeBoef made a rather controversial speech from the pulpit of that church a few years ago. Secondly, are you aware of some kind of fortified stronghold that this minister, your former minister, the Right Reverend Aaron Samaritan, has up in the Clearwater Mountains in Idaho?"

"I think I read something about that, yes, that's one of the reasons I . . ."

"Apparently the reverend is heavily into guns and politics. I have a hot team on the way by helicopter but it will take some time. Have you ever been to this fort of his, Mr. Vice President?"

"Of course, I haven't. What the hell do you think . . ."

"Mr. Vice President, are you aware of any particular significance of today's date—in relation to Reverend Samaritan?"

"Today? No. Why?"

"Just curious. Your former pastor seems to have some rather radical ideas. Has he ever discussed the possible overthrow of the United States government with you, Mr. Vice President?"

The vice president, red-faced, sputtered, staggered to his feet.

"How dare you, you . . . I was serving this country when you were . . . take your questions and shove them up your ass!"

"I'm sorry I offended you, Mr. Vice President. I am simply asking for your help. When was the last time you spoke to Reverend Samaritan?"

"Go fuck yourself!"

Bassett ignored that entirely and turned his attentions to the secretary of defense. He asked Veissbrott for more information on the missing pilot. Veissbrott said he had nothing of significance.

"I'll take whatever you have, Mr. Secretary," Bassett said.

Veissbrott said his aide was on the phone with the officer who bunked next door to Guiteau in the batchelor officers' quarters at the Kuwait air base in Kuwait City. He said that the missing pilot ate breakfast in the mess hall, filed a flight plan and stopped by the chapel. After lunch, he packed his kit and took off. Nothing unusual to report.

"I'd like to speak to the officer, please," Bassett said.

"My aide can ask him anything you want," Veissbrott countered. "This junior lieutenant is not cleared for all this."

"I'll be careful, Mr. Secretary. Put him on, please."

Veissbrott reluctantly did that and the officer introduced himself over the speaker phone.

"Lieutenant, I'm with the FBI. This is very important, son. Did Guiteau take anything with him on that flight?"

"Uh . . . no sir, just his overnight kit and equipment, sir."

"He didn't bring an extra bag or any cargo?"

"Uh . . . no sir, there's not too much room for cargo, sir."

The officer was obviously scared. The FBI chief wondered whether it was just the call from the secretary of defense or something else. He gave it a shot.

"Don't shit a shitter, son!" Bassett barked. "What else did he take? This is a direct order."

Before Veissbrott could protest, the lieutenant spilled.

"Uh . . . he may have taken some . . . alcohol, sir," the lieutenant blurted.

"Alcohol? Did you see it?"

"Yes sir. Oz collected it from the APO before lunch. It comes for him from the States like clockwork, sir. There's no booze on the ship and shore leave in Saudi is dry as a bone, sir. Their religion forbids alcohol. You can get it but it costs a fortune if you buy it there."

"So the military postal service delivered a package of alcohol for him and he picked it up just before his flight?"

"Uh, yes sir. Sir? Oz is a good guy, is he . . ."

"How big was it, son?" the director asked. "How big was the package. We don't have much time."

"Twelve quarts, sir. In a box. Whiskey."

"Have you ever seen the booze?"

"Sure."

"But not this time, right?"

"Uh . . . right. How did you know that?"

"I do this for a living, Lieutenant. How many bottles? How big was the package?"

"Always a dozen quarts. Say thirty inches long, maybe a foot wide."

"Not in a square box?"

"No sir, always flat like that. Because of the space where he had to put it behind the seat, sir."

"So, when he took off he had a heavy, flat, sealed box about a foot thick and thirty inches long?" Bassett pressed.

"Yes sir."

"Mr. Secretary, does that sound like your package?" Sheila Preston asked.

"That's classified," Veissbrott shot back.

"Not in this room," said Preston.

"So, did the whiskey catch fire, sir?" the lieutenant asked. "Is that what happened to Oz?"

"We don't know yet, son. But thank you for your help, Lieutenant," the director said.

A visibly angry Veissbrott warned the lieutenant to keep his mouth shut and ordered the call off speaker phone. Bassett quizzed the secretary on triggering methods. Veissbrott deferred to his aide, who explained that the portable devices were a low-end option of a SEQUOIA package of battlefield release weapons. They were equipped with digital timers for up to twenty-four hours. They could also be detonated by satellite signal. They only had five of the usual seven safety "locks."

"Are we sure about this?" the president asked up on the big screen. "That our own guys are involved?"

"Mr. President," the FBI director said, "I now think we have to assume that the plotters were able to ship one of the weapons via military post a few days ago and it was secreted onboard this Jump Jet for some as-yet-unknown reason. The other nuclear weapon is either on the hijacked jet or perhaps in a major city. We don't know."

"Let me get this straight. They mailed a nuclear weapon?"

"Through the military postal system. It looks that way, sir."

"That is not a fact yet!" Veissbrott insisted. "That is utter and possibly specious speculation."

"Okay, so, if one of them is all the way over there, that's good, right?" the president asked. "Then it can't go off here."

"Mr. President, we have to assume that whoever did this did

so with a plan. Perhaps part of that plan is nuclear blackmail by a terrorist organization or a terror state, like Iran."

"If they were going to blackmail us, I think we would have gotten a call by now," said the director. "The plane thing may have been stopped. As they descend, we will find out if the hijackers have rigged a barometric trigger to set off the device before we can reclaim it. If Islamist terrorists are behind this, which I do not believe, I would say they moved one to the Mideast so they could nuke Israel. But if this is of domestic origin, as it may be, I'm at a loss as to what their target might be."

The head of the State Department spoke up to suggest that heads of friendly governments in the Mideast should be alerted to the possible danger.

"I don't think that's a good idea, Mr. President," the vice president said. "That would open up Pandora's box. We have to keep this close to the vest."

"I do not agree," Sheila Preston said. "I believe we owe it to allies such as Great Britain and Israel. They should be given an opportunity to protect themselves and also to help us. I agree with State, Mr. President. We should take our close allies into our confidence. They may have pieces of the puzzle."

The vice president and secretary of defense each launched into multiple reasons why that could spell political and military disaster. Preston's PDA on her belt vibrated, startling the national security advisor. That never happened during such linked meetings because everyone who ever could beep her was already in the room or on a screen. She pulled it off her belt and punched a button. There was an e-mail message marked URGENT. The PDA had a security filter, which was supposed to keep out all e-mail except preapproved addresses. But Preston did not recognize the originating address, a long series of numbers and letters that contained the phrase

YMCA@amman.jordan.org. How odd. She called up the message and it flashed on the screen.

Miss Preston, One of the items you seek is likely stationary at location twenty nine point zero five seven degrees north latitude, forty three point seven eight seven degrees east longitude. Original course was southwest. Please act quickly. Message ends.

# 47.

Matt entered the new numbers into the autopilot system after trying them on the laptop simulator program first. Jerry had told him how to use the fast-forward function and Matt watched the cyber-jet fly at warp speed over the landscape, go into a dive to low altitude and make a final left turn and come in for a landing. As the computerized 767 neared the desert floor, a WARNING box appeared that said the spot was not an airport. There, the game froze. Matt was not happy. Jerry explained that the game programmers had simply not envisioned such a scenario. The simulator was not a shoot-em-up game for teenagers but a hyperrealistic teaching tool for pilots.

"In other words, it's boring," Jerry said. "No imagination. Don't worry about it."

They had no choice. Matt carefully entered the numbers in the real autopilot.

"Do you want me to doublecheck the numbers?" Teddy asked, leaning over Matt's shoulder.

It was a good idea, especially considering the marshal's head injury.

"Sure, go ahead. Make sure I did it right."

Teddy looked back and forth from Matt's laptop numbers to the real thing and then agreed that they were exactly the same. Matt looked at Ed.

"I'm ready."

"Hold it," said Ed. "Teddy, go back and tell people what

we're doing, so nobody freaks out this time, okay?"

"Okay, Marshal."

Matt waited until he heard Teddy announcing that our new vector was being entered and that we would begin to descend and turn but it was okay, we were going in for a landing soon. There was a smattering of weak applause from the few remaining passengers who still believed in a happy ending. Teddy told the other passengers they were going to land at Death Valley. Something about the kid using the word vector troubled Matt. From the coach cabin, Emmett's voice, reciting the Twenty-third Psalm, could be heard.

"Yea, though I walk through the Valley of the Shadow of Death, I shall fear no evil, for thou art . . ."

"Marshal, there's something about Teddy that bothers me," Matt said in a low voice, glancing back toward the cockpit door. "I think you should keep an eye on him."

"Teddy? He's a good kid. He has been helping us all the way. You're still pissed he took a shot at you by mistake. You missed what he did back there. He finished all those bastards off. He's got guts."

"Yeah, I know. But I think he's also weird. He has this . . . I'll talk to you later."

"Okay," Teddy said, back in the cockpit. "I told them."

Matt looked at Ed and asked the marshal if he wanted to push the button.

"Sure," Ed smiled.

"Make it so, Number One," Matt said, imitating actor Patrick Stewart's British accent. "Engage."

"What?"

"Never mind. Just a bad *Star Trek* joke. Go ahead."

Ed hit the engage button. Matt clicked on the identical simulator button at the same time. Both real and virtual autopilots bleeped. Moments later, the plane began making a gentle turn to the west. Once the turn was complete, the autopilot in the cockpit and the one on Matt's laptop screen bleeped again. The nose of the plane slowly dipped, putting the aircraft into a shallow descent.

"Any idea how long until landing?" Liz asked from the door.

Matt looked at the simulator clock on his laptop.

"If this is right, thirty-seven minutes and fifty-three seconds."

"Great."

All the coffee Liz had given Matt had worked. He was wide awake but he had to piss like a racehorse. He closed his laptop and made his way back to one of the first-class bathrooms. When he emerged, Ruby was in the seat and had his laptop open on her lap.

"Ruby, no!"

"I didn't touch anything, Matt. I was just looking. What game is this?"

"It's not a game," Matt said, taking the computer back and replacing Ruby in the seat. "It teaches people how to be pilots."

"So you and Teddy are learning how to fly the plane? Cool. Can I learn, too?"

Matt noticed that Teddy was sitting on the floor outside the cockpit, with the hijacker's laptop open again. He remembered what Fiona had e-mailed him.

"As soon as I'm done, you will be able to play games. But right now, sit down for a second, while I look something up, okay?"

Ruby plopped down at Matt's feet.

"Shall I tell you the secrets now, Matt?" she asked.

"Sure."

"When he was on the phone, Teddy was saying stuff like he was going to get to go to Hollywood or Las Vegas and get ruptured."

"What? Ruby, are you sure?"

"Yup. I read his lips from way over here. He said first we would go to the desert but then he would fly to Hollywood and get ruptured. Or Las Vegas."

"Ruptured? This is when he spoke to everybody about landing a few minutes ago?"

"No, before that, when he was on the phone with Avery Samaritan."

"Okay. Anything else?"

"He told Avery that there was only one gun left and that the marshal could barely stand up. And more praying stuff."

"Thanks, Ruby."

"Is it still secret?"

"Yup. For a little longer, thanks."

She wandered off. Matt called up the links about Teddy's minister that Fiona had logged. There was page after page of websites and articles about the Right Reverend Aaron Samaritan. Fiona had placed red stars on some of the entries to draw them to Matt's attention. The first was a magazine profile about the fundamentalist minister who wore a crown of thorns and saved souls at Texas motels, including the president. He was a former Army chaplain who left the military after he openly prayed for the defeat of all religions other than Christianity, including Islam.

A *New York Times* piece said Samaritan was an apocalyptic preacher and "Zionist Christian," who was eager for the final predicted battle of Armageddon and who had accused high members of the current conservative Republican administration of "treason, blasphemy and surrendering to the mongrel, Antichrist forces of degeneracy and liberalism."

Another article was about a fundamentalist Christian belief of Samaritan's in something called the Unitary Executive theory. Samaritan and others were pushing the idea that the President of the United States overruled all other branches of government and could, essentially, act as a king.

A red star had also been placed over Samaritan's own website link and Matt clicked on that next. The home page of GOD'S SEVENTH CHURCH OF ZION appeared. Two figures flanked the words. On the right was a photo of a puffy-faced white man with beady eyes, in a white suit and white tie, with suspiciously black hair. On the left was a white-robed image of Jesus, with eyes that looked just like the guy in the suit. Matt looked again. Samaritan's eyes had definitely been Photoshopped in. A little tune began playing and Matt smiled. "Onward, Christian Soldiers." Actually, it looked like a good website, a cut above the usual lunatic fringe site that nobody pays any attention to. There were links for Samaritan's radio and television stations, his newsletter, videos, books, retreats. The guy was a conglomerate, probably loaded. There were odd green boxes to click on, such as THE COMING BATTLE BETWEEN DARKNESS AND LIGHT as well as MOSLEM ANTICHRIST and others. There were also red rectangles with titles like INNER CIRCLE and THE THREE SEVENS.

Inner Circle sounded good, so Matt double-clicked on it. A pop-up box with a space for username and password appeared. He typed in "username" in the username spot and "password" in the password spot, hoping to find a quick way in. Instead he got an error message warning him that he was not authorized to access the site. Matt backtracked and tried THE THREE SEVENS. Same thing. If he had time, he would crack the site but he bailed out and went to the next link Fiona had sent.

It was an executive summary of a 2007 B'nai B'rith Anti-Defamation League report about Samaritan. Fiona had highlighted a section that read: "Samaritan preaches that the final battle between Good and Evil will commence on the seventh day of the seventh month of the seventh year, in keeping with his use of mystical Christian numerology, an analog of the 666 of the Old Testament. His most recent Doomsday prediction, for July 7th, 2007, failed to come true. However, that has not dissuaded Samaritan from predicting a future Armageddon on that date."

Matt looked at his watch. The little square windows for the day, month and year were perfectly aligned: SAT JUL 7. This was the seventh day of the seventh month, Matt realized.

Today.

# 48.

Paul raised the weapon when the next plane approached. He ordered the trembling blonde woman to open her eyes but she did not. The noise rose until the ground shook and Paul fired. Jennifer screamed and fell onto the muck of the shoreline, as black stuff sprayed all over. She lay motionless on her back in the foul mud, her blonde hair in the oily water.

"Jesus, Paul!"

"Relax, Cindy. She just fainted. You saw me fire into the mud."

"It doesn't smell like mud. It smells like shit. I'm wearing it."

"Help me get her up," Paul ordered, ignoring the complaint.

They pulled the unconscious ticket agent into a standing position. Paul pinched her nose between his left thumb and forefinger and Jennifer's eyes popped open. She looked at them like she had no idea who they were or where she was.

"Welcome back. You are a lucky girl," Paul said in a sympathetic voice. "You have been born again. You were just about to tell us about the bombs—where they are and who has them, remember?"

"Yes. No. I can't," Jennifer said, looking back and forth between them.

"Sure you can. It's easy. We're here to help you. Where are they?"

"I can't. He would . . . I can't," she sobbed.

"Now we're getting somewhere. I told you, Princess, I can

read you like a comic book. I fought the Viet-fucking-Cong when I was younger than you. You are a day at the beach. I know you, Princess. I know what you're thinking. You're a sad, lost little girl who is probably doing it for a boyfriend or some daddy figure or both. You might die for whatever thing it is you have been told but you don't want to be hurt. Or disfigured. Am I right?"

Jennifer watched Paul like he was a cobra, her mouth open.

"For example, right now, you think I'm psychic or something, right?"

She did not disagree. She gazed, stunned, mesmerized.

"Or maybe you think I'm the devil?"

"God help me."

"Enough with the God shit. Bite your tongue. His name in your mouth is a sin. You think you can go to Heaven with this on your soul? Are you high? You are going straight to Hell, missy. In fact, it's time you got a little taste of what your new home will be like. Take off your top."

"What?" Cindy asked.

"Cindy, help her take off her shirt."

Paul looked at his partner. Cindy hesitated but then pulled Jennifer's T-shirt up over her head. It stank from the swamp mud and Cindy tossed it back toward the more dry muck on the path.

"All of it," Paul ordered, waving the gun at Jennifer's pretty white camisole bra.

"Paul . . ." Cindy started.

"ALL OF IT!"

Cindy stripped that off and Jennifer stood naked to the waist. Her pink nipples were slightly elongated. There was another black beauty mark on her pale left breast. The blonde hugged herself to hide her chest.

"Nice rack. God made that. Such a shame. One more time,

Princess—who and where?"

"I can't . . . I should die before . . . he . . ."

"No, Princess, you misunderstand me. I'm not going to kill you. I think you like the idea of a quick martyrdom too much. But I notice you don't like to be hurt. Funny, isn't it? From experience, I am totally against torture but there is an exception to every rule, Princess, and this is it," Paul told her. "You're right-handed, aren't you? Hold out your left arm."

Paul tossed his stogie into the stream. Jennifer held her left arm out to Paul, using her right to cover her nakedness.

"No, out to the side all the way up," Paul said, as he holstered his Glock and stepped back, moving Cindy away also.

"That's good. Hold it there, please. See how long you can hold it steady, okay, Princess? Great, thanks. Like I said, unless you let us help you, you are damned, so I want you to imagine what it's like to burn in hell before you actually go there. I want you to know what the millions of people you are about to kill will feel when those bombs go off and burn them alive. Close your eyes, please, and imagine what it would feel like if you arm were on fire, okay? Can you try that? Keep your eyes closed. Great."

Paul quickly pulled something from his right pocket with his right hand and something larger from his left pocket with his left hand. He aimed his left hand at Jennifer's arm and a clear liquid arced over to the blonde's arm. At the same time, he flicked open his lighter against his leg, snapped the wheel and tossed it forward. The lighter hit her elbow and fell onto the ground. Her arm popped into blue flames. Jennifer opened her eyes wide and looked at the sight in complete disbelief, like she was a kid witnessing a magic trick. Paul placed his shoe on Jennifer's arm on the front of her chest and shoved her off the bank. She splashed backwards into the dark water and vanished.

"My God, Paul!" Cindy yelled.

Paul's open lighter, now out, and the yellow can of lighter fluid were sitting in the mud. Jennifer erupted from the fouled stream, which was only a few feet deep, clawing for air. Paul planted his feet on the muddy bank.

"Give me your right hand," Paul told the dripping girl.

She held out her left arm. It was pink and smelled of burnt hair.

"No, Jennifer, your other right arm. That's it. You're fine now. We're police officers. We're here to help you. Welcome back from Hell. Scary, wasn't it?"

"Yes."

Paul pulled her back up. Jennifer looked at her pink arm, with a puzzled expression. She did not try to cover her breasts.

"Jennifer, I've decided you're right. You have been very brave. You did what he told you to do. Nobody wants your pretty breasts to catch fire next, or your face. So, we all have decided that you don't have to tell me anything."

"Okay," she said vaguely.

"You're going to tell Cindy."

"Okay."

"I'm going to go over there, so I can't hear, okay?"

"Okay," Jennifer said, turning to Cindy. "They were supposed to blow up the president because he is a traitor and a sinner. The other one is to destroy the shrine and the city of the Antichrist," she told the female cop.

Cindy was so shocked by the flaming event and by the sudden change in their prisoner that she was momentarily at a loss for words.

"Uh . . . right. Okay. We heard about the plane trying to do that. What city are you talking about?" Cindy asked.

"Mecca."

"Jee-sus," Paul said.

"You mean . . . like in Saudi Arabia?" Cindy stammered.

"Of course. God told him that we must do this to the city of the Antichrist, the enemies of God. First the purifying fireball for the traitor in the White House and then the same for the Black Cube. Each will blame the other and God's Final Plan will begin."

"I see. Uh . . . who is he? Who is doing this, again?"

"The Right Reverend Aaron Samaritan," Jennifer explained. "The opener of the Seven Seals."

"I know that name," Paul said. "The plane. Matt. Cindy, please ask Jennifer where the good reverend is right now."

"He's at the stronghold in Idaho, opening the First Seal."

"Cindy, please ask our friend Jennifer at what street address this seal opening is taking place in Idaho."

"My arm stings," Jennifer said.

"I'm sorry. We'll get you something for that," Cindy said. "Here, put your clothes on and we'll go get the first-aid kit from the trunk. Let me help you, Jennifer. What was that address?"

Jennifer gave Cindy the name of a street without a number in Samaritan, Idaho.

"The town has the same name as your reverend?" Cindy asked.

"Yes, he bought the whole town and renamed it."

"Cindy, please ask Jennifer how they are getting the second bomb to Saudi Arabia."

"I don't know. What happened to the hair on my arm? Eeee-www, it stinks."

Paul flipped open his phone and hit last number dialed. He stooped to retrieve his muddy lighter.

"Kevin? Paul. My witness says the guy behind this is a mutt by the name of Reverend Aaron Samaritan. Yeah, like in the Bible. She says he is in a stronghold on Bitter Well Road in Samaritan, Idaho, if there is such a place. Correct. Go ahead.

There is? Good. The ticket agent says he bought the town and named it after himself. That guy, Matt on the plane, he asked me about this reverend a while ago. No, no clue. Okay, if he exists and the address is real, then we got it. Wait, she says they wanted to blow up the president first and then use the second bomb to nuke Mecca in Saudi Arabia. No, I'm not. Yes. She said she does not know. She said each will blame the other. This asshole is trying to jump-start the Apocalypse, Kevin. Yeah. Why don't we check before she lawyers-up? Good. Can you rig that fast? Hold on."

Paul pulled out Jennifer's cell phone and displayed the phone number, which was in the 718 area code. He read the full number back to Kevin.

"Got it?" Paul asked Kevin. "How long will that take? Really? Damn, that's fast. It takes us weeks. Okay, I'll try it now and get back to you. Go get the prick."

Paul redialed Matt's number on the plane. He got voice mail.

"Hi, this is Sergeant Paul Ambrosino. Why did you ask me about this Reverend Samaritan? We now think he is behind all of this. Call me as soon as you can."

Back at the car, Cindy had dressed Jennifer and was putting burn cream on her arm, which seemed incredibly normal, except for what looked like a bad sunburn. She asked how her arm got burned.

"Chemical burn. When you fell in that polluted water. We'll have a doctor look at it later, okay?"

"Okeydokey."

"How are you feeling, Jennifer?" Paul asked.

"Okay, except my arm stings and is hot."

Paul held up the cell phone he had taken from her Volkswagen.

"Jennifer, do you feel up to making a quick phone call?"

# 49.

Sheila Preston reported that the mysterious e-mail she had received appeared to have originated from a YMCA in Amman, Jordan.

"It's an obvious hoax," the vice president said.

"Actually, although we do not know from whence the message came, one of our FIELD HOCKEY radar satellites has just now located a small aircraft at the precise location mentioned in the message," Veissbrott said. "It is, in fact, the same type of plane. Colonel, could you put that up on a screen, please?"

"It could still be a hoax," the vice president insisted.

"That is within the realm of possibility, George, but we cannot take that chance," said Veissbrott. "Colonel?"

"Yes sir. The aircraft is apparently secreted in this very small valley in a very large, remote desert area called the An Nafud, as you see in this real-time imagery. That location is also consistent with the earlier reported southwest course from Kuwait. The infrared signature—that glowing there in the afterburner and nacelle areas—is consistent with an aircraft that landed and has been idle for several hours. We need more than eyes on this, fast, Mr. President. We can scramble fixed wing from Kuwait and be there in about twenty minutes, sir."

"Do it," the vice president ordered.

"Absolutely, I agree," the president said.

"Yes sir, Mr. President."

"Mr. President, I would like to apologize," Veissbrott declared. "I am responsible for this terrible situation. My service has been used and corrupted, it would seem, and I had no earthly clue. You have my resignation at the earliest convenient moment, Mr. President, if you so desire."

That stopped all chatter in the bunker and elsewhere.

"Stop foolin' around, Pappy. This is not your fault. You're doin' a great job."

"Mr. President, I wish that were true. I will do my utmost. I hope it is good enough."

There was an awkward silence in the underground stronghold. Lieutenant Alice St. Thomas broke into the void, to point out that the television news channels had the story.

"What do you mean, they have the story, Alice?" the vice president demanded. "What story?"

"The story, sir. The nukes. But they got it wrong, as usual."

She put CNN up on one of the screens, with audio. A red NUCLEAR ALERT banner stretched across the top of the screen. The announcer said the office of Homeland Security had announced that Saudi Arabian terrorists had apparently smuggled a homemade nuclear device aboard hijacked Flight 1787 but that U.S. marshals had foiled the plan and, along with the passengers, killed the Islamist terrorists. The announcement also said the entire American government and military was on full alert to locate any other possible weapons of terror and protect the public.

A shot of a press release under the official OHS letterhead appeared on the screen.

"What the fuck is this?" fumed the vice president.

"We didn't put out any press release!" the Department of Homeland Security chief protested. "It's not true!"

"At least they don't have where they came from," Veissbrott offered.

"True," the vice president agreed. "I'm going to rip those assholes at CNN a new asshole. The full Dan Rather treatment."

"Mr. President," said Sheila Preston, "even if we deny this, there will now be mass panic. We have to take measures to deal with that, sir."

"Sheila is right. But I think we have to continue to deny the story until we are on top of this," the vice president added. "Until the plane is down and we find out what's going on in Kuwait."

Preston agreed and said that if the weapons were not secured by nightfall on the East Coast, the president might have to suspend habeas corpus and impose a curfew.

"Something strange on Fox," Alice announced, changing the channel on the screen.

A man with milky skin and jet black hair appeared. Across his chest, a LIVE logo and his name: Right Rev. Aaron Samaritan. The clergyman, who was sitting in a windowless room in front of an American flag, was praising the work of the government, especially the brave marshals, for ending the hijacking on the plane.

"I support the remaining moral members of our government in their crusade against the godless Islamist terrorists—again from Saudi Arabia. In fact, I urge the president to make a preemptive strike at the heart of this plague as soon as possible, before they hit us again. My contacts tell me that is even now being debated in the high halls of power. America would be completely justified in using the terrible might God has placed in our hands to destroy this Evil. God bless America. That is the end of my statement."

"Who's running this candy store?" FBI director Bassett wondered out loud.

"That good ol' boy is as crazy as a shithouse rat," the

president chuckled. "Like we'd nuke our oil."

No one chuckled with him.

Turner Black tugged at the vice president's elbow.

"What?"

"It's him again. Samaritan. He just sent you an e-mail with a video attachment."

"Tell him to shove it up his ass."

"I can't. You need to look at this," Black said, swiveling the screen toward his boss.

> Let the hijacked plane land safely. Call off the fighters. Do nothing. There is nothing that can be done. Any other course will result in the attached video file being released to the press and the government immediately. I know you will do the right thing. God bless you.

"What video?"

Black opened the attached file and handed the vice president an earbud headset. The video was grainy. The vice president and Samaritan were sitting in two easy chairs, chatting. Their haircuts and clothing were different. The vice president was somewhat slimmer, making it obvious to a careful observer that it had been filmed years earlier. There were glasses of whiskey in their hands.

"Mr. Vice President," Samaritan said, "this country has always been ruled by white, Anglo-Saxon Christian men. God is outraged by the rampant perversion in Hollywood and New York, even in the government. What can we do?"

"Well, R.R., as you know, the Declaration of Independence preserves our right to alter or abolish the elected government," the vice president responded.

"Exactly. What we need is a new revolution to clean out all the queers and traitors and miscegenationists. You know, I saved the soul of the president but he seems to have lost it again."

The usually calm, sleepy eyes of the vice president widened, as he watched.

"Well, between you and me, R.R., he's not so much lost as forgotten," the vice president guffawed in the video. "Don't you worry about Junior. He does what I tell him."

The video froze. The vice president gasped.

"Fuck! We were alone in that cabin. That's impossible!"

"You mean the video is real?" Black asked.

"No."

"So, it's a fake. Thank God," Black said. "So we can tell everyone that he is trying to . . ."

"Hold on, Turner. Of course it's fake. I mean, I was there but I never said anything like that. They must have fiddled with the sound. That goes without saying. But if we let this out, all hell will break loose. This is a fucking set-up. Let's not fall into their trap. Let's just keep this to ourselves right now, okay? This could be the Democrats."

"Working with Samaritan? Are you sure, sir?"

"No, I'm not fucking sure. Goddamnit."

"Mr. President," Colonel Gunning said. "The Jump Jet just started his engines!"

"In Kuwait? Fast work, Colonel. Great," the president replied.

"No sir. The Harrier out in the desert. We're scrambling F-16s from Kuwait. I don't have engine start there yet. They're just getting the orders now. Damn. He's already dusting off, Mr. President. You can see it on the screen."

"Shit!" said Sheila Preston, who never cursed.

"What do we do, Colonel?" the president asked.

"Alert the Saudis right away, sir, they have an air base much closer."

"Are you seriously suggesting we tell the Saudis that a mutinous U.S. Air Force officer with a nuclear weapon is inside their country?" the vice president asked.

"Tell them what you want, sir, but do it quickly. It looks like he's done waiting. He's in the air. He's heading southwest again. That would take him toward the Red Sea. But he'll run out of fuel when he gets there. The problem is, the F-16s may not catch him."

"Do it!" Preston said.

"Mr. President?" the colonel asked.

"Yes, but don't tell them about the bombs, right?"

"Yes sir."

"Mr. President. He may be heading for Mecca," FBI director Bassett announced, hanging up his red phone. "NYPD has located a member of this conspiracy and she has confessed that one weapon is aboard Flight 1787 and the other is to be used to destroy the Islamic holy city, which is where our plane is now headed. This Samaritan character is apparently trying to start a war, Mr. President. A holy war to trigger Armageddon."

"Holy shit," the president said. "Are you sure about this?"

"As sure as I can be. It comes from good people on the ground. They're in the process of obtaining hard evidence but I think the performance we just saw by that kooky preacher says it all, sir."

"Colonel, can the Saudis catch him?" the president asked.

"Probably, but I doubt they'll take him down."

"Why?"

"Our guys are too good."

Everyone started talking at once: the president, the vice president, the secretary of state, Preston, Veissbrott, and others.

"This may force our hand, here," the vice president said loudly, in his booming baritone, getting to his feet, sweat dripping down his face. "If we are presented with a fait accompli—a detonation here or in Saudi Arabia—we will have to protect ourselves. I suggest we consider preemptive strikes against Iran and possibly Pakistan. Anyone who could seriously hurt us with weapons of mass destruction."

"That is completely irrational," Preston observed, breaking her usual habit of discretion. "That makes no sense, Mr. President."

"I'm afraid I am forced to agree," said Veissbrott. "We have to concentrate on preventing this before we start picking other targets."

"Mr. President," the colonel jumped in, "the director appears to be correct. The Jump Jet course is flying directly toward Jedda, which is the international airport serving Mecca. That is a course that would not arouse undue suspicion and would put him within a few air-minutes of the shrine, which is a no-fly zone. We are alerting the Saudis and providing them with the aircraft type, location, course and speed. Mr. President, I suggest we issue a flash traffic message to our forces that hostilities may be imminent."

"Sir? Are you okay?" Preston asked the vice president.

The vice president was still standing at his place, red-faced, muttering curses and tugging at his shirt.

"I'm fucking great."

His eyes rolled up in his head and he bounced off the conference table and hit the floor with a distinct thud. He disappeared from his video box on the wall screen.

"Oh, my God!" said Preston. "Someone get the medics."

"Woody?" the president called from the big screen. "Where'd ya go, buddy?"

# 50.

Matt stared at the screen, gaping at the information about Samaritan's belief that the end of the world would happen today. Talk about a self-fulfilling prophecy.

Teddy.

Matt looked up. Teddy was typing away on his laptop. He seemed calm. Ruby was sitting next to him on the floor outside the cockpit, looking at the screen, and giggling. Matt heard a third voice, also, on the audio line of Teddy's machine. There was a commotion back in coach. Matt noticed that CNN had a NUCLEAR ALERT warning on the screen. Matt saw the crawl letters on the bottom of the screen: "TERROR A-BOMB MAY BE ON HIJACKED JET, HOMELAND SECURITY SAYS." The rest of the passengers were just learning about the bombs. Matt could hear Jim and the others trying to reassure the passengers that there was no danger. A pop-up flashed on Matt's laptop screen with a little tone just like a doorbell chime.

> You have an urgent instant message from A. Samaritan. Please click to read message.

Matt got a chill. The originating address was "breadcrumbs.02" The same name as the programs on the hijackers' laptop. He clicked on the box and the IM window opened.

> Hi, Matt. I know your secret. Say nothing and do noth-

ing until landing.

Or you will all perish in the fire.

Matt typed "Who is this?" and sent it.

A. Samaritan. You tried to contact our website.

The same guy on the phone? Fuck you. You want to kill us all anyway.

No, we will set you free.

Who is we?

We will set you free.

Bullshit. I don't believe you.

Matt cradled the laptop in his left hand, waiting for him to reply. He stood up and took a step toward the cockpit, toward the marshal. Another message popped up:

Sit down. Believe this.

Matt froze in his tracks. How could Samaritan on the ground know whether he was sitting or standing? He looked over at Teddy. The youth was now glaring coldly back at him. His laptop was still on his lap but one arm was now around Ruby. Over her shoulder, unseen by the eight-year-old, Teddy wiggled one of those black half-moon blades, just inches from her throat. Matt sat back down. Teddy typed. A few seconds later, another message appeared on Matt's screen:

Good. Stay there. Stay quiet.

It was Teddy, pretending to be Samaritan? Teddy was sending his instant messages up to a satellite, down to the ground, back up to a satellite and into Matt's laptop, from about thirty feet away. Something out the window caught Matt's eye. Purple and

black mountains were level with the descending plane. A huge jet, a 747, floated into view. "FLAME TAMER" was painted in fiery red letters on the side. It waggled its wings and pulled ahead, out of sight. Matt's phone began to ring. It was the flying fire extinguisher guy. Ed was probably busy talking to him on the radio. The computer said he was calling Matt. They were much closer to the ground but Matt couldn't tell how low they were. Under one thousand feet the autopilot's Autoland function had to be reset manually or they would fly into the ground. Matt looked at the running simulation program. The virtual altitude gauge, in thousands of feet, read 5.630. Five thousand, six hundred thirty. It was rapidly rolling backwards.

"Matt?"

It was the marshal, calling from the cockpit, wondering why Matt was not there.

"May I have your attention, please?"

It was Liz, back in the coach section, on the loudspeaker.

"We are on final approach. Please return to your seats, restore them to their upright position and fasten your seatbelts tightly. Close your tray tables and prepare for landing, please."

"Leave her alone, you sack of shit," Matt said out loud.

Teddy's face filled with rage. He shoved the laptop aside onto the floor and jerked Ruby upright. His left hand was around her neck with the blade.

"Hey," said Ruby. "That hurts."

"Take any pillows, blankets or coats and put them on your laps," Liz continued over the loudspeaker. "When I tell you, I want everyone to double over forward and put your heads to your knees to brace for landing. If you wear dentures, please remove them now. Everyone take off your shoes right now."

Matt put his computer aside. He had no choice. If he waited, they would all die. He stood up.

"I told you to sit down," Teddy said.

"So is Samaritan behind all this, Teddy, or is it just you and your friends, pretending to be him?" Matt asked.

"We're not pretending."

"You were in the Instant Message just now. You claimed you were A. Samaritan."

"I am. Aaron Theodore Samaritan. Junior. I am his only begotten son."

"Oh, my God!" Anna screamed.

"Momma!" Ruby yelled back, struggling to break free of Teddy's grasp.

"What the hell is going on?" Jim demanded, rushing forward. "Let her go!"

"Nobody move!" Teddy warned.

Matt moved slowly forward, ignoring Teddy. When Teddy yoked Ruby so tightly she gagged, Matt stopped a few yards away. The marshal was calling from the cockpit, asking what was going on but he could not see the scene in first class. Teddy looked toward the cockpit and Jim started moving again.

"MARSHAL!" Teddy yelled. "Get out here!"

Teddy tossed the black blade toward Matt, who instinctively tried to catch it. At the same time, Teddy shoved Ruby violently toward him. The blade cut Matt's clutching hand, as Ruby slammed into him. They staggered backwards. Ruby's young reflexes tugged Matt back, just as the marshal emerged from the cockpit. The marshal saw Matt grabbing at Ruby, who seemed to be trying to get away and Matt bobbling the hijacker blade, as it fell to his feet.

"Marshal," Teddy yelled, "Matt's one of them! He's trying to hurt the girl!"

Ed pulled his gun and leveled it at Matt, as Matt and Ruby tumbled onto the floor. Matt and Ruby and her parents were all saying no at once but Ed didn't get it.

"I knew it," Ed said, "I . . ."

Teddy smashed his arm cast across the back of Ed's head. It sounded like a baseball bat hitting a watermelon. He did it again and again and again, the cast and Ed's skull cracking. Ed went down like a tree and Teddy was on top of him. The others rushed forward but Matt and Ruby blocked the way. Teddy popped up with Ed's gun in his right fist. Everyone froze. Ed did not move at all. Teddy ordered them back and squatted down, ready to fire. Ruby ran to her mother and they all backed up. Teddy used his left hand to pull apart the cast on an arm that was obviously never broken.

"Teddy said he was a pilot and was going to fly us to Hollywood," Ruby said. "He's crazy."

"In the name of God, stop it," Emmett pleaded, walking forward up the other aisle, over the bloody *New York Post*s on the carpet.

"I am doing this in the name of God," Teddy replied.

"I thought you were a hero. You helped us save everyone," Emmett said.

"You're not heroes. You just want to save your skins. We will save the righteous and destroy all evil. The war begins today."

"No," Emmett said, "I am no sinner. Teddy, please think. What would Jesus do?"

Teddy seemed to consider that for a few seconds and then he fired. The round hit Emmett's wrist, ripping his right hand off. The second shot hit his chest and he tipped backwards onto the carpet, face up, pouring out blood.

"Oh, my God! Emmett! Sweetheart!" Emmett's wife, Valerie, wailed, running up the same aisle and standing over her dead husband. "You're one of them, Teddy? You killed my Emmett, you evil bastard. I'll kill you!"

"Stop!" Teddy ordered.

"I'll kill you!" she repeated, stepping over her husband's body and walking steadily toward Teddy, her bare hands held out to choke him.

Teddy fired again, aiming up. It struck her left breast and she spun around. She hit the floor, dead, lying next to Emmett, an arm over him.

"Who's next?" Teddy asked.

No one moved. He picked up the blade and ordered them back into the coach cabin, down the aisles.

"You know the drill," Teddy said. "Everyone to the back of the plane. Except the children, this time. They stay with me, just in case you decide to try anything. If you do, I will fire through your children and kill you. If you cooperate, I will let you all free when we land. If you come at me, I have a lot of bullets. I will do whatever God requires of me. Your choice."

Teddy moved everyone back into coach and gathered the kids around himself, seven of them, including Ruby. They held hands and formed a daisy chain around Teddy, facing outward. He ordered the men to put two carts back to block the aisles. But this time, they were tipped onto their sides, spilling out the soda cans and booze and cups back toward the passengers, who were prisoners once again. Even with the plane angled down the heavy carts could not be used again as battering rams. Teddy stood, triumphant in the open area, surrounded by the children.

"The seventh day of the seventh month," he beamed, ecstatically. "And seven little children as my shield and buckler. God's will be done."

Teddy moved his entourage over to the port side porthole in the exit door and peered outside. There were mountains all around. He looked at his watch. Right on schedule, the plane made a gentle turn to the left and came around to almost due south, to align with the long axis of the landing area. The turn brought the port windows down, giving everyone a view of the ground, a white hot sea of sand. The plane leveled off. Still nosing gently downward, the jet descended into the mountainous bowl, toward the shining desert floor below.

Death Valley.

# 51.

Vice President George Franklin Yarwood was flat on his back. His face was no longer pink, it was blue-gray. His eyelids again looked sleepy, his face calm. Two officers performed CPR on his unresponsive body without effect. Moments later, military medics arrived with a gurney and rushed him to the infirmary.

"How's Woody doin'?" the president asked from the screen.

No one answered for a moment.

"It appears to be a heart attack," said FBI director Bassett. "They're not getting a pulse, Mr. President. But the doctors here are the best. They're working on him now."

"Christ on a crutch, I can't believe this," the president said, shaking his head.

Preston's PDA vibrated on the conference table. She had a new message, again from the YMCA in Jordan:

> Miss Preston, your target is on the move.
> Can you stop it? Yes or no?

The national security advisor quickly typed a reply and sent it back to the mysterious source:

> Who are you? How do you know this?

Loyal friends. For good reason, I can only tell you in person. We are on the same side. Waste no time trying to find out who or where we are. You need help. That is a lovely pearl necklace you are wearing. Please, can you stop it? Yes or no?

Preston's manicured hands automatically went to the distinctive water pearl strand around her neck. She had just bought it on vacation a week earlier and was wearing it for the first time to work today. She looked around at other members of the government but no one was looking at her. All of the other faces in their screen boxes, the other agency heads, could also see her. It couldn't be any of them. This was not the time or place for a childish prank. The FBI director was talking to the president. Preston looked at her image on the screen, her pearl necklace sparkling. They are watching our live secure video link, she realized. That was impossible. Or, it was supposed to be. Who could do that?

"Excuse me, Mr. President," said Colonel Gunning. "Our F-16s are on the way. The Saudis are also in the air and we have directed them toward the Jump Jet. We have also tried to reach the pilot on the radio. No answer, sir."

"So, I have to give the order to shoot him down?" the president asked.

"No sir. Our guys are still out of range. The Saudis will get first shot at the Harrier."

"What do the Saudis think is going on?" the president asked.

"Well, sir, I told them the truth. I told the head of their air command that one of our planes went missing from Kuwait and was flying toward Jedda and did not respond to our commands. The Saudi general asked me if we thought it might be anoxia."

"You mean, you told them he passed out because his oxygen cut off?" the president asked.

"Yes. Well, no sir. He asked and I said we did not know but anything was possible."

"We should tell them the truth, Mr. President," Sheila Preston protested. "They need to know. They might waste time trying to raise the pilot on the radio or something."

"No they won't," the colonel disagreed. "I also told the general that anything was possible and that we understand that they will have to take direct action to protect their country. They deserve that, sir. Believe me, he got the message. As you can see from the tactical big board, three Saudi fighters are heading toward the Jump Jet. Considering all that is going on, I got a hundred bucks that says those one hundred choppers they got lined up for the Royal Family at the Bin Sultan airbase are warming up right now."

As the colonel spoke, the Jump Jet figure vanished off the big screen. Instantly, dozens of other jets appeared over the An Nafud Desert, heading in the same direction.

"Uh-oh. Sorry, the Jump Jet has turned on his ECM jamming," the colonel said. "He went stealthy and is propagating all those phony bogies to confuse the Saudis. Now he'll speed up and change course and altitude. Hold on a sec. Let me take his ghosts off our screen. There you go."

The fake targets disappeared from the screen and the Jump Jet appeared again, along with the three Saudi jets. As the colonel had predicted, the Jump Jet was performing a hairpin turn away from the approaching fighter planes, back the way he came.

"Is he running away?" Preston asked.

"No, Ma'am, sorry," the colonel replied. "He's in combat mode. He'll do a paper clip maneuver and jog back onto his original course once he loses them. Yeah, there he goes. Shit. Excuse me, Ma'am. I'm directing the AWACS plane that is feeding us this data to vector the Saudis toward the Jump Jet because he is totally spoofing their radars. They can't see him. This is a problem."

"And, by a problem, you mean what, Colonel?" Preston pressed.

"Well, Ma'am. Our guy is pulling heavy G's and doing the paper clip. Yup, here he comes back the other way. Except this time, he's not aimed at Jedda. He's vectored right at Mecca, Mr. Director. He's going down to coconut level, pedal to the metal. This boy is good."

"Colonel."

"Look at the screen, Miss Preston, the Saudis are chasing the ghosts. By the time they figure it out, he'll be there. Mecca has a ring of SAM 6 antiaircraft missile locations but he's too good, too low and too fast. He'll get into the city but they'll get him coming out."

"What if he doesn't plan on coming out?" Bassett asked. "What if he just wants to detonate the bomb over the city of Mecca? And himself with it?"

"Then he wins," the colonel said.

"So, can we stop him?" the president asked.

"I'm sorry to say I think that is very unlikely, Mr. President," the colonel responded. "Mr. Secretary, as we discussed, I recommend we issue a NUDET warning. A flash traffic message to our forces that nuclear detonations may be imminent. It could save lives, sir."

"American lives?" the president asked.

"Yes sir."

"Okay. How many people live in Mecca?" the president asked.

"More than a million and a half," the secretary of state answered. "Fortunately, it is not holy month, or you'd have a million more civilians there on pilgrimage."

"Oh," the president said. "That's still a lot of folks."

"Mr. President," said Veissbrott. "The infirmary just called. They tried their best. George . . . Vice President Yarwood is dead."

"I can't believe it," the president said. "That's impossible. Woody can't be dead."

There was a moment of silence.

"I would like everyone to join hands and lower your heads in prayer," the president said.

The president joined hands with his Secret Service agent and his political aide. A large portion of the United States government at the table in the bunker joined hands, as the leader of the free world prayed for Jesus to welcome the soul of George Yarwood into Heaven.

Preston did not join hands with the secretary of defense when he reached out. She respectfully bowed her head and looked down at a black shoe on the carpet, next to an empty chair. One of the vice president's. Who could be watching us, Preston wondered? Was it this psychopathic minister and his lunatics? Why would they give away the fact that they were watching our secret deliberations, taking the risk that we might lock them out? If it was the terrorists, what harm would it do to reply truthfully? She could think of none. Preston found it hard to believe that these Christian terrorists were capable of eavesdropping on the most secure channels of communication in the world. Might there be greater harm in not responding? She picked up her PDA and sent a reply message out to her unknown source:

No, it seems we cannot stop it. The answer is no.

# 52.

Matt, along with Jim and Anna and Lester and Bob and Gordon and Danielle and Toni, was back in the rear of the plane again.

"We have to rush him now," Matt said. "I have to get up there and reset the autopilot in a few minutes or we're done."

"Did you hear Ruby?" Jim asked. "She said Teddy was a pilot and was going to fly us to Hollywood or Vegas."

"But no one is a pilot, we asked everybody before," Danielle protested.

"He lied, Danielle," Gordon told his wife. "He's one of them."

"Oh. Well, he said he'd let us go."

"He's lying," Matt said. "But maybe not about Hollywood. That sounds like the kind of place these right-wing Bible beaters would want to nuke. Also Vegas."

"But he helped us kill those people," Danielle insisted. "It was his idea to make signs so the fighters wouldn't shoot us down."

"It was in his interest to do that. He also had to survive, so he could betray us," Anna said. "He did it for himself, or his cause, whatever that is."

"You know, Hollywood is not very far from Death Valley," said Bob. "I grew up next to LA, in San Bernardino. Hollywood is, like, only about a hundred and fifty miles away from Death Valley. We're turned to the south—we're now pointed right at LA. He could get this thing there pretty quick, maybe fifteen minutes, if he gunned it at full speed, which is probably about five or six hundred miles per hour. Vegas is even closer."

"Won't the fighters shoot him down?" Gordon asked.

"Maybe, but I haven't seen any fighters for a long time," said Jim. "I think they're gone. They may not be able to get back up in time to catch him."

"I agree," said Matt. "They missed the president and now Plan B is Hollywood. He's been hiding, pretending to be one of us, helping us, but all along he was just waiting for his chance. We have to go again, guys. Right now. I have to get up there before he shuts the autopilot off."

"You aren't going," Anna said. "We are. Matt, you are the only one who can land this plane. You stay here and keep down. We're lucky he didn't just shoot you. That was a mistake."

"She's right, Matt," said Jim. "Hang back this time."

"He's still here because he wants to keep us away from the cockpit," Matt said. "But he has to go there to take control. We can't wait that long. We have to go now."

"So this kid is hooked up with some kind of Christian militia?" Lester asked.

"Yeah. He's the son of the head guy," Matt said. "They want the country to be run by white Christians."

"Sounds like the Klan without the sheets," Lester observed.

"Yeah," Matt agreed. "It does. But these guys are committed. The most committed wins."

"We took down six of these motherfuckers and we can take down one more. He can't have too many more bullets left," Lester said. "It's been a pleasure flying with you folks. Let's go."

"Wait. He has the children. We need a plan," Anna said.

"I can talk to Ruby," Jim said. "Let her know what we're doing."

"Yes," Anna agreed.

"If you say something to her, Teddy will hear you," Gordon said.

"No, I won't say it out loud. She can read lips. She'll understand," Jim explained. "I can tell them when we're going."

"Good," Anna said. "We can't change the ground. We have to go up both aisles again but we need something else," she said, her eyes darting around. "Something . . . anything to get him off balance . . . Yes. That's it. Marathon," Anna said, striding forward to the beverage cart.

"What Marathon?" Matt asked her.

"The Battle of Marathon on September twenty-first in 490 B.C.," Anna said, lifting her skirt and hurriedly pulling down her pantyhose. "Or, the Retreat of the Ten Thousand in 401 B.C."

# 53.

Paul sat on the backseat next to Jennifer. She was soaking wet and smelled like shit and burned hair. He was holding Jennifer's cell phone. He asked her how she was feeling and she said she was okay.

"Good. Are you up to that phone call yet?"

"To my lawyer?"

"Later. First, I thought you might like to talk to Reverend Samaritan. You know, just to let him know you did what you were supposed to do at the airport?"

"I already did that."

"Oh. Well, how about just calling to say hello?"

"I'm not supposed to call until he calls me."

"Unless it's an emergency?"

"Right."

"Your arm. You were in an accident and burned your arm. That's an emergency, right?"

"Yes. That's an emergency."

"You could ask him if you should go to a hospital or not."

"Yes, I could."

"Also, you're very curious about everything. You know, where the bombs are, things like that—how the plan is going?"

"We don't call them bombs. We call them Keys of Fire."

"That's very interesting. Okay, you're very curious about the Keys of Fire, where they are, how things are proceeding, would that be okay?"

"Sure."

"Okay, Jennifer, what number are you going to dial?" Paul asked her.

She said the number and repeated it for Cindy in the front seat, who was writing it down. Paul dialed the number and handed her the phone and she held it to her ear.

"It's ringing," she said.

"Remember, Jennifer, it would be better if you didn't mention Cindy and me to the reverend just yet, okay?"

"Why?"

"Well, we don't want him to get the wrong idea, do we?"

"Uh, no, I guess not, okay . . . Hello? Reverend? Hi. It's Jennifer. No, everything's all right. I did what you asked me to do at the airport, with changing the names in the computer. What? Oh, well, actually, I was in an accident and I hurt my arm, so it's kind of an emergency. I think I hit my head on something. I feel kind of funny, you know, dizzy? Reverend . . . No, not in the car. I fell into the water. No, the policeman pulled me out. I'm fine. I don't know. I'll ask him. Am I under arrest?" she asked Paul.

Paul did not answer. He was shaking his head.

"Yes, he's right here, Reverend. He wants to talk to you," she said, handing Paul her cell phone.

"Hello, who is this?" Paul asked.

"This is a wrong number," the man said. "Who is this?"

Paul identified himself, loudly and clearly, so the NYPD tape would get it.

"Before you hang up, Reverend Samaritan, I want you to know that we know what you have done and what you intended to do with both bombs," Paul said.

"What bombs? I don't know what you're talking about. I told you, this is a wrong number."

"Really? So you did not steal two nuclear weapons from a

U.S. military base and put one on a hijacked plane and the other heading toward Mecca in Saudi Arabia? That's a different Reverend Samaritan? Sorry for the mix-up."

The line was quiet. Paul took a quick look at the phone screen, which still registered CONNECTED.

"If Jennifer told you that, it is a damned lie from the pit of Hell," Samaritan said, finally. "That poor child is a former drug user who has damaged her brain. I wouldn't believe a thing that poor soul says, Sergeant."

"I see you know her name. Suddenly, you're not a wrong number? You're not Joe-fucking-Blow from Idaho? Well, now we've got your number, pal. And your location. And you're not in Tora Bora, are you? Peek-a-boo. We're on to you, asshole."

"It doesn't matter, Officer. It's too late," Samaritan said. "The seal is about to open."

The line went dead.

"What did he say?" Cindy asked.

"Something about a seal. He said it's too late."

Paul got out of the car and dialed Kevin. He flipped it on speaker, so Cindy could hear.

"Did you get that?"

"Yes, Paul, we were listening live, thanks. The FBI is about to knock on his door."

"Great. You were listening live? Jesus, that's scary. He said it's too late. What does he mean?"

"The FBI says there is a plane heading toward Mecca and they think one of the bombs might be onboard. The hijacked jet is about to land at Death Valley in California."

"Death Valley? You're kidding me."

"No. We still haven't confirmed the location of either bomb. If we're right, Mecca and Death Valley may disappear before dinner."

"Too bad, I've never been to Death Valley," Paul said.

"Paul, if Mecca goes and we are blamed, a billion Moslems will be after our blood until the end of time. It is the worst possible scenario, which is exactly why this loony is doing it. We are well and truly fucked, buddy. America will be at war forever or they will make it their business to nuke us back."

"So I did this for nothing?" Paul asked.

"Did what for nothing?"

"Threw away my life, my career, my freedom and the bomb wasn't even here, Kevin. Do you know how I got the information out of her so fast? You remember what I used to do on my first job? In my other uniform?"

"No, and don't say it over this line. That will never happen, Paul. Bring her here. Now, before she lawyers-up. We will take care of this."

"Okay, Kevin. But she's going to need a police surgeon. And a shower. She's cute but she doesn't smell too good."

"You didn't do it for nothing, Paul. One of the bombs was here. At your airport. If it wasn't for you, we wouldn't know any of this. Get over here now. Lights and sirens."

# 54.

Anna picked up a silvery can of seltzer from the pile in the aisle from the overturned beverage carts.

"We're all thirsty. Everybody is dehydrated. Get a can of soda," she said. "No, we're very thirsty. Everybody take two cans and pass them on."

"We don't have time for a drink," Gordon protested.

"No," said Anna, "just pretend you're thirsty. There are our weapons. Slings, catapults, artillery, bullets, whatever. We are stuck with the same ground—but worse, because it's barricaded. We pass out the cans and throw them at the same time as we attack. The men throw cans and attack, the women throw cans, also. It's all we have. Let's get ready."

Anna tied one end of her pantyhose around her right wrist and held the other end in the same hand. She placed the shiny can sideways in the crotch of the pantyhose and swung it gently at her side.

Bob picked up a can from the pile.

"This is a weapon?"

"Yes," Anna replied. "The metal is thin but it's filled with heavy liquid. Drop it on your toe. In the ancient world, they stoned people to death, you know, like the women would stone an adultress? One stone is a bump and a cut. Hundreds of stones is a painful death. A stone from a sling can break bones."

Bob dropped his can onto his foot.

"Hey, that hurts," Bob agreed.

Anna continued gently swinging the filled tan pantyhose at her side, stepping back and forth, hefting the weight.

"What is that supposed to be?" Gordon asked, pointing to her device.

"A sling, best I can do on short notice. It's all we have to hurt him, distract him until we can get over the carts and take him down."

"Got anymore pantyhose?" Lester asked.

"No, only in my luggage. Have you had experience with a sling?"

"A slingshot when I was a kid."

"That's different. Also, I'm going to have to do this overhanded, in one motion," Anna noted.

"Have you had experience with this . . . thing?" Gordon asked.

"Not using pantyhose, but I did my masters thesis on slings in ancient warfare; battles where slings were a major factor. You know, could David really have killed Goliath with a sling, that sort of thing? He certainly could have stunned him or knocked him out. Slings had greater range than archers. The Greeks used lead bullets. The Rhodian slingers actually turned the tide of battle against the Persians."

"You did a paper?" Gordon asked, sarcastically. "This guy has a gun."

"I spent a summer in Greece, making and using slings with the original materials, in the original locations," Anna said. "I got a lot of practice. Pass the cans out to everybody in the seats. Tell them what to do. Quietly. I'll say when, okay?"

"Momma!" Ruby called out from her place near Teddy in the front of the cabin. "The little planes are back!" she said, looking at a window.

Several of the passengers in seats also noticed. Emily taunted Teddy that they were here to shoot him down. The fighters pulled even with the descending plane and waggled their wings. Then the warplanes peeled off and flew away.

"I don't think so," Teddy said loudly, with a nasty grin. "They're leaving. His will be done. He is my shield."

Matt watched Teddy, who kept looking back out the window, at his small human shields, at the others in the back and then back forward, toward the cockpit. You could see the wheels turning in his head. He was trying to figure out how to keep everyone at bay and still get back to the cockpit to take control. Once he got back to the cockpit, Teddy could easily hold everyone off with the pistol.

"We have to go now," said Matt. "I think we're already below one thousand feet."

"Everybody got sodas?" Anna asked the women. "Wait, this is no good. Teddy is over to the side. I need him in the middle, where the ceiling is highest."

Anna rushed over to Danielle and whispered something. Danielle went to the right side of the plane and looked out a window.

"Ready?" Anna whispered to the men. "Danielle first, then the men throw and go, then the women throw. Matt, stay here. Get down."

Anna waved to Danielle on the other side of the plane. Danielle nodded and peered out the window.

"Oh, my God!" Danielle wailed loudly. "The fighters are back! They're over here!" Teddy's head jerked around.

"Over here, let's go," he snapped at the children surrounding him, shoving them toward the other side.

As they worked their way into the middle of the open area, Ruby noticed her dad waving at her. She waved back. Then she said the word yes out loud. Teddy did not notice. Neither did he notice that Jim's lips were moving but he was not making any noise.

"Okay, dad. 'Ring around the rosy,' " Ruby began to sing,

tugging the other kids around Teddy in a circle. " 'Pocket full of posies. Ashes, ashes, all fall down.' "

The kids all plopped onto the carpet.

"Get up!" Teddy said, tripping over two little boys.

"Is that a missile? I think they're shooting us down!" Danielle screamed, quite convincingly.

Since Anna had not shared her trick, several women holding soda cans in their seats screamed at the fake news. Teddy jumped over the children, leaving them on the floor and sprinted toward the other side to see for himself.

"MEN, NOW!" Anna yelled.

Teddy turned back at the noise, as the men threw their first cans. The air filled with two dozen Pepsi and Diet Coke and Sprite cans, arcing toward Teddy, who was instantly torn between getting back to his little hostages and dodging the missiles. He tried to do both and succeeded at neither. Almost half of the cans hit him almost simultaneously, in the head, legs, chest, crotch, shoulder, stomach, staggering him backward.

"UUUUFFF!" he grunted.

One hit his right elbow as he brought the gun up, knocking it down. The gun went off. Some men threw a second can and a few connected. Men scrambled over the carts on both sides. Teddy, blood on his face, raised his left hand to shield his head but most of the cans were coming from the other side. A gaunt figure appeared in the aisle. Matt, peeking over the seats, recognized the TV guy, the drugged-up cancer patient. He had been sitting in his seat the whole time, watching TV. The man walked steadily like a zombie toward Teddy, who shot him. He bravely kept walking and Teddy fired again and again. The man didn't go down until the fifth shot snapped his spine.

"WOMEN, NOW!" Anna yelled. The women stood up in their seats and let fly with their cans.

Another half dozen cans hit Teddy, two hard in the side of

the head, sending him reeling. The men were already over the carts on both sides. Teddy fired blindly at the first two men who rushed him. Lester and Bob. The shots and the screams and grunts came too quickly to count and the two men fell at Teddy's feet. Teddy raised the gun again. The other men froze or jogged sideways, away from the gun, as Teddy decided who to kill. He settled on Jim.

"TEDDY!"

Teddy turned to Anna's voice and movement, accompanied by a whooshing noise. Anna was halfway down the port aisle. She whipped her improvised sling backwards and brought her straight arm windmilling over her head, like an English cricketer bowling. Teddy, blood in his eyes, swung the pistol at Anna and fired, just as she launched her sling like a hand grenade, with a smooth overarm throw of the right arm that stopped at eye level. A shining, spinning cylinder shot out, trailed by one leg of the hosiery, which remained attached to Anna's wrist. She went down. The can flew at Teddy with incredible speed and struck him with a dull clunk directly in the face, on the bridge of his nose. His head jerked back, he flopped over backwards and the men were on him.

Matt ran forward. Jim and Gordon and two other men were holding a dazed Teddy down in the middle of a field of soda cans, some of which had ruptured and were fizzing and spritzing their contents and rolling around. Blood was pouring out of Teddy's nose, his face welted with gashes. Anna's slung can had knocked him cross-eyed. Danielle rushed up and hit Teddy several times with one of her high heels on the head until the other two men pulled her away. Jim snatched Teddy's gun out of his hand by the barrel.

"OW!" Jim yelled, dropping the burning metal, which tumbled a few feet away. "That's hot."

Emily limped up on her cane, shaking her head, tears welling in her eyes, as she looked at the new murders. The kids were crying, except Ruby, who was staring, wide-eyed. Jim and Gordon each had several small, bloody holes in their left arms, buckshot from bullets that had passed through the other men's bodies. The TV man was dead. Lester was lying face down, with Bob lying sideways next to him, holding the larger man's hand. They had died together.

"Goddamnit," Matt said, looking at the bodies.

"Is he dead?" Emily asked, scowling at Teddy.

"No," Jim said. "Unconscious. He's breathing. His nose is broken, though. He's messed up. Maybe we should tie him up. Where's Anna?" Jim asked, looking around.

No one answered. Jim got up and went back to look.

Gordon found the black blade nearby and threw it aside. Teddy slowly put his hand into his right front jeans pocket. He lazily pulled out a bloody cell phone, as if he wanted to make a call.

"Stop that," Emily said to Teddy. "What's he doing?"

Teddy did not stop. He brought the wavering phone up to his face, trying to blink the blood out of his swollen eyes. His other arm came up toward the phone.

"We should tie him up," Gordon said, shrugging.

"No, I don't think so," Emily replied, standing over Teddy.

She had the pistol in her hand and was pointing it down at Teddy's chest.

"Whoa, lady!" Gordon said. "Be careful!"

"I am. You shoot mad dogs before they can bite anyone else," said Emily, firing a shot through Teddy's chest, causing more screaming and panic.

Teddy spit blood from his mouth and dropped the cell phone onto the carpet. Gordon rolled away from the shooting. The old woman fired until the automatic slide popped back. No more bullets. She dropped the gun onto Teddy's corpse. The weapon bounced off his stomach and landed on the wet carpet, next to the bloody cell phone that he had taken from one of the dead hijackers.

"The children have had enough," Emily explained, turning and limping calmly back to the kids.

# 55.

The president was watching the screen and cursing a blue streak, as the rogue American Jump Jet inched toward the holiest city in the Moslem world.

"Goddamnit, Pappy, are we supposed to just sit here on our asses and watch this crazy son-of-a-bitch nuke Saudi Arabia?"

Veissbrott just hung his head and said nothing.

The secretary of state again suggested the president call the Saudi King to warn him. Veissbrott protested again, weakly. After some more cursing, the president suggested a prayer.

"Dear God," the president intoned, looking at his tactical screen. "Please help us in our hour of need. We need your grace and mercy to prevent terrible destruction and suffering, we ask you to . . . what the fuck is that? Whose planes are those? They're moving like bats out of hell."

Two red dots had suddenly appeared on the screen of Saudi Arabia, moving faster than the Harrier or the Saudi interceptors on the screen. Both red dots curved in a tight arc and veered directly at the Jump Jet.

"I have no idea, Mr. President," Veissbrott confessed.

"Those are missiles, Mr. President," Colonel Gunning spoke up. "Too fast for jets. No pilot could survive those G-forces. Looks like Mach six. I have no idea where they came from. They're heading south, so they came from somewhere north."

"Could they be the Saudi SAM sites protecting Mecca?" Sheila Preston asked.

"No, Ma'am," Gunning said. "Wrong location. Also, these were air-launched at . . . looks like twenty seven thousand feet. What the hell?"

"How come I can't see the planes that fired those missiles on my screen?" the president asked. "Are we having more communications problems?"

"No sir, Mr. President," Gunning answered. "They're not on our screen, either. Our radar satellite is not picking them up, which is not possible, and neither is our airborne AWACS theatre radar. All we're picking up is the hot exhaust from the missiles. We can't even image the missiles themselves. The planes and the missiles are invisible to our imaging, sir. It's impossible, but that's what we are seeing."

"Did we give the Saudis stealth fighters when I wasn't looking?" the president asked.

"No sir," Gunning said, his voice wavering for the first time. "Sir, FIELD HOCKEY can track our own stealth aircraft. If these were our aircraft, we'd see them. This is something else. This is something better. And I have no fucking idea who."

Veissbrott buried his head in his hands on the conference table.

"So, what is happening?" the president asked. "Can't our fighters get over there and see who it is?"

"It's dark over the Kingdom now, sir," Preston pointed out.

"It is? Oh, right."

"My only guess would be SHAPESHIFT technology, sir," Gunning offered.

"What's that?"

The colonel explained that SHAPESHIFT was a theoretical technology, in which radar frequencies are not just absorbed and deflected, as in stealth planes, but are actively reemitted in phased and polarized form that make the plane completely invisible and create one or more false targets of choice with the incoming radar energy, even on the ground, using a supercomputer to create fake mountains, buildings, anything, like in a video game.

"So if we have this shape shit, why aren't we using it?" the president asked.

"We don't have it yet," Veissbrott said. "We're working on it. If it is possible, the technology is years away. You remember, Mr. President, I briefed you on the top secret program out west last year?"

"No."

"Mr. President, look at the screen," Gunning said.

Both red dots converged on the Jump Jet.

"Our pilot has no idea, poor bastard," Gunning said, shaking his head.

"Poor bastard?" the president said.

The red dots and the Jump Jet converged and grew into a larger red dot that pulsated and faded away, leaving only the Saudi jets and the F-16s still on the screen.

"Is that it? Did they shoot him down?" the president asked. "Or did the nuclear bomb go off?"

"There was no nuclear detonation, sir. Our IR satellites would have registered the double pulse and the heat. It looks like he was brought down, sir," Gunning said. "I'll order up close coverage by the FIELD HOCKEY satellite to look for wreckage. We need a Marine weapons recovery team in there ASAP."

"Is there radiation?" the president asked.

"If the weapon casing was breached, there might be radiation contamination, sir, especially if there was a secondary detonation of the high explosive inside the weapon itself. Actually, that is the best scenario, Mr. President. I'm saying a little prayer for that right now."

"What do you mean?"

"Well, sir, I would prefer that by dawn we have a bunch of

Marines in moon suits vacuuming up sand dunes out in the desert, rather than having one of our portable nuclear devices sitting under a palm tree, waiting for the first radical Islamist to come along and pick it up."

"But the Saudis are our allies," the president said.

"Uh, yes sir, but that is not the case with many citizens of the Kingdom, I'm afraid."

The president asked what was happening with the hijacked jet out west. He was informed that Flight 1787 was coming in for a landing at Death Valley.

"Our fighters were bingo . . . I mean, they ran out of gas, so we pulled them off. The civilian passenger jet is coming in completely by wire, sir—on the autopilot."

"How can they do that?" the president asked.

"Theoretically it's possible," the colonel replied, "but this will actually be the first time in history that anyone has attempted to land a big jet that way. I wouldn't give a fiddler's fart for their chances, sir. Again, that's not a problem for us. If they crash, that is terrible, but we should be able to recover the device. If there is leakage of radioactive material, it will also be contained in a remote desert location. More Marines in moon suits, sir."

"So, it's over?" the boss asked.

"Maybe, sir. Stay tuned. We have assets on the ground in Death Valley and on the way. We have cleared the tourists out of the area. Let me switch birds and put Death Valley up on the TAC screen."

Sheila Preston's PDA began rattling on the table again. She snatched it up and opened the message.

> Miss Preston, we stopped it. I think you know the location. Can you stop the other one? In the other dry place closer to you?

Yes, I believe we can. Thank you.

What are friends for? We'll talk. Is Monday good for you?

I will clear my schedule for Monday morning. Who are you?

I'll call.

Preston put the PDA back on her belt and smiled. She listened to discussions about the Death Valley landing site for a few minutes. When there was a pause, she asked a question.

"Mr. Secretary," Preston said, addressing Veissbrott. "What other countries possess the SHAPESHIFT technology?"

"Sheila, you know perfectly well that no one on the planet has this yet. It's Buck Rogers."

"Really? Well obviously someone has it. We just saw a demonstration. I have another question, Mr. Secretary, how secure are the video links we are using right now?"

"Completely inviolable."

"So you are as certain of that, Mr. Secretary, as you are that no one else has what we just saw with our own eyes?"

Veissbrott's mouth opened, but, for the first time in a long while, nothing came out.

Preston looked back at the map. The invisible planes had come from the north, in the direction of Iraq and Jordan. Neither country had the resources to accomplish what the United States had not. Jordan might help but Iraq certainly would not. The e-mail address of the messages was in Jordan. That had to be fake. Someone wanted it to appear that he or she was Christian and in an Arab country. Preston's eyes traveled across Jordan to the neighboring country just a short distance away, on the Mediterranean. That country also had access to the Gulf of Aqaba, a short distance from Saudi Arabia. She turned to her aide.

"Clear my schedule for Monday morning. Set up in the situation room. We're going to have a guest. Make sure we have plenty of bagels, lox, and cream cheese."

"Who is Buck Rogers?" the president whispered to his political aide.

# 56.

Matt stared at the bodies of Lester and Bob and the man with cancer, whose name he never knew, lifeless on the killing floor. They died for us. Strangers. Americans. And they knew they were doing it. Why should that surprise me? Matt wondered. Nothing should ever surprise me, ever again.

"Shouldn't you be up front, Matt?" Gordon asked him.

Matt shook it off and ran down the left aisle toward the cockpit without waiting to see what had happened. He jumped over the bodies of Emmett and his wife, Valerie. More dead heroes. He dashed into the cockpit, where there was a lot of beeping and computer voice alarms were also going off. It was impossible to tell how high up they were. They could be at one thousand feet or at one hundred feet above the white, featureless floor of Death Valley. It didn't matter. He pushed the reset button on the AutoLand system on the autopilot system. It prompted him to okay flap settings and landing gear. Matt had no clue if they were correct. Jerry had told him that any big change in wind direction or speed or the barometer could screw it all up. Kaboom. Matt okayed everything and reengaged the system. They were committed. The beeping and voices stopped. Except one.

"Come in, Anytime 1787! This is Flame Tamer One, come in. What the hell is going on? Hello?"

Matt picked up the radio set. He was trying to remember which part was which, when Liz sat next to him in the copilot's seat and helped him.

"This is Matt, I mean, 1787, sorry."

"Buddy, this is Danny Carroll in the 747 right in your face, Matt. You are in landing mode, correct?"

Matt looked up. A huge 747 was floating above him.

"I think so, Danny, thanks for coming. Yes. Yes we are. I see you. We had a problem but I reset the AutoLand function and it looks okay. I think."

"Glad to hear it. You're not a pilot, right, Matt?"

"Right."

Matt felt a heavy vibration beneath his feet.

"What's that? Something is making noise."

"That's okay, Matt, your gear is coming down. Your flaps are set, you're looking good."

"Oh, God," Liz said. "Lester. He was going to open the other emergency exit door. I have to get someone else to do that. Matt, I know you can land this plane."

Liz kissed Matt on the cheek and rushed away. Back in coach, Matt could hear singing. It sounded familiar. We all live in a yellow submarine.

"Uh, Danny? How high up am I?" Matt asked. "I can't tell. I forgot where the altimeter is."

"Stop looking out the window, amigo. There's no reference in this landscape. Just look at the instruments. You're probably about three hundred feet, coming in fine."

Things began to beep and buzz and lights began flashing in spots all over the instrument panel.

"What the hell is all that?" Matt asked. "I left my laptop in the back."

"I can only hear it, Matt, read the letters under the flashing lights."

Matt began reading them out, a series of letters that made no sense.

"Okay, Matt, you are getting low pressure readings in several key hydraulic systems. Any other warning lights?"

"Yeah, it's like a Christmas tree," Matt said, reading the other indicators over the radio.

"You also are having some strange electrical problems. Did this just start?"

"Yeah, just now. This is all new. Maybe all that shooting did it."

"What shooting?"

"I don't think I have time to tell you. Some of it might have gone through the floor. Danny, the ground looks really close."

"Yeah, it is. I think you should shut off your engines, Matt. I'm going to give you the short version. Ready?"

"Don't we need them to land?"

"You're going to have to coast. If you have an electrical fire or your gear collapses, I want your engines off."

"Oh. Okay, tell me."

Danny talked him through the steps. The engines did not suddenly shut off, they just slowly wound down until all Matt could hear was whistling noises and the beeping and buzzing.

"Now look down, see the switches for your engine fire extinguishers? Flip all of them right now, Matt. Better safe than sorry."

"Okay, but I don't see any fire."

"I want it to stay that way."

"Got it."

"Is your seat belt on, Matt?"

"Uh, no."

"If you're going to stay there, put it on. You don't have to stay. I suggest you get to the rear and get out as soon as you can. You did as much as you could."

"Isn't there something for me to do?"

"Yeah, but if anything happens, you have a better chance of

getting out alive if you're not in the cockpit."

"I'll stay. What do I do?" Matt asked, fastening the seatbelt.

"Good man. Hold the wheel firmly but don't turn it. If you go into a sharp turn, keep it straight, if you can. If you can't see because of my fire retardant, just look at your compass. Good luck, Matt. Here it comes."

The bigger plane pulled up and ahead. A gigantic red cloud poured out of Danny's 747, blocking out the sun, like a curtain of blood. It pelted the windshield of Matt's cockpit like a biblical plague. All Matt could see was red. The plane got dark, filled with a weird Martian light. Matt looked at the compass, like Danny had told him, and held the steering yoke, his hands sweating.

The plane's gentle floating descent stopped with a bump and a screech. Matt squeezed the wheel tight.

"You got wheels down, amigo!" Danny told him. "Ooops!"

The plane floated up a bit and then screeched down again.

"Stay down, Matt. You're not pulling the wheel towards yourself are you, amigo?"

"No."

"Good. Don't touch the brakes."

"I don't know where they are."

"That's good. Keep her steady. Do you hear or smell anything funny, Matt?"

"No, it already smells very bad. It's suddenly really hot in here. Why?"

"Just asking. You're looking good. Your air conditioning may be off. I want you to pull the electrical plug now, too. I'll walk you through it, okay?"

Danny directed him to several circuit breakers, which Matt shut off.

"We're on the ground right?"

"Yup. You did it, amigo, you just have to slow down enough

to . . . oh crap."

"Danny?"

"Matt, you still holding onto the wheel?"

"Yes, why?"

"You can't see it. Little bump in the road coming up. Get ready. No problem, just keep it straight and level . . ."

"I thought this place was supposed to be perfectly . . ."

The plane hit a hump and lifted up, leaving Matt's stomach on the ground. He flew out of the red rain. He was back in the air. The wheel wobbled back and forth.

"Terrific," Matt said. "What do I do, Danny?"

"Don't take your hands off the wheel. Keep it straight. Stay cool."

"Is the autopilot still engaged?"

"You bet. Just make sure it stays straight, okay? Just maintain. You're coming down again. Just keep doing what you're doing."

"I'm not doing anything."

"Okay, good, hold on, I'm going to hose you again, amigo. Keep that bird down this time, Matt."

"Talk to the autopilot."

The red cascade fell again, darkening the cabin. The wheels screeched again, as Matt continued to hold the yoke with his sweating hands. He waited, his muscles tensed, ready for anything. His arms and legs began to cramp from the strain but he did not move. They were slowing down. He looked at the compass. Was that the same as it was a minute ago? He couldn't remember. The plane was definitely moving slower but Matt kept his hands tight on the wheel.

"Nice job. Get out of there fast, amigo," Danny said.

"Not until it's over," Matt answered.

"It's over. You're stopped. Welcome to Death Valley. I'm low on fuel, I'm out of here. Get everybody out."

Matt looked out the window, as the red stuff trickled down.

The 747 was nowhere in sight, just white sand and mountains, through red glass. He saw a clump of rocks below. It wasn't moving. They were not moving.

"I didn't feel that," Matt said. "Thanks, Danny."

"You did it, amigo."

"I didn't do anything."

"Matt you landed the plane. That's something."

"I didn't do any of that. The autopilot did it."

"The first time, yeah," Danny said. "It was off when you hit the bump and became airborne. The breakers were off. You shut them off. You went up maybe a hundred feet. I saw you right the aircraft. You kept it steady and brought it in. Not bad for a first lesson, amigo."

"Holy shit."

"Now get the hell out of there."

# 57.

PAUL sped onto the Gowanus Expressway in Brooklyn, toward the Battery Tunnel to Manhattan. His squad car was the only vehicle on the roadway. On the other side of the divider, civilian traffic out of the city was bumper to bumper. There were accidents, breakdowns and fistfights. He had to stop at the tunnel entrance, which was blocked by an NYPD armored personnel carrier and large Department of Sanitation dump trucks filled with sand. He breezed through the tunnel and into Manhattan. He went quickly through another security gantlet getting into police headquarters. He pulled onto the sidewalk at Park Row and Pearl Street, below the red brick fortress.

"You Sergeant Ambrosino?" asked a cop in a flak vest and helmet, toting a shotgun on his hip.

"Yeah."

"Let's go," the cop said.

Several other cops with machine guns surrounded them, scanning around for threats.

"Officer Bernstein and your prisoner are going to central booking in the basement for an accelerated booking. Officer Bernstein is the arresting officer. The prisoner gets treated and cleaned up and placed in protective custody. Intelligence will then question her. You are to come upstairs with me, sir."

Paul was taken to the Executive Command Center. Inside, he saw his brother-in-law Kevin at the big conference table, along with dozens of other bosses and personnel. There were more heavily armed guards. Kevin rushed over and grabbed Paul in a bear hug. Other bosses slapped him on the back and shook his hand. The room was surrounded with drive-in-movie–sized TV screens, with talking heads, people at desks, security cams. It looked like a James Bond movie. Kevin pulled Paul to a seat next to him at the table and told him there was news.

"The second plane is down," Kevin announced.

"There's a second plane?"

"Oh, sorry, the FBI found out that one of the stolen weapons was overnighted to Kuwait by the military postal service a day or two ago. Two-day service, I guess."

"We sent it there?"

"Yeah, scary, isn't it? It was apparently put on a Harrier Jump Jet headed to Mecca, just like your prisoner said. They shot it down and are out looking for the dingus now. The passenger jet from JFK is also down, in Death Valley."

"Yeah? Damn, that's too bad."

"No, it wasn't shot down, it landed. That guy Matt did it with the autopilot, it looks like. It just happened, the FBI said. No word on casualties yet."

"Hey, that's great. Some good news, for a change."

"The feds aren't telling us a lot but they swear they will let us know as soon as both nukes are recovered," Kevin continued. "The FBI is kicking in the door of this minister Samaritan in Idaho. The guy you nailed on the phone. Sean? Can you hear me, Sean?" Kevin asked, talking into a speakerphone on the table in front of him.

"Yes sir."

"Paul, Sean is one of our guys on the Joint Terrorist Task Force over at Federal Plaza."

"The NYPD–FBI thing?"

"Exactly," said Kevin. "Sean, any news from Idaho?"

"The team is taking heavy fire from the compound and the

surrounding woods, apparently from several positions. Small arms. I'm listening in on their relayed tactical frequency over here. They won't let us listen directly, sorry. Hold on. Uh-oh. There have been explosions. Several explosions. The scene commander says the explosions are walking toward them. Sounds like mortar fire, to me. Uh . . . this does not sound good . . . They have people down, casualties. They are pulling back, sir. Sounds like they are seriously outgunned. Wait one second . . . the Agent-in-Charge here has asked me to tell you that the team is pulling back. Reinforcements are on the way. Military reinforcements . . . tanks . . . are on the way. I'll get back to you as soon as I have anything else, sir."

"So, it's not over yet?" Paul asked.

"It would seem not," Kevin said.

"Oh, your captain was looking for you," Kevin said. "They located those two missing Anytime Airways baggage guys you people were looking for."

"Where?"

"Out in some weeds off Rockaway Boulevard. Throats cut ear to ear. Funny thing, their pockets were filled with cash."

"Dumb bastards. Probably figured there would never be any blowback taking money to smuggle something into Mexico. The people who hired them were looking for a different payoff," Paul said. "They don't care about the money."

"Yes, true. The good news is it looks like they were not planning to hit the city."

"Kevin, do we know for real that the bombs were actually aboard either of the planes yet?" Paul asked.

Everyone around the table exchanged hard glances. One by one, they all began shaking their heads.

"No," Kevin admitted. "Remember, we have to depend on the feds for a lot of this out-of-town information. The jets detected radiation aboard Flight 1787 but nothing is a lock yet.

Until they get onto that jet in Death Valley and find that wreckage in Saudi Arabia, we won't know for sure."

"So, one of the gadgets could be up the Statue of Liberty's skirt, for all we know?"

"Logically? Yes," Kevin replied. "But we have found nothing in our raids, our roadblocks, wiretaps, nothing. But we can't know yet. That's why we are still looking. This is the question I brought you here to ask you, Paul. What's in your nose? What kind of feeling are you getting now?"

"Feeling? Oh. I've been too busy to think about my feelings. I don't know. Let me think about it."

Paul thought about his day, the twists and turns. As he mulled the events, the people, the words, the expressions on faces, he drummed his fingers on the table. He thought about Jennifer and that skel Samaritan on the phone. The heads of NYPD watched Paul think and twiddle his fingers.

# 58.

Matt unclipped his seat harness and scrambled out of the pilot's seat. He exited the cockpit by stepping over the unmoving body of the marshal, jogged left to avoid the bodies of Emmett and Valerie. The windows were covered with the red stuff, bathing the whole passenger cabin in pink light. Lines of tiny sparkling white lights on the floor were moving like on a Broadway marquee, lighting the way to the emergency doors. In the open area of the coach cabin, Matt came up behind Liz, who was pulling the starboard side door open, a crowd of passengers behind her. Brilliant white light flooded into the plane, along with searing heat, as the thick emergency door opened wide.

"Are we on fire?" a woman asked.

"No, we're in the desert," Liz answered. "It's probably over a hundred degrees out there."

She hit buttons on the wall near the door and a bright yellow rubber chute inflated and flopped down to the sand below. Hot air blew like a blow dryer through the plane, along with a smell like a rubber raft. On the port side, Gordon and another man were copying Liz's actions. Another group of passengers was lined up there to exit past the pile of hijacker corpses.

"Alright, one at a time," Liz ordered loudly. "No shoes. Jump out and sit. Slide to the bottom and move away quickly. You two men first, go down and help people off, please. Emily, then you go. Faster, please. Then Anna and her family. And the other wounded people."

Matt saw Jim and Ruby supporting Anna between them.

"Momma got shot in the butt," Ruby explained to Matt.

"The hip, actually," Anna said, limping along with her family. "It really hurts."

Teddy was still lying on his back, staring at the ceiling, the empty gun and a bloody cell phone nearby, amid dozens of soda cans. It turned Matt's stomach to see the bodies of the cancer patient and Lester and Bob, also still lying where they fell. Every one else ignored them, busy getting out. Liz pulled people toward the door, shoving those who hesitated. When Ruby went down the slide, Matt heard her yell.

"Wheeeee!"

"Matt, look around," Liz said over her shoulder. "We can't leave anyone behind."

Matt climbed over one of the soda carts and dashed to the back. The bathrooms were empty. He quickly ran to the other side and back down the port side aisle. As he was about to climb over the other beverage cart, Matt noticed a fat man and a fat woman were sitting in their seats, eyes closed, unmoving. The man's mouth was open. Teddy's bullets must have gotten them. The man suddenly made a noise like a pig. Matt jumped, startled. He leaned over. They both stank of booze. The drunks. He shoved the man, who snored again. Matt reached over and shoved the woman, who made a cranky whining noise. Matt shook them.

"Hey, wake up!"

They did not respond. Matt grabbed the first can he could find on the floor. Ginger Ale. He popped it open and emptied the fizzing contents onto their faces. They both opened their eyes and sat up.

"Wake up! Time to leave!"

The couple stood up, looking around through half-closed eyelids. They were still loaded. Matt walked away disgusted. He walked over to Liz, who was helping the last three people onto the chute. The other side was wide open, everyone there was gone. The drunks lurched out of their seats and staggered wide-eyed around the pile of hijacker bodies over to the port side door.

"No!" Liz yelled at them.

The couple was not listening. They walked out the open door and vanished.

"Is that it?" Liz asked Matt.

"Yeah. No. You go, I have to check something."

"No, Matt, we have to get out."

Matt jogged back up front to the cockpit.

"Marshal? Can you hear me?" Matt said to Ed's bloody head.

Ed did not respond. He seemed dead. Matt squeezed his wrist and waited. He felt a weak, quick flutter. Matt reached under Ed's arms and started dragging him backwards. He was really heavy.

When Matt got to the escape chute, Liz was still there, throwing can after can of unopened liquids down the chute. Then she tossed out a large, white first-aid kit.

"Is he alive?" she asked.

"I think so. Maybe not for long."

Liz called out to others below and helped Matt shove the unconscious marshal down the slide.

"Now you," she said.

"No, wait, my laptop."

He dashed back up front, shoved his laptop back into his bag and ran back.

"You are crazy," Liz told him.

"Is that a problem?"

Matt and then Liz slid down the chute. It was blistering hot, the sun heating every part of them, the scalding desert floor burning their bare feet. Matt tasted salt in his mouth and realized he was standing on a huge sea of ancient, dried salt. It was a giant, gray cracked mosaic as far as the eye could see. People had gathered in the shade of the wing and were hugging and laughing. The men had dragged the marshal into the shade. One of the women was bandaging his head, using the first-aid kit.

Liz and Matt walked over to the group. Matt looked at the prostrate form of the marshal and at Anna, who was also stretched out on the salt. He looked around. They were in the middle of nowhere, a flat desert that stretched for miles and miles in every direction to surrounding walls of distant mountains. The plane above them looked like a murdered bird with its pockets turned out. Dead and plundered. The fuselage and wings were coated with dripping red stuff. White foam was oozing from the silent engines, which were making hissing and cracking noises. Looking back down the endless track, Matt saw a red gash on the salt flats where they had landed. There was nothing and nobody as far as the eye could see. It was eerie, like they had landed on Mars.

"There he is!" Gordon said. "Let's hear it for Matt! I don't know how he did it but he brought us back safely."

The passengers gave Matt a round of applause.

"Thanks, but I'm not quite sure we are back safely yet," Matt said.

"What do you mean?" Gordon asked. "We're down. We landed."

"It's brutal out here," Danielle complained.

"Yes, where the hell is everybody?" Gordon demanded. "Do they just expect us to stand here and roast alive?"

Liz said they should move away from the aircraft but most resisted.

"It's like an oven out here, dear. This is the only shade," Emily pointed out.

Danielle told Liz she needed her travel bag, with her makeup kit, from the plane. Liz explained that it was not possible to get back on the plane without airport equipment.

"It's a safety factor, so no one tries to go back in and dies for something stupid," Liz said, smiling sweetly at Danielle, who glowered back.

Gordon asked Liz why no one had arrived to help them. She explained, patiently, that they were not at an airport. They had landed in a desert and it might take quite a while for help to arrive.

"Also, they're probably not too eager to get close to our atomic bomb, which is why we're here, in the first place," Matt said. "You know what they say. 'One nuclear weapon can ruin your whole day.' "

"Excuse me," the heavyset drunk man interrupted. "Where are we? This isn't Cabo, is it? What the hell is going on?"

Matt and Jim couldn't stop laughing hysterically. Someone else took the tipsy couple aside to explain the situation.

"They won't believe you," Matt said, still laughing and wiping tears from his eyes.

"It's not over, is it?" Jim asked, wearily.

"Doesn't feel like it," Matt said. "We landed. We got off. But we're still nowhere."

"Are you saying they didn't think we'd survive?" Jim asked Matt.

"Probably. I didn't, either."

"You think maybe they didn't want us to make it?" Jim pressed.

"Maybe."

"Why would our government want to harm us?" Danielle asked.

There was tired laughter.

"I mean why would they still want to harm us?"

"Good question," said Matt.

"They almost shot us down," Toni said.

"I understand that," Matt said. "That makes sense. But this whole nuke thing, I don't know. It's like we're still up in the air."

"But hotter," said Liz.

"They could kill us and claim we crashed," Toni suggested.

"That's ridiculous," Gordon said unconvincingly. "Paranoia."

Again, Liz said they should get away from the plane. Jim said he agreed but they couldn't get far enough away to escape an atomic explosion. Also, he said, there were wounded who couldn't do that. Danielle said they could all die out in the desert.

"Look!" yelled Ruby, pointing under the wing, to the horizon behind the plane.

A light dot against the sharp blue sky was growing larger. There was no sound. By the time they realized it was another fighter plane, it flashed one hundred feet overhead. The screeching roar of the engines arrived just after the jet sped away. A storm of choking salt dust whipped at them. Some passengers were waving and shouting, happy, as the fighter disappeared into the distance.

"Over here!" Gordon yelled, waving his arms.

Jim and Matt looked at each other, unsmiling.

"That is not a rescue. That is a fighter," Matt said.

"What are you saying?" Gordon asked. "You think they're going to attack us? Why would they do that?"

"I could think of several reasons," Jim answered. "I think we should get away from this plane."

A heated discussion about whether to stay or go began. Matt ignored it and sat down on the hot desert floor in the shade of the wing and opened his laptop. He reduced the flight simulator program and wrote a fast spam message:

> This is Matt Newton we just landed Flight 1787 in death valley and got off we need help there is no one here and we have wounded people call the white house call everyone you can think of pictures coming.

He broadcast it to all of the addresses in his cyber address books. Then he plugged in his video and speakerphone link to Fiona. He tried to talk to her but she was too busy crying. Eventually she told him that CNN had a guy on the phone from Death Valley, who said he saw two planes landing close together that must have collided, because he saw a huge red explosion in the distance. Matt assured her he was alive and signed off. He dialed CNN on the same hookup.

"What are you doing?" Jim asked.

"Insurance," Matt replied, as the cable news desk picked up the line.

# 59.

The president and his political advisor Ben Andre were having a side discussion on Air Force One about how to publicly handle the crisis, when the word came in that the computer attacks on U.S. government sites had stopped. From the underground Maryland bunker, Secretary of Defense Veissbrott announced it as if he had won a battle. But, as Colonel Gunning explained, the cyber-assaults just stopped on their own. They had all come from Samaritan's Idaho bunker, over hundreds of satellite telephone data lines. The National Security Agency was in the process of isolating and jamming the lines when the attacks shifted to Arab websites, mostly Al Qaeda and Jihadist sites. Samaritan was now using large numbers of remote proxy machines called Zombies to jam almost six thousand radical Islamist sites, along with a few official Arab government sites, mostly in Saudi Arabia. The colonel said the National Security Agency was still systematically locating and jamming Samaritan's lines but it was a big job.

"Why are we bothering, now that he's stopped?" the president asked. "He's going after the bad guys."

"I have no problem with him taking down terror sites, sir. I wish we did more of that. But any time you have a chance to pull your adversary's claws before he can use them against you again, you do it, Mr. President," the colonel explained. "If you remember, sir, the backpack nukes can be detonated by satellite signal, if they have overcome the safeties."

"Oh, right. You bet."

Three pieces of news came into the bunker at the same time from the Pentagon. Veissbrott announced them triumphantly: The National Guard attack on Samaritan's bunker had begun. Flight 1787 was on the ground in the Death Valley salt flats. And U.S. Marines had arrived by helicopter at the Saudi desert site of the crashed fighter. They had located the bomb on the Jump Jet, which was apparently undamaged, and were guarding it until a larger force arrived.

Veissbrott sounded rather disappointed when he announced the landing of the hijacked jet. Sounding more confident, Veissbrott said a flyby showed that the plane had landed in one piece and some of the passengers were outside.

"Mr. President," Veissbrott continued. "This is almost over. I recommend we immediately neutralize the aircraft before the terrorists have a chance to set it off. The collateral damage is unfortunate but, even in so remote an area, a nuclear explosion inside the United States would be a feather in the terrorist's caps. The fighters are standing by."

"Are you actually proposing to kill the hostages, now that they are free?" Preston asked in disbelief. "That is disgraceful. Mr. President, I suggest you accept Secretary Veissbrott's resignation and ignore his outrageous advice."

"I'm for whatever gets the toothpaste back in the tube, boys and girls," the president replied. "If we can do it without hurting those folks, great, but we need to get it done."

"Exactly, Mr. President," Veissbrott said, "if there is a detonation, not only will it kill the hostages but it would be a great victory for the terrorists. The fallout from such an explosion will scatter the radioactive signature of the device into the atmosphere. In a few days, detectors in Russia, China and everywhere in the Northern Hemisphere will analyze the fallout and conclude that the bomb was one of ours—from our stockpile.

The American people and the world will know it was stolen from one of our bases. That will have a devastating effect on this administration and our ability to fight terrorism and run this country."

"You mean it will have a devastating effect on your career and reputation, Secretary Veissbrott," Preston snapped.

The president held a whispered conference with his political advisor before speaking again.

"Pappy, that is exactly what Ben and I have been talking about," the president said. "This is your problem and you need to clean it up, pronto. I agree with you. I need to sign a National Security Finding that all news of where these weapons came from is now Top Secret Compartmentalized Intelligence. No one can find this out. That's the deal."

"Mr. President," Preston said, standing up. "I do not believe that plane would have landed in that remote location if it was still under the control of the hijackers. You cannot order an attack on American citizens."

"I'm not, Sheila, I'm ordering an attack on the plane with the bomb in it. To save lives. They could blow it up by satellite, right?"

"Mr. President," she continued, deliberately, "too much has happened. Too many people are involved—in and out of the government. You cannot keep this secret. If you order that plane and the passengers destroyed, it will come out. Everyone will know what you did and why. I strongly urge you to wait until the recovery teams get into the plane."

"That will be too late," Veissbrott objected. "And who is going to divulge the secret? You, Miss Preston? Are you suggesting that you will commit treason if the president orders you to remain silent?"

"I am suggesting that it is treasonous to kill our fellow Americans to hide your mistakes and avoid the political consequences of incompetence."

"Sheila," the president interrupted. "Are you willing to accept the consequences if you are wrong?"

"Yes, I am, sir."

"Well, that's good but I still agree with Pappy. I think we have to protect the whole country. Any loss of life is tragic, especially such heroic folks, but we are acting for the later good."

His political operative whispered urgently to him.

"The greater good, I mean. Right, the greater good. We're putting together a speech right now. Then, later, we'll announce the sad news about Woody. Pappy, if you think we have to . . ."

"Excuse me, Mr. President," interrupted Lieutenant Alice St. Thomas from the bunker table. "What you are discussing right now? It's on CNN live. I put it on a screen. Do you want to listen, sir?"

"What?" the president asked. "Uh, sure. Let's see it."

The lieutenant turned up the sound. The jerky phone video showed a crowd of people standing or sitting on a bright surface. A voice was panning the camera around and narrating.

"A lot of people have been wounded and need medical attention," Matt's voice explained, his voice echoing slightly. "This is Anna, she was shot when we took out the last terrorist, a guy named Teddy. He told me he was the son of Reverend Aaron Samaritan, the man behind all of this, the man who stole the nuclear weapons from the U.S. Army base somewhere in the south. The fighters who followed us detected radiation and they think one of the bombs is on the plane here. Maybe that's why no one from the government has come to help us."

Matt panned the camera in a three hundred sixty degree arc, from the passengers, to the red-splattered jet, to the desert and mountains, and back again.

After a slight delay, the CNN anchor asked about the second incident. Matt pointed the laptop webcam at Jim.

"Teddy pretended to be one of us and actually helped kill the other hijackers," Jim said. "But just before we were about to land, he attacked the marshal, took his gun and started shooting people. We had to do it again, take back the plane but lots of people died, including Lester and Bob and Emmett and his wife, I don't remember her name. We hit him with soda cans and jumped on him. Teddy, I mean. What?"

Matt was prompting Jim.

"Okay, right. What about the bombs? The nuclear bombs? Why is the government denying what happened? What are they hiding? These were not Arab terrorists. They were all Americans. What is going on?"

In the bunker, Veissbrott looked daggers at the screen.

The CNN anchor asked if Jim or Matt had seen the bomb. Matt had to admit they had not but they believed it was somewhere in the cargo hold. In fact, apparently two cargo workers at the airline were missing.

"Goddamn it!" the president said. "Who let this out?"

FBI director Bassett clenched his teeth but said nothing. Preston said this only proved her point, that the news could not be contained.

"Bullshit," Ben Andre shouted. "You heard them. They never saw any bomb. It doesn't exist if we say it doesn't exist. It's too late to blast the plane. That would look great on CNN. Get those assholes away from the bomb and clean this up. None of our weapons were stolen. It was just terrorists, probably secretly working with Islamist terrorists, who tried to get nukes—but they failed. Brave soldiers died defending our blah, blah, blah. The hijackers on the plane had some kind of fake bomb, that's all. It's just a hijacking. Nothing happened in Saudi Arabia. End of fucking story."

"You heard him," the president ordered. "Do it. I'm going to get ready for my speech."

# 60.

Matt related to the live CNN audience how Teddy got pelted with soda cans, according to Anna's plan, and then shot. He also described the landing. The anchor then told him the White House was completely denying all rumors about nuclear weapons and saying they were part of a terrorist plan to panic the public, along with computer attacks.

"In fact, Mr. Newton, a highly placed government source has just told us that the hijacking was the work of foreign terrorists and anyone who said otherwise might be part of the problem."

"They're lying," Matt replied, into his webcam.

"Do you have any proof?"

"Yes. Do they? Can you hold on? I have a call I have to take. I may have more information when I come back."

Matt hung up on CNN and took his incoming call.

"Sergeant?" Matt asked.

"Call me Paul. I'm looking at CNN. I can't believe you people had to do that twice. I see you landed the plane. Way to go. How the hell did you do that, Matt?"

"I have no idea. What is going on, Paul?"

"I have no idea. Apparently they shot down a plane in Saudi Arabia that had the other bomb on it. That part is over, looks like. They're assaulting Samaritan's hole in Idaho. Suddenly, NYPD is only getting news from CNN. Now the feds are denying everything. The good news is, that means it might be over soon. The bad news is the feds are in charge of the news. So this Teddy guy was Samaritan's son?"

"That's what he told me. The government can't deny that."

"Obviously, you don't know these guys too well. It's your word against theirs. Unless you've got something that says different."

"My laptop. Their laptop. But I left theirs on the plane."

"Get it. Then get the hell out of there, buddy. I'll see you when you get back to New York. Good luck."

Matt hung up. Liz told him the only way to get back onboard was to hoist someone back up the inflated neoprene chute, which was sagging in the torturous heat. It was well above one hundred degrees. Matt's camera phone line rang. He thought it was CNN but it wasn't.

"Matthew Newton?" the familiar voice with the southern drawl asked.

An angry face appeared on Matt's screen. Booms and rattles could be heard in the background.

"Mr. Samaritan," Matt said, moving his mouse and clicking on an option.

"Reverend Samaritan," the older man corrected.

"Reverend my balls, you worthless piece of shit. Your dickhead son and your other scumbags killed a lot of good people. I'm told your little plan to nuke Mecca has also failed."

"That would explain why both Teddy and our other pilot have stopped communicating with us," Samaritan agreed.

"I can also hear that you have some loud company out there in potato-land."

"Yes, I do," the preacher admitted. "I understand you killed Teddy?"

Uh-oh. He also was watching CNN.

"No, actually, someone else shot him . . . but he's not dead," Matt lied. "He's wounded."

"Really? Where is he? I'd like to talk to him."

"He's up on the plane. We can't get back on."

"Your lies ring hollow in my ears. You're a nonbeliever, aren't you?"

"I don't believe in what you preach. I believe in nature. I also believe in evil."

"So you believe in the Devil?"

"You bet. I'm talking to him."

"I am God's anointed messenger."

"So was Satan, I believe."

Several loud bangs interrupted their chat.

"I'm afraid I have no time, apostate. I wanted you to be the first, or the last, to know."

"Know what?" Matt asked.

"That you have lost. That I will now hang up this phone and open the first seal. It would have been better if Teddy had reached Hollywood or even Las Vegas with the bomb but this will have to do."

"Wait! You'll kill Teddy if you do that!"

"We both know he is dead. I feel his spirit. He is telling me to dial God and begin the End Times. To cleanse with fire. Once, I do, I know my government will act and do the right thing, I . . ."

His voice stopped in midsentence, replaced with a loud intermittent bleating noise, like an angry electronic bull from hell.

"Hello?" Matt said. "Hello?"

Matt hung up and tried to dial the number back. He kept getting a recorded message.

"Please stand by, while the satellite phone provider tries to locate the subscriber."

He gave up and looked around at his fellow passengers. Some were still arguing about staying or leaving. Jim was looking at

Matt. Jim asked him who he was talking to. Matt told him who and what.

"Anna, Ruby, we're leaving. Let's go!" Jim announced, helping Anna to her feet.

"Jim . . ." Matt began.

"I have to try," Jim explained, limping with his family away from the jet.

"What's that?" Ruby asked, pointing to tiny black and yellow squares on their side of the horizon, dancing in the heat like a snake.

"They're coming!" Gordon said.

"The cavalry?" smiled Anna.

"Yes, but are we the settlers or the Indians?" Jim asked.

Matt thought of talking to his crew on the laptop one more time but decided to try CNN again, knowing his employees would also be watching. CNN put him on live just as he pointed the webcam at the caravan approaching quickly over the white salt flats. The dark rectangles resolved into four big motor coach buses with tinted black windows. Behind them were six large yellow school buses.

"That's not the cavalry," said Danielle.

"They look good to me," Gordon disagreed.

The black buses stopped in a semicircle several hundred feet away from the starboard wing. The signs over the tinted windshields all said PRIVATE CHARTER. The sides of the buses all had different, large painted logos: ALADDIN CASINO, MGM GRAND, CAESAR'S PALACE, BELLAGIO'S. Gambling buses? No one got out, the buses just sat there idling. Matt noticed that the gambling coaches all had bulging domes of black glass on the front of the roof.

"Could a Mr. Matt Newton please step forward?" a loudspeaker voice said.

Matt, aiming the camera at the buses, walked forward.

"I'm Matt Newton," he said, loudly. "Smile for CNN, guys. You're on live."

"Yes, we can see that. If you could please shut that camera off, Mr. Newton, we can help everyone, thank you."

"You don't want America to see you helping us?"

"You know why we're here, sir. I don't think you want to stay here. I believe you know you are wasting time we may not have. Do any of you folks have a pacemaker?"

No one said they did. A loud hum came from the tinted dome on the closest bus. Matt could hear a voice from CNN on the laptop, telling him not to shut the camera off. He looked at Jim and the others, bloody, exhausted and scared. For the first time he noticed that everyone had blood on their bare feet, from wading through gore. He looked back at the jet and thought about what was inside. He closed the laptop and put it in his bag. It was time to leave.

More buses arrived. Yellow school buses drove forward, past the casino buses, to the front of the plane. SHOSHONE PUBLIC SCHOOLS was painted in black on the sides. The loudspeaker from the lead casino bus asked the passengers to please board the air-conditioned school buses as quickly as possible.

"Air conditioned?" Danielle asked. "I am so there."

"The injured first," Gordon scolded, helping Jim support Anna toward the closest bus.

As the passengers moved toward the school buses, the black buses drove closer to the jet. One backed onto the escape chute, ripping it, as it came to a halt just inches away from the open exit door. The bus doors opened and maybe three dozen people emerged from the casino buses. They were all wearing either silver moon suits or green camouflaged moon suits, like alien astronauts or frog astronauts. The guys in the frog suits were carrying black M16 assault rifles, some pointed at the plane, some at the ground between themselves and the passengers. USMC letters were across their backs. The silver suits had red NEST letters across the back.

"Spacemen," Ruby said. "Cool."

Several of the guys with guns unfolded a green stretcher and quickly carried the marshal to one of their casino buses. Two other men with bad wounds were also helped into the same bus. A dozen of the frog space suits clambered up a rear ladder of the bus next to the plane. One Marine tossed something inside. There was a flash and a bang and they jumped inside, one after the other.

At the entrance to each school bus, a silver suit and a frog suit were waiting, flanking the door. The frog held his finger on the trigger of his machine gun, while running a metal detector wand over everyone and everything. His partner in the shiny suit also used a different, larger tube that he moved up and down over the passengers. When both spacemen had wanded a person, they hurriedly waved them onboard. They're afraid, Matt realized, as he got on. A gaunt, wrinkled guy in a dingy T-shirt was behind the wheel. No space suit. He was dragging on a cigarette, like he did this every day. Onboard, it was probably about eighty degrees but it felt wonderful. Everyone was overheated and light-headed from the heat. Matt sat alone, near Anna and Jim and Ruby and the others. When the bus was about two thirds full, the spacemen got onboard. Hiding it behind the seat back, Matt opened his laptop again. It wouldn't work. The computer would not boot up. He tried three times but nothing happened. He looked at his digital watch. It had stopped. The doors shut and they took off. The driver quickly accelerated to at least eighty miles an hour. Small stones or chunks of salt from the mosaic salt pan pelted the underside of the bus. The driver paid no attention to it. Matt turned and looked out the rear window of the bus. The dark image of the jet through the smoked glass was receding. Go, Matt thought. Faster. Get away.

The guy in the silver suit began asking questions of the passengers. Emily told him all of the hijackers were dead. He asked where the last terrorist's body was on the plane.

"Teddy? Right inside, on the floor, with all the soda cans," Emily told him.

The guy in the shiny suit asked if he had any electronic devices on him.

"He had a cell phone but I . . . we stopped him from making a call," Emily said.

"Actually, he took that phone from one of the original hijackers," Matt added.

"And where is this cell phone now?" the suit asked.

"Somewhere in all those cans, near the gun," Emily replied.

"When did he try to make a call?"

"After we took him down," Matt said. "You think he was going to use the phone to set it off?" Matt asked.

The suit ignored Matt's question and walked to the front of the bus, obviously talking on a radio built into his protective suit. Matt could hear him describing Teddy's body and the gun, the soda cans and the cell phone. Matt could only hear one side of the conversation. A few moments later, the silver suit was talking in a low voice on his suit radio again.

"Negligible here. Just background. Did you get it? Affirmative. How about the cargo? Labeled what? Skis and boots? Damn. It was a backpack? All the safeties? Jesus. Status? Outstanding. Copy that. Phase two. Out."

The silver suit gave a gloved thumbs-up sign to the Marine and they high-fived, their gloves making a soft thumping noise. Under their face plates they were smiling.

The windows of the bus were so dark it was hard to see outside, despite the bright sun. The bus bumped off the salt pan over a sand dune and onto a paved road before accelerating again. There were no other cars on the road. They drove for miles and then pulled off the main road, past a stone and wooden sign, too fast for Matt to read. The bus circled and then came to a halt in front of a low, stone building.

The bus door opened and the guy in the silver suit waved everyone off. The Marine with the M16 stood to one side. No one moved.

"I'm not going anywhere until you tell us what the hell is going on," Toni declared. "They know we're down and all safe! The world knows we're safe. If anything happens to us, the world will know."

The silver suit pulled off his head cowling hood, revealing a sweaty face with blue eyes, topped by black hair.

"Now, why would anything happen to you nice folks?" he said in a Southern drawl. "I'm Captain Englehardt of the Nuclear Emergency Search Team from the Department of Energy. We had to check the aircraft to make sure there was nothing unusual onboard. That is standard procedure. I hope we didn't alarm you."

"Oh no, nothing alarms us," Anna laughed.

"I have been advised that everything is fine and there are no problems," the captain continued.

"When are you letting us go?" Toni demanded.

"Letting you go? We're not holding you. The terrorists were holding you. We're the good guys."

"What about the bomb?" Matt asked.

"Fortunately, there was no bomb," the captain smiled sincerely. "It's all over now. We will have your luggage for you later. As soon as we can arrange it, we will have buses to take you to Las Vegas. The visitors center is right this way, please. Anybody hungry or thirsty? The rest rooms are inside," he said, walking off the bus.

The Marine with the rifle followed him, leaving the door open. Toni looked confused. Matt reopened his laptop and turned it on. It worked. He looked at his watch. It was working again, as well. What the hell was in that dome on the bus, Matt wondered? He stood up and helped Jim with Anna. Outside, in the bright sun, they were in front of a public building with an empty parking lot.

FURNACE CREEK VISITORS CENTER
U.S. Park Service

# 61.

Kevin Toomey, NYPD Deputy Commissioner for Counterterrorism, listened to his brother-in-law Paul talk on the speakerphone to the Flight 1787 passenger in Death Valley. It was a disturbing conversation.

Kevin picked up the red phone on the conference table. The head of the mayor's police detail answered on his radio. Kevin asked to speak to the mayor. He relayed the news about the passengers landing the plane and being stranded in Death Valley with wounded, waiting for rescue from the feds. He suggested the mayor might release the information to the press. Moments later, one of the screens in the Executive Command Center at NYPD Headquarters showed the mayor sitting down in front of a camera in his emergency center, getting ready to go live with a statement. It couldn't hurt, Kevin thought.

"Do you believe that shit?" Paul asked Kevin, once he got off the phone with Matt.

"I'm afraid I do," Kevin said.

"What's happening with the Princess?"

"Who?"

"Jennifer, the ticket agent, Samaritan's girl."

"Oh. Intelligence Division is debriefing her now. They can't shut her up. That was an incredible piece of work, Paul."

"It's been a long time, Kevin. You, know, that was the first time a fast break interrogation worked and the information was actually true. In Khe Sanh once, the ARVN had this VC courier, this girl, and they were going to . . ."

"Hold it, Paul. We need to have this conversation in one of the small conference rooms, okay? Follow me."

Kevin led Paul to a door with a vertical window into a small, windowless room nearby. When the door was shut, Kevin continued.

"Everything at the table is digitally recorded," he explained. "No one needs to hear your stories of watching Vietnamese soldiers torturing and executing Vietcong soldiers."

"Oh, yeah. Thanks, Kevin."

"We are not being taped in here."

"Okay. As I was saying, I was in-country for two tours, you know. Along with the South Vietnamese Army soldiers, we handled thousands and thousands of intelligence reports and I saw our allies torture hundreds of suspects. Almost all of whom were guilty, by the way."

"Almost all."

"Yeah. That was the problem. It was maybe one or two. I've told you that before. This is why I'm against torture. Not a single one of those intelligence reports was right. Not one in all that time. Nothing that came from torture was true. It all came from the enemy. We had a perfect record. The VC never broke under torture. They died or were executed. They got so good at jerking us off that they actually began sending people for the ARVNs, the South Vietnamese troops, to break. Some were really good actors. Of course, we didn't know this until much later. One guy didn't pretend to break until they cut off his ear. Then he fed them a line of bullshit about a fake tunnel that got a dozen ARVN wasted when they went out on it. One of my guys, too. Kevin, you have to remember that our men were getting blown up every day. But it was all for nothing. We lost. All torture got us was what we wanted to hear. From the hard-core guys, I mean."

"So this ticket agent today was not hard core?"

"No way. Cream puff. Just like this college girl from the Cholon district in Saigon. You know, smart, beautiful Vietnamese girl, also spoke French and English, wearing a white silk ao dai. I called her Princess, too. I did the same thing to her. Worked like a charm. She was so pretty."

Kevin listened carefully. In a lifetime, he had never heard this story from Paul.

"She was cool at first because she thought we couldn't touch her because her daddy was an ARVN captain," Paul explained. "Wrong, Princess. She also fainted when I fired my gun. I didn't even have to light the lighter fluid on her arm. She freaked and started crying like a little girl and sang fast. That was my only fast break on record. That was the only time torture ever worked. That's why today, when this . . ."

"What did she tell you?" Paul asked.

"Who? The Vietnamese girl?"

"Yes."

"The truth. Everything," said Paul. "And I never really hurt her. She told us everything she knew. Unfortunately, she did not know that her VC contact at the university had told her nothing but bullshit, a cover story, a fairy tale that distracted us from what they were really doing. They used her and faked us out. Got more good people wasted with a bicycle bomb. So my success story was really a disaster, like the rest of it."

"Until today."

"I guess, yeah. Jennifer's shit checked out. That's true."

Paul stared at the blank wall. Kevin knew he was thinking about his dead brothers; he had that look.

"Paul, you did the job, man."

They both knew what he meant.

"Thanks, Kevin."

"You have to retire, put in your papers," Kevin told him, abruptly.

"My cloth parachute? Not until next year. You know that."

"Paul, listen to me. You probably saved a lot of lives today but you have to retire. Today. I spoke to your inspector. You are on terminal leave as of now. This ticket agent is talking to us now. She has agreed to join our witness protection program. But if you are still on the force, you would be at risk if she lawyered-up and decided to change her tune sometime down the line. She would own you. I won't let that happen."

"I didn't have that problem with the girl from Cholon," Paul remembered.

"What happened to her?"

"Nothing good, buddy."

"You will receive a medal from your department at your retirement ceremony next week," Kevin continued, ignoring an officer knocking on the closed door. "Next month, out of the blue, you will get a call from a major security firm that will offer you an excellent position as a security consultant for a major corporation. This is to protect you and your family, Paul."

"Also the department and the case against the ticket agent, so she can't back out," Paul added. It was not a question.

"Correct."

Paul thought about it silently, looking at the table. The officer knocked on the door again.

"Kevin, what would you think of me retiring a bit early?" Paul asked, with a grin. "I think it's time to move on."

"I think that's a great idea, buddy. Congratulations."

They stood and shook hands. Kevin spoke to the officer outside the room and returned with more news.

"The feds are still quiet but they have lowered the defense alert status two notches. I think it's over. You did it, buddy."

"Did I? I think Matt and the passengers did it, especially the heroes."

"You mean the dead ones?"

"Yeah."

"Also, the tanks are blasting Samaritan's place in Idaho."

"Did they get him?"

"I don't know. It's on CNN live," Kevin said, looking through the open door back at one of the wall screens.

Paul stepped out and looked at the TV screen. All he could discern were flames, black smoke, explosions and a big green pine tree.

"It would take a miracle to walk out of that shit," Kevin said.

"Let's hope," said Cindy, joining them.

Paul took out a new cigar, flicked his Zippo, and lit it, puffing the slate-colored smoke around his head. He told Cindy he was retiring.

"About time," Cindy answered. "Got another one of those things?"

Stunned, Paul took out another tube and lit the cheap cigar for his partner. Cindy noticed that the smoke, for the first time, had irritated Paul's eyes. They were moist.

"This does not taste like victory, Sarge," Cindy coughed. "This tastes like bitter shit in my mouth."

"Exactly," smiled Paul.

# 62.

Matt walked into the Furnace Creek Visitors Center, which was beautifully air conditioned. Passengers were lined up for the four pay phones in the lobby. Some were able to get through to their relatives and were having tearful reunion conversations. Others could not get through due to jammed lines around the country. It made Matt think of the people still on the plane. Lester, Bob, Emmett and his wife, Nancy the blonde flight attendant, the rest of the flight crew, the marshal, all the bodies. He couldn't stop seeing them in his mind.

Most of the passengers were in the cafeteria, where several partially eaten lunches on tables showed how quickly the tourist spot had been evacuated. Two Marine corpsmen, both women, were bandaging and treating the wounded at one end of the room, including Anna and Jim and Gordon and the two guys who got shot in the first attack. Matt could not remember their names and felt guilty to be in one piece. The marshal was still unconscious but alive. Another marine was on a radio arranging for a helicopter to evacuate the beaten marshal and the other wounded to Las Vegas. Liz, the only surviving crew member, was helping.

A man in a brown Park Service uniform was handing out cold waters, sodas, sandwiches and snacks. One of the Marines with a rifle announced that everyone had to stay until the FBI arrived from Las Vegas to interview everyone.

"How long will that take?" one passenger asked.

The Marine explained they had been ordered to clear out a local lodge for them and that they could be there for a day or two, sparking groans and protests. The Marine ignored them. He said that after the FBI was done, buses would be provided. They could go to Las Vegas or Los Angeles to make plane connections. A group of passengers watching the TV news on a set on the wall, wailed at the suggestion.

"Fly?" one woman screeched. "I'm never getting on one of those things again."

"Why not?" Emily asked. "It's like lightning. It couldn't possibly happen again. I'd get on another plane right now. I'm cured."

"I don't know about that," Jim chimed in. "Logically, I agree with you, but . . ."

"I know I probably shouldn't say this but I'm too old to care. Don't you feel lucky?" Emily asked. "I can't wait to get to Vegas."

The CNN anchor announced they were switching live to an undisclosed location for a statement from the President of the United States. Everyone turned back to the screen. After a few seconds, his face appeared. He was smiling that peculiar twisted grin of his.

"My fellow Americans," the president said. "Today has been a tragic and difficult day for many of our countrymen and women. A plane that left New York's Kennedy Airport was hijacked by foreign terrorists this morning. Their insidious plan was to decapitate this government and leave the American people in a state of panic."

"What did he say?" Matt asked, incredulously. "Did he say foreign terrorists?"

"Their evil plan was to crash the plane and kill me and my family, even my young children, and spread terrifying rumors—in the belief that we would panic and give them a great victory. Well, my friends, that has not happened. Reports are still coming in and there are still many false rumors circulating about the possible involvement of others, but I can tell you that the hijacked airliner is safely on the ground, thanks to the work of brave federal marshals onboard. The hijackers and some passengers appear to have been killed in that battle in the skies over America today. We salute those brave men. They have made us all safe again. Unfortunately, a small group of foreign-born terrorist suspects are still at large. We need the help of every loyal American citizen to stop the rumors, which can kill as surely as a bullet or a bomb by jamming vital lanes of transport and communication that our economy depends on. I want to say this as clearly as I can. The terrorists onboard that one plane wanted us to believe they had a weapon of mass destruction. Wild press reports still airing on television even claim atomic bombs were stolen from one of our military bases. Those reports are completely unfounded. Let me say that again. Those reports are not true—they are false rumors fostered by the evil forces that want to steal our freedom. I appeal to you, do not pass on any unsubstantiated rumors. I also appeal to the press to be more responsible and not instantly report every crazy rumor. That kind of behavior causes panic and aids and abets our enemies. The danger is over for now but the threat continues. Together we can beat this danger to our liberty and the traditions we hold dear. Please remain calm but be vigilant and responsible. Thank you and God bless America."

"That lying son of a . . ." Toni spat.

"How can the president just lie like that?" Emily asked.

"Nothing about Mecca, either, or the other bomb and nothing about Samaritan," Matt said. "I feel better already. None of this ever happened."

"He doesn't want anyone to know we were a nuclear guided missile," said Jim.

"If we were," Gordon said. "I don't blame him."

"C'mon, Gordon, you know we were. What were those space suits for? Rumors? Did you see them high five on the bus? They found it."

"But we can't prove it," Gordon pointed out.

As the others discussed the surreal developments, Matt put his laptop on a table and sat down. He logged on with his crew and updated them and sent an audio file. He asked Fiona what other valid media offers had been made to the public website. As she began to list them, he stopped her and had her send only one group to him. He read them quickly. What balls on these guys, Matt thought. He wrote an e-mail, mentioning his degree in film from NYU and a brief outline of the untold story and sent it to every one of the eleven men and women who had e-mailed him while he was in the air. In minutes, the auction had begun. When he was done, he advised his staff to make it happen as soon as possible. The he returned to the group watching the television.

"The press is now backing off everything," Jim told Matt, "and qualifying it with 'allegedly' and 'reportedly' and 'unconfirmed reports,' stuff like that."

"That's okay," said Matt. "I just released a recording of Samaritan. Let them deny that. It doesn't matter—we'll tell it all in the movie."

Everyone laughed.

"No, I'm serious. I just made a deal with 20th Century Fox studios to do a screenplay about today. All of it, everything. They want all of you to sign on, also, so they can use your individual stories. I started out to do this, actually, movies. I sort of got sidetracked on video games and hacking and then cyber security. Who wants to make a movie? We all get a piece. All of us, including the people who never made it off that fucking plane. Or, at least, their families."

"You're not joking," Jim observed.

"Not at all. The lawyers are working it out now. I'm definitely doing the screenplay. The president is going to love it."

"Holy shit," said Toni.

"You are a fast worker, Matt," Emily said.

"Yes he is," Liz agreed, moving closer to Matt. "Who will play me?"

"Salma Hayek, or somebody prettier," Matt said.

"Who will play you?" Liz asked.

"Who cares?" Matt said, grinning at her.

"I'm not married," Liz said.

"I figured," Matt replied.

After a TV report about the inferno at Samaritan's place in Idaho, the TV anchor gave an awkward, rambling statement about doing their best to confirm rumors on live television. He said they had been able to fully confirm a late development that was possibly—but not definitely—related to today's hijacking. The NUCLEAR ALERT banner had vanished from the screen. They went live to a home somewhere in Tennessee, where a homeowner was talking live to the camera.

"I was in the bathroom, taking a shower when I heard this big boom," a brown-haired, balding guy with a goatee was saying. "I thought the whole house blew up. What? Sure, c'mon in, it's right here in the friggin' living room."

The TV camera light illuminated a couch crushed by a large blue chunk of something, surrounded by smaller pieces, everywhere, with objects frozen inside.

"It's Blue Ice," the homeowner explained. "You know? From a airplane toilet? But that's not the deal. Look what's frozen inside 'em."

"What are they?" the clueless reporter asked.

"Cell phones. Maybe a hundred," the man said. "They been dipped in shit, frozen and dumped on my fuckin' house."

The cable news network cut off the live shot, leaving the

flustered anchor to apologize for the language.

"Sorry, but that's live TV, folks," he said with a shrug.

"That's network news for you," Toni said to the screen. "Nothing but shit."

The group laughed until tears ran down their faces.

"Hey, Ranger!" Matt shouted to the Park Service guy. "Is there a bar in this place?"

"Yessir, right through those double doors, but it's not open yet."

"Could you please open it?" Matt asked. "We insist. I want to buy all of my new friends, and partners, several drinks. We're on vacation."

# ABOUT THE AUTHOR

**Sean Michael Bailey** is the pen name of an investigative reporter and *New York Times* best-selling author of nonfiction, who felt compelled to disguise his identity to tell this story. This is his first novel. For further information visit seanmichael bailey.com.

| DATE | | | |
|---|---|---|---|
| | | | |
| | | | |
| | | | |
| | | | |
| | | | |
| | | | |
| | | | |
| | | | |
| | | | |
| | | | |
| | | | |
| | | | |